THE

BORDER

OF

PARADISE

The Unnamed Press
P.O. Box 411272
Los Angeles, CA 90041

Published in North America by The Unnamed Press.

3 5 7 9 10 8 6 4 2

ISBN 978-1939419699

Library of Congress Control Number: 2016933947

This book is distributed by Publishers Group West

Designed & typeset by Jaya Nicely
Cover art by Leonardo Santamaria

THE
BORDER
OF
PARADISE

A NOVEL

ESMÉ WEIJUN WANG

FOR CHRIS.

Here we are,
the constellation of
a coupled single star.

A prison becomes a home if you have the key.
— George Sterling

Real goodness was different, it was irresistible, murderous, it had victims like any other aggression; in short, it conquered. We must be vague, we must be gentle, we are killing people otherwise, whatever our intentions, we are crushing them beneath a vision of light.

— James Salter, *Light Years*

CONTENTS

PART I

THE NOWAKS

DAVID

(1935–1954)

I've never known a man who has taken his own life, and so I've never read a suicide letter, seeing as how the final words of such uncelebrated and self-condemned souls are so privately guarded. Still, I can't help but think such letters all must be the same, because what else can be said but, over and over again, *Sorry, sorry, I am so sorry,* in the way that someone newly smitten can only say, *I love you, I love you, I love you,* like one of the Wellbrook patients I grew accustomed to in my incarcerations. In particular I am thinking of a schizophrenic woman with chin-length, ashen hair, stooped in her wheelchair, who repeated the word *plum,* such that the hum of that word faded into the background of everything, including the screams of other patients, the soft rush of water, *plum, puh-lum,* until the word shed its meaning, becoming nothing but sound.

This motel room is not as depressing as I thought it would be. Someone has taken pains to make the place palatable; I have yet to see a cockroach. Only one or two flies the size of kidney beans occasionally dive-bomb the air. The bed's comforter itches, but is printed with an assortment of nice English roses. Note that a man conflicted about his suicide will reflexively stop and smell the proverbial roses. The cheap blue curtains let the light through, and when I first walked to the window to pull them shut I saw that one of them had been carefully stitched near the edge, where I'm assuming it was once torn, and in the end I take this all to mean that this place is as good as any to die. I didn't want to end things anywhere near the house, where my wife could find me—or, even more horrible to consider, my children. If I had my way, I'd hang myself peacefully from one of the trees in our wood, but that seems more blasphemous than this, somehow, and I'm grateful to this humble little Motel Ponderosa of no significance, which is a small grace.

I had breakfast this morning miles from here with my son, William; my daughter, Gillian; and Daisy, who is my wife. We had bacon, and fry bread cooked in the grease, and eggs fried in whatever grease was left. I watched William sop up the yolk with a crust of bread. I watched Gillian scrape her plate, her hair in a little topknot tied with a red velvet ribbon. I watched Daisy, whose face in the light was worn smooth like a rock under the same persistent current of worry. *Click, click, click,* I thought, committing them to memory to be preserved and then destroyed, because even in my moribund state I could see the simple beauty of it, and silently I asked the Lord to bless my family, even if neither he nor they will ever forgive me for my desertion. Those three were persistently beset by trouble, and worse, they still loved me; so how this can be anything but a betrayal and an unfairness, I don't know.

I've been returning to *The Confessions* more than to the Bible these days, but it's become difficult to understand what I mean to accomplish through any style of confession. I have sinned, and I had hoped to expose and atone for my sins. I hoped to cast them out, as Christ cast the demons into swine, so that the Lord might take pity on my soul—this, despite the saying that God never gives a person more than he can handle—but what about despair? For so many years I have thought I ought to be able to handle this, and the only refrain that returned to me was *I'm in pain, I'm in pain, I'm in pain.* "Spare Thy servant from the power of the enemy," said Augustine. And yet Augustine achieved sainthood, an achievement for which not even I am insane enough to dream.

———————◆———————

I was born with good fortune, the only son of Francine and Peter Nowak; and my father, whom I called Ojciec, was the president and owner of the Nowak Piano Company. Nowak pianos are less known now. For a handful of decades they were nearly as well known as Mason & Hamlins, or even Steinways, because of their combination of quality and affordability. Our name was significant in a city full of significant names. But for most of my childhood we were at war, with our manufactory building gliders to carry troops behind enemy lines, and during this time we made only four pianos, sent overseas to the troops for entertainment's sake.

War meant instability. I was only four when the war began, and I can't recall life before it, but I had absorbed enough to know that the war shoved everything off-kilter. The radio threatened us with new forms and styles of entertainment as much as it threatened its listeners with news from the front. My parents refused to buy one on principle, which meant that news reached us a beat after it hit everyone else, or else we caught snatches and bits of it from family friends; but this, too, seemed to be a purposeful, buffering act. Ojciec visited the factory as though our lives were no different. In watching the rib press, he peered over his glasses at the torque wrench, which had already been double-checked by the workers; he paced vigilantly in the gluey conditioning room and examined the bridge press for inaccurate gauges; he came home smelling of instruments pregnant with music, of chemicals and wood. He came home tired, but the factory also gave him substance. To Ojciec, being the paterfamilias of the remaining Nowak clan meant little if it didn't involve our pianos as well.

A slender, fair woman with a bump in her thin nose, my mother, whom I called Matka, was primarily occupied with caring for her only son, and secondarily occupied with spending money, albeit in an abstracted, halfhearted way. She brought me with her to estate sales in Blenheim, in Lysander, in Hastings, where we sifted through abandoned belongings and plundered what we wanted, returning to our brownstone with armfuls of yellowing Edwardian dresses and stuffed toys worn with love before being left behind like Moses in the reeds. As I headed up the stairs to my bedroom after such excursions, my arms laden with toys, my mother would put her cool hand on the back of my neck, lean down, and anoint the top of my head with a kiss. It wasn't as though we were *oblivious* to what was happening overseas, although I see the oddity now of what Matka and I were doing: buying up the belongings of the dead while the dead piled up away from home. We did, financially and emotionally, feel the pinch of war less than most of Greenpoint. We were utterly grateful to Our Lord for this.

◆

Very early on I realized that I was not like other boys I knew, or not as good at pretending to be anything other than what I was. What energies I had were sadly misdirected, scattershot, toward obscure targets. While I ran around with the other kids in McCarren Park, getting my shoes muddy and looking like any other golden-haired son of Polish America, I was also fretting about my bunny Flopsy's left eye coming loose as his right one had, until I had to stop and catch my breath, a rising panic looming in my chest and forcing me home. While playing stickball I made myself ill, and even vomited in the grass, from dwelling on Leo the Lion's head, which had fallen off its crumbling spring. I'd attributed to these dolls a kind of anima or animus. I wouldn't say that I believed them to be truly living, but I did invest enough of my emotional attention into each one that they may as well have been alive. I kept them in the bottom dresser drawer, away from Ojciec's disapproval, and dressed them fastidiously in the mornings and again at bedtime. Leaving these chores undone would undo me; it was the beginning of my so-called neuroses, though at the time I had no word for it.

Generally, I tried to mind my p's and q's when I was with my fellow children, putting up the best front I could. I threw rocks at Louise Bielecki, for example, and I called her snaggletoothed, the memories of which are enough to make me weep into my hands.

At the age of ten I borrowed a slender volume from the library, titled *The Man Who Loved Wolves*—a tell-all biography about William P. Harding, the infamous *National Geographic* writer and photographer who lived for years among wolves, and who was known best for being the first man to expose the phenomenon of wolf cannibalism. On the cover Harding posed in a runner's crouch atop a cliff, with his hands on the backs of two large, sitting wolves. His facial expression suggested a deep-seated anguish extant since birth. What drew me to this book was not the cover, however, but Harding's quote on the dust jacket: "Man and wolf are the same creature—brutal, beautiful, and not meant to be alone." But while I sprawled out on my bed, slowly paging through the saga of Harding's life, the scenes of wilderness and wolves gave way to a lurid depiction of his alcoholism and suicide, and this I could not comprehend. To be sure, my parents drank; but they had never fallen down a flight of stairs and broken four ribs and an arm, as Harding had, nor had they even considered (I was certain of this) leaping off a cliff to be picked at by vultures for days before their rotting corpses were discovered, again as Harding had.

Remembering it today, my bafflement is almost touching. That a man could purposefully end his own life, and in so doing give up his most beloved things, was truly beyond my understanding. Yet from my childish, perhaps preconscious aversion to the idea of Harding's suicide, I can discern an attraction—an inability to let go of the horror, as I had failed to set aside my concerns for Flopsy and Leo.

I can safely say that William P. Harding was solely responsible for my becoming a preadolescent insomniac. My attempts at sleep tangled with images: Harding's plummet; a pack of wolves swarming upon its weakest member; blood spurting thin as water, leaking thick as honey. Panicked, I ran to my desk, grabbed the book, and shoved it into my trash can, beneath the tissues and papers, but even that wasn't enough. I snuck the can outside my bedroom door and closed myself in. I remember holding my hand palm-out as some kind of protection. I know that such inclinations and incidents may not seem like much, and that they are not my fault, but the fault of circumstances beyond my control. But to this day, I suspect that I planted the seeds of my own suffering without having any notion of consequence.

The doctors rarely used clinical terms to address my sleeping problem. They said I had nerves, and recommended to Matka pharmaceuticals with futuristic names. I never told anyone about William P. Harding because, from the beginning, they seemed determined to be the ones with the answers; I've never known any profession to be surer about its own expertise than the one with the stethoscope.

There is a possibility, although I try not to think about it, that my children will inherit this madness. In other ways I've given them the most I could. I wanted to give them everything. I tried to teach William and Gillian about the Bible and Virgil and the importance of language, which is not easy to do with their mother being the way that she is; but they are quick studies, and I can tell they have the potential for outstanding intellects. It's too early yet to tell if there's something unsavory lurking, but if there is, I haven't seen it. No one deserves this, least of all those two. If I could do anything, anything at all, I'd ensure that their realities remain strong as bricks, as solid as diamonds.

◆

Naturally, insomnia interfered with my schoolwork, which I became too dull-headed for; and when Matka, upon receiving my report card, tentatively visited my bedroom after dinner to ask if everything was all right, I vaguely gave a half-truth, which was that I was having trouble sleeping. A groove folded between her eyebrows. She sighed, the paper in her hands creasing into her lap, and said, "I'll have to tell your father." She meant the grades, of course, never the insomnia. And Matka turned to me and smiled one of those smiles propped up by many things, but not by happiness. She loved me all her life, but I did wonder how many children she would have wanted if she'd been able. At that age I knew only that I'd never have a brother or sister, let alone a pack of them, but not why. She did tell me later, when I returned to Greenpoint with Daisy, that she'd had a near-fatal hemorrhage when I was born, and everything had been removed—uterus, fallopian tubes, ovaries—which saved her, but meant I would always be her only child. She said this bitterly, tapping a cigarette into the sink, her hands trembling so that she almost dropped it in with the dishes. That medical crisis also made her sick, I realized later, as a consequence of depleted estrogen.

Insomnia. Wolves. Matka's concern for me. My grades. The war had ended by then, and the atmosphere at home and school seemed perpetually on the brink of a great unraveling. No one close to us had died. My parents' closest friends, the Pawlowskis, were childless, though apparently Mr. Pawlowski had a nephew from Long Island who lost a leg in combat, and some of the kids I knew from St. Jadwiga had lost a brother or had a brother newly, and I assumed happily, home. For us the end of the war meant that the Nowak Piano Company would return to making pianos, although whether those pianos would then find buyers was a new anxiety to be conquered. This question gave Ojciec ulcers, which I'm sure Matka was disinclined to make worse with my disappointing report card.

But as she'd said, she did have to tell him, and he was unhappy. I'd always been decently athletic and scholastically impressive, and the new Cs and B-minuses bewildered him. "What's gone wrong with you?" he asked at breakfast. "It's not a girl, is it?"

"No."

Ojciec was a small man, not where I got my height; he was compact and had a thin flop of dark blond hair across his pate, which he managed with pomade, and wore a pair of small, round wire-rimmed glasses that were always slipping down his nose. And he was always hot—standing near my father, you could feel the energy radiating off him. He put down his fork with a clatter and said, "You're growing up, David. It's important that you learn to take responsibility. As you get older, the responsibilities you take on will be more than letters on a piece of paper." He nudged my report card. "Screwing up ends up meaning losing thousands of dollars, means losing your shirt. And the older you get, the more ways there are to screw up."

That was the end of his lecture. He pushed his plate away and stood, hurrying to ready himself for a day of factory oversight. Matka, who had been putting away dishes, walked Ojciec to the door, her hand on his back, saying nothing.

But the following week he announced that I was to attend an important meeting with him because I was growing up, and thus needed to go to the manufactory with him. He said that I needed to see how the pianos were put together because the Nowak Piano Company was a family business, and had been since my *dziadek* had passed the business to him, as Ojciec would to me; I was responsible for carrying it on as the last child of the Nowak line. I'd need to learn every aspect of the company's operations, including how to manage the workers so that they would only go so far as to gripe about their wages and hours, but would not rebel or leave or, worse, unionize; how to recognize whether a piano was finely tuned or no better than any heap of wooden garbage thoughtlessly nailed together. I needed to understand the intricacies of *voicing*. I would watch my father negotiate with new dealers, who were cads and cheats in comparison with the men who had known my grandfather years ago, and used to treat the Nowak name with respect, but were now out for themselves because they, too, had suffered when the war came, and shrewdness mattered more to them than decency. If I continued to "refuse to grow up," as he obliquely referred to my slippery grades, and to behave no better than a modern-day boy without a shadow, I'd never be a capable successor. He would bring me to an important meeting in the coming week. "It will be part of your education," my father said.

I had no say in the matter, and little understanding of what it really meant to be a Nowak son. The myth of the Nowak Piano Company—a Polish immigrant arriving in America with nothing but a Bible, a tuning fork, and a knife! The notion of an affordable, but still beautiful, piano! The immigrant's ingenuity and his consequent success as a piano maker in an inhospitable land!—this tale was as essential to our family as the story of the birth of Christ. When it came to the modern-day workings of the company, my understanding of their importance came from my parents, who spoke of our pianos as though they, and thus we, were crucial not only to the esteemed world of music, but to America itself. I believed this not because I saw with my own eyes, on the way to the park or school, a Nowak piano in every living room window, or because of other children's reactions upon hearing my name; I never saw such a thing, or heard any envious tones. I believed in our importance only because my parents overtly stated it all my life. And I was proud to be a Nowak, and relieved that my father still considered me the company's heir, because it was essential that I honor my parents. It was necessary that I should have the chance to demonstrate my ambition, and to put my smarts to work as their son.

But I made sure that my children would grow up without this on their backs. They believe that the pianos in our living room state our names because they belong to us, in the way that a mother might carefully embroider a shirt label with EMMA or MARK.

——◆——

Oh, Gillian, my little Artemis: you would not be surprised to hear that you are my favorite in the family. I think that became clearest when I began to teach you taxidermy, but William is fussy in a way that you are not. I have always been proud of the way you handle yourself around blood and viscera. Do you remember the first time I had you make your own rabbit's foot? Your delicate fingers moved with such confidence, and when your small hand wrapped around the penknife I thought, *How powerful she is!* I have always been proud of you.

◆

Though we were well known in Greenpoint, only a few were truly in my parents' circle. George Pawlowski was my father's right-hand man, and had been since my *dziadek* passed on and willed the company to Ojciec. Vicky Pawlowski was by default my mother's closest friend, though Matka never seemed quite intimate with anyone who didn't live under her roof; and when Mrs. Pawlowski and Matka did socialize at our home, their conversations were full of halting pauses that made me squirm. But for my mother, it was clear that Mrs. Pawlowski served a crucial purpose—the woman tethered her to society. Once, and only once, did I overhear Mrs. Pawlowski's sobs as she spoke in a roundabout way about infertility. This explained the Pawlowskis' lack of children, and perhaps also the bond between Mrs. Pawlowski and my mother.

Mrs. Pawlowski was the first to note the Orlichs' appearance in the neighborhood. From the beginning, she was *unconvinced*, as she put it to my mother. Their only boy, Marty, was my age, thirteen, and he began to show up in my classes, more often than not sitting next to me because of the alphabetical rows. Marty quickly became infamous for his foul mouth, which simultaneously titillated and unnerved us, his peers. He was of average height and build. He had a sharp face, with a pointy chin and nose and slashes for eyebrows, and when he smiled it was like he was leering at the world.

At the dinner table my father said, "You know that new family, the Orlichs. Well, Benjamin stopped by the manufactory today."

"Oh?" Matka said.

"Yes. It was shocking what a ridiculous little man he revealed himself to be. He introduced himself, briefly. Apparently he's an accountant, and the whole family is from Chicago. He came to ask if he could buy a baby grand for *three-fourths* the price."

"Three-fourths? What on earth would make him think you'd say yes?"

"I said something to that effect. He said, 'Because our sons are in the same class.' As if this made us family. David, do you know his son?"

"Yes," I said.

"And what do you make of him?"

"Marty? I don't know him well. He gets in trouble a lot with the nuns, I guess. He's stellar in Latin."

"Well," Ojciec said, sawing into a pork chop, "if he's anything like his father, I'd say you'd best stay away from him. It would be one thing if Mr. Orlich were merely foolish, but I could tell from ten paces that the man has a temper. Though he knew better than to duke it out with me." He shook his head. "Imagine! As if we were a charity."

"I loathe Chicago," Matka said. "It's so cold there in the winter."

"Whenever a new family moves in, it's like a roll of the dice," said Ojciec.

Yes, it was a roll of the dice, or can we say it was Fate that brought the dysfunctional Orlich clan to Greenpoint. It was Fate that the Orlichs should have a daughter, too, named Marianne, whom I would love, and still do love, with my utterly fallible—my utterly human—heart that is still beating.

The first time I saw the Orlichs as a family was at Christmas. Our little clan—at first just Daisy and I, then with William and, later, Gillian—has had a number of Christmases, but the sort of Christmases I had as a boy were nothing like the ones we've enjoyed. These were loud affairs. Crowded. Upward of eighty people were invited to the Pawlowskis' Christmas party on a yearly basis, and everyone who was invited came. It was a lavish show for George and Vicky Pawlowski, especially for Mrs. Pawlowski, who used her pent-up maternal energy spending days decorating their home in tinsel, votive candles, glass ornaments that broke if you so much as gave them a stern look, and a gigantic tree by the staircase, which hung heavy with what she explained every year was inherited Mazowsze glass. When I was very young I saw the Pawlowski party as a family obligation and a bore, but the older I became, I sensed that there was a desperation that haunted the Pawlowskis, and this desperation came to a shrill plateau from Advent to Epiphany. The hunger for adoration, for festivity and friends, was played out in the party itself, with too much high-pitched conversation and people posturing, and the tension dissipating only when all hosts and guests had imbibed a healthy amount of booze.

On that particular Christmas we were the Pawlowskis' first guests, and Mrs. Pawlowski immediately descended upon Matka as I drifted into the sitting room.

"We invited the Orlichs," Mrs. Pawlowski said.

"Oh? Are you friendly with Caroline?" Matka asked, and there was a tinkling of wineglasses in the kitchen.

"No, I don't know Caroline, and George barely knows Benjamin—I mean Bunny. They sort of invited themselves. You know how the Christmas party is our special occasion, but they approached it as though it were the ball drop. A sort of 'come one, come all.' I didn't know how to say no. I didn't want to be impolite. I fear it will be strange for everyone else, though. No one really knows them. No one in our circle, I mean."

My mother said, "So many people are coming, though. It won't make a difference."

"Caroline basically *insisted* that her daughter sing at the party. She flat-out assumed that we would want to hear her sing. So now her daughter is going to sing 'O Holy Night,' I think."

"I love that song."

"I do, too. It's my favorite carol. When done well, it makes me cry. I honestly shed tears, real ones. But you should have heard her, Francine. She said, 'Well, Marianne is an excellent singer, and she'd be honored if you had her perform at your party.' I was so shocked! Really—inviting yourself to a party, and then inviting your daughter to perform, too? It was like she'd heard about the party for *years* and finally decided that it was high time they make the list. Before I could figure out what to say, she said, 'She does a *truly* beautiful "O Holy Night." She'll be so pleased.' And by then it was too late, they were as good as invited by George himself."

"Goodness."

"Maybe they won't show," Mrs. Pawlowski said. "Maybe they'll get in a horrible car accident. Did I just say that? I've been drinking wine all day, just sipping while cooking, and I don't know what I'm saying anymore. But we've known each other forever, haven't we? You won't tell anyone?"

The doorbell sounded. "Oh," Mrs. Pawlowski said, and went down the hall. She peered through the peephole, and then she opened the door for the Orlichs. Coming in was balding Mr. Orlich, who had absurdly round cheeks, and Mrs. Orlich, who held the wine. There was Marty, who was now taller than I was, although I would be quite lanky and nearing six feet by the end of senior year, and he had on a lumpy red-and-white-striped wool hat that I presumed a relative had knit for him.

But Marianne. That moment in the sitting room was the first time that I found myself paying any attention to a girl, let alone a girl slipping into the shape of a woman. If I was neurotic about stuffed animals as a child, as an adolescent I was even more neurotic about girls, who seemed not quite human to me. Yet here she was, a sylphlike fourteen-year-old, wearing a red angora sweater with a matching skirt and low heels with girlish white stockings, and there was her startlingly white-blond hair, which had a slight wave to it, and here was a broad smile that spanned her round face. I invented none of that; that is exactly how Marianne looked that day when she walked into the Pawlowskis' house.

She followed her family into the sitting room, where they hovered over the canapés, and chose their cucumber sandwiches and treats, before settling together on a love seat kitty-corner to mine. Marty stuck his tongue out at me. I did not respond.

"Does anyone need anything?" Mrs. Pawlowski asked.

"No, no, everything looks fantastic," said Mrs. Orlich, "this is quite the spread you've got here." She looked at her daughter. "Marianne? Isn't there something you wanted to ask Mrs. Pawlowski?"

Marianne stared at her mother for a moment, and then asked Mrs. Pawlowski if she could sing "W Zlobie Lezy" before dinner was served.

"Oh yes, of course—George and I are dying to hear it. I can even accompany you on our Nowak grand." She looked around. "Please, everyone, enjoy the hors d'oeuvres. There are plenty more in the kitchen. Caroline? Benjamin? Something to drink?"

I kept watching Marianne, unaware of how strange I must have looked, but when Mrs. Pawlowski took everyone's beverage requests and returned to the hallway, Marianne stood and followed her, saying, "Excuse me," and I was alone again.

Soon the house was crawling with people. Most of them came from our church, St. Jadwiga, but many of them were neighbors who knew Mr. Pawlowski because he was an affable man and the sort who knew everyone. One of the Stopka children, a six-year-old named Emily, took it upon herself to attach herself to me, her pigtails whipping as she swung her head with her tongue out. My memory of six-year-old Gillian is so different from my memory of Emily Stopka, so much brighter. As I searched for Marianne I gave Emily a *paluszki* to eat, to keep her occupied, but she maintained her attachment as though she were in love, and the adults were too busy socializing to pry her from me. Emily followed me into the enormous piano room when it was time for Marianne to sing, and put her small hand in mine. I was irritated at the time, but now when I think about that little blond girl I feel the need to cry. I'll lie down for a spell, while the feel of candy-floss hair lingers still in my hands, and I'll say a few prayers, too. There is a bit of sun soaking the curtains, I've noticed. Marianne sang; I was enchanted. That's all there is to say about that kind of beauty.

———◆———

As soon as I could escape the postprandial hubbub I retreated to the library, which was Mr. Pawlowski's great pride, and was floor to ceiling with books in musty jewel tones rubbed pale by many fingers. I was slipping *Phaedrus* back into its place when Marianne came up behind me. She tapped my shoulder, and when I turned she was crouching, eyes bright, looking as though she had happened upon a prize.

"Sneaky you," she said. "But I won't tell. I don't like parties, either."

"Why not?"

"They make people lose control of themselves. I like to know that everyone around me is in their right mind. Why are you hiding?"

I shrugged.

"Maybe we can find an atlas," she said.

We searched for a while until I finally found one low enough for me to reach and heaved it onto the floor. She knelt and randomly opened it to the Orient. I showed her the Silk Road, tracing its route with a finger, and named as many spices as I could think of. I spoke of Magellan. I worried that she would leave if I failed to keep her attention, but I was wrong about Marianne's capability for patience: her eyes never drifted, she didn't interrupt.

When I stopped, she said, "Men are always exploring. Adventuring. I've been reading about the Gold Rush—it's interesting how much men are willing to put themselves through when they think there's something to gain."

"'That the trial of your faith, being much more precious than of gold that perisheth, though it be tried with fire,'" I said.

"California. The land of gold and fire," she answered. And then she asked, "Have you been abroad?"

"No. I haven't even left the state. Why, have you?"

"No. But I think about it." She drew a circle on the page with her finger. "I wouldn't go to Paris or London, though. Somewhere in Egypt, where they need missionaries and nuns. I'd like to do something useful like that. I'm not interested in going to some posh bistro and toothpicking snails out of their little shells."

"Oh? Why not?"

"Glamour doesn't interest me."

"I'm not sure I really understand glamour, not being a woman and all," and when I said this, I was thinking of my mother, who wore rouge and daubed carmine on her lips.

"Men can be glamorous, too," Marianne said. "Look at this library! It's all a show, a show of going beyond the ordinary—Mr. Pawlowski wants this house to be glamorous as much as his wife does, even if her view of it means ornaments and tinsel, and his is leather and wood. Do you see what I mean?"

Her tone pricked me. After all, I lived in a fancy brownstone, and my parents were not only wealthy but famous; granted, Marianne had never been inside our home, but it would be easy enough to guess that we had original paintings by esteemed artists on our walls, or that we laid elaborate Oriental rugs on our floors. But Marianne saw my discomfort and apologized, putting her hand on mine. "I say things without thinking," she said. "It's a fault. One of the few things I have in common with Marty."

"You don't curse as much as he does," I said, very aware of the feel of her hand on mine, and she laughed.

"No," she said. "I don't. He gets that from our father."

"Did he—Marty—say anything about me?"

She said, "He told me you were a bit strange."

But why had Marty said this? Could he have been watching the bloat of my sagging eye-bags, the same eye-bags that evidenced my nights of insomnia? Were there not infinite reasons for not sleeping? Did I betray myself more than I thought I did? Why did I already care *so much* about what Marianne Orlich thought of me?

"Strange? Really?"

"He did. So far, I don't see it."

"Did he say why?"

"It doesn't matter," she said. "He says whatever comes into his head most of the time."

We fell into a natural silence. Finally she removed her hand, tucking a strand of hair behind her ear. "If you *are* crazy," she said firmly, "that's not so bad. So many of the saints were thought to be insane. Only later were they canonized."

"I'm not a saint," I said. "Sorry to disappoint."

"I didn't say you were." She laughed. "You're a very serious kid, you know that?"

"Yes. I don't know why—it makes life difficult."

She turned the pages of the atlas, stopping at Egypt. "Here," she said. "Someday, I'd like to go here." We stared at the full view. I tried to imagine her there, a missionary of some kind, her milky skin gone leathery from sand-soaked wind. She would ride camels and pet the trunks of elephants; she would be exotic beyond my American imagination.

———◆———

That winter—an unusually cold one—was the winter of the Or-lichs. I saw Mrs. Orlich at the butcher's, clutching her purse to her side. I saw the family at church. Here and there they appeared, all of them holy by virtue of being related to Marianne. Even Marty shone. Here he was, her brother, who had seen her grow up. Who had probably bathed with her as a child.

Caroline Orlich was Marianne writ large, taller and with thicker bones and a face covered in cracking makeup, including her lips, which were heart-shaped like her daughter's and peeled in the winter. In the dawn of my ardor I saw Caroline as the future version of her pious daughter, so I loved her, too. I did think of it as love; what else could I call the connection I'd felt so immediately, and with nothing like it before her? I barely knew the girl, but it was this precise fact that made her so easy to adore. She was a churchgoing, compassionate girl, and I took this to mean that she had deep thoughts about morality, God, and how to live.

But I did worry. Her accountant father, through social manipulations like those committed by her mother, began to play weekly poker with Mr. Pawlowski, and I assumed that Mrs. Orlich gleaned any and all information about me through her gossipy husband. And while I tried to keep my neuroses hidden, there were certain things that I absolutely could not help. I won a Winter Latin prize in the first week after the holiday, which was as much a triumph for Ojciec as much as it was for me; yet my mind had grown increasingly confused outside of my fascination with Marianne. Already, back then, there was a sickness growing. I worried about my body and its dividing cells, because the idea of my skin covered in invisible pores repulsed me in the way that gaping stomata repulsed me in biology; and then I became afraid that my soul would leak out through those holes, and the abandonment would leave my body a shell for me to prop up through the endless, terrible days. I popped my pimples till my skin was spotted with scabs, and then I picked those scabs with the conviction that immaculate skin would be underneath, but such ministrations only made my face painful and wet and inviting infection.

Nothing looked right on my newly gawky body, either. At times I peered at myself in the mirror, and reflected back at me was a dwarf stretched squat, wide, and obese, and no matter how I turned and posed, I couldn't make the horrible image change. How could I have gone for so long without knowing that *this* was what I looked like? The first time, I ran to the bathroom and double-checked my reflection there, not knowing what I would see, and there I was, seemingly myself without the distortion; but the feeling that I had transformed, or been lied to, remained. Was there any way that I could know for certain if any mirrors were honest, and how had I gone through life believing that these flat and magical pieces of glass would reflect my true self? I describe the expression of these neuroses with the bewilderment of someone who still can't understand them, and the embarrassment of someone who knows how ridiculous they sound—but if I didn't check the mirror, pick the scabs, change in and out of clothes in hopes of winning back a normal body, and so forth, the problems would only multiply. The only control I had over them was to be watchful and to attend to them.

But *why* these strange rituals? I was able to dress for school easily; thanks to the uniforms, I had no conflict or confusion about what to wear on weekdays. Weekends, and particularly Sundays, were another story. The idea of choosing clothes appropriate for Mass seemed almost an insurmountable task. What should have taken a few minutes dissolved into hours. Increasingly, Matka had to pull me out of the room, rushing me downstairs where my father watched the clock, and me, dubiously. Even though we both knew I was too old for it, Matka took to organizing my Sunday clothes for me on my bed. In some ways, her suggestions only made things worse, and we suddenly found ourselves tussling over my wardrobe, my mother fighting with her adolescent son as if he were a toddler. When I finally refused to go on a grim, late January morning, my father said nothing, and he and I both watched as my mother trudged disconsolately out the front door, which Ojciec next shut behind him without so much as a glance in my direction.

Would it be so unlikely to claim that I didn't want to attend Mass, I didn't want to worship, I didn't want to sit with the waves of Latin rolling over me, I didn't believe in God, and God knew— as well as my dead relatives, including my grandfather, rest his soul—that I was making up this ridiculous problem that wasn't actually a problem, what with my hidden loathing for God and all that was holy, this secret blasphemy hiding so deeply within me that I could delude my conscious self, though I could not delude my parents, and of course not God, which would inevitably lead to damnation? Such convoluted explanations allowed me to make some sense of my idiosyncrasies, but my beliefs and behavior were ultimately attributed to a disordered mind rather than some kind of religious antipathy. I am not sure which is preferable.

While I fought with my clothes, poor Matka, who had no idea what to do with her strange son, removed the mirror in my room ("Boys don't need mirrors anyway," my father snapped), and I sensed my body stretching like taffy while I simultaneously feared Hell, or feared that I was already in it.

My February and then March absences from Mass spurred the gossip machines to begin whirring; such chatter finally alerted the Orlichs, and in particular Mrs. Orlich, that something was wrong with me. My parents' friends ran the gamut from purely cultural Catholics to the extremely religious, most of whom were immigrants born and bred of the Polish Catholic denomination, and while neither of my parents was strict observers of the faith, my parents prayed, said grace before meals, never missed church, and were self-conscious about how they were perceived in the churchgoing community. That they'd given up on trying to get me to attend meant that I was lost, despite my efforts. I sat in my underwear atop the covers on Sunday mornings next to a pile of cast-off clothing, daring myself to try on another shirt. *Just go ahead!* I told myself. *Just go ahead and try to take it off—I'll knock your teeth in!* But I always took it off, my parents left, and when my paralysis let up I wrapped myself in Matka's terry-cloth robe and went to the kitchen, where I sat at the table and waited for my parents to come home.

On one of those days I was sitting on a stool in that robe when the bell rang. I got up and peered through the peephole at Mrs. Orlich. The fish-eye effect of the peephole made her look like a Kewpie doll in an enormous camel coat.

"Hello?" she asked. "Francine?"

"No," I said.

"Oh! David? Are your parents home?"

"They're not back from church yet. They'll be here in a little bit."

"Oh."

I wondered if she wanted me to invite her in to wait. Not wanting her to, I didn't ask, and she didn't inquire. Finally she said, "Do you think they'll be very long? I'd like to speak to your mother."

"They should be back soon."

"All right." She turned to look back toward the street. It wasn't snowing, but she must have been cold, because her nose and ears were bright pink, and she shivered even with that coat on. She didn't seem to want to leave. "I'm praying for you," she said. Then she hurried away, and I watched her leave with astonishment. Praying for me? Did the Orlichs chat over dinner about how David Nowak was damned? Did they speculate about whether he still said his prayers? (I did, fervently, daily, nightly, as if to make up for my lost Sundays.) What must Marianne think? I began to chew on my lip, shortly feeling the hot sting of a wound. I'd convinced myself that Marianne, whom I hadn't spoken to since Christmas, hadn't noticed my absence, but if Mrs. Orlich was praying for me...

My parents came home soon after. I was still at the kitchen table. "What's wrong with your lip?" Matka asked, unbuttoning her coat.

I said something about biting down wrong on a piece of toast. "It looks like it hurts. Put something cold on it." She removed her coat and hung it in the hall closet. "We have leftover pot roast." She glanced at my father, who climbed the stairs without acknowledging either of us, and in his silence I was certain he blamed me. All of Greenpoint knew that the heir of the Nowak Piano Company was ready for the funny farm, thanks to my sartorial prohibitions.

"When did you have your toast?" she asked.

"Breakfast."

"You still want pot roast? Your father is probably going to want to eat soon." She entered the kitchen. "And you're wearing my robe. I don't know why you do these things—these things that you know Ojciec won't like."

I tugged at the belt. Finally I said, "Mrs. Orlich stopped by."

Matka opened a cupboard. "What did Caroline want?"

"She wanted to talk to you, but she didn't say about what."

"Did she leave a message?"

"She didn't say much," I said, and hoped that would end it.

"You mean you don't want to tell me what she said. Go on."

"She really didn't say anything to me," I said. "She said she would come back and tell you herself."

It was true. Hours later, my father was hidden away in his study, my mother was cleaning the kitchen, and I was in my room, reading, when I heard the doorbell. Mrs. Orlich had returned. Sensitized to the sound of my name, I put down my pen, went to my open bedroom door, and stood in the hallway to the left of the top of the stairs, which allowed me a view of Mrs. Orlich's cobalt hat through the railing.

"Please, come in and have something to drink," my mother said.

"No, no," said Mrs. Orlich. "I'll be out of your hair in a moment." She said something else, so quietly that I couldn't hear, and then: "Francine..."

"Yes?"

"I want you to know that I don't think ill of you or Peter at all. Not because of David. I know that you're doing the best that you can with him."

"That's kind of you, Caroline."

"I mean it. I wouldn't come to your house, in this weather, without Bunny, if I didn't mean it. I—I know you're good people.

I know that David is a good boy. You see, I think that his type of neurosis is only temporary. I know an analyst who says so. Now don't worry—I didn't mention your family by name, of course, but I'm acquainted with an analyst, a very good one, and I took it upon myself to ask him what he thought of the situation as I presented it in the abstract. He said that David was unlikely to have any serious, permanent neurosis. A phase. Hormones. Adolescence. Boys, especially very bright ones, are so likely to have trouble." In a louder rush she added, "I also wanted to let you know that my Marianne has taken an interest in your son. I think he made quite an impression on her at the Christmas party. I know she's been looking for him in church; I guess you could say she has an infatuation. And I know they're still young, and these matters are so far off, of course, but I'll let you know right now that I'd be happy to have Marianne marry your son one day. Out of all of the boys in the neighborhood, you have such a sweet, good-looking boy. I don't think ill of your family in the slightest."

I was afraid that my mother would climb the stairs and see me, so I ducked back into my room and sat in my chair, staring at my World's Fair poster with its painted, abstract sphere. In my room the walls were a patchy white, and there was a single window above my bed for the moonlight and the nightmares to come crawling in. As I'd guessed, I soon heard Matka's footsteps, and then she was standing in the doorway, leaning against the frame with her arms crossed.

"My bug," she said, though I was too old to be called that childhood nickname. She studied me for a while as if deciding something, and then she left. I hadn't said a word, but my mind was shouting, *Marianne!* I even found myself smiling. And then, in the middle of all that happiness while I dazed and dreamed, I heard my mother shriek my name, and as if waking from a deep sleep, I staggered down the hall and into their bedroom.

My father was lying on the floor, pulling his shirt from his chest and moaning. I'd never heard him make such a sound; it was like a noise that I'd think a moose would make, but it was Ojciec crying out, and it terrified all the happiness right out of me. My mother screamed my name again, and told me to call our doctor.

As my mother drove us to the hospital behind the paramedics, I thought of things to say and then discarded them. When you've got so many things to say, you end up saying none of them; there's never any way to know what is the right thing to say, and I didn't want to upset her further. But the truth was that I resented Ojciec for interrupting my tiny moment of triumph—one that even Matka could share in.

He'd had a heart attack. The stress of reviving the manufactory after the war had done a number on him, and Dr. Herms said it was nothing to sniff at. But my father's "ticker," as Dr. Herms called it, could last Ojciec to old age if he took better care of himself. He listed a number of suggestions, which Matka took down in her notebook. God willing, Dr. Herms said, Peter would live to see his great-grandchildren's christenings. I couldn't help but daydream that those great-grandchildren would have Orlich blood in them, mixed with mine. What kind of son thinks these things in such calamitous circumstances?

———◆———

I thought Matka would burst with joy as we walked to St. Jadwiga. She'd sneak looks at me, making sure I was still there, and then look at Ojciec as if to say, *Look, I have done it.* I'd been to the Cloisters with my parents on occasion, more for "tourism within New York" reasons than anything, on par with visiting Lady Liberty, but St. Jadwiga was the holiest place that I knew, and entering the double wooden doors was obviously my return as the prodigal son. I didn't know what to expect. I didn't know who would treat me as though I had never left, and who would act as though my afflictions—whatever they knew of my afflictions—were contagious. I was afraid that someone would accuse me of heresy, or possibly worse. But I came in flanked by my parents, and immediately we were greeted by the Orlichs, who descended like a flock of friendly gray pigeons, including Marianne, who had on an ashy sweater glittering with beads. "David, it's *so* good to see you," she said, her face brightening, and she grabbed my hand. I was so surprised by her warm skin that I flinched and almost pulled away, but she drew me close to a pew, and let go to briefly kneel and make the sign of the cross before scooting deep into the center, where she patted the wood beside her for me to sit down.

My parents were still talking to the Orlichs. As I moved closer to Marianne, while still maintaining a safe distance of about a foot and a half, I saw Mr. and Mrs. Pawlowski approach them. The group enfolded my parents, and everyone immediately looked at me. Their voices lowered even though I couldn't hear what they were saying to begin with, and in their murmur I heard someone say "immense disappointment." The phrase leaped out at me like a jackrabbit.

The church began to fill—the hefty butcher, straining in his suit, with his wife and three girls like something out of a fairy tale; the moron with a flattened face, who brought his widowed mother sorrow, and who also had a persistent cough that often interrupted holy contemplation; the Stopkas with young Emily and her older, tomboy sister, who was at that time twenty-two and neither married nor dating, and who I am sure is a lesbian somewhere now and surely happier than I am—all the people came in, and Marianne put her hand in mine, and I squeezed it, mostly from terror, but hoping that she would interpret it as affection. "Look," she said, the interior falling to a hush, "let's make room for our families."

———◆———

Though she never said so, my return to St. Jadwiga also sparked Matka's next suggestion: that I spend time tutoring Marianne in Latin. She was interested in Latin, and the local girls' school, St. Agnes, wasn't an institution that placed much importance on the education of young women other than to make them amiable brides, or maybe nuns. And I'm sure that Mrs. Orlich had a hand in the arrangement, too, ending in a conspiracy of study sessions that doubled as playdates, with Marianne and me being lightly supervised in living rooms while our mothers sat at someone's kitchen table and drank tea or wine.

In the beginning there was the bright spark that was Marianne; next there was the magnetism that drew us together and prickled my skin; and then, finally, the intimate conversations that served as kindling for a bonfire.

She wasn't naturally gifted at languages. Her grammar was awful, and she found it difficult to retain almost any amount of vocabulary. Still, I liked spending time with her, this girl who brought beauty into my life and kept my afternoons from being long and empty. Later I realized that this—to not have to ask for anything from a person, and to be contented still by her existence—is a great gift, and one that I wish I'd appreciated more when I had it.

On one of those infinite, limited days, in the early weeks of summer, Marianne asked, "Do you think I would make for a good nun?"

"A nun?" I thought of the nuns at my school in their habits, smacking students with rulers. "I can't imagine you living that kind of life."

The corner of her mouth twitched, and I hurriedly added, "But what do I know? The only nuns I know are the ones at school, and I've never known anyone who's become one."

"I know how ridiculous it sounds."

"No, not ridiculous," I said, knowing that I'd disappointed her, and she rolled her eyes at me.

That summer, Marianne spent an inordinate amount of her time in St. Jadwiga, praying for hours, and when she wasn't praying, she was helping Father Danuta with feeding and clothing the poor. Marianne didn't tell me any of this herself; I learned of it from Mrs. Orlich, who had become attached to Matka, and now came to our house two or three times a week to see my antisocial mother.

"That girl," Mrs. Orlich said, "will be the death of me. Of course, we consider ourselves as observant as any other family in the neighborhood, but this is an extreme Bunny and I just don't feel comfortable with."

Matka said, "It can't hurt for her to do some charity."

"It's not just charity. Of course I'm fine with charity and good works, but she prays for hours, too. The amount of time she spends praying, she might as well be praying for everyone in Greenpoint, one at a time. And she keeps mentioning joining a convent after she graduates."

"I wouldn't worry too much about that. It's not unheard of for girls to be intrigued by a religious vocation when they're young. I imagine it's a phase."

"What if it's not? She's a beautiful girl. She ought to be going on dates and daydreaming about what to name her beautiful children." Mrs. Orlich sighed. "At least she'll have less time for these things when school begins again."

In the meantime Marianne would call, rarely and randomly, and ask if she could visit. I always said yes. When she arrived on the stoop, her forehead damp and her armpits charmingly sweaty through her blouse, I'd fall for her all over again. The thought of her in a convent, unreachable, gave me a knotted stomach and a sudden inability to breathe.

On one of these visits she followed me into the kitchen, where I poured her a glass of iced tea. She had a few swigs. "Where's your mother?"

"Headache. She went up to bed a few hours ago."

"I'm sorry to hear that."

"She'll be all right—she gets them in summer when it's too hot out, and I bring her damp washcloths for her head. How's your day been?"

She said, "I helped Father Danuta for a few hours, cleaning out the Sobczak house. Then he told me to skedaddle before I got heatstroke." Her glass was now empty. "Thanks for the tea."

Mrs. Sobczak had died a few days prior. I knew her as the old lady who wore the most elaborate hats in church, and had been a widow since she was barely twenty and saddled with two kids, who later died in the Great War; I doubted Marianne knew anything about her. But I was proven wrong when she continued: "I tried not to get depressed about it. Father Danuta said she was beloved by so many people—and so she wasn't lonely, even though her husband and sons had died—but as I was going through her house I kept thinking, *This is the hallway she went down every day,* or *This is the stove she boiled hot water on,* and I couldn't help but imagine her in that house, doing all of those things alone for so many years."

"I think about growing up and being alone all the time," I said. "You're my only friend."

When I said this, I was certain that I was also Marianne's only friend, and yearned to hear her say so in return. Instead Marianne continued, as if she hadn't heard me: "When I told Father Danuta what I was thinking, he said, 'Well, Mrs. Sobczak had Christ with her. She had faith to keep her company, just as all of God's children do.'"

I'm not sure what I said to her then. I probably waited for her to change the subject, or maybe I put her glass in the sink and went to the broom closet for a box of checkers. I knew better than to ask her if she believed fully that Christ kept Mrs. Sobczak safe in all that emptiness. I wish I could tell that girl now that mortal love is no bulwark against loneliness.

Those curious months came and went like the seasons I'd marked them with. One moment she was the Church Girl, which was Marty's unclever nickname for her, and the next she was no closer to the religious life than any other neighborhood girl. My neuroses loosened their grip—on Sundays Matka still picked out my clothes, but I no longer needed her to dress me. I grew brave enough to glance at myself in mirrors, or shop windows, and see my true and rapidly maturing self. I attributed these blessings to Marianne, my guardian angel, whom I would walk to my house from St. Agnes for Latin and board games and whatever else entertained us. I interpreted her change from Church Girl to regular Jane as a sign that in the battle between the nunnery and the sacrament of marriage, the latter had won; I only hoped that it meant I had won, too.

Then during geometry class one of the sisters came to fetch me, a rare interruption. I was too nervous to ask her why. The halls were long and empty, dotted with too-short water fountains, and we silently walked through clouds of foul air erupting from the boys' bathrooms.

Mr. Pawlowski was sitting on one of the leather benches outside of the principal's office. He stood when he saw me.

"Davy," he said, "I've come to take you to the hospital. Your father's had another attack."

"You'd better go," the sister said, and put her hand on my shoulder, which made me flinch.

After Mr. Pawlowski started navigating his Rolls-Royce away from the curb, I expected him to say more. He did not. Finally I asked, "How did it happen? Is he going to be all right?"

Mr. Pawlowski sighed. "Your mother is already at St. Mary's" was all he said, and we sat in silence while I fretted.

When we got to the hospital, Matka saw me and stood, and she blinked in confusion as though trying to figure out why Mr. Pawlowski had brought a monkey to see her.

"How is he?" Mr. Pawlowski asked.

She looked at him and shook her head. Obviously she had been crying. Her thin arms wrapped around me, and she put her head on my shoulder. She said, "He's alive, Davy. It will be all right."

———◆———

We entered the new decade with my father in a coma—and yet instead of getting worse, my neuroses seemed to be abating. Father Danuta had been making appearances at our home for months, going up the stairs with his bag, and for hours he sat with my father and mother in their room, praying. I prayed, too, with them and alone; yet Ojciec remained in his hospital bed, which had been moved into our house by loyal factory employees, as December of the previous year came and went. The fact that we had skipped the Pawlowskis' Christmas party that winter weighed on me more than I'd expected it would. Marianne told me that she'd sung again for the party, and she sang the carol again for me alone when my mother went upstairs, her voice breaking in parts from the softness of it.

One day she and I stopped on the way home from weekday Mass. I was still fourteen. She was still fifteen. On the wet bench I touched her pale, cold knees. It felt like early spring and the snow was melting into its customary dips and hollows, and when Marianne asked how my father was doing I was afraid to answer, because the more times she asked, the more I felt the unkind passage of time. She looked at me expectantly, her eyes the same mossy hue I see at the bottom of the river when I swim with the children. I said, "Father Danuta and my mother say it's in God's hands."

"Of course it is." She put her hand on mine. "Don't you like me, David?"

I almost said, *Do you need to ask?* but laughed instead. We'd been such a curious neighborhood twosome for years, with each having no friends but the other, so I did the bravest thing I'd ever done: I kissed her. I want to say that she tasted like sugar, but she didn't taste like anything. Kissing her was like dipping my lips into the rising stream of a water fountain, and perfectly blissful. I kissed her again and again with my fingers in her hair, and she kissed me back until she gently put her hands to my shoulders and pushed me away.

"Not here," she said. "Let's go somewhere more private. I know a place."

As we walked, Marianne asked, "Do you think you'll marry me?"

I tried not to stop dead, forcing myself to keep walking as I said, "Why, do you want me to?"

She smiled. "I asked, didn't I?"

I held her hand. She led me down streets and familiar alleys till I saw that we were going around the back of St. Jadwiga, where there was a ladder attached to the side, leading to the flat part of the roof. She began to climb with determination; I followed without arguing. I could see up her skirt and saw that she was wearing a pair of white panties with lace trim, and I saw her caramel-colored pubic hair sprouting from the sides. Immediately I paused on the ladder, embarrassed and excited by my body's reaction. She hauled herself over the side.

Next we were on the small roof. All of a sudden we were closer to Heaven, and I was lit up with hormones and fireworks, and closer to jumping, too. I had never felt my blood beat so hard. I could see the neighborhood all around, its bricks and streets and parked cars, and the people milling about with their hats on heads and jackets buttoned tightly around themselves, and I saw stray cats prancing into alleyways. Then she turned and beamed her bright smile at me, and I loved her. I reached for her hand and kissed it. I said, "I love you," and she laughed in a manner that could to my ears only mean *Yes.* We stood on the roof and looked out at Greenpoint. She pulled me to her, biting my bottom lip with her square teeth, pressing a thumb into the side of my neck, and I thought I would turn to ash and fly away on the wind.

The roof is where we rendezvoused then, both of us taking great care to preserve her innocence. I never even kissed her on the neck, which seemed like one dangerous erotic breach of many. To think of putting my hand or hands on her breasts or thighs was out of the question. I took care to be a gentleman out of gratitude and respect; I was also still feeling the remnants of a disgust with my own body, so I was happy with what we had—butterfly kisses, mouth kisses, embraces. Mild Marianne, my girlfriend, was the most stable thing in my life. For most of the year I went to school and she went to school; then I accompanied her to daily Mass; then we went back to the Orlich house and I tutored her in Latin until six o'clock, which is when Mr. Pawlowski came to fetch me, and I ate dinner with him and my mother in our dining room while my father was comatose in his bed upstairs. In the summer Marianne and I had even more free time to ourselves, and then came fall again, which is when Marianne insisted on celebrating my birthday because no one else, including Matka, had remembered its passing. There was a surprise yellow cake, which she had baked and carried in a wicker basket. We ate cake on the roof, saying very little to each other, though she did sing the Polish equivalent of "Happy Birthday to You." "It's a song that means 'May you live for a hundred years,'" she said, and put her hand on my thigh for a moment before tucking it back under hers.

I worried, in the meantime, about Mr. Pawlowski. As my father was indisposed, Mr. Pawlowski naturally took over certain aspects of the manufactory. He'd served as my father's assistant since my grandfather died, and I'd turned a mere fifteen in the year Marianne sang to me. All responsibilities therefore fell to him, but purely in duty and not by name. There was the chance that my father would return to us, and his name, after all, was the one embossed above the keys. Still, I feared that Mr. Pawlowski would usurp my position as the owner of the Nowak Piano Company when I was the only son of Peter Nowak himself.

So it was a miracle when, in the middle of one Tuesday night, I was awakened by a flurry of activity in the master bedroom. It was the Polish nurses and my mother, who slept in a cot beside my father; they were all exclaiming that Ojciec was awake. When I entered the room, Matka ran to the door and grabbed me. "Davy, look!" she cried, her face wet. "Our prayers have been answered!"

I did look. He was propped up in the bed now, his gaze watchful. Soft bags drooped beneath his eyes; the lamps drew blobby shadows across his face. He was also looking directly at me, unblinking, and then he beckoned me to come closer. He smiled and said, "How have you been, David?"

The room went quiet—the nurses, who were scrambling for a glass of water; Matka, who was weeping—everything silenced itself.

"I've been well," I said, which sounded ridiculous in its ordinariness. "It's good to see you're awake."

He nodded. "Good marks in school?"

"Yes."

"Good. Do you remember what the pin block is for?"

"It holds the tuning pins in place."

"And what kind of wood do we use for our pin blocks?"

"Beech," I said.

He nodded again. "Good. Good."

"Ojciec," Matka said, "I'm going to call Dr. Herms."

"All right." Ojciec closed his eyes. One of the girls tapped his shoulder, then lifted the glass of water to his lips, dribbling water on his chin.

◆

The prognosis was not good. Ojciec went to the hospital and returned with pills and the knowledge that it was very likely that he would have another attack, and whether he would survive that one, no one could say. He was stoic as he faced the possibility of a premature death. There were matters to be attended to, one of those matters being the question of the factory and its ownership. It was as much of a surprise to me as I'm sure it was to Mr. Pawlowski when Ojciec insisted that I be named the owner of the Nowak Piano Company without delay. The act of signing papers with a lawyer was both ordinary and momentous; I, the only son of Peter Nowak, had triumphed, but the context for my triumph certainly wasn't a celebratory one. I was shocked to find that I felt no better—no prouder, no loftier—after being named the company's president. I was in tenth grade, and still going to high school. What kind of company president wore his school uniform to the office, and came in each afternoon after school was out?

"You like it here?" Mr. Pawlowski asked. We were in his office after a week into my new position. The radiator was broken; I could see his words forming clouds in the cold air. He was planning to move up to my father's office, which I'd wanted for my own. We were talking about how it would be better, in his opinion, if I took his soon-to-be-former room so that I could learn how to keep my eye on things.

"I like it fine."

"Managing your school and work responsibilities all right?"

I resisted the urge to scoff and simply nodded. I was irritated that he wanted to take my father's office. It was supposed to be mine, regardless of how little I knew or how much authority he commanded over the workers. At the time, I believed that were I really strong enough to be in charge, I would take control of the situation and tell him that he couldn't have it—nonsense, in hindsight, for a young man following a full-grown adult every day like a mule.

"You'll love this room," he said. "Ah, the things I've done here. The conversations your father and I had. The decisions. You're lucky to be getting a head start in the business world, Davy. You'll learn a lot from me. I owe it to your father to help you out, same as he helped me out after your grandfather died. You do need help, you see. Running a business is no small potatoes. You don't think it's small potatoes, do you?"

"No."

"Because that would be a mistake. Learn from me and you'll learn from the best. I know you're the one with the keys to the kingdom. Don't think I don't. I have to admit that I was a *little* bit hurt"—and here he held up his hand to indicate a centimeter of space between thumb and forefinger—"to know that you were taking over. But no hard feelings. You're his only son—of course he would let you take over. Selling to me—well, he'd never do that, come to think of it—he's too proud. The only thing—the *only* thing that surprises me—is that he gave you the company when you're so young. That's really the only thing. What other people say about your problems, your personality, that's not something that I bother with. It's really the life experience that I'm thinking about. But with me on your side, that won't be a problem at all. I'll guide you as though you were my very own son. Have I told you that I think of you as my very own son? If you like, I'll tell Vicky to help you decorate your new office. She's got an eye for the aesthetic. In fact," he said suddenly, "since I think of you as my son, I want to ask you something. I don't mean this to hurt you, and I don't want you to take this the wrong way. I mean it in the way that your father would be caring for you if he could. Davy, you seem quite fond of that Orlich girl."

I shrugged, though I was cringing inside. He meant well; I already knew this, but I suspected something unpleasant coming as he thumbed the underside of his chin in upward strokes.

"Because—and again, I hate to say this, hate to even *suggest* this—but the Orlichs are not, shall we say, the most trustworthy of people. You know that they aren't on the same level as we are, financially, and they have a certain amount of envy."

"I hadn't noticed."

"It isn't even Marianne who is being devious, most likely," Mr. Pawlowski said, "but her parents. At one point, none of us knew them. They were new to our neighborhood, and we gave them every opportunity to belong. But almost everyone sees their true selves at this point. They're interested in—how shall I put this—what your family has, and what they do not. They live off of Mr. Orlich's accounting income, which is serviceable, but they also live beyond their means. You can see this by the way they dress, the things they have. And the way that they can best get at a different life altogether is through Marianne. She seems like a good girl and loves her parents immensely, I would imagine, and probably would do anything that her parents tell her to." He paused. "Do you see my point? You see my point. I don't mean to burst your bubble. Your bubble isn't burst, is it? Like I said, Marianne is a good girl. And that's all I'll say about that," he said. "You just think about that. It's part of growing up. You see eyes through the life of business and that's when everything becomes business, everything as transaction. Are your hours up for the day? Should I drive you back home?"

I wanted to walk. The trip from Manhattan to Brooklyn, with all the public transportation included, would take a long time, but I didn't want to be in the same small space with Mr. Pawlowski anymore, and especially not in his Rolls-Royce, which reeked of pipe smoke. As I walked, I was not following the rules of New York sidewalk etiquette; people practically shoved me into the street as they bustled by. But a movie reel was unspooling itself in my mind, with kisses and songs. I knew Marianne so well that I could summon, as though she were standing beside me, her reedy laugh. Frame by frame I asked myself, *Is this a lie? Could it be possible that Mr. Pawlowski is right—if not wholly, then at least partially?* He was a businessman. He'd acknowledged his own cynicism. He didn't understand that Marianne accepted me without reservation, and so what if the piano company was a part of that? We gave and we took and we received mutually. We spent our afternoons running through alleys, chasing each other, the chaser always kissing the chased. The roof at St. Jadwiga, our second home and a safe haven. She wrote me letters, long letters, and signed them in slants and loops: *May our hearts be ever blessed.* I trusted her; I wanted to believe her, so I deliberately refused to believe that our love could be a lie.

———◆———

My father died in November of my senior year. As the pallbearers lowered him into the ground I watched Matka shrink into herself like a blooming flower in reverse, nothing but a bud afterward. My mother took a three-month-long holiday in Minnesota, where she drowned her anguish in the twenty-below chill with her sister, the "Midwestern harlot," as my father had called her. Who knows what he would have thought of his wife hiding in a snowdrift town called Monserrat, drinking vodka out of the bottle and swaddled in fur. It was after Peter died, everyone said, that she lost her grip on her natural eccentricity; after all, what kind of mother would leave her son for three months after such a tragedy?

She came back at the end of winter. Her suitcase was gone, and so was the coat. She'd given both of them to Penelope, she said, who had barely anything. Gosh, you've never felt that kind of cold, she said. She was wearing a lot of makeup, but I could tell that she looked awful underneath. Her foundation didn't quite match her sallow neck. Have I mentioned that my mother's once-placid face, after my father's death, now had a perpetually bewildered expression, as though to say, *How did I wind up here?* After she came back from Minnesota I was under the impression that she had become absorbed in the cold there, and that it was impossible for her to materialize fully as flesh and not frozen, fluffy water.

I am confident this is where the true sorrow—sorrow? I lack the correct word—began, when I learned that it is possible for *I hurt, I hurt, I hurt, I hurt* to be my only heartbeat. *Puh-lum. Puh-lum.* Of course, it seemed natural for me to grieve. Matka, after all, was grieving. My peers and teachers at school knew that Peter Nowak had died, and his son, David, who had just inherited the Nowak Piano Company not so long ago, surely must be grieving as well. Marianne, God bless her, particularly mothered me. She had a gift for not making me feel like a child even as she sat with my head in her lap, stroking my hair in silence.

All of this in hindsight seems ordinary. It was ordinary and then—when I realized I was mourning something more than my father—it turned into something monstrous. My despair sprang from an awareness that whatever I had suffered from before, whatever *neuroses* had been dormant for this brief period while my father slept and Marianne walked tall and golden by my side as my only companion, had returned. It was a feeling that eventually metamorphosed outside the realm of human emotion. This unnameable thing I eventually called "vitaphobia" as a feeble attempt to get at the nastiness that was neurosis turned inside out—the fear of everything else turned into the fear of actually being alive. In simplest terms, vitaphobia was the fear of the sun shining or not shining, of opening my eyes or keeping them closed, of eating or not eating, of eating too much or too little, of darkness and light, of all the colors and hues of the rainbow, of every texture that my body could touch. Everything that I could register caused paralyzing fear, and the only solution to this that I could think of was to be dead. I am trying to keep this from becoming maudlin as much as I'm compelled to just open the window and scream, or writhe around on the floor right now. I ask the Lord, *Do you know what you've been asking of me for all of these years?* But of course. *And how can you ask me to continue? All those nights in the woods, praying, hoping for an answer I could use!*

Yet I didn't kill myself then. There was something keeping me alive that I've since lost: a pessimistic optimism. One frantic afternoon I tied a belt around my neck in my bedroom and yanked hard, but I choked for only a second before I pried the pathetic noose away from my throat and threw it across the room. I didn't tell Marianne. In the worst of it, I wanted to protect her, which was my first adult instinct; but not telling someone that you've got vitaphobia is like telling someone that you're not covered in blood when you are—it doesn't work, and you look the worse for denying it. She came to my house and I could see the fear that slipped over her face like a mourning veil. I lay in bed and she prayed at the foot of it, usually the Memorare, over and over, but I slept through most of it, and even my sleep was painful and shallow. I dreamed of Matka. Where was she? When she spoke, hovering over my face, I smelled the faintly sweet burn of vodka on her breath, her teeth the color of piano keys. I conflated her and the Virgin Mary as she cradled my head in her lap. Eventually I was my old self again—though hardened and glossy, having gone through a crucible—and later, as an adult, the doctors would explain to me that this was the natural course of my illness; even unmedicated, there would be times when I was well and times when I was sick, but I didn't know that for years, and I attributed my wellness or lack thereof to whatever seemed an appropriate precipitant, like the seasons, or, later, the ups and downs of my marriage, or a nasty encounter at the K & Bee Grocery. It wasn't a spiritual illness, they explained to me. *And what are your spiritual beliefs?* I asked them in turn. One said he was uncomfortable disclosing such a thing to a patient. Another said he was Lutheran. There were a few more, but even the Catholic one didn't put his hand on my shoulder and say, *Go, then, to a priest, and have yourself exorcised.*

"I did," Marianne informed me toward the end of my senior year, "talk to Father Danuta. I said to him that you might be possessed. It was naive, of course, but he was kind. He listened to the things I said, and then he asked me some questions, like a doctor palpating a pain. He said that you were very sick, but that you weren't possessed by the Devil, and that the Church performed very few exorcisms to begin with. Is it strange to say that I was—"

"Disappointed?"

"No, not that..." (But she was. At least a demon could be cast out.)

She finally said, "I was afraid for you. I didn't know what to do for you but pray."

Eventually I was functioning again, but what had happened to my mind left me hobbled, as if I'd been hit by a car instead, and with poor healing to show for it. I graduated with mediocre marks; I suspect I avoided failing entirely only because adults pitied me, couldn't help me in any other way, were too embarrassed to offer a kind ear, and so raised my grades. *Good for you,* I thought as I stared down at some written exam of mine, too beaten down for truly enthusiastic sarcasm. At the top was written *70.*

And Mr. Pawlowski, my surrogate father now, squeezed me almost entirely out of any company matters, having me sign here and there on various dotted lines on papers I never read—not that I blamed him. What could he do, when I was the one who really owned everything, but could do almost nothing. Nothing, that is, but sell the company.

"If you're going to sell, sell to George," Matka said. "He knows what he's doing." But I still couldn't forgive him for what he had said to me about Marianne, so I nodded and said, "Of course," with no intention of following through; Matka would love me no matter what, though selling the company would give us both more than enough to live on for the rest of our lives.

There was a businessman from Maine who was interested in moving to New York. He was willing to keep the name intact, and

offered $10 million for the factory and everything associated with
the factory, including its workers and unsold pianos. I tried to get
more because I was proud and hurt, which is a terrible combination for partaking in a business deal. He said, "Don't you have
an adult to handle these things for you?" I said, "Fuck you," and
hung up.

I thought there would be more offers, and there was one man
who had dealt with my father before and seemed serious about
making a purchase. There were two caveats. First, he would change
the name of the company to Norris & Sons. Second, he would pay
$8 million for the company, and no more. Having said no to the
previous man, I felt compelled to say no to this one as well.

Mr. Pawlowski, then, having heard about my pathetic attempts, offered $20 million, and he would keep the name. I had
always known he was wealthy, what with his extravagant car
and lavish parties, and what funds he did need to raise were
easily coaxed from his multitudes. What did I care if he took my
place? I'd lost my marbles, or I was possessed. Either way, there
was no hope for the future of the company with me at the helm. I
made the choice to sell the factory, the brand, and the whole rest
of a mess of it to Pawlowski. This is where the Nowak fortune
is from. Half of it went to my mother, and the rest to me. This is
the money that I've been living off of; this is the money that will
be left behind for Gillian and William and Daisy when I'm gone,
which ought to bring me a modicum of comfort.

News of the sale must have spread quickly, because it was
only two days afterward that Mr. Orlich came to our door, his
face flushed and blurry through the peephole like a poorly taken
photograph, and I knew that if I opened the door I would only
be inviting more of the bad fortune of which I already had an
abundance. He rang the bell over and over, and then he resorted
to banging with his fist. I had every intention of waiting him out.
He could stand there and throw a tantrum if he wanted, I decided, and then I went upstairs, where the sound of his undoubtedly drunken anger continued to rage.

"What in God's name is that?" I heard Matka call from her
room. "Who's there?"

"No one," I said.

"Well, tell *no one* to go away."

"He'll go away when he's tired."

I had underestimated Mr. Orlich's capability for persistence. He continued his campaign to have the door opened while I debated calling the police, and then I remembered that he was still Marianne's father. To sully his name would do no good. For Marianne to know that I'd been the one to sully it was no better.

Finally I opened the door, and there he was, barking, "Why have a goddamn doorbell if you're not going to answer it?" I couldn't see Marianne's face in his at all. He was, in fact, the exact opposite of her: the picture of a face so accustomed to scowling that it had hardened into cruelty.

"I'm sorry," I said.

"I heard you sold your family's company," he said. "I heard you sold it for a substantial sum."

"I did sell it."

"And you want to marry my daughter. My Marianne."

This was not how I had imagined asking for Marianne's hand in marriage. I stuttered yes.

"What are your plans for this money you have now?"

I said nothing, noticing that he hadn't asked to come in. I was grateful for this because I had no intention of letting him in, even if he was Marianne's father. He smelled like liquor—I was becoming accustomed to the smell, thanks to my mother, and it made me anxious—and he seemed to be rapidly approaching some point.

"So what are you going to do with yourself? All day long, day after day."

It was, in fact, a good question. My plans were to live off the money and try not to lose my mind, but Heaven help me if I allowed honesty to dictate the conversation.

"You've been after Marianne for some time now. She has known no other beau, as I'm sure you are aware. She is a pious, hardworking young lady. She is going to provide a home and children for you. That is your expectation, I guess?" He was gasping now, spluttering with rage and unwept tears and the desire to tear me limb from limb. "And what will you do then? In this home my girl provides for you? Have you considered it? Are you going to sit there in your fancy house, counting your money, and thinking of ways to embarrass her with your insanity? Because that's all I can imagine you doing with no company, no job, no responsibilities."

I opened my mouth and closed it. He was right. I was worth less than nothing, and would be worth less than nothing to his daughter. But I loved her, and I selfishly wanted to be with her no matter what this furious, drunken man was saying to me, even if it was the truth.

"So, then, David Nowak," he continued, "why *did* you sell your family's company? Because you're a lunatic. Everyone knows that you are *fundamentally* incapable of living a functional life. And still we supported you. Gave you the benefit of the doubt. When people talked, my wife and I insisted on giving you a chance to prove yourself. To take forward everything your father has built. You dare insult me, my wife, my son, my daughter—*my daughter!*—by doing this—giving up the one thing that could save you. And now you think that you can be my son-in-law. Is *that* what you think?"

I was not going to say yes. I was not going to say no. I began to close the door, but Bunny Orlich was a quick drunk. He hurled himself against the door, and before I could realize what was happening his fist was slamming into my face with a noisy cracking sound, which sent me blindly backward and clutching at my nose.

"Do you hear me? Leave her alone, and I'll leave you alone. But I find out you're an even bigger idiot than I think, and your poor mother will be all alone in this big house of hers, with no husband to sleep next to and no son to see her on Christmas, and with two gravestones to lay flowers on." He stared at me, flapping his punching hand. Had Matka heard? Was there even a commotion? There were drops of blood on his fingers. Matka in Monserrat. Matka underground. Please, never let her know about my Motel Ponderosa. Let her be dead.

———◆———

Something was visibly wrong the next morning when Marianne came to my home, the sky blue-black behind her. Surely it pained her to be there, but she was that kind of girl—and I say "girl," but she was a woman dressed in a floral blouse, a wool skirt; the girl whom I had loved was already grown, and the boy who I had been was still halfway in front of her and hardly a man.

"Your nose," she said. She reached out as if to touch it, and then drew her fingers back. "I can't believe he did that. And your eye. Oh, it looks so terrible. Is your nose broken?"

"I don't know. Maybe. Probably."

She began to touch my cheek with the very tips of her fingers, patting the skin.

I asked, "Did you sneak out of the house?"

"Yes, but it doesn't matter. I'm so sorry." She told me that she was leaving for Chicago. It was her parents, of course. They didn't want her in Greenpoint anymore, never mind that I hadn't attempted to see her since Mr. Orlich came. Better to assume the worst of me. She was so beautiful, and was growing only more beautiful by the day, I was certain of it. Her eyes had a perpetual-ly soft sleepiness to them; her silvery hair was mixed with cream. Already I was ticking off her attributes in my mind—*good-bye, good-bye...*

I said, "That's ridiculous. They don't own you. You're an adult. We could marry. I have more than enough to sustain us financially." Briefly I thought of Mr. Pawlowski. "You've always known this."

"You want me to marry you. You think we can have a full and happy life together."

"Yes. Of course. Why not? Isn't that what you've thought all this time?" But when she raised her eyes to me again I saw how sad she was, and how plain her doubt was at that prospect, per-haps imagining herself as a nursemaid to me as I disappeared further into lunacy; then I felt the gentlest flicker of hatred in my rib cage, where all my love for her was living, and soon we were both crying out of stupidity and helplessness and uncertainty.

"Come in."

"I—no. I do, I want to, but I don't think I should."

"Just come in. For God's sake."

"Why? What difference does it make?"

"To talk. To figure something out."

"No, it's all set up, I don't have a choice. It's my parents, I swear, it has nothing to do with how I feel."

"You're going to Chicago? And where will you go after Chicago?"

She wiped her eyes. "I don't know! I don't know anything. He said he would kill you. No matter where we went, David, he would find us."

Quickly Marianne turned around and hustled her solid body down the stoop. I watched the back of her head and its inelegant, lopsided bun travel, bobbing slightly of its own accord, moving like a head gently agreeing yes, but it was only hope, I was frozen, it was only a dream, and I finally called out, sure that she could still hear my voice: "I love you. Write to me."

PART II

DAVID

AND

JIA-HUI

WIFE OF DAVID

JIA-HUI (1954–1968)

in translation

In Mandarin the words for suicide are 自殺. In literal terms this means "self-kill." My husband David has self-killed and it has been four months now. I knew this would happen once I found him crashed to the floor from attempting to hang himself. I knew that it was only a matter of time.

Or yes I knew this when I was first told that he was crazy by his own mother. But who can believe one's mother-in-law, especially when that mother-in-law refers to you as a souvenir without batting an eyelash, and burns with anger in your presence simply because you exist and have small eyes and skin with the undertone of ripe star fruit. Or yes I knew that he would 自殺 while in a penthouse suite in San Francisco, when we were surrounded by luxury and William was in my belly, and I awoke to be confronted with a floor of broken glass. I'm afraid to admit that I was ever so naïve. What other things do I not know, when I thought I knew so much?

David was the one who changed my name. It was Jia-Hui Chen until I was nineteen, and who I was then bears little resemblance to who I am now at thirty-three, with two children and a dead husband who behaved as though we had always lived in this wooden home in these woods, in this former gold mining town like an inserted memory. I am much older, for example, than the Daisy Nowak who walked into Saks Fifth Avenue in the summer of 1954. In the air-conditioned building scented with perfume I stood next to my new white husband, who was willing to spend "two thousand dollars or more" on his wife, whom he called an "Oriental lamb" not only to my ear in passionate love but to anyone willing to indulge him in listening; David, who only knew of money and not of pretty clothes; and I not knowing the ridiculousness of what two thousand American dollars meant, or the extent of David's irrationality or wealth. But I looked at the salesgirl, whose hair was a helmet of distinct red curls, each a perfect sculpture, and I read in her round face the answer as the corners of her mouth pulled back and her eyes shot the accusation, *Who do you think you are?*

I emerged from the multi-mirrored dressing room in the first dress, which exposed the soft hollow above my collarbones, and fit at the waist with a full skirt. I felt the flutter that I had known when, at the bar, David first put his scarred hand on my waist. When I felt it through the silk of my dress. (Fatty asked me later if the scarred hand was worse than the white men's thicketed arms and legs. Was it worse than their pale koi bellies, she wanted to know.) The sight of myself in the multiple mirrors, dressed like a Hollywood starlet out of a song-and-dance magazine, was like seeing a chicken with the head of a lizard. I could never become the girl that the dress was made for, but would be an entirely new creature. I smiled. The black-haired girl in the mirror smiled. Blond David grinned like a child. You think that these details are not important, but they are. In Kaohsiung, as the daughter of a mama-san, I could have had the red-haired woman's face kicked in by thugs. But as Daisy Nowak, wife of David? I could only smile.

◆

Who are you being an Oriental girl, the daughter of a mama-san and a mob boss father, a young woman who hunted girls to hire like a wolf in the woods.

One might think that a sixteen-year-old girl would be so young as to not have any power or authority over other females, especially ones who were older than she. Let me reassure you that this is not the case. A certain repertoire of cutting looks and bitch-mouthed retorts, plus a sharp sort of attractiveness, makes a girl like me as intimidating as any tattooed thug. Part of this was nature, but the other part was a consequence of the cutthroats who raised me. I also had an uncanny ability to see past pouting lips and clotted-on makeup, deep into whether a girl could be transformed into a bar girl and, more important, a moneymaker. I had no formula for making such a decision; it simply came to me. Another girl in my position, had she a lesser eye, might have chosen a potential bar girl with predictably appealing characteristics. But on occasion I would select a rather flat-chested girl, with the secret knowledge that her flirtatious tentacles touched not only myself, but also anyone whose favor she wished to curry, and many of my mother's best, and most eccentric, girls came to her from my cultivated choosing. By my eighteenth birthday I was seeing up to three or four girls a day for evaluation. Some, having heard that the Golden Lotus was a more hospitable refuge than their own sorry homes, had come to meet me at the market (always in the morning, before the heat descended, and when I was at my least ill-tempered). Others I'd found while prowling the streets, searching for girls running errands for their families. I'd ask them, "You want a better life?" as they hurtled past with their baskets and bags. Leery, yet grateful for the interruption, some would slow their pace. The pretty ones knew what I was after. No one would call Fatty pretty, which is why I had given her the job that I did.

———————◆———————

With David I was the girl who, when we returned to the White Hotel, chopped apples and oranges with a cheap knife on the hotel desk, and who said, "Fuck!" (my first English obscenity, taught to me by a sailor with an ear like 燒賣) when juice got into a cut on her finger. And David said, "You don't have to do that," as I arranged them on a brand-new platter, and I said, "It is polite for your mother." Because at the bar I was the slut who learned "Whiskey in the Jar" for the hilarity of the sailors, but I was also the girl who knew what it meant to have piety, with a mother who heaped too much pork and so many pomelos on the ancestors' altar.

I brought that fruit platter to the Nowaks' brown stone house. I wore a lemon-yellow sundress with an embroidered bodice and kept stopping my fingers in midstroke as I felt the thick stitching, correcting my motions so that it wouldn't look like I was caressing myself sexually, with the platter resting in my lap and my new purse the color of fresh milk beside me. The air, which walloped us as we got out of the taxi, reminded me of home with a slap of damp heat. David put his wallet back in his pocket and moved to the trunk to take our suitcase from the driver; David, who was taller than any other man I knew and gangly, and made a swallow's nest of his hair by yanking it when he was nervous. I reached up and smoothed it down because I loved him. David said firmly, "So let's go ahead and do this."

It was all a dream; I was sleepwalking through everything. We were going to tell his mother that we were married. We were even going to, depending on the level of our bravado, tell her that I was pregnant, though the child in my belly was barely a month old and not yet stirring, and only known to us because of my otherwise precise menstrual regularity and symptoms of soreness and sickness. We were visiting her during our honeymoon early in July. We did not know what we were going to do after that. But Taiwan already felt very far away, as if it were itself a dream, and there was nothing around us to remind me of its fragments. The wisps of memory were already fading and being replaced by this also dreamlike reality. David banged the knocker twice.

A woman came to the door. I knew that she was Mrs. Francine Nowak right away. She had his blond, nearly white hair pulled back with no fringe, and the same twitchy mouth, which jerked slightly as it smiled as if on a hook.

"Davy," she said, hugging him, patting him on the back as though he could break, and then, looking over his shoulder: "You brought a friend."

His father was dead and he had told his mother nothing about me. He was a simple man and had not wanted a big wedding, and we had gone to the town hall. He was passionate and had wanted to marry me as soon as possible, without his mother's interference, and we had gone through all the hoops, the visa and paperwork, to do it. He loved his mother, but she had grown, in his words, *difficult* over the years. My English was both good enough to assume this was the case and bad enough to cause misunderstandings. This peculiar state of being in the vaguest language space was enough to paralyze me if I thought too much about it, because there was much that I could misunderstand. In Taiwan

I had been proud of my ability to manipulate language to my advantage. Here I was lucky if I understood most of a sentence.

"Her name is Daisy," he said.

"Charmed," Mrs. Nowak said. "I didn't _____ you were bringing someone. You really should have told me—I haven't _____ prepared. I _____ she can sleep in the _____ room."

David said, "It's _____ hot."

She backed into the hall, pulling the door open as she did so, and she stood behind the door as we entered until we were inside (her disappearance strange for a moment), at which point she pushed the door shut and double-bolted it. The air was cool and thick with pipe smoke—but who smoked a pipe in this house of a dead man? I looked deep into the brown stone house, which had entryways into other rooms on either side and opened into a large room at the end, where I saw plush green sofas and a lamp. In the safety of her home Mrs. Nowak now looked at me more closely.

"I cut this fruit for you," I said, still holding the plate.

"You _____ did," she said. "Bring it into the kitchen. I have some _____ _____. David, I'll bet you haven't had a good _____ in _____."

"Don't you live alone?" David asked.

She nodded; she looked like he had accused her of something.

"Well, it _____ of pipe smoke," he said.

"It's a new bad habit, you could say. We all have them."

"I suppose," David said, "that we do." He glanced at me briefly and smiled. Already I was unmoored. Mrs. Nowak began to walk down the long hall as we followed. I looked at the photographs on the red velvet walls, including one of David at a grand piano. The Nowaks used to make pianos and that was the source of the Nowak fortune; that much I knew. Then we turned to the right and entered a kitchen more glorious than any of the stony kitchens I had entered in my nineteen years. The stove gleamed white, with two oven doors beneath it. The cabinets were the pale pink of watermelon milk. Buttery containers of three sizes sat on the countertop, and they were the exact color of the yellow tiles.

"_____ for your friend?" Mrs. Nowak asked, moving to the icebox. She removed a large bottle.

"She's never had it," David said. "I don't think she has. Champaaaagne?" he asked. I shook my head, smiled. He asked if I wanted some. I nodded. The less I said, the better it would be for all of us. "You can put that down," he added, pointing at the platter, and I looked for a suitable surface.

Mrs. Nowak took the fruit from me. She was smiling again. She wanted to speak to David alone about me, but instead she retrieved three tall, thin glasses with single legs while David popped open the bottle, and he poured me a glass of something full of bubbles. I waited for them to drink first before I took a sip, but if there was anything I knew how to do, including crying only when I wanted to and dancing the twist, it was how to drink. I didn't startle when it went down my throat and I felt like I was inhaling water.

"Delicious," I said.

Mrs. Nowak said, "Excuse me?"

I said it again. She looked at David. He said, "She said, 'Delicious,' _____."

"Ah. So," she said, "is this your Oriental souvenir?"

She may have thought that I didn't know what *souvenir* meant, but David had bought me many: a flattened penny with the Statue of Liberty on it, a metal Times Square key chain for keys I didn't own.

I thought, *Eat dog shit,* and the place between my ribs stung.

David said, "Don't start."

"So who is she?" she asked. "I _____ she wants _____. Don't tell me you've already married her?"

He paused, and seemed unsurprised that she had guessed. "I have, actually."

"David!"

"Well, I *have*," he said, and he did not sound the way I wanted him to, like a grown man, but like a child who was promised something and failed to receive it. He was tugging at his hair. I wanted to say, *Stop it,* and wished that he had the same self-awareness that I'd had in the taxi. "And," he added, "I love her! I'm happy. I'm doing much better now."

"Oh, Davy. You were barely gone! The _____ still give me looks at _____! And already, a wife? Were you even _____ by a _____?"

David said nothing. He gestured at the air.

"Oh," she said, and took a gulp of champagne before setting it down, but the glass was too fragile for her gesture to have force.

"What do you expect me to say? How can I be happy, when she's not even a _____ [emphasis]? Does she even know who Jesus is?"

"I know," I said, although all I knew of Jesus was that he was related to missionaries—the only Americans who came to Kaohsiung were missionaries and sailors, with David being a gadabout and an obvious exception. Fatty had encountered a missionary one day, she told me. Most missionaries in Kaohsiung spoke both English and Mandarin, but this one had not; he gave her a pamphlet with a pencil drawing on the cover of a man hanging on a cross, but her English was much worse than mine, and the missionary had given up on trying to explain. "He said something about a 'word,'" she said, and I said, "*Word* means 字. What 字?" She shrugged. I could have said something to Mrs. Nowak about the word, but then she would have wanted to know more. She might even ask me what the word was as a test, and I had no idea even though I had thought very long about the puzzle. Maybe it was *love*, or *happy*, or *man*. But I knew it was not *woman*. There was no woman strung up beside the bad man, but that was because she was not important, made into a figure to be revered or reviled.

When I said that I knew who Jesus was, Mrs. Nowak gave me a cross look. She said something that I didn't understand even a little bit, and then she had another gulp of champagne.

"We can go back to the hotel," David said, a threat. He touched my shoulder.

Yes, I thought, *let's go back to the hotel*. I thought of the bed that was more comfortable than any bed I had ever lain in, where I could fall asleep and dream a million dreams without moving a centimeter. But then Mrs. Nowak's face went soft and sad, and she touched her son's shoulder.

"No," she said. Her voice sounded like the cracked shell of a tea egg, full of networked maps of where the injuries had been sustained, and then she wept, her free hand moving to her leaking eyes. "No, please stay. Don't go. I think about you every day—where you are, if you're okay..."

"Oh, don't *cry*," David said, seeming more frightened than irritated. He put down his glass and wrapped his arms around her. "We won't go." The back of his shirt was coming untucked. "I'm fine. Really, I'm okay."

I felt the need to vomit. I put my glass down, and everything swam. Without explaining myself I turned and walked down the hall until I found a small door, slightly open, and pushed my way inside. I ran the water to cover the sound of sickness, and then I vomited for a long while into the sink, the sour champagne burning my throat as it returned, and then I rinsed and wiped the sink with toilet paper before rinsing my mouth. When I looked in the oval mirror, I saw that my lips were pale again, and I realized that my purse was still hanging from my elbow like a forgotten limb. I threw the soiled toilet paper into the trash and reapplied my lipstick.

For the longest time I found bathrooms in America to be comical. American bathrooms, no matter where we were, seemed palatial in comparison with Taiwanese bathrooms, which were, at their best, little more than outhouses even in a wealthy home. To void oneself in this American bathroom was to sit in a jewelry box with jade-colored wallpaper. A closer look and I could see a print of tiny women with parasols. I pulled down the toilet lid and sat, not eager to return to the kitchen. My new life was broken. Everything was concealed by the secrets of language, and even that which was spoken was concealed by another layer of secrecy that I could sense on my skin but not fully understand.

By the time I returned to the kitchen, Mrs. Nowak was gone, and David was pouring himself a glass of what looked like whiskey. In my pregnant state I could smell its familiar odor from where I stood.

"Your mother is where?" I asked.

"Lying down," he said. He raised his glass. *"Gan bei."*

I toasted him with my champagne. The tiny click made my back teeth hurt.

"Were you sick?"

"Yes."

"I told my mother that you weren't used to the champagne. So that she wouldn't _____." He pointed at my stomach. For the most part, he was good about using words that I could understand, and I was good at asking him about the ones I didn't know. Still, we were in a place with a woman who knew him much better than I did. I didn't have the words to pierce through my confusion. My blood mouth filled with sand.

David's childhood bedroom was bare except for a white wooden bed and white nightstand, a white dresser, and a single poster of strange and painted shapes, which now hangs, curling, in William's room. He said, looking around, "The _____ _____ of my child _____."

"What?"

"Sorry," he said. "At home it's easy—it's easy for me to forget what is okay to say to you. I'm sorry about my mother. She loves me. I've always been close to her. Understand?"

"Yes," I said, and sat on the bed. He sat beside me, his glass half-empty. I said, "Your mother is beautiful."

"Well. Yes. She—in the past, people would turn their heads to look at her as we walked down the street. But she never really _____ or cared. God. All that about *Jesus*. I'm sorry. She has certain ideas about me."

"Yes."

"I came here to show her that I was okay, because I know she worries. But this has been a mistake. We can leave. We won't eat dinner here. We'll go back to the hotel, just the two of us."

"Yes."

He lay onto the bed, as if merely speaking of these possibilities exhausted him. The small amount of whiskey left in his glass, held aloft, sloshed and dripped onto the sheets. "Come here," he said, and awkwardly lifted his glass to the nightstand.

My heart sighed. I curled up beside him in my fancy dress, avoiding the wetness of whiskey, and pressed my face into his ribs. He rubbed my head in slow circles, and I thought, *I am happy, I am happy, I am happy.* I inhaled the aftershave he had splashed on that morning that smelled of something dark and sour, like small animals and the color brown and himself. When we lay together there was no need to speak, and I preferred it that way because when we didn't speak we could be any husband and wife, with no struggle in it. We lay in that bed and kissed tenderly, and then we took our set of matching luggage and left. I imagined Mrs. Nowak lying in bed with a towel over her forehead. She didn't try to say good-bye.

David and I took a taxi back to the hotel because I didn't like the subway, and he was *hemorrhaging* money in those days. David booked a new room, and then he was hungry; he liked diners to the exclusion of all else, and for the longest time I thought that all American restaurants were diners, and that all American menus contained hamburgers and french fries and malts. This particular diner was cramped with people smoking cigarettes and chatting loudly in their booths, if they were lucky enough to have a padded red booth. David and I sat in dirty-white hard-backed chairs at a sticky table.

By then my husband had tufts of hair sticking out all over, as though a dog had been chewing on his head. He no longer seemed all right about leaving the brown stone house. I imagined that he felt guilty about abandoning his mother: a sad woman who had the same mouth as he did, who likely gave him everything he wanted all of his life, and only wanted his attention and love in return. It suddenly felt selfish to leave without acknowledgment, and I pitied Mrs. Nowak, even if she had called me a souvenir.

The waitress came. "I don't know yet," David said. "We'll have some coffees. Black."

He kept looking through the menu. I looked, too, but there weren't any pictures. The only words I recognized were *hamburger* and *eggs*, and I didn't want either of those things. I watched him as he flipped from the front to the back, from the back to the front, and again. Finally he put down the menu. I smiled at him. I imagined that the right thing to say would be clear to me if we didn't have a language barrier. He was staring not at me and my smile, but at something in the center of the table. When the waitress came, he took the coffee from her and drank his without waiting for it to cool. I could have said,. "拜託你告訴我所有的實情,我會了解的." I could have said, *I love you*. I could have kept smiling until my face broke. I could have cried. But I didn't know what he was thinking, and I could only guess.

"There's nothing to *eat* here," he said, and got up. He pulled his wallet out of his pocket and threw some money on the table, and I followed him out of that diner into the open air. We stood on the sidewalk, where no one could bother to move us as the crowd flowed every which way. We might have stood there until we grew roots and turned into coconut trees if not for the sudden shift in the wind, which started from a single woman sighing, shaking her head, and saying, "_____ me," because Americans were always muttering to themselves and sounding annoyed by unknown slights, and like all the disgruntled people before her, the woman kept walking, though she continued to wag her head from side to side. But more people noticed what she had seen, and then we, too, looked at the man on the roof across the street.

I don't remember what he looked like except for the hat he wore, which was a newsboy cap of the kind that David wore sometimes to protect his head in the rain. The man on the roof would back away from the edge, and then return to it with a new enthusiasm, even peering over to such an extreme that I knew for sure he would fall, even accidentally, but he didn't make a decision one way or another, causing people to yell things at him that I didn't understand—to jump? or to save himself?—and I thought of Fatty's father, Farmer Chu, who had starved his pigs and then thrown himself into their pen to die. My mother refused to say that Fatty's father's death was tragic because Farmer Chu was batshit insane, and if he was so crazy as to feed himself to his own pigs, he deserved to die, did he not? When people did things that she didn't understand, my mother would always tell me that they were batshit insane, probably to keep me from doing them. I thought of Farmer Chu's hand dangling from a pig's mouth as I looked at the man on the roof.

David said, "He's only three stories up."

"Pardon?"

"Three stories. Three floors?" He gestured with his bad hand, holding it parallel to the ground and then miming the distance: one, two, three. "He won't die. He'll break his legs, but he won't die."

"So why he is doing this?"

"I suppose he wants to do something."

"Break his legs?"

"Kill something," David said. "But he won't die."

I understood the words, but not the meaning. I said, "Dangerous."

"He'll be all right," he said, and started walking. I followed him two blocks to another diner, where we sat at a booth and ordered corned beef hash with fried eggs, and he ordered a strawberry milkshake for me, which was my favorite at the time. So suicide has always followed me, you see.

David wanted to go back to the brown stone house. A whim, or the sudden breeze that cut through the heat, or the four cups of black coffee had changed his mind—no, I knew that it was the man on the roof who did, or did not, die that day that pushed him back. David had been so calm, watching him. Now he was resolute about going back to his mother. In the taxi he reached over and held my hand. "My Oriental lamb," he said, and kissed the side of my head, breathing into my hair.

We pulled up to the curb.

Mrs. Nowak answered the door again and said, "David!" I saw that she'd been crying, and had not bothered to fix her makeup. "You've come back," she said. "Where did you go? I didn't think you'd come back," and she opened the door wider. She said, "I'll start dinner." It was approximately three thirty. I could barely remember the woman who had frightened me so upon first arriving at the house—a woman who had been scared out of being and left this ghost behind. "Help me cook," she said to me. David touched my shoulder and said, "All right," after which I pulled my skirts around me and followed Mrs. Nowak down the hall, back to the kitchen. I wondered how she could possibly cook anything in that white dress of hers.

"We'll have an early dinner tonight," she said, looking at the stove and the icebox, at everywhere but me. "We'll cook David's favorites—some old _____ _____ that he likes."

She tied on a full-length pink apron without offering me a covering of my own, even though my dress was clearly more expensive than her dingy tablecloth of a garment, and we worked in silence, which was a relief. She passed me food to chop and clean, and I caught on to the essence of the dishes being prepared without trouble. There was something with pork knuckles, which she butchered expertly, and potatoes, which I washed and peeled with a paring knife. I took care to be deferential to my mother-in-law. I even avoided brushing up against her as we moved in the kitchen from the counter to the stove to the ovens, but this choreography may have been because I dreaded the feeling of her skeletal body against mine.

Still, neither of us relaxed, and finally she said, chopping in a way that punctuated her every syllable, "I-love-my-son. Do-you-un-der-stand? I do not want you here for his money. I do not want you to take _____ of him. All right?"

I kept my face blank, though what she wished to express was probably lost on me. What was I not supposed to take from him? His money? That wasn't what I wanted; I'd had money in Kaohsiung. Was I supposed to tell her that I didn't understand? Was it best to pretend that I did?

"Do you know? Do you know what I'm talking about? He's _____ _____." She repeated these final two words with emphasis. "Oh, for _____, what _do_ you understand? He's _crazy_. Do you understand that? Crazy. David... he's very _____. He was _____. And if you know that, and if you're taking _____ of him because of it, I'll figure out a way to send you back. I don't care if you're married. Whatever kind of marriage you have, it's not one I _____, and I doubt the government _____ it either."

She watched me for a reaction, but I had none.

"I do not want to take something from your son," I said. Crazy, that I understood. His mother seemed certain of this. Indeed, she'd been crying in our absence—but for what reason? David's craziness, or her son's unacceptable marriage? My own mother thought I was crazy, and to my face she'd called me a pervert and a whore. But David and I were bonded now, with our baby in my belly and rings on our fingers, and I had to remember where I was now, and how impossible it was to return to where I'd been.

(Is this the moment when my fate could have gone in a different direction? Or had the doors already closed behind me?)

As I searched for something more to say, or waited for Mrs. Nowak to say something in reply, we both heard the piano intoning its solid, clean sound. In Taiwan only people who were both wealthy and of high class owned a piano, and my mother was one but not the other. I stopped chopping onions so that I could catch the melody, which drifted like a kite on a soft wind.

Mrs. Nowak sighed. She said, "You can always tell who's playing by the way they touch the keys." She leaned against the counter with her eyes closed, listening. "If you're really going to be his wife, you need to take care of him. Promise me that."

"Yes," I said, and I meant it.

That was the last time I saw David's mother. It was one day, that July day in that brown stone house, when I cooked with her and made a promise that I couldn't keep. I tried to send her some of his ashes, but they were returned to me. Apparently she had moved away from New York after David left Wellbrook, because mothers know their sons; he said something once about her being from the middle of America, and I assume that is where she went in the end, like an animal crawling into a hole to die. He called it the "heart's land." It sounded like a safe place to me.

———————◆———————

Fatty had come to look for a job. She wanted to work for the Golden Lotus, and when she approached me at recruitment hours, where I sat at my usual shaved ice stand, I laughed upon seeing her plump body and misshapen arm cloaked in a buttoned blue dress. She had no redeeming physical features—not a prim, aquiline nose in the middle of that doughy face, nor a clear complexion to make up for the abundance of her body. She was simply not pretty, and also simply fat.

"Is this a joke?" I asked.

A thinly lipsticked smile. "No."

"I seek out girls for the Golden Lotus, not pigs for the slaughter." I waved my hand at her. "Leave me alone."

She seated herself across from me, bringing with her the odor of a sweaty body mixed with cheap Western perfume. Who knew where she had gotten those few precious sprays? She said, "You're Jia-Hui Chen, the mama-san's daughter?"

"Yes."

Fatty was looking quite comfortable. Despite myself, I was intrigued by the lump beneath the upper sleeve of her dress.

"What's wrong with your arm?" I asked her.

"I broke it," she said. "It didn't heal correctly."

"There are doctors who can set bones, you know."

"You're right," she replied, and smiled again. "I want to work at your mother's bar."

"Ah, that again."

"I'm a virgin."

"Many girls are virgins. And many of those girls don't look like a sow in a dress."

Did she flinch? Do I imagine it, now?

She said, "I am the *tongyangxi* to my brother. My parents bought me when I was a little girl, when both my brother and I were too young to understand marriage. My parents had *expectations*. But my brother didn't want to marry me, in the end, when I turned out fat."

The tradition of raising girls as *tongyangxi*, the sisterly wives to their adoptive brothers, was already taking on an old-fashioned flavor at this time. But there were still families, even in a major city such as Kaohsiung, who sought out impoverished young girls for marriage to their sons.

Fatty continued: "My father broke my arm. I was not taken to a doctor, and then my family kicked me out. I need to make money, and my arm prevents me from doing manual labor. I can't find work as a maid, I can't work in a field or farm, I am good for nothing. But I am sure, Jia-Hui, that I have more personality than any of the girls in your bar. I'll entertain the men who come while the other girls offer their bodies. I can live from nearly nothing. I request only shelter and food."

"My mother," I said, "will never allow it."

"Ask her."

"She'll beat me for even suggesting it the second she sees you. I'm sorry. If you were less fat, there is a chance that—" and I wanted to say, *she could overlook your arm,* but there was suddenly something so tragic about it that I couldn't speak the words.

"I know I'm fat," she said. "I can't help it." She looked right at me. "They told me not to eat rice. So I didn't. Then they said, 'No meat, only vegetables; I did that. I did lose some weight, but not enough for my brother. Then they said, 'You can't eat anything at all,' and it made no difference even though I was starving. So if you say no, I'll leave you alone. I have enough experience with eating bitterness."

"No," I said. But she didn't move. And then I said, "Wait."

It wasn't that I never heard tragic stories in my line of work. It wasn't that this girl had been beaten or starved. I saw plenty of that. I met girls who were raped by their fathers and their brothers and their uncles and gangs of men who tore their bodies open. I met girls who had scars up and down their backs from bamboo cane lashings. So you become accustomed to this kind of thing. I couldn't hire them all. What ghost then possessed me to give Fatty my day's pocket money, and to ask her to come see me the next day at the same stand at ten A.M.? For a long time I believed that it was temporary madness. Now I think that it was when she said about her fatness, "I can't help it." It was the helplessness being voiced in combination with her certainty that she had other things to offer besides her helplessness, her fatness, her arm. She also looked me in the eyes, which almost no one did, and I admired that.

———◆———

After we left New York City, David wanted to show me America. With heaps of cash he bought a Buick, and we filled it up: spare change, aluminum foil gum wrappers smelling of wintergreen, empty bags of potato chips, our clothing thrown on the backseat, our sweat seeping into the fabric. I didn't know a place could be so big, or that one piece of land could be so different from one place to the next. It was mountains and jagged red holes in one place and flat as a steel plate in another. In Kaohsiung things were sea-foam green, and if they weren't sea-foam green, they were gray-black sand, and if they weren't gray-black sand, they were the color of banana leaves drying in the sun, or the wet crimson of a bar girl's mouth. In America people were the color of milk and the inside of a split piece of wood, dark as char, smooth as caramel. From state to state there were more souvenirs than I could fit in the tote bag that we'd purchased for that very reason, each souvenir representing a state or monument we visited while I said, "Beautiful," and I said this about everything with honesty.

My mouth hurt from speaking English. The muscles around my lips and my cheeks ached. In my dreams voices stretched into long, silly words that meant nothing, and I woke up saying "milk" or "glass" before tumbling back into the sleep of nonsense dreamers. Soon I vomited over and over at the side of the road while David reached over and rubbed my damp neck, and then I craved all kinds of things: hot buns filled with pork, cold and briny seaweed, red bean popsicles. The sudden craving was monstrous, like a thing already in my mouth that could not be tasted or swallowed and just between my frozen teeth with a jaw stuck open, and my longing for these foods was not a longing in my stomach but something jammed deep in my throat. I awoke in fancy motels with mouthfuls of blood, the insides of my cheeks chewed ragged and raw, and I spat and spat into porcelain basins while clutching my belly. I was inconsolable in the most beautiful of hotels and I sobbed on a ledge of the Grand Canyon, where I was sure that my longing would push me in. David said, over and over, "Oh, sweetheart." He understood the vomiting as morning sickness and something that all women experienced in pregnancy. He understood the mood swings as common, and understandable for a biological process that would result in the production of a human being who was our baby and our joint accomplishment. He washed the blood out of my pillowcases. He stroked my hair, and I loved him. And yet I continued to vomit everything that I put into my mouth, my throat hot as my eyes watered and burst bloodshot, until finally I pushed away a basket of french fries that sat before me in a blue-and-white-checkered diner, where the flies landed and rose, and I was resolute: I would not, and could not, eat those french fries, hamburgers, or bowls of chili any longer. If I continued, I would vomit until the baby, whom I suspected was a boy because of his sense of entitlement, dried up in my womb. But how could I explain this? Instead I said, "I am not hungry." In fact, I was hungrier than I had ever been in Kaohsiung.

I drank milk. I could have cold milk from bottles through a straw like a child, and our baby would not force it back up. David bought a dairy crate and put it in the backseat. Every hour he reached behind his seat and handed me a sweaty bottle, from which I drank while watching the scenery. Still, I craved the taste of things I couldn't have, including their delicate saltiness, the unique pillow of a 包子 crushed flat between the tongue and the roof of the mouth, and in my hunger and bloody craving the milk took a pink tinge to it, reminding me of the strawberry milkshakes I no longer wanted.

"You need to eat," David said. He dragged me from diner to diner. All the names ran into one another. "You need meat. Vegetables." I shook my head, starving, teeth itching.

We were at a truck stop near Eugene, Oregon, with lights that flickered like sleeping eyelids. I sat in front of a closed menu and a glass. I didn't want milk. I was, in fact, tired of that clotted feeling on my tongue and the mucus it formed in the back of my throat. I was exhausted from not eating, and David seemed exhausted, too, as he blinked and blinked.

"Why don't you take a look at the menu?" he said. He hadn't asked me to look at a menu in days.

I opened it. I looked at the words. They were all the same words that I'd seen in every other diner in America. I closed it. David asked me what I wanted. The restaurant shimmered, felt dangerous. I said, "A hamburger."

The hamburger came. It was the size of my hand, and the top had a crease like the inside bend of an elbow. Even thinking about it made my stomach lift. I looked at the limp pink tomato inside, the pale lettuce. I moved my hand from my lap as if to touch it, or to pick it up, and then, under no will of my own, the hand lifted and pushed the plate away. Whip-fast, David reached out and grabbed my wrist. *This is it*, I thought. I went limp with his hand wrapped around my wrist, which grabbed so tight and held me for so long that I thought my fingers would go numb. David let go. Finally he said, wearily, "I don't understand."

Of course he didn't understand. We didn't understand each other except when we were touching, and neither one of us could crawl into the guts of the other. But the pain in my arm woke me.

I said, "Our baby does not want America food."

"Our baby doesn't. What does our baby want? Does our baby want Taiwan's food?"

I nodded.

He tugged at his hair. I was sure that he would leave me. The lights continued to flicker. The air filled with late-night smoke. "All right," he said. "Well, we're not going to get it here." He raised his hand for the check.

Our journey, once slow and meandering, became hurried as he drove to San Francisco, the Old Golden Mountain. I drank milk in the passenger seat to survive and filled the backseat with empty bottles that tumbled and clanked at sharp turns, but I did not vomit, and he only stopped at truck stops to buy himself burgers, which he ate one-handed with ketchup dripping down his palm while driving south. We went through the never-ending grasses, which were fields, and I dreamed hazy dreams of the boy growing and snarling inside of my belly.

◆

David persuaded the owner of the Hotel Grande Royal to let us live in the penthouse for as long as we could pay. I never saw money change hands, but we stayed in room 333 until William slipped out of me, howling, on March 8, 1955, in the four-post bed.

Our room was as extravagant as the Nowaks' brown stone house had been. A velvety parlor beside the bedroom, crammed with knickknacks—coral-colored crystal vases, tins filled with spiced potpourri. The same delicate, reflective surfaces all over, forming mirrors upon infinite mirrors. A pink chandelier. A grandfather clock that did not chime, but loomed in a corner with a grave face. The bed was its own marvel: four-poster, king-sized, with pillows piled atop layers of custard bedding. In that bed I could lie and look up at the tin ceiling, which yielded an unfurled and floral universe. We spent more time in that bed than we did anywhere else in that suite, including the claw-footed tub, the chaise longue, or the white sofa in the parlor. I would not be surprised if, when the maids finally entered almost a year later and stripped the bed of its comforter and sheets, the women saw the shapes of our bodies burned into the mattress. Why leave? Why would we want to?

The Hotel Grande Royal was six blocks, David told me, from Chinatown. Despite our proximity, I refused to see that Oriental facsimile for fear of my heart and liver being seduced by the old dream. No, best to write down the names of the dishes on a scrap of paper and have my white husband go and bring things back for me. Best to have David bring me the dishes the baby craved: oily bags of sweet 菠蘿包 for breakfast and 叉燒包 for lunch. The first thing that he brought back was a bamboo basket of soup dumplings, and, like a mutt, I took my basket of treats to the corner. With no concern about appearances, I sat on the chaise longue and lifted a saggy dumpling to my lips, barely getting the lukewarm 小籠包 to my lips before it burst and spilled hot juice down my chin and into the space between my swelling breasts. My eyes dampened, then wept. My shoulders shook with joy. I devoured 三杯雞 for three weeks, and then I craved 鹹魚雞粒 炒飯, which took David three days to find; but the salt in those crumbs of fish on top of fried rice satisfied me more than that of any greasy paper boat of fries. David watched with fascination as I ate. He had eaten only street meats in Kaohsiung.

"Not salty crab?" I asked. "Not an oyster pancake?"

"No, no," he said, "but you look so happy."

We ate at the desk side by side. He ate his hamburgers and I ate my food from Chinatown. The food, though familiar, had a different flavor from what I was accustomed to; still, it was better than a hamburger, and I pitied David for his limited diet.

I ate and ate. My arms and legs remained slender while my belly swelled. No longer able to wear my dresses, I lounged in underwear with my hand splayed over my navel, and said that I was going to give birth to a boy the size of Formosa. In San Francisco David laughed, and I delighted in being able to create that sound with my words. He laughed like a little girl, like a tickled child; it bubbled out of him in waves. He bought a radio and we slow-danced around the parlor as I waddled; he came home with different things every day: a dictionary, magazines with bright covers, red lipstick in a fancy tube. He pulled wrapped caramels out from behind his ear. He sang to me a Polish folk song, and I mimicked, *"Matka, matka,"* while pinching his thin nose.

I redoubled my efforts to learn English, paging through the dictionary and *Life* magazine. I kept a notebook of new words, as I had in Kaohsiung, and studied it daily as I circled entries in the dictionary. In September David's words, and the strings of them, came to me more clearly, and then more often. Fall passed with little fuss, accompanied by a light breeze that we allowed through the window until the end of November. By December I was large enough that my back hurt with too much standing, so we lay in bed in a valley of pillows. He'd put his hand on my belly as he spoke in low, conversational tones: "I know that one day, Daisy, you're going to be able to speak a lot of English, and we're going to be able to have real conversations. I'm going to be able to ask you about your family, and you'll tell me all about what it was like for you, growing up where you did. We're going to have a real nice life together. You, me, and the baby."

"I now can speak English well," I said. "I now know what you say."

"Good." He ran his hand up and over the hill of my stomach. "That's very good, lamb."

Sometimes he would bend me over the bathroom sink and make love to me from behind, tilting my face upward so that I could watch myself in the small, speckled mirror, and I was always bewildered by what I saw. The solid white shape of the man behind me, with his ghostly golden hair, as well as my own careful expression, which then, predictably, erupted into a sexualized grimace, and then I would avert my eyes for the ugliness of it. With my pleasure came ugliness. I had to remember this, and yet it did me no good.

———◆———

There are moments I can pinpoint in my life where I look and say, "This is where it decayed." Like the first bruises on a fruit that suddenly rots without warning.

One morning I woke up and the chandelier was askew. The paintings of flowers—even the flowers had seemed to wilt—tilted on their nails. Our clothing was everywhere but not shed from our bodies; rather, someone had pulled them from their hangers and onto the floor and the chairs. I thought I was dreaming in the light and pulled myself and my heavy belly out of bed. I pressed my fingers into my skin and felt their strength: I wasn't dreaming. It was February. Morning fog clouded the wide windows. I called David's name, and when no one answered I checked the bathroom and then the parlor. What was new and what was old? How had I not noticed the paper containers stained with grease, the bags on their sides like fallen soldiers? David was gone, and I was too afraid to leave.

In the afternoon he came back with his peacoat buttoned and his shirt wrapped around his bleeding hand. I had been chewing the insides of my cheeks and flipping through old issues of *Life*, not reading any of it but needing to do something with my fingers.

"Your hand, what happened? You went to where?" In panic I pulled him to the sofa. He seemed confused. "Where?" I repeated. I tried to unwrap his makeshift bandage to see what had happened. He resisted, but my terror was stronger; I had never seen him behave this way before. His hand was covered in haphazard, deep gashes split with open sides: palm, back, fingers, a map on top of a map of scars, wounds so open that I thought the sides would never come together, and I pressed my own hand to my mouth to keep from screaming.

When Farmer Chu died, Fatty told me that her mother believed he had been possessed by a hungry ghost. My mother was not as superstitious as Fatty's, and I wasn't raised with such beliefs. But Fatty was adamant about the reasons for her father's death. In his drunkenness he often wandered the streets at night, where any hungry ghost could have taken possession of his body. He could have encountered a snake or fox, or even fucked a beautiful ghost-woman in a neighbor's field. Why else would he feed himself to pigs? I searched David's coat pockets and found a bloody knife, and I cried. Yet I was in America. There were no hungry ghosts in America. I thought about Mrs. Nowak, and what she had said about her son: "He's *crazy*." The question was where the craziness came from. Was it in the spirit, or in the blood? I kept crying as I rewrapped the shirt around his hand. He sat on the couch until I told him to get into the bed, and he did that, like an obedient child, still in his peacoat, and stared at the ceiling and muttered to himself.

I was afraid to leave David in the room alone. I washed the knife and kept it in my purse until I could throw it out the window. I disposed of it in the middle of the night, chanting prayers as I did so, and then I watched him sleep with a bloody rag wrapped around his hand, red spotting the sheets.

He slept for only one or two hours at a time. The rest of the time he continued to stare at the ceiling. Sometimes he talked to himself, or shouted. Maybe he was talking and shouting at me, but I wasn't certain. I had a difficult time understanding what he was saying, and I didn't know if it was because he was speaking nonsense, or because my English wasn't as good as I wished it to be. I stayed awake by pinching myself, careful not to pinch myself too hard lest it disturb the baby, and I also sang to myself all the old songs I knew, and the American bar songs, too. I lay beside David in the bed, crawling under the blankets, and I sang to him, but after accidentally falling asleep once I stopped lying in the bed with him and walked around the bedroom instead, in circles like a mindless donkey.

Day and night came the same. The fog swelled against the windows, and then the rain, which pinged on the glass and then pounded at it.

I took his wallet on the third slow day and put it in my purse. I checked the room for anything dangerous before I left. I had to return quickly so that nothing could happen, but I had to leave because there was no more food, not a single stale bun or grain of rice, and I was both dizzy from hunger and afraid for the baby. I took the elevator down to the lobby and stepped into the daylight, where crowds were scurrying up and down the sidewalk, teeming with the small, icky motions of their arms and legs.

I had not been outside of room 333 in months, and the emergence felt like falling. The sky seemed larger—I wasn't standing beneath the heavens, but feeling the heavens suck me up in all directions. In a cloud of voices I waddled toward the biggest street that I could find. I'd had to fashion clothing to accommodate my belly: one of David's shirts, tied at the waist; a yellow dress turned upside down and tied with a leather belt for a skirt. Everyone looked, frowning at my getup—looked at me, my small-eyed face, the darkness of my hair. A woman stopped and shook her dandelion head. I walked until I found a food store, and swiftly I picked up a loaf of white bread, a bag of oranges, and cheese, even though I had never liked cheese, but David did. I went to the counter, where a man with hair the color and sheen of tar was smoking a cigarette. He sorted through my things. No, I couldn't care about the looks I received, or the shame, because I needed my thoughts to be so powerful that David would remain sleeping until I got back to the hotel. I was focusing with such concentration that I didn't realize the man at the counter was speaking to me, but I didn't care to understand because I needed to pay and leave, and I needed to get back to my husband or something terrible would happen. He said it again anyway: "_____ Chinatown?"

I nodded. Of course. I paid him. To hell with him, to hell with Chinatown, to hell with all of them.

I could barely walk, so heavy were my things, so heavy was my belly, but I went back to the hotel. My heart was thumping, thumping, thumping. I gave the black man in the elevator a coin, and then I ran to the door. Again I felt myself on some kind of brink. I unlocked the door and I banged the door open and then closed as I went through the ruined parlor into the bedroom.

David was awake and sitting. His eyes were red. The skin beneath them sagged. "Where did you go," he said. His bandaged hand lifted, and swatted at the nothingness in front of his face.

EROTICISM

DAVID (1954–1956)

I admit that for too long I only knew my wife as erotic. I don't mean that she was wild and thrashing, or frothing at the mouth with her hand up her skirts. I meant that she was exotic to me, and that was the primary pleasure that I derived from her, I confess.

One might ask: Do I regret that we hadn't had a Catholic wedding? I regret that I had to, in a sense, instruct a blind man in the art of color theory. I met her on her terms. Off the plane after a long-haul flight, I felt the new air first, a wet blanket that smothered everything, that smelled of not-quite-rotting garbage and, faintly, sewage. On the cart into the port city of Kaohsiung, with the wheels rattling below me such that my teeth clattered and clacked unless I clenched my jaw shut, I heard the words of people cawing in the same steady waves as the warm air that never lifted, the same air that pressed against the windows like hands.

Taiwan wasn't what I had expected. If you weren't there when I was you can't know what I mean. If you've been there recently, and seen the modernity of what was once a third-world country, you know half of it. Imagine the roofs barely held together and the billboards covered in mysterious slashes and dots. Such a conflagration was the only thing I could understand after New York. I'd gone down to my white bones. I'd scalped my skull, cracked it open, and seen the putrefying brain beneath. The last thing I wanted to think about was how hard it was to be a person and how hard it was to be alive.

In Taiwan I was staying in an apartment above a teahouse. Marty, of all people, had handled my arrangements, having joined the navy immediately after graduation. Though I waited, bereft, for a letter from Marianne, it was Marty whom I received a letter from that June, which began with apologies: for his father's violence, his parents' scheming, his sister's behavior. Crede mihi, he wrote, *when I say that Marianne has less control over her life than you think.* He then went on to describe his life in Taiwan, which intrigued me—so many bicycles! Stray animals everywhere underfoot! Banana farms, and did I know bananas grew in bunches on trees? The letter ended by saying, *I know this must sound crazy, but I wanted to see if we could have a correspondence.*

I didn't write back to Marty right away. I felt that I should wait until I heard from Marianne before I spent any energy on her brother. His letter sat in a desk drawer while I tended to Matka, making her gin and tonics with just a splash of olive juice, the yellowy tinge clouding against the ice cubes. So many gin and tonics there were, and no letter came for one month, and then two months, and then three months, at which point I stopped hoping, or convinced myself that I had stopped hoping to hear from Marianne Orlich.

So I wrote Marty back; after all, I was lonely, too. I asked, among other things, if he could tell me anything about where Marianne was, or how she was doing. The reply, which took weeks to arrive, made no mention of his sister. I knew it was a deliberate omission, but what could I do? Soon Taiwan became so appealing that I asked if he could help me make arrangements. Really, though, it could have been anywhere. I just wanted to get away.

He'd planned my stay by contacting his former lieutenant, who was still active in the American intervention. I would meet Lieutenant Archibald Winner at a given day and time, and he would show me to my apartment. When the lieutenant had a spare moment, he would help me to acclimate myself to my surroundings. On the fourth day, I planned to meet up with Marty, who would be returning from a tour of the nearby seas.

The lieutenant liked me well enough. His smile was avuncular when I first met him, as though I were an old relative that he had grown up with, or perhaps lived on the same block as, for years. He was happy to do me favors. He was the sort who would have done well as one of Proust's bourgeoisie, so aware of and respectful of class was he. He called Michigan a shitty place, and referred to New York City as the center of the world with reverence. He was Protestant, but appeared to have no problem with Catholics. He was not Polish, but respected the Polish community "for their brio," and was disappointed to hear that I didn't speak Polish. This disappointment faded when he learned of my predilection for Latin. The lieutenant was in his late thirties, but had already gone entirely silver-gray, and had three deep lines permanently carved into his forehead regardless of facial expression. For long stretches of time he would disappear, I presumed due to his naval duties, and then he would show up at my flat above the teahouse, out of his navy whites, looking small and ordinary in a fresh T-shirt and khakis with dusty shoes on.

About the Golden Lotus he'd said, "It's a place to go, if you want to meet pretty girls."

"And you don't?"

"Ah, well, it's essentially a whorehouse, and I wouldn't be able to keep my wife from knowing I'd dipped my pen in some other girl's ink. She can read volumes in the twitch of my left eye. I go for drinks, for company, but I keep it in my pants."

He asked if I was interested. I shrugged. We were the only two people in that teahouse with its low, screened windows. We sat on benches. Flies and mosquitoes sang and swam around us, their dances strange and ever present despite the violent zappers that hung from every window, each bursting occasionally into flame.

He said, "It's not like your New York, is it? Not like anything else, either. I've been here for five months, and something new surprises me every day. It's not just the food or the filth or the Orientals. It's even the sun in the sky—it doesn't feel like the same sun. The moon isn't the same moon."

Nothing was the same, but I was relieved by the difference. My neuroses had all but disappeared since arriving in Kaohsiung, though I missed Marianne. In her absence my hormones broke viciously through, and I spent hours regretting that I hadn't, at the very least, felt her beneath her blouses and skirts when I had the chance. I was convinced that she would be softer than anything I'd ever touched—as soft as the centimeter of skin behind my earlobe, as soft as Matka's chinchilla coat, the quality of skin as hot and damp as the inside of a mouth. The mere consideration of her body gave me a hard-on.

When I didn't hear from Marty by the end of the fourth day, I mentioned him to the lieutenant. He pursed his lips, which I'd never seen a man do before, and then he said, "Martin is no longer in the navy, I'm sorry to say."

"What? Why? When did that happen?"

"You'd have to ask him yourself."

"Well, do you have his information? A contact?"

He shrugged.

I thought about going home, and then dismissed the idea. Nor did I complain about Marty's flightiness, though I was curious about what I perceived as the suspicious circumstances of his departure; I'd gone around the world to experience something else, and it didn't matter if Marty was or wasn't there. I could fend for myself.

Later the lieutenant said, "The girls aren't the same here. You're how old? Eighteen? Nineteen?"

"Eighteen."

"Old enough to know a bit of the difference. You see it in their eyes. They don't have much here. It's not a wealthy country, but maybe not quite third world, either. You see it in the bars as though whoring were ordinary. There's one girl I ran into when I was with one of my fellas, about to go in for some drinks and company. One of them—the Oriental girls, I mean—she took no money. She was dressed in Western dress. Not in one of those *qipao*. She was dressed like the girls back home, and that threw me off. Anyway, she had her eye on my sailor. Just grabbed his arm, laughed in a way that made my skin crawl, and tugged him in the direction of the big house behind the Golden Lotus, out by one of the northwest banana fields."

"And he didn't go."

"Oh no," the lieutenant said, sipping his tea. "He went! Seemed happy enough when he came back. It was no effort for him, and he didn't have to pay. I asked him what it was like. He said it was heavenly. 'China girls know how to move,' he said."

I tried to imagine this girlish apparition appearing. As a virgin it was harder still to imagine the sex, the moves, or that kind of female desire.

"'Like a dream,' he said. I would have thought he was lying, if not for the fact that I'd seen her myself. Almond-shaped eyes. Long black hair. Sexy as all hell. There's no making that stuff up."

I said, "That's so strange."

"Something about being here, I guess. There's no dignity in it. It's different here. There's no dignity in the way these girls live." We changed subjects then, but the *jiu jia* lingered in my thoughts, as did the notion of an Oriental girl in Western dress— looking like Marianne in the garments she chose, but with a different species of face and pitch-black hair. I imagined her arching her body so that her belly pointed toward the sky and her soft breasts rose pale from her firm chest. When I returned to my flat, the window was open, breezeless, and I was sweating through my clothes. I turned on the radio. I went to my bamboo mat, parted the curtains of my mosquito tent, and lay down within its web, running my hand down the waistband of my slacks to feel myself, my nerve endings waiting for something to come into contact with, all the aching electricity of sex thrumming like cable wire, and an imaginary body made of swampy heat climbing on top of mine. I didn't caress or linger, but squeezed and trembled. I closed my eyes and moaned between gritted teeth.

———◆———

The lieutenant said, "You know, it's possible to never go to the open-air market, if you eat street meats for every meal. But if you're inclined to cook for yourself. . ." And he held up his cuttlefish skewer and thrust it in an easterly direction. "Or even if you don't cook. It's a madhouse, but may hold some interest for a man interested in foreign cultures." I told him that I would go. How different could a market be? What kind of blood-soaked dirt forming red-black islands, hog heads' eyes bulging white, the stink of fish and meat attracting looping flies? I went midweek. The lieutenant insisted on coming with me. He had a taste for what he called *lian wu*, a type of apple, and the oranges, he said, were sugar-sweet. Hurriedly he pulled out his cap, which was not a navy-issued hat but a Detroit Tigers cap, and he adjusted the brim such that the lines in his forehead were in shadow.

The nearest market to my teahouse faced the port and was propped up by ramshackle constructions made of tin and wood, shielding leathery women and men from further sun as they sat, legs open, elbows on their knees, behind their goods, which were laid out on the ground atop blue tarps. It was loud, very loud, and the smell nearly knocked me over like the butcher's back home, except with no ventilation and captive beneath a bell jar of heat. Everyone yelled at one another as though perpetually arguing, hollering again and again in surges of nasal noise.

After ten minutes of the lieutenant pointing out that exotic item and that unusual creature, some in buckets or flayed on tables, I had purchased exactly one bag of hard-boiled eggs stewed in soy sauce, and I'd had enough. If our olfactory senses are the most direct pathway to memory, what does it mean when every scent is strange?

Then the lieutenant stopped, grabbed my arm, and said, "There!"

He pointed at two girls at a round table, eating shaved ice. One girl was fat, the other thin. The fat girl laughed with her mouth wide open, head tilted back, her large breasts shaking beneath her blouse, and she wore sandals that exposed candy-apple-red toenails. Something was wrong with her arm. The thin girl beside her smiled, her hair tied up in a bun, exposing a long, slender neck with what was—I was sure of this—a hickey on the side. It was the only mottled and ugly thing on her otherwise flawless self. Oh, she was beautiful, of course, in a way that I didn't understand. I was already beginning to fall for her without truly seeing. And I only sense this in hindsight, but I was filled with excitement over something foreign that could serve as a vessel inside which I could put all of my longings and hopes. I didn't like myself. I didn't like where I'd come from. Therefore, I was forced to like something different. It's really no different from any other exoticism—say, the exoticism of something so beautiful that to try to describe it falls into a series of clichés: "startlingly blue eyes," "shiny hair," "full lips." Beauty, if you're like most un-truly-beautiful people, is unlike the self, with its strangeness being part of what makes it novel, and therefore pleasurable. To love something different and inexplicable is a natural state of the human condition.

She wore, as the lieutenant had explained, expensive-looking Western clothing. I assumed, wrongly, that she was a kept woman. Her breasts were the size of my fists. She had pointy elbows. Later, I would adore these elbows beyond reason. Her legs were not bare like her friend's, and she wore white kneesocks and saddle shoes that looked as though they had been polished that morning. Her shoulder bag hung at her side, sadly drooping, cast away.

But the hickey. The hickey was dirt, it was sex. It couldn't be brushed away, marking her till it disappeared of its own volition.

"Are they sisters?" I asked.

"They're not sisters, no, they don't really look anything alike," he said. "You get used to looking at them after a while. They begin to look as different as Marilyn and Audrey."

I thought she was beautiful, but how could I have? All that I saw was that bruise, and then my mind's eye saw her on a bed, without her expensive clothes. That was my wife, Daisy, and her name was Jia-Hui then. They didn't notice us. The two girls giggled and ate their shaved ice, and I continued to sink into filthy reverie until the lieutenant said, "Go talk to them. The pretty one speaks English well enough. She's educated, somehow, despite being no better than the whores. Why, you could take her home with you this afternoon, I'm sure."

"No," I protested, embarrassed.

"Eighteen? Wealthy?" He nudged me with his knuckles. "Go on, go ahead. Her friend with the fucked-up arm will understand."

Despite my refusal, the lieutenant grabbed me and pulled me toward the girls. The sight of these two tall white men rapidly approaching them caught the attention of both young women, who looked right at the lieutenant as he came forth with me in tow. Whereas the fat girl tensed and frowned, her shoulders lifting, the thin girl picked up her spoon and sank it into her bowl of ice, twirling it slowly as she waited for us to approach. Neither of them spoke.

"Do you remember me?" the lieutenant asked the thin girl, who crossed one leg over the other and brought a spoonful of ice to her mouth. Her lips glossed with sticky water. She shook her head as if she didn't understand. She looked at the other girl and said something, and the other girl laughed.

"Let's go," I said to the lieutenant.

But the lieutenant was affronted, and would not come. "She knows me. This one does," he said.

"Yeah," the thin girl said, and it was this word, *yeah*, coming out of her mouth that surprised me—not *yes*, but the colloquial, broad *yeah*, as though she were Louise Bielecki on the playground, and I was holding stones.

"You slept with one of my men."

She shrugged.

The fat girl obviously admired her, and, emboldened, said, "I work for little money. You want?"

And then the thin girl said to us, "You go away."

The lieutenant frowned. He was a dignified sort, by most accounts; still, he was a navy officer, and in my experience of navy officers, they will brook no fools—not even a fool woman. He muttered, "China girl bitch," before putting his hand on my shoulder, and walked us both away from them. I heard the thin girl mock, "White son of a bitch!" and both girls laughed again, the sound of a flock of proud birds.

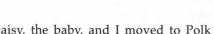

Daisy, the baby, and I moved to Polk Valley in Northern California. It was there that I bought our small, absurdly cheap house from a man named Frank, whose parents had died in that house two weeks prior. This was in 1955, and I liked the place immediately despite its oddities. The water-stained wallpaper sometimes hovered from the wall in gluey strips. Frank and his brother had removed their parents' furniture and goods, but for whatever reason had left the calendar collection hung, and from room to room all calendars exhibited different months and years, curling at the edges—1932, 1944, January, a sentimental and snowy December landscape that didn't remind me of anywhere I'd ever been—and though a calendar in the middle of an entire wall, orphaned, made much less sense than a calendar beside a light switch, so it went that there were so many calendars, and all haphazardly placed. A wall in the living room lacked any paint or wallpaper. Drywall. But there were charms, too: pale and ornate molding along the crack between wall and ceiling, and around every entryway; a well-built shed; solid wood floors with dark knots; an unusually pristine stove. The house was laid out like a smaller version of the first floor of my parents' brownstone, which may or may not have been a point of attraction. Unlike the Greenpoint house, there was no foyer, only the mouth of a short hallway that led straight down to the master bedroom. Along the left, in order: a space for a living room, a bedroom, and the kitchen/eating area. Along the right, in order: a bedroom, a bathroom, and a third bedroom.

But the true win was the land. "Part of the deal," Frank said as he hunched over a piece of paper pulled from his pocket, marked up with a rudimentary pen drawing of the area, "and here are the Sierras." We owned the house and the raggedly triangular plot, with two points along the Sierras borderland and the third point deep in the woods that had no name, as far as Frank knew. We were close to the Yuba River, he said, but it was a substantial walk. No one called it the Yuba River, he added.

"What do you call it?" I asked.

"The river. Just the river."

Frank took his money from us and was happy, and we took the house and the land from him and were happy. In March the Sierras were still puckered with frost, but the valley had already begun to warm, the snow melting into water running riverward. I hired men from the town to improve the house. These men reminded me of men from the factory in age and heft, and they coolly accepted my money, as they no doubt saw me as a wealthy, snot-nosed interloper, probably an orphan who'd inherited a boatload of cash and would eventually turn wild beauty into beastly lawns. The men came and I played with William on the porch while Daisy brought out a tray of fresh-squeezed lemonade.

There was nothing obviously inappropriate about the way my wife behaved in front of the workers. She barely spoke to them, though her English was passable by then, and she handed them their glasses of lemonade before coming to me and saying, "I bring one glass for you." In front of the men she kissed my waiting mouth, and set a sweaty pitcher on the steps. She sat beside me and chucked William, who sat on my lap, under the chin. We'd named him William for no specific reason other than liking the name; no lineage, no homage to Shakespeare or the conqueror. The men had taken the lemonade while silently assessing her in the way that men do. I didn't fault them. But I didn't fault her, either.

It started with small isolations. First we were shut up in that San Francisco penthouse, where Daisy first saw me without my human mask on and did not leave—although in hindsight I ask

myself, How in the world could she have?—and next in the rural fringe of Polk Valley, America's greatest producer during the
Gold Rush, which I had chosen at random from the McNally
map in the glove box. By instinct I was suspicious of how the
world perceived us, so I thought a rural location would be a de-
cent place to live our lives out in peace. A repeated survey of
townsfolk demonstrated that there were, at maximum, two Negro families and one Oriental family, who, Daisy informed me,
were Japanese, not Chinese. The still-fresh memory of Japanese
colonialism in Taiwan gave her mixed feelings about the Okis.
We had no feelings, one way or the other, about the two Negro
families. We suspected that they were related to each other, as
they appeared together more often than most merely friendly
families, and the wife of one family had the same strong jaw as
the husband of the other. We did wonder what had caused them
to move to Polk Valley, which was blindingly white.

Polk Valley chiefly consists of two parallel streets: Main Street,
divided into North and South, and Laurier Street, which emerges like a victorious snake from a Gordian knot of dirt roads and
barely paved paths. Main and Laurier run parallel until Laurier
tributaries into Main; the five blocks that follow are known as
"downtown," or simply "town." Downtown is a hodgepodge
of Old West historical buildings and saloons-turned-bars. South
Main Street exits Polk Valley shortly after the town's lone gas
station, to continue in a no-man's-land of brush and woods to
Killington.

We live on a path that, as far as I can see, has no name. Our
nearest neighbors, the Boones, are a half mile off, and they have
never come to introduce themselves in our thirteen years of life
together. I know that they're called the Boones only because their
box is the closest to ours at the end of Sycamore Road, where a
clump of mailboxes holds each family's mail. I'm not saying that
Daisy and I live a monastic existence, but I'm suggesting that
some vestige of that desire for solitude still thrives in me.

The reconstruction of our home took the bulk of April. We slept
on the floor of the master bedroom with William between us.
One night I jerked awake from a nightmare, and saw the shadow
of a mouse scurrying across Daisy's foot. I was sure that she'd
notice, but she didn't stir.

After the workers left our first major purchase was a huge, rectangular wood table—a disproportionate enormity in our small home. Like most inappropriate purchases, I hadn't thought twice about buying it, let alone how it would get through our small doors. The table could not be dismantled, so I had the men come back and widen both the front door and the opening to the kitchen while the table stood, like an aggrieved houseguest, on the porch. Next came the bed, the mahogany bookcases and dresser, the food staples to fill the pantry, the cold goods to fill the icebox, the unmatched chairs for every room, the rugs more like carpet than the thinning Oriental rugs of my upbringing, the utensils to fill the drawers, the pots and pans, the lamps with delicate shades like butterfly wings, the lace curtains aflutter. A mix and match of the upscale, the backwoods. A home.

◆

It bothered me that William didn't look like me, no family resemblance at all. His hair was neither the inky black of Daisy's nor the white blond of mine, but something in between that always reminded me of what a mutt he was, like a puppy of unknown origin, a head of hair the insignificant color of wet leaves rotting after a rainy autumn. And his face, too, was a mix of ours, but far more Oriental than mine. He had small eyes that peered out in perpetual suspicion, and though he did have jaundice as a baby, it turned out that he also had a yellow tinge to his skin as well, which Daisy claimed was my imagination; but how would she know, or be able to see it? She was blinded by adoration for her child, as any mother should be, not to mention having grown up being surrounded by individuals of the same shade. It's the father who's permitted to lack absolute absorption in his offspring. The fact that William didn't look like me made me nervous, not because I feared that I'd been cuckolded, but because he was my own son and yet alien, looking like nothing I'd previously known. "Hold him," Daisy would say, and she'd put him in my arms, and I'd become incredibly self-aware of whether I was feeling *absolute love* for our baby. For example, I had a fear that when she put William in my arms I would throw him out the window without realizing what I was doing, or drop him unintentionally with my arms suddenly going limp of their own accord, not out of maliciousness or evil, but because I was lukewarm to my own child, and even my body knew it.

The nervousness that I felt around William in those early years may have been another symptom of the nervousness that I was beginning to feel about my marriage. We had finally settled down in a place that we could call our own, with a family that we could call our own. I saw Daisy as exotic; I assumed that, with her improved English, we'd be able to satisfactorily live together and love each other. I naively thought that love went beyond language, but in the foothills of Polk Valley, in our little house in the woods, I struggled with the fruits of these assumptions.

And who was there to tell? I longed to speak to Matka about my loneliness, but having earned her disapproval already, I hated to admit that I might have done something wrong. This was less about my dignity, and more about my fears of her worrying over my condition. I didn't speak to her for years, and she didn't know that William existed until he already had a sister, though she never met either of them. She may even have forgiven me a divorce, but that wasn't what I wanted, even if I could have had one. Daisy was, and is, an excellent wife. Her fervent pursuit of mastery over the English language put Marianne's Latin learnings to shame. She spent her days doting over our son; when William was asleep, she would dote over me. I am ashamed to say that this made me more irritable than pleased at times. In the first year of our life in Polk Valley we went into town frequently enough that people recognized us and knew our names no matter where we went, and she accepted this notoriety without complaint, despite the funny looks she received. I cringe to think of how embarrassed I became when we went into town and she'd attempt to speak English to someone, whether it be a shopkeeper or a cashier, because the listening party certainly couldn't understand her. I became her translator in those situations, and it humiliated me. Yet this was actually a great accomplishment on her part. She was speaking a language that wasn't her own, in a country that wasn't anything like her own, with an aplomb that I couldn't manage when I'd been overseas; and she was doing it because she loved me. To this day she'll say things like "What happen to Joan?" and I'll say, "Who's Joan?" to which she'll reply, "She every time buy canned pea and bag of potato at the supermarket." When I'm gone, she'll still remember those people, though she'll rarely see them, and she'll still have our children. Of course we knew that this was coming. In San Francisco, an inkling blotting itself.

For example.

By the eighth month in Polk Valley I could not spend too much time in the house, and would pace the hallway, the kitchen, and the living room until Daisy suggested that I go for a walk. By then it was November and colder than it had any right to be in my vision of California. I learned that in winter, in the foothills and mountains, it would snow, and there would be snow in the field behind our house, and it would pile to the top of the porch steps and whisper dangerous secrets that only I could hear. But in November it was simply cold.

She held William—who was already clever by then, and had a perpetually solemn and nearly melancholic expression on his face—up with her hands so that he hung high in the air with his feet dangling. She nipped at his naked toes, and he stared at her until he finally turned away, wriggling, and this rejection made me sick. Daisy's response was to pull him closer, and to murmur things to him in a language that I didn't understand.

"Please don't do that," I said.

"What?"

"Don't talk to him in Chinese. I don't understand what you're saying, and he'll get confused."

"He is Chinese baby."

"He's an *American* baby."

I tugged on my heavy boots, a wool sweater over long johns, an overcoat, a scarf. I put on an old hat with fur earflaps, and I opened the back door. I looked out at all the land before me, but even the sight of the field and the trees beyond the field didn't calm me, not with the irritation climbing my throat.

"Bye-bye," Daisy said. "Say 'Bye-bye, Daddy.'"

I didn't turn around.

"You think you will go where?" she asked me.

"Into the woods," I said, "to get a bit of fresh air. I won't be long."

I walked out onto the back porch, where we had a rocking chair and a few label-less tin cans with my cigarette butts in them, and I walked into the field, feeling a shadowy fear put its finger to my heart.

But I'd been wrong about the possibilities of the land. The air was good. It was the sort of air that I'd come to Polk Valley for, fresh and unsullied by the smells of people and their machines, and I felt better almost immediately. In the clean air sounds rang out; the crunch of my boots pressing into the snowy field crackled for what seemed like miles. I saw a pinecone that looked like a corncob, and another one that looked like an armadillo, though there were no trees till I reached the line of the woods, and when I reached the line of the woods I saw that these tightly packed pinecones were everywhere if I only kept watch for them. I walked deeper and deeper into the woods without thinking and without concern for whether I would be able to find my way back. It was my land, wasn't it? How pathetic it would be, to be lost on my own plot. And just when I was about to turn around and pick my way back (I had some sort of half-assed notion of following my own tracks back to the house), lost in my thoughts and the pleasure of getting to know my property, I saw a long shape lying in the dirt behind a tree a few yards away.

I steadied myself. The head of a deer—a buck? No horns. A young deer, then, or a doe. Dark, wide eyes open, frozen. I thought about the animals I'd seen at the American Museum of Natural History. Those creatures brought new meaning to the phrase "still life," and here was an animal, dead, with guts still inside—did blood congeal?—and how had this deer or doe fallen without a predator to kill it? Illness, then. It was probably full of poisoned maggots feeding on poisoned blood. Yet I walked toward it, and when I saw its entire length spread out before me, tears pricked my eyes, and I sat on the dirt in front of the animal. I thought about touching it. Its face was so peaceful, unlike my father's in his coffin, whose face had been twisted in unceasing agony even in death. But here was this animal that could very well be resting, and just as I sat down in front of it with all intentions to enjoy its calm presence, I blinked, and it was gone.

But what could I do with a moment such as that one, or with the hundreds of moments like it afterward? I have been to Wellbrook several times; I have been to doctors. My options have been psychoanalysis, electroshock, or medication with more side effects than treatment functions. There is no taught method of coping. What the doctors never told me is that a percentage of the crazy are also living a crazy lifestyle. Others are more fortunate. For them, being mad is like a cold. They don't even call it an illness. They say, *I was melancholy, I was under the weather. I was panicking in the supermarket by the grapefruits and my hands went numb, but now I'm sitting in front of the television with a glass of wine and some pills, and I'm doing all right.*

I do miss my adolescence, when they simply called me a victim of neurosis.

The doctors said, *Try this, try that, try this,* never, *You're a lunatic for life,* so that every time it came up it was a surprise in the way that a paper cut is surprising.

Maybe the key is to not be surprised.

The doctors don't give you much in the way of options, which is why so many of us madmen choose to go full stop. As though the problem were a matter of, say, picking the right location or knife or piece of rope, and not the horror of knowing one's own wretched selfishness. Such solipsism: a crime with a punishment worse than death. I am fully aware of the choices I've made.

———◆———

I walked back to the house. By then it was getting dark, and with the dark came a deeper cold. I stepped onto the porch and saw, through the window, Daisy in the kitchen with William. Only the overhead kitchen light was on, and because Daisy and William were sitting beneath it, their heads were suffused with a white glow; her dark one and his slightly lighter one were both encircled by halos of light. The religious nature of this image was not lost on me. She had a book open on his lap. She was reading to him in her slow words, words that sounded incorrect to my American ear, but wasn't it enough that she was trying? Without her, I was alone. Without me, she was alone.

I opened the screen door and then the back door, and Daisy finally looked up at me.

"American book," she said.

"I know," I said. "*Goodnight Moon.*"

"You take him," she said. "I will make dinner."

I came up behind her and put my hands on her thin shoulders, feeling the taut muscles that connected to her bones. I leaned into her and sank my nose into the crown of her head where the hair was soft and thick, and I breathed in her warm hazelnut smell. William fidgeted. I heard his small hands slap the pages of the book, and I said, "I love you." I waited for my heart to pound in the old way; I swear that I wanted it to so badly, but it only beat steadily enough to keep me alive.

"I love you," she said.

"We have a nice family."

"Yes."

"We're going to be all right," I said, and then I added, "I love you."

"Yes. Here, take him." She closed the book and put it on the kitchen table. She handed me the baby. I sat at the table and lifted him into the air, swaying him from side to side. He kicked like a frog swimming and laughed. I thought, *How could I ever ask for more than this?*

◆

On the first visit to the Golden Lotus I was assigned to a petite creature whose limbs gyrated like she was made for sex. She was the kind of thing that I could reach out and eat like a ripe, skinned mango. I watched her wriggle her hands up and down, moving them in slow spirals around her body, and then she bent over so that her ass was in my face. How she did this in the constricting *qipao* I do not know. When I was younger I would have been embarrassed, but I was no longer, as I had conveniently forgotten my faults. The point of sex, then, is to become an amnesiac regarding the horrible parts of the self and to absorb oneself only in the friendliness of sensation—to be inhuman for once. I let her degrade herself in front of me because I'd paid money for her and this was what she was, a fleshy being swaying before me for the purpose of my arousal, the only thing that could get my mind off my self because I did not want to think of my self. I wanted to only think of warm skin wrapped around me, and I had paid enough money, hadn't I? All I was good for was money.

After the girl danced for a while she opened the paper sliding door and called out, and then she came and sat next to me at the table on the floor. She still had that absent presence. She asked me what my name was. I told her.

"David," she echoed.

"And your name?" I asked.

"Mei-Ling."

We sat in silence. I didn't touch her, and perhaps it was still leftover childishness that held me back, or a softness that came over me when I heard her gentle voice. In ten minutes there was a rap at the door, and she called out again before the door slid open. The fat girl I'd seen at the market came in with a tray with a bottle of liquor and two tumblers. She didn't appear to recognize me.

"For you, whiskey," Mei-Ling said. She watched as the other girl poured. They said something to each other in Mandarin or Taiwanese, the latter a pungent dialect derived from Hokkien, and the fat girl left us alone again.

Mei-Ling pushed one tumbler toward me and I touched it to my lips. She nodded, lifting her glass to her own swollen mouth. I swallowed. I grew increasingly drunk as the second girl popped in with more whiskey, and with Mei-Ling occasionally asking questions in broken English. What did I do? Did I like Taiwan? The drunker I got the more I saw her as a variety of different animals: doe, lynx, mouse, house cat. The whiskey splintered the air between us. She was only a girl, really, but with makeup on she looked older, her carmine lipstick forming a bow on her full lips, the heavy ermine-white powder on her face forming a feral apparition. Doe, deer, female deer, feline, fox. I'd succeeded in getting as far away from my old life as possible. Her hair, inky. Compact body. Small breasts hidden beneath her dress and not the heavy sway of Marianne's, Marianne's hair the color of the sun. Mei-Ling put her hand between my legs. The feeling of falling. Remember that I was a virgin. She grasped my hand and slid it up her leg to the softness between her legs where there were no undergarments, slipping my fingers inside her (soft as the inside of a raccoon) while she massaged my aching groin, and that was all it took—I shuddered and spasmed without meaning to, my body jolting as I ejaculated into my pants. I blushed, and then I hated her. With an inchoate and abstract desire I wanted to beat her senseless. I even saw the red handprint on her white cheek that I did not make. Red, white, black: those terribly dramatic colors. Even the room smelled violent.

Without letting any surprise at my ejaculation show, she moved so that we were separate beings again. Here was a small clean towel from out of nowhere. I undid my pants and wiped myself off like a child: disgusted, embarrassed. Meanwhile, Mei-

Ling undid and then fixed her hair. It was my underwear, and not my trousers, that bore the brunt of the damage, which was a small relief. She patted her bun, and opened the door to call outside again.

An older woman in a heavy kimono came; later I would learn that this was Daisy's mother, the mama-san. "Mei-Ling is requested to go," she said. "You will come back. We would like to see you tomorrow."

I nodded, surprised by her forthrightness, but already I was thinking of coming back. After the mama-san left, I said, "Good-bye, Mei-Ling."

"Good-bye," she said, surprised. "Okay?" And she sounded a bit frightened. I guess I must have seemed angry, and I wouldn't be surprised if she'd gotten knocked around in that place. Then she said something I hadn't expected at all, which was "What happened?" And she pointed at my scarred hand.

"I hurt it," I said. "I cut myself."

She nodded. I didn't know if she understood, so I took my grand-father's knife out of my pocket, flipped it open, and pretended to slice the back of my hand with the blade. "Like this," I said.

"Why?"

"Haven't you ever gotten hurt before?"

"I gotten hurt. No..." She pretended to cut herself. "No like this. I gotten hurt..." And then she slapped herself, her head whipping to the side.

I laughed. It seemed the correct response at the time. And she laughed, too. We laughed a little hysterically, I'll admit. I'd had a few glasses of whiskey, but she was, as far as I knew, sober, and had barely sipped her first drink.

When the laughter died down it seemed that we were adrift again, without connection—but having had that connection, I wanted more. So I said, "How long have you been a bar girl?"

"Pardon?"

"You are a bar girl? How long?"

"Pardon?"

"Forget it. Are you happy here?"

"Happy here..." She picked up her hand and swayed it back and forth. *Comme ci, comme ça.* "No one happy. Yes?"

And I got very quiet. I lay down on the tatami, and I covered my eyes with one arm so that I couldn't see anything. In my mouth was the taste of all of that whiskey, and in my loins was the memory of spasms. I thought I wanted to come back. I didn't know a damn thing about anything. I got up and left the paper room, wove through the sailors in their hats, stumbled into the hot air that felt like sickness. Now that I was away from home, I missed America. I thought of New York fireworks, and of the pews at St. Jadwiga that I knew so well, worn almost soft beneath our bodies, and I touched my slicked fingers to my mouth, which brought me no pleasure.

I wasn't far from the entrance of the bar, and there was some-one calling to me, I realized, through the haze of voices and dogs barking. When I turned I saw that it was the pretty girl from the market. It was true what the lieutenant had said—they *didn't* all look the same. This girl had high cheekbones and a thin nose. She was wearing a striped and belted green dress, socks, Oxfords—the dress of a schoolgirl or aspiring bobby-soxer. Her hair, loose past her shoulders, hid the bruise on her neck. But I knew it was there, and the knowledge reinvigorated me.

"You forget your knife," she said, and handed it to me.

"Thank you."

"Mei-Ling tell me. You like Mei-Ling?"

I nodded. I was still drunk—the soggy air didn't help that. But it was true that this girl was beautiful, and I felt momentarily brave.

"Do you want to come to my apartment?" I asked her.

She laughed. "You want sex?"

"I want *you.*"

"You want sex with me?"

"I want to spend time with you."

"Spend time?" she said.

"I want to be with you."

"Ah. I want to listen music," she said, and delicately pinched her thumb and forefinger together in the distance between us, lifting them an inch or so in the air, and then swinging her arm in an arc before gently dropping them onto an imaginary record. "You have music?"

I nodded. She swayed slightly, rocking back and forth from foot to foot; from this she might sound like someone unsure of herself, or physically awkward, but Daisy has always been any-thing but awkward, and was merely hypnotizing me—and the serpentine symbolism of her movement does not escape me, but it's never that simple, is it? She makes that swaying motion now only rarely. In fact, she usually stands quite still.

We went to the teahouse, up the stairs to my apartment. I fumbled for my keys, still drunk, and she said, "You are nice."

"Oh, I don't know about that," I said.

"No, I know, I know," she said, and wrapped her arms around my waist, pressing her warm lips to my shoulder. "You are a nice man."

She waited for me to open the door. When I did, she slipped in past me and strode around the room, examining things such as a canvas rucksack, or my briefcase, or a pile of books that I imagined she couldn't read, her fingers stroking the few shirts I had hanging in the alcove that I called a closet. I thrilled to anticipate the shape of her breasts beneath that belted dress, the curve of her ankles beneath those cream-colored socks that matched the paleness of her silly Oxfords exactly, and I wanted to be on top of her. No—I wanted *her* to be on top of *me*, controlling me, doing as she pleased with me. This Oriental girl would not mind seizing me. After all, according to the lieutenant, she had fucked plenty of white men because she enjoyed it.

Daisy turned to me. "Shall we," she said, and I loved the word *shall* in her mouth, its formality, "listen?"

"What do you want to listen to?"

"Mmm," she said, pressing her lips together, "you have what?"

"Well, let's see. I have," I said, "see here, I have a lot of classical music, like Mozart and Beethoven and Bach, but especially Beethoven. I love Beethoven. Have you heard Beethoven?"

"Beethoven?"

I hummed, as best as I could, the opening bars of the Fifth Symphony. She shook her head. The notion of someone having never heard the Fifth Symphony surprised me. Then again, I reminded myself, we were fundamentally different. I went to the record player and I took the requisite record, tilted the sleeve, and let the black vinyl slip into my hand, and as I arranged the system to play I could feel Daisy watching from behind me, so close that her head was almost resting on my shoulder. I felt electricity flickering between us in that small space, and my back went hot and prickly sensing it.

The symphony began. I turned to look at Daisy and saw that she was curled up on her side, with her wrists positioned such that her paws pressed against her chin. With her eyes closed, she looked even more like a child, even with her lip color and rouge. And after ten minutes had passed, and after she had still not moved, I wondered if I'd made the wrong decision in having this girl come over. I was no Don Juan, and she was making no attempt at being a seductress. I was about to ask her if she liked the music when she exhaled suddenly in a rush, and then snored very lightly, but it was still a snore, and I was annoyed in the way that a young man is annoyed when a beautiful girl prefers falling asleep to Beethoven over unbuttoning his strained pants. But what could I do? I removed the needle from its groove. Still, she did not move. I wondered if she was deprived of sleep. The bruise at her neck, exposed, stared up at me like a black eye. As I went to my bed to fetch her a sheet, I realized that she couldn't sleep there; the mosquitoes would eat her alive.

So I tapped her on the shoulder, and then I shook her lightly. Her eyes opened.

"You'll be bitten by mosquitoes," I said. "Sleep underneath the tent."

"Mosquitoes?"

I mimicked an insect, flapping my arms and making a whimpering, whining sound, and then I pointed at the bed. I parted the curtains of the tent and climbed inside, and then I said, "Come here."

She did, and then she fell asleep again. I lay beside her, aching, and put my arm around her, which she didn't seem to mind. I tried not to touch her with my body from the waist down. I pressed my face against her arm and breathed the scent of her skin, which smelled like nothing, but felt warm. Even though she was asleep, I already felt less alone, and I think this is how I began to fall in love with her. You feel alone and something comes to take away the knife-edge of your loneliness. The more mysterious, the better; there's less to prove you wrong. I lay next to her for hours before falling asleep myself, and in that time I felt myself coasting on waves of anxiety that dipped down into black relief, and then I floated gently onshore. I rested. In the morning I awoke, and I was unsurprised to see that she'd left without saying good-bye. But instead of feeling angry or annoyed, as I had before, my flesh was suffused with tenderness for her. For her, I was no ordinary man, but someone whom she felt comfortable enough with to sleep beside. I evoked no anxiety in her. She'd slept like a child. It was a revelation, and I was moving on.

———————◆———————

My relationship with Catholicism had fluctuated to a low ebb in my time overseas, but when I discovered the beauty of St. Joseph's Church I immediately loved its charming stained-glass windows and modest pews, which were not unlike the ones in St. Jadwiga back home, and I told Daisy that I would like to take our family to church on Sundays, which she only vaguely seemed to understand, but agreed to nonetheless. The morning before we went to church we sat at the kitchen table, where I attempted to summarize Catholicism in the simplest way possible. As I began to deliver my explanation I realized that Catholicism was, in fact, difficult to explain to a non-Westerner without verging on ridiculousness. Daisy nodded gravely at everything I said, but I wouldn't have blamed her if she thought I was spouting gibberish.

When we arrived at St. Joseph's, Daisy seemed bewildered by the rituals. She tried to mimic everything that I did, though she crossed herself in the wrong order, and was slow to realize when we were to stand and sit; I strained to appreciate her efforts. William sat in her lap with *Goodnight Moon* in his, ignoring the ceremony and rites until it was time for Communion, and when I stood to approach for the wafer and wine, he reached for me, the book sliding to the floor with a bang.

"No," I whispered, hoisting him by the armpits to sit him back down again, "you two stay here."

"I want," William said, and he wasn't loud about it, but people began to look at us—which they did anyway, because of the kind of people we were.

"No," I said, panic rising hot behind my breastbone, and I told Daisy, "Keep him in his seat," before I hurriedly exited the pew and into the line. I looked back, and my family was the only one still seated; I flushed at seeing their dark faces, including William's miserable one. He looked like he was about to shout. As I took the host upon my tongue I closed my eyes and saw, behind my lids, young, smiling Marianne patting the pew beside her.

After Mass had concluded, and we exited St. Joseph's into the frigid air with our coats on, Daisy said, "We do this every week, Ba?"

"I hope so," I replied. We were in a small crowd of Polk Valley denizens who chattered about potlucks, none of which we were invited to, and my wife looped one arm through mine while holding William with her other. She asked, within earshot of everyone, "How there is so many of Jesus's body to eat?"

I opened my mouth, and then I closed it. I drew my family away from the crowd. "It's very complicated," I said. We made our way to the car. "It's—it's very complicated. When your English is better, I'll explain it to you."

Later that night, as we settled into bed and I turned off the bedside lamp, Daisy said, "I like church."

"Yes, lamb?"

"Yes."

"What do you like about it?" I asked.

She didn't say anything more, and in the dark I thought she'd fallen asleep. Finally she said, "Many times, I do not understand you. Church helps me."

"It helps you to understand me?"

"A little bit."

"How?" I asked, but the question would be fruitless before it was even planted. I couldn't imagine how she'd be able to explain.

"I see you love something," she whispered. She reached for my hand, and we intertwined our fingers, and we said good night.

I admit that I was, and am, an elitist. I didn't want my son to wait until he was seven to begin his schooling when I felt that he was smart enough to begin serious learning when he was four or five; after all, it's not uncommon for expert pianists to begin their lessons so early, and yes, William did learn to play a scale when he was three, when I began to teach him what I knew on an upright at home. I didn't dare attempt to have a Nowak shipped out to us from the factory; there was no way that I'd slip past undetected. So I'd found our homey, well-worn secondhand Nowak upright in the city paper for a perfectly reasonable price.

He would not go to school with other children. Daisy and I agreed on this together. Neither of us wanted him to be shunned or mocked for his otherworldly looks. And she wanted to keep him close; there was nothing more she needed than to be with him at all times, pulling him to her whenever he wandered within arm's length, and lifting her eyes to observe him every few moments like clockwork. Twice she tentatively brought up the notion of a second child, for William's sake, but I stood adamantly against this. I, the Catholic, felt guilty about but insisted on contraception, not wanting to feel the same eerie sense of alienation that I suffered with William, and I hated that sense for existing. Of course I did not hate him. I'm not a monster when it comes to my only boy. I know all too well from my own father-son relationship that such relationships are complicated, and I tried—oh, I tried!—not to let William feel unloved, unwanted. I hope I haven't failed in this.

But about education. I spent a lot of time attempting to distill a concentration of essential books. There was the Bible, of which I preferred the King James for its stride. I wanted him to know Latin, too, and I considered acquiring a textbook, and then moving on to Julius Caesar's *Gallic Wars*, and so forth. We would need a dictionary, of course, a good one. We could find a copy of the abridged *Oxford English* somewhere, or have it mailed to us. We already had *Goodnight Moon*. He was reading that on his own before he was two, sounding out the words based on a teaching style that I cobbled together, pulling together consonants and vowels, singing the alphabet, and drawing letters onto sheets of paper. Until William was six and Gillian was four, I didn't begin to teach my children in earnest, but I had a list of books that I wanted to keep in the house for them: *Physicians Desk Reference to Pharmaceutical Specialties and Biologicals*, a world atlas, a few dictionaries in other languages, a field guide to North American birds. I made a short list, and those books are all in the shelves now, save for the King James that Ojciec inscribed for me, and which I keep here with me in my briefcase but will soon enough find its way back home, I imagine, when the police arrive. I trust that my children will be able to take the reins from here.

◆

After a year of living in Polk Valley, our existence had become tightly circumscribed. We three went into town only to purchase groceries and dry goods, because staying home was easier than trying to appear normal when I was ailing; and Daisy pressured me, too, stating that she felt stared at by what she referred to as "strange people," and I was too tired to explain to her that we, and not they, were the strange ones. We no longer went to Mass, although this was less a consequence of Daisy's feelings and more due to my discomfort with attending church. After all, we'd had a civil, and thus secular, wedding ceremony, as Matka had suspected, and I did want to raise William to be a good Catholic, but how would I do it without Daisy's help? At times I heard her chanting, singsong, to William in her language. I told her to stop, and we fought, and she cried, and I screamed at her that I wasn't raising a foreign child in my own home; I reeled with how out of control my life had become. For a few weeks I took William to Mass alone, insisting that Daisy remain at home, but he seemed to understand his parents' religious conflict. He stopped paying attention. He refused to stand and sit when he was supposed to, and he whined loudly for his mother, the embarrassment nearly killing me. I stopped taking him, and then I stopped going, too. It all felt pointless, too pointless.

It was this limited life that brought back the ghost of Marianne Orlich, never quite forgotten, who now possessed in my mind even more of the holy attributes that I'd once put upon her. I sat in the kitchen with William in my lap, sifting through flashcards while he placidly absorbed them, and he repeated things with his dull, thick tongue. I worried about his accent; he did have one. (And I tried to shake it out of him, but I'll go to the grave with the knowledge that my boy, my own flesh and blood, sounds off-key.) As I absentmindedly turned the cards that my wife had so diligently made, I watched said wife as she stood at the counter and sliced potatoes. She was humming to herself a song that I didn't recognize. With Marianne in my head I saw only the parts of Daisy that were decidedly not white. She was small, and her black hair was in a thick braid down her back, and with her left foot crossed over her right one I wondered why her feet, which I had once been so enamored by, were so tiny, and could think only of things like barbaric foot-binding rituals; when had such things ended, anyway? Her questions about Mass made me cringe. So did her blunt disbelief with regard to transubstantiation—these were all things that had hurried along our domestic conflicts. I wondered why I'd set such traps for myself. I was living with someone whom I loved, but in so many ways she was a stranger to me, and with our handicapped communication I felt lonelier than ever.

So to the painfully obvious question of why I had married this woman in the first place, I would say that I adored her sharp and almost jagged elbows; I loved how inappropriate it felt to remove her saddle shoes, which she still let me do as part of sex in our shoeless home, and I always unlaced them to reveal her white socks and what I then considered to be her marvelously shaped feet. I loved how she was mouthy when she got drunk and never pretended to be more decorous than she really was, but would occasionally slip into what she called *sa jiao*, a sappy, sloppy girlishness that made my nerves squirm with delight. She lounged in my bed under the mosquito tent, dressed in her un-buttoned silk blouses and underwear. She would sprawl out on my small bed, stroking her own hipbone with the back of her fingers as one would a cat, staring at the ceiling. At times I thought my heart would take a running leap out of my chest; at times all I wanted was to look at her forever. Why else do people fall in love? What sense does love ever make for itself, especially young love, which is so desperate to be satisfied?

"Nowak, let me tell you," the lieutenant had said. "You *pay*, you *play*, but you never let them *stay*."

When I had asked her to marry me, she laughed. She traced her finger in a thin oval on my bare and tanning side. "America?" she said. Her breasts were paler than the rest of her torso. Her upper arms were the darkest part of her. She had delicate hairs that sprouted from her areolae. I loved to bite her brown nipples till she moaned.

"Yes," I said. "You can have anything you want."

"Whatever I all want I have here. Why don't you stay here? Stay in Taiwan, be here, be happy with me."

"I can't do that. I don't speak Chinese. At least you know English."

"At here everybody know me, I have power."

"In America," I said, kissing her forehead, "everyone will know you. I promise. I promise, I promise, I promise. My lamb. I promise you, you will have a good life with me."

"I have a good life here."

"I want to be with you. And so you must come with me."

Nothing. She rolled onto her belly, the curvature of her back smooth as driftwood. "I'll never leave," she said. The ring, pure gold, was still in my hand.

We spent our days together in my apartment or at the Golden Lotus, and there was no in-between, which I believe led to a rapid increase in the sexualization of our relationship. After I asked her to marry me and she said no, I searched for her in the ordinary places, but couldn't find her for days, and I was afraid that I'd scared her off with my proposal. And I feared that the old insanity would come around again as I wandered the filthy streets of Kaohsiung with bicycles swirling around me, my armpits sweating, being followed by dogs with their ribs showing and their shrill barks sounding; I waited for the abyss of fear to open in my belly, pulling everything I'd managed to make of a life into that deep hole, but I thought I could scare it off with distraction. I spent several nights at the Golden Lotus so that I could drink—alone, chastely—with Mei-Ling, the first girl, and I asked her if she knew where Jia-Hui was. She shook her head. I reached into my wallet and pulled out three nights' worth of yuan, which was nothing to me, but which I knew would be everything to her.

"This is yours. Not the mama-san's. Yours."

She pushed the money back at me. "I take your money, mama-san finds out, I get hit, kill. No."

"I want to know what happened to Jia-Hui."

Perhaps Mei-Ling heard something in my voice, because she went still then, and when she spoke again her voice was quiet. "The mama-san. Only because Jia-Hui is mama-san's daughter is she alive. She is bad." The word *bad* held weight. It loaded down the space between us with a thousand tons.

"Bad?" I echoed.

"The most dirty. People know Jia-Hui and the whites have sex for no money. But she is even more dirty. More bad."

"What are you talking about?"

Mei-Ling gave me a hard look. "I know you like Jia-Hui. So many men like her. But she has a poison. I tell you, she is worse than animal and worse than whore."

I pressed her for more, but she added nothing to what she'd told me already, so I weighed my options. Mei-Ling was frail and would be easy to bully. She reminded me of the girls I taunted in my youth, and it wasn't so different now. If I hurt her it would only be a means to an end. I could break her wrist by clenching it in one disfigured hand. Even now, I wonder, what happened to Mei-Ling? Did she ultimately make a misstep? Was she killed for an error, or did she grow old in that whorehouse? Did a white knight carry her away on his pale, gaunt horse? I cared so little about what she had to say about Jia-Hui's poor standing. I was obsessed. I would eviscerate myself for Jia-Hui, but I did not hurt Mei-Ling.

On a night that is only important to my memory because of Jia-Hui's role in it, I exited the bar. I walked home as I had done so many nights before. The few lights in the windows doubled themselves and shimmered. Dogs snapped at my ankles. They circled me in a ragtag pack, one not belonging to another, snarling and woofing in hopes of a scrap, or perhaps in hopes of devouring me. I walked and they followed, leaping. A Chinaman passed with his head down, looking briefly at me before hurrying elsewhere. Here she was to chase them away, my ghost-girl. I felt her grab my arm.

"Take me to America," she said in a rush, her breath in my ear. She sank her face into the side of my head, whispering, "I want to marry you."

◆

Daisy finished cutting the potatoes. William laid his head against the inside of my elbow, signaling that he was tired of flashcards. Four o'clock: he needed a nap.

"William's sleepy," I said, still thinking of Daisy's small feet, and my memory of Marianne's larger ones, pink from traipsing inside wool socks and boots in the snow, the size of which she was embarrassed by. I lifted William into my arms, and he rested his face on my shoulder. I carried him into his room and settled him to bed. There was no such thing as a crib for our wee one; he slept in a twin bed with an assortment of stuffed toys. I tucked two bears around him and pulled the covers to his chin. He did not suck his thumb, as I had. He said, drowsily, "Love you."

"I love you, too." I kissed him on his crown.

Next I entered the master bedroom, which was sparsely decorated. I'd thought all women were interested in interiors, but Daisy was not. The only additions that she made to our bedroom were a few of William's drawings—taped, not framed—to the wall above our iron headboard, and a corny, coral-colored vase of fake carnations that she'd bought from town and placed on her vanity table. I'd chosen the furniture: the wrought-iron bed, the matching mahogany night tables, the wardrobe with its elaborately carved doors, and even the vanity table and mirror, which I'd assumed that Daisy wanted because she was a woman, and which she did use, though I never did know if it brought her pleasure.

I closed the door and locked it. The phone sat on my side of the bed, on my night table. My wife, after all, had no one to call.

"Number, please."

I gave the switchboard operator the Orlichs' number. I waited, and through the crackle of the line I heard a familiar voice: "Caroline Orlich speaking."

"Mrs. Orlich," I said.

"Who is this?" Did I hear something resigned, tired, upset?

"It's David Nowak."

"Oh. Well," she said, "this is a surprise."

"Is this a bad time?"

"No. I'm completely unoccupied at the moment. Isn't it true that you broke your mother's heart a few years back?"

The fact that Mrs. Orlich knew this shocked me. Matka was a private person, and wouldn't even have allowed anyone to know about my father's death if it hadn't been an unavoidable concession. Carefully I asked, "Do you speak with her?"

"No. I see her at the supermarket sometimes, but she's always thought that she was too good for me. Look where that's got her. Anyway, I heard from George that you had some kind of fight with her. That's all. She looks miserable, by the way—skin and bones. Wrapped in furs like a bag lady. Why are you calling?"

"I was wondering," I said, God help me, "if I could—I'd like to get in touch with Marianne."

"Is that right. Well, if you're looking to scoop her up, you're barking up the wrong tree. She's living in a convent now." She laughed. "Is that all you wanted?"

"I'd still like to talk to her," I said.

"I don't think they accept phone calls at the convent, dear. Probably too busy praying, and I haven't spoken to her since she left. It's somewhere out in California, out in the middle of nowhere. Near Sacramento. Did you know that Sacramento is the capital of California? Who knew?"

"What sort of convent is it?"

"Oh, I don't know, the kind where they pump out nuns like parts on an assembly line. The town is Killington, I just remembered. What an awful name. Killington. I can't believe my daughter lives in a place with a name like that, can you? Like a land of murders."

Killington. She was forty-five minutes away, in the next town over. My heart felt oversized, pumping rushes of blood to bloat my head full. Was this the greatest news of my life, or the most terrible? I vaguely recalled Marianne telling me of some dream to live in Northern California. Had I, without knowing it, steered my family in this direction?

"That's too bad," I said.

"Is that all you wanted to know? These calls are expensive. I don't even know where you are."

"Nowhere. Good-bye," I said, and hung up.

I sat on the bed with my hand on my chest. Had I imagined the conversation? Had Caroline Orlich really told me that her daughter lived a short distance from where I sat? Marianne was in a convent, of course, and I was married, with a son, but she was out there: no longer in Chicago, but doing what she'd wanted to do for so long, and it couldn't be a coincidence that she was now so close to me, but an act of Fate. Because while I'd found a woman to marry, I'd never snuffed out my flame for that girl from the Pawlowskis' Christmas party. If monogamy is measured in the heart, I must say that I'd never forsaken Marianne, the specter. In the marrow of my bones I'd carried her with me from New York to Taiwan, around the United States, and finally to Polk Valley.

My one regret was this: it was not that I'd lacked the courage to chase Marianne to Chicago, or even that I'd fled to the East and chosen to marry the woman I named Daisy, but that I had but *one life* with which to make such choices—and that damned inflexibility immediately left me greedy and grasping, with my hand still pressed against my sternum as though to hold in the heart beneath.

Within the week I told Daisy that I had business in Sacramento. She didn't ask what that business was, but nodded, hugged me, and told me to be safe. "Be safe" was a habit of hers, and it makes me wince to think of it now, because I left this morning without saying good-bye to her or to the children, which means that I escaped the plea or superstitious ritual of hers. (Lord Jesus Christ, have mercy on me, a sinner.) On the drive to Killington I lost myself in dreams. Frankly, I'm surprised I didn't drive off the road; I was busy thinking about Marianne's body, but it would be too simple to say that my interest was purely sexual. I had no intention of seducing her, because the Marianne I'd known as an adolescent would never allow herself to be seduced, and the Marianne who had chosen to become a nun would be even more impossible to bed. It was the substance of her that I wanted to be near. I loved anticipating the sight of her body, even if it was cloaked and hidden; but I also wanted to just talk to her, to hear her gentle voice, to ask her if she remembered the days on the roof, to remind her of eating cookies in her living room, which felt threadbare to me at the time, but now seems far warmer than my Polk Valley living room, which has a small bookcase, a sofa and easy chair, and the twin uprights, but not much else; I wanted to ask her if she ever thought of me, because I was lost and I often thought of her; I would tell her that I continued to pray, but that I felt as distant from God now as I did when I first lost my mind. Most of all—and here my eyes misted, and I could barely see the road—I wanted to tell her that I missed her.

Right as I crossed the border into Killington, I made my plans. I decided that I'd claim to be Marty. I feared that I wouldn't be allowed to enter without being a direct relation. And yet I was terrified that Marianne's disappointment upon discovering my lie would make her angry, and that she'd send me away without a chance to explain. When I arrived at Killington I drove aimlessly, not sure of what to do or where to go until I found a filling station, and asked the attendant if there was a convent in town. He said that there was. I asked him, a tautly muscular young man with a mild overbite, if he knew where the convent was. He asked if he looked like the kind of guy who would know where a convent would be, and I said, "I suppose not." I asked him if he knew how I could find out where the convent was. He shrugged and looked over my head at the mountains. I reached for my wallet and gave him a five-dollar bill. "And how can I find out," I said, "where this convent is?"

He put the bill in his pocket and went into the garage, and when he returned he said, "The convent's the Monastery of the Sacred Heart, on the only hill in Killington."

As I drove toward the singular hill, I saw a bar on the main road. It, like most buildings of that area, and of Polk Valley, resembled a saloon, complete with swinging doors and a block-font sign, which read THE MINE SHAFT. I wanted courage. I parked the Buick in the dust, and I entered the open bar, where I sat on a stool and spoke to no one but to order my drinks. I knocked back whiskey till my face went numb. Yet I was in possession of all of my faculties. I didn't stumble, I didn't slur. I merely felt more confident when I thought of what was to come. I took care to rinse my mouth with soda, and then I paid my tab and stepped into the light, where the light was so blinding that I felt myself surrounded by angels.

———————◆————·

At the convent I said I was Marianne's brother, Marty, and the abbot directed me to her. I entered the kitchen in a daze. I was aware of a long counter and a long wooden farm table at the center of the room. On the wall closest to the door hung a crucifix and several small paintings in frames, but I only glanced at those; Marianne, standing alone, was all that I truly saw. She was making bread, with her hands and forearms covered in flour. Lumps of dough sat on the counter on wax paper.

Marianne turned, wearing a shapeless brown dress beneath a simple white apron at her front, and her likeness was that of a drab female bird. Her face had matured and thinned—the rounded cheeks were pulled sharply inward, and her nose gave her face a leaner, more beaky profile—but her lips were the same soft shade of blessed pink, her eyes green-blue, and when I say "drab" I mean no insult; only that her looks were more modest than Daisy's spectacular ones, and simultaneously more angelic. Her face tensed. She said, "David? How did you know where I was? They told me it was Marty. Why are you here?"

"I wanted to see you," I said. Her face was as holy as anything in that convent, I thought. Her head was uncovered, which surprised me, and my eyes traveled from her face to her hair, and her hair glowed, the experience of it like opening a window in a stuffy house. But I had to deal with the reality of where I was, and with whom I was speaking. I did try to rein in my heart. I struggled to remember that we were two human beings, each with our own commitments. (At her throat lay a simple cross. On my left ring finger clung a simple band.)

Marianne took a stool from the farm table and dragged it out. Flour dusted the seat. "Sit," she said. "I need to deal with these loaves before they turn to stone. I'm not the best baker, but I'm learning." As she punched the dough, she said, "They told me that Marty was here. I thought you were going to be Marty. You know," she added, her fists thudding steadily, "they would've let you visit me, regardless. Our order isn't known for being strict. You didn't have to lie about it."

"I'm sorry."

"Yes. Well, it isn't as bad as all that. I don't mean to sound cross. I'm glad to see you—it isn't as though I forgot about you." These last words disrupted her movements for a second, and then she continued. "You look unhappy."

"Is that a divinely inspired insight?" I asked, trying to joke, but feeling like death.

"No. I just know you." She smiled. "Do you still pray?"

"Yes. And with my son, too."

"Your son," Marianne said, and paused again. She lifted the loaf and moved it, replacing it with the next ball of dough before resuming her small movements. "So you have a son. Goodness, how time flies. What's his name?"

"William."

"William. I'll add him to my prayers. And your wife?"

"Daisy."

"I'll pray for Daisy, too."

She was polite enough to ignore my uncontrollable twitching. How serene, I thought. Why was it so simple for her? Daisy's name from her throat had a wretched effect on me. I imagined that the name, which in that moment I found anything but charming, had caused Marianne to feel safer in my presence, but I didn't want her to feel safe. I wanted her to be on edge and shaking with complicated emotions, the way that I was on edge and shaking because I wanted to throw myself at her and run away all at once. I wanted her to be vulnerable, and even to come over and put her flour-flecked hand on mine. My eyes settled on a vase on the counter by the sink. Coming out of the clear glass was a sprig of something with round green leaves, and a number of bright pink flowers sprang here and there from its branches. From that counter she overlooked a lawn with trees, and I saw women huddled in the dirt outside, digging and planting.

"Well," she said. "I'm going to be doing this for a while. Then I have prayers at four. Don't you have somewhere to be? I don't expect that you have a job now. Or do you? Where does your wife think you are?"

"I don't have a job, no. And I told Daisy that I was visiting a friend."

"Ah. That you are. Funny how quickly things change. You look so grown-up now."

"And you," I replied, "said that you would devote your life to God. Here you are." I wanted to add, *You never wrote*, but I knew that to say so would jeopardize everything.

"Yes. It took some doing. My parents weren't pleased. But it was God's will. You know that summer, when I was doing volunteer work with Father Danuta? When I was praying all that time? I was asking. I was searching for guidance."

"I remember. You came to my house. You were cleaning out that widow's house, and I barely saw you for months."

"Well. My father was drinking, which I've forgiven him for, and more importantly, I'm not afraid of him now. At the time, though, I was terrified. I would have done anything he told me to. The whole family did."

We both thought of my broken nose and my black eye. I saw it flicker across her face as it danced through my brain.

She said, "You know, my family never tries to make contact with me these days. That's why I was so surprised when the abbot told me Marty had come. I haven't seen him since he left for the navy, do you know that? I hope I didn't seem angry when you came in. It is truly good to see you. I just miss my family."

"I wasn't offended."

"This is the life I'm meant to live, but it isn't without sacrifice."

I said, "I admire that."

"In a way," she said, "it's easier than you might think. Doing a thing that some people consider difficult—it's a lot easier when you don't have options. Or no longer have options."

"What do you mean?" I asked.

"You know," she said, frowning, and looked away.

"No," I said, "what *do* you mean?"

She said, "*When*, for a while, it looked like I was going to marry you. Don't misunderstand. I did... *love* you. I did. Of what I know of love, that *is* what I think it was. I was torn between my spiritual calling and hoping to be a good Catholic as your wife. I must have spent hours praying over it, asking God what he wanted from me. Then there were my parents, who saw me as their meal ticket. All I had to do was marry you. But that all changed for them when you got sick."

"I assumed as much."

"I was glad to get away, but I'll say this again—my feelings hadn't *changed* when I left for Chicago. I need you to understand that. I was always very fond of you," she said. "It just didn't work out for us. But that's all right, it seems. You have your family, and I have this. We've found our own ways, haven't we?"

"Yes. You're right," I said, but I wanted to laugh and cry at the same time.

"I'm glad to see you, though. You're looking... well."

"Am I? Do you mind if I stand next to you?" I drew circles in the flour. I drew a heart without meaning to. Then I turned and kissed her cheek. She didn't pull away, but I felt her grow rigid as I touched her.

"Please don't make things difficult."

"I'm not trying to."

"You have a wife."

"This and that are not mutually exclusive," I said. "I'm here as a friend."

"David," she said.

"I'd still like to see you as a friend." I wiped the flour heart onto the floor.

———◆———

That night I checked on our son, and came to find Daisy sitting at the kitchen table, sniffling and swiping at her eyes. She smiled. "Hi," she said.

I'm ashamed to admit that the sight of her sadness irritated me. It shouldn't have. I ignored her tears, and then I feared that she'd accuse me of infidelity, although she had no right to; I hadn't done anything wrong. I'd seen Marianne once. I'd spoken to her, and then I'd left her there in the kitchen baking bread as feelings roiled in my every cavity.

"William's asleep," I said. "How's dinner?"

"Dinner will be at six o'clock," she said.

I knew but never dealt with the fact that Daisy was prone to occasional fits of melancholy, which she always tried to hide from me, and her ability to make that effort causes me to suspect that she was crying more than I was witness to. I'll never know why she cried, but maybe what's most important is that she had so many reasons to cry, which leaves me with the conclusion that perhaps she was weeping for all of them at once. I hope that one day, if the luck that's escaped me in this life can find me in the next, I can speak to her plainly. I would ask her to please tell me the story of her life, including the story of her life with me. She deserves that much, I know.

From moment to moment the air was like sheets, like walking through a hallway of clotheslines. Everywhere I went I was saddled with warnings. I went to visit Marianne again the next week, this time carrying a satchel of fresh cheese and a hunk of dark peasant bread, red grapes, wine. Fake-Marty-the-brother took his sister into the woods behind the monastery and he found her a great oak to sit beneath. Her face was beautiful in its plainness; she was happier than I could have hoped for. I was happy to see that she was happy, even if it was a tentative happiness. I could hope to have our old joy back.

"Once upon a time," Marianne said, lying in the grass with her arms stretched overhead.

"There was a young man," I said, "who had everything."

"He had a cloak that rendered him admirable to the selected few."

"There was really only one of the selected few."

"Yes." Marianne was, what, twenty-two at the time? It was autumn. The oak had shimmied off half its leaves. She said, "She was a girl trapped in a castle, and she had a cloak, but hers was tattered. And she adored the young man who had everything..."

"He lost it all, his mind, everything."

She sighed. "Oh, the story is becoming sad."

"It is a little sad, isn't it?" I took the bottle of wine and corkscrew out of my satchel. Daisy and I rarely drank—she lacked the Oriental propensity to redden from alcohol, but still she preferred not to drink it, which I never would have guessed, given her origins; so I stopped drinking, too, remembering Matka and her dragon's breath. But on this visit with Marianne I brought a bottle of wine, and I uncorked the bottle and drank. I handed it to Marianne, who held it with one hand at the neck before swal-

lowing from it with the help of her other hand tipping it back at
its base, a thin stream dribbling down the corner of her mouth. I
wiped the drips away, and she smiled.

Before I knew it I was corrupting her. The Marianne I visited
this time felt fundamentally different from the one I'd seen before. This time I touched her arm, and then I was brave enough
to touch her thigh. She didn't move, but her stillness seemed like
permission. The seduction was immediate. I yanked up her dress
and waited for a reply. She went still again, and then I heard her
breath, shallow and wanting, before she pressed her forehead
against mine, and that was enough for me. I thought momentarily of consequences. I'm afraid that I could not be convinced
of how terrible those consequences could be. We made love in a
field absent of insects, with the only sound around us the crackling of the dead grass, the dry leaves, and the agonized sounds
that slithered from the back of her throat. She wrapped her legs
around my back. I thrust slowly and with concentration; we
gulped air in turns. We were the center of the universe.

She went quiet as she gathered her clothes, and I watched her
muscles move beneath her skin. I asked her what she was thinking. She shook her head. I put the remnants of our picnic in my
bag, and when it was all finished she said, her teeth purplish,
"You never think that you have an impact on people, David, but
you do."

"What do you mean?"

"You're not careful, you think that you're the only one that
anything happens to. It's blindness."

I needed to leave, but I didn't want to leave on those terms,
so I waited. She asked me where I lived. I said Polk Valley. She
wanted to know exactly where. I almost said that it would be
better if she didn't know, but I knew that to say so would be a
slap in the face. I gave her a description without an address, and
then I asked her why.

"I just wanted to know something about you that I didn't already," she said. "Having you here makes me think that nothing's changed. I can't afford to think that."

I saw her a few more times. The next time, she was reluctant;
her gestures were less hungry, but still she reached for me. When
I saw her for the third time she looked sick. I told her, half joking,
that she was a classic example of Catholic guilt. She told me that

I was ruining her, that she loved me, but she didn't know what to do.

A month and a half later the air became frigid, and I went outside to have a cigarette when I opened the door and there was Marianne in her long-sleeved dress, which was damp at the armpits.

"David," she said, and I thought I was imagining her until I opened the screen door and she looked behind her at a car in our driveway behind the Buick, holding up her hand to someone I couldn't see, before coming into the hallway. As she and I walked into the living room Daisy poked her head in. She looked at Marianne.

"Hello," Marianne said. She seemed as though she had just woken from an unsatisfying but much-needed nap.

They were in the same room now. Daisy came in and stood next to me, while Marianne sat on the sofa with her knees tightly pressed together, one hand atop the other in her lap. Daisy looked at me. "This is who?" she asked.

Marianne told my wife her name, and said that she was an old friend.

"Ah," Daisy said.

"This is Daisy," I said to Marianne. "Sweetheart," I added, "could you please go play with William? I need to speak to Marianne alone."

Daisy squeezed my arm, hard. "Okay," she said.

When she left the room Marianne said, "She doesn't know, does she?" and I was aware that my wife might be in the hallway, listening.

"No," I said.

"I didn't think so."

"No."

She rested her hand on her belly in a way that I recognized from my wife long ago, so that Marianne didn't have to say it, but she said it anyway: "I'm pregnant, David."

"Oh," I said, and I had no excuse for two fools who had hoped themselves untouchable.

She said that she had left the convent. I did not say the word *procedure*, though that was what came to mind. I knew that she would never have one, regardless of whether she was in the convent anymore.

She looked like something that had been hollowed out and stuffed with wet feathers.

She said again that she didn't know what to do.

And yet in my state I could think only about what the baby would look like. It would be a girl, and she'd be beautiful. But what did that matter to Marianne, who was pregnant and seated before me, whom I still loved and wanted to embrace in joy as the mother of my child?

"I'll give you money," I said. "I'll write you a check right now."

Marianne looked around the room, taking in her surroundings with her hand still resting on her belly. I realized that my checkbook was in the kitchen, and I didn't want to leave the living room if Daisy was spying in the hallway. I preferred to remain ignorant, and the pregnancy was enough to contend with. Instead I reached for my wallet and sifted through it. There were five twenty-dollar bills, which I gave to her, and then I asked, "Where are you staying, if not at the convent?"

She said that she had just left the convent that day and had nowhere to go. I realized that she had come in with no suitcase and was likely to have no possessions. I had no idea who it was that had driven her to my home, or how she had determined my location. She was in my home because she'd earned the right, through my poor judgment, to trespass.

"I'll write you a check right now," I said, though I had said the exact same words before, and then I got up and barreled into the hallway, where Daisy stood illuminated by the hallway light. I avoided her eyes. I walked past her into the kitchen. As I sifted through the drawer where I kept my checkbook, my hands were fluttering of their own accord, reminding me of Matka's winglike hands with their long fingers, and my mind spun with how fucked up everything was and what would my mother think? No matter what I did—even if I spent the rest of my life performing acts of goodness—here would always be the fact that I'd ruined Marianne's life; perhaps worse, and selfishly, there would be an emptiness in me that could not be filled by anyone but Marianne.

I took the checkbook and Daisy was not in the hallway, but Marianne was still in the living room.

I said, "I'll write you a check for..." and I scrambled for a number that seemed appropriate, but what was an appropriate number for this type of situation, anyway? It seemed farcical. "... four thousand dollars. You can find somewhere to stay for a while."

She took the check, not looking at it, and stuffed it into her dress pocket.

"How did you get here?" I asked.

"I went to St. Joseph's," she said, "and found someone who could drive me."

She was so beautiful. I had to let go of her now, truly; I have had to let go of her and everything else.

"Is there anything else you need?" I asked. "Is there anything at all that I can do for you?"

There was a long silence.

Marianne crossed the room. As she passed me I smelled the dark odor of her body, and a lingering trail of the oil from her hair, but neither of us made the effort to touch. I heard the wooden door open, and then the screen door. I heard both doors shut, and with the sound of their closing I didn't allow myself to cry. Instead I went to the sofa and sat. I waited for Daisy to come. I am sitting now and waiting for—I'm not quite sure what I'm waiting for.

———◆———

I have one last story. Jia-Hui and I were in the firefly village on the outskirts of Kaohsiung, where the ponds and banana trees were plentiful, and where my blood was being sucked out of me by mosquitoes that whirled and wheedled everywhere we went. It had taken more than two hours of walking to reach this village. I'd found the trip eerie; unlike the ramshackle, noisy, cosmopolitan Kaohsiung, the borderlands of the city were silent, and we heard nothing but our own footsteps as we traveled. The firefly village was far, Jia-Hui had said, because the bugs with blinking lights could not meet where there were so many people.

"Here there are many kinds," she said, meaning the fireflies. "They come different times."

And yet I didn't see any as we stood on a small bridge, staring into the darkness with her small hand in mine. I supposed aloud that perhaps the recent rain had something to do with it. Maybe, I said, the fireflies wouldn't come out if it had been raining.

"No, no," Jia-Hui said, "firefly use umbrella." She let go of my hand to mimic opening an umbrella over her head, and I laughed. She was going to marry me. I didn't know what had changed her mind, but she would be mine.

She'd wanted me to see the firefly village before flying to New York the next day. It was important, she said, for me to see the most beautiful thing in her country before we left it and got married in my country. In the meantime, I was still trying to think of a fitting American name for her. I thought something floral might be appropriate.

A spark. A shimmer. "See"—as the world lit up around us— "so, so much firefly," Jia-Hui said.

Amen.

KNIFELESS

JIA-HUI (1956–1968)

in translation

Years ago I was putting William to bed when someone came to our home, but no one ever did, not then and not now. The three of us lived far from the nearest neighbor, miles up the mountain from town, and the voice seemed like nothing. But then I heard David. He said, "Marianne." After William settled in, I came into the living room and there was a white woman in a brown dress, sitting on the sofa with her hands in her lap. She introduced herself as Marianne.

"This is Daisy," David said. "Sweetheart, could you please go play with William?"

"Okay," I said, but I didn't. I went to the hallway instead, and I listened with my big ears. This is how I learned that the flat-bellied woman carried his baby inside of her. When I heard this, I quickly gathered my senses. I said to myself, *You can't shatter open.* Instead of crying, I stumbled to the kitchen and made chamomile tea. When the water boiled I pressed my finger against the hot kettle, and I left the finger there for a few seconds before removing it. The skin was then bright pink, and a shape lifted from the flesh to form a proud, puffy blister. I sat with my teacup at the table and lifted it to my mouth. My tongue burned to sandpaper, which shocked me out of numbness. So what was this? What did it mean, to be woken to this life here?

◆

When David finally came into the kitchen after the blond woman left, and he saw me sitting with my empty cup, quiet as a stump, I had already explained the situation to myself: he was a man; I knew what men did; I had, from my smallness to adulthood, served girls to men just like him. As a result, there could be no disappointment, only naïveté, in forgetting that he was the same. But I was surprised to see that he was scared, that his face had gone the same color as his hair. He was as frightened of my opinion as he was frightened by knowing about the pregnancy.

"Daisy," he said.

I said nothing. I was angry at him for being weak, and I was despairing, too. What can I say about love now when I could barely express how I felt about him to his face when he was alive? It seems unjust to expose myself this way when he couldn't understand me even after all of my efforts, which afforded us hundreds of words of English that were kilometers from enough. Fatty, at least, had understood everything.

"You listened," he said.

"Yes."

"Daisy, that was a woman that I had one time with. It was a single time, and a terrible, single moment. I was drunk, very drunk... I don't love her. I love you, Daisy. You're my wife. I can't live knowing that you hate me. Daisy, I'm begging you. Go ahead, _____ me."

"_____?" I asked.

"_____. To have something happen to me. Because I've done something bad."

"Punish."

"Yes." A pause. "Daisy, please say something," he said.

It wasn't the correct tea that I was drinking, or even the right kind of cup, and I was not in Taiwan.

"It is okay," I said. "We later talk about this. William will in a moment wake up." I was horrified to discover inside a want to cry.

"Daisy," he said.

He was the father of another woman's child. The other woman would birth the child and that child would have blond hair. It would have light eyes and skin and it would look like him and not me. Never would it look anything like me. David watched me rinse the teacup, dry it, and put it back in the cupboard. I was doing everything right. He watched me leave the room, but as I passed him, he didn't touch me, and I was glad.

When I came to William, who was still asleep, I sat on the bed and lifted him into my arms. He stirred without waking. I put my hand on his back and rubbed my hand in circles, more to soothe myself than to soothe him, and his legs twitched against my body.

He opened his eyes. "Ma," he said, and I said, "乖寶寶, my baby." He nestled his face into my shoulder, I laid him back down, and then I lay down next to him and closed my eyes. I put my arm over my child. I fell dead asleep. I didn't expect David to come in. I am sure that he was afraid to.

And this ritual of tea-making, and going to bed, was the same thing that I did years later, after the phone rang and rang and I didn't answer it, because David had left that morning as he was so prone to disappearing, and he was the one who always answered the phone. The phone rang again. It was not until the third attempt that I answered, but I had a terrible chill.

"Is this Mrs. Daisy Nowak?"

"Yes," I said.

"Are you sitting down?" he asked.

But that was a different time, and a different shock.

◆————◆————◆

For months we said nothing about the white woman. It could have been four months, maybe less. To an outsider I'm sure that we looked the same as we had before. But I think even William noticed the difference between us, when David went from room to room like a ghost. The way that he touched me changed; his good hand would, for example, alight on my shoulder, nervously rubbing the outermost layer of my clothing, and when we slept in the same bed he edged toward me so that his lower back pressed into mine, but he did this with less confidence, while at the same time he seemed scared to let us ever not be touching in our unconsciousness. I thought I could feel him strain to stay aware enough to be touching me in that casual way even as he tried to fall asleep. I noticed everything. I was sad to notice them, but I did.

He had started to bandage his hand again. I said nothing. Blotches of blood seeped through the gauze.

On the last day of this there was a knock at the front door, and I knew before David let her in that it was the white woman. This time I was on the living room sofa, playing games with William, and David said her name again with the same amount of solemn moderation. I was already in the living room and what could he do? He could bring her into the kitchen and talk to her there, but it would be ridiculous if he avoided me and had to pass the entryway of the room with Marianne for me to see, and it was possible that the white woman would turn to me, and we'd look at each other with embarrassment, or fear, or too much politeness.

I think that he thought the same thing, because he brought her into the living room. It was the obvious wrong choice, which made it the right choice. She was wearing the same dress that she'd worn when she first arrived, although it looked funny now that her belly had grown low and round like a ripe yellow melon, and when I had a good look at her I saw that she was as miserable as I was. Her unwashed hair, oily and limp, was the color of a beard of white corn. Still, I admitted to myself, she was pretty in the ways of white women. We had one sofa and one easy chair. David let her sit on the easy chair, and he sat next to William, who sat between us.

"Daisy, this is Marianne. Marianne, Daisy," he said, although he had introduced us before.

We said hello to each other. William looked up at me, and I smoothed his bangs down over his forehead.

"I'm sorry to have come back," Marianne said. "But I didn't know what else to do."

"Do you need help? More help?" David asked.

Marianne: "Money again?"

"Money... Tell me what you need and I'll try to provide it for you."

"David... I left the _____. I'm pregnant. I have no husband. What am I supposed to do? Will you tell me? Don't just push money at me." As she spoke her eyes darted toward mine, zigzagging between David and myself. "Does she understand?" she finally asked.

"She understands most things," my husband said, which I hated.

The woman began to cry, quiet and dignified.

David said, "Do you want us to take the baby?"

This made Marianne cry harder.

He looked at me. I said, "That is not my baby."

"Baby?" William asked.

"We'll talk about it, Marianne," David said. "If it's something you want to do."

I wanted to say, *I am your wife, not her,* but I held my tongue.

David went to the kitchen. Eventually Marianne stopped crying and wiped her eyes with her sleeve. She said to me, "I'm sorry, I'm really sorry that this is happening," and still I didn't speak to her.

My husband came back with a glass of water. He held a check in his other hand. She took a few sips and passed the glass back to him. She said, "I can't raise a baby on my own."

"We'll talk about it," David said again.

Marianne stood.

"Wait," David said. He handed her the check. "I know you don't want this, but you need it."

She took the check and looked at it briefly before putting it in her pocket. "For the baby," she said. She turned toward the hall and was gone.

David stood in the middle of the room. Now that the stranger had left, William crawled into my lap and pulled on my lips. When David continued down the hall and into our bedroom, I felt betrayed as soon as the door clicked shut, so I didn't follow, because so what if he suffered? He deserved to suffer for what he had done. Instead I absorbed myself in playing with William, who was in a bright mood, and he said in Chinese, "Sing me a song?" I sang about a little girl carrying a doll and walking though the flower garden. The doll cries and calls for its mother, and the birds laugh at her crying. It's a common song.

The distraction worked for a while. At the same time, David was hanging himself in the bedroom. There are high beams in every room. I was playing with our child, and David was tying a rope to a beam. I don't know how he learned to tie a knot like that, but he hadn't thought about the strength of the rope, which might have been half rotten in the damp of wherever he retrieved it from, or maybe he knew that it was a gamble. I heard a crash and I screamed. I wouldn't have had such a reaction if the sound were less violent. It was the sound of something gone truly wrong, and not just a lamp knocked over. It was declarative.

There was no answer after I cried out. I lifted William, who was crying, into my arms, and I hurried to the bedroom. I yanked at the locked door. William said, "What's bad?" I yelled David's name again, and when he didn't answer I took William to his room, sat him on the bed, and said, "Stay." Then I closed the door. He was scared. I didn't blame him for his fear. He shrieked for me, but I couldn't let him see.

I am glad for flimsy doors and the strength of frightened wives. With a hammer from the kitchen I smashed a hole in the door and reached inside to unlock it, the splinters scraping my skin like teeth. When I stepped inside I saw that a swaying rope, like a fishing line that had nonchalantly lost its prey, was hanging from a ceiling beam, and David was on the floor, lying next to a toppled chair with the rope's remainder around his neck. I thought, *You're a coward. You can't leave me here.* I think I may have also thought, *This is it,* but I thought this so many times between then and the end, when what felt like possible endings were not really endings, when he died a little bit more by the year, by the month, by the day. And yet I'm surprised that I didn't actually think he was dead. It was shock, I think, that let me believe he could be alive, and it was that which coaxed me into going to him. I could save him. It would be like bandaging his bad hand. If only I could make the blood go away. If only I didn't have to see the redness everything would be all right. I rubbed at the floor with my bare arm until I remembered that I had to tug at the loop around his neck. I was numb as I untied the rope chafing against his skin, and I shook my husband, thinking it was possible that he had so badly hit his head that he would be gone quickly. It was possible that he would die, and it was possible that he would live, but either way his death was staring at me whether it was now or later, then or now—the possibility of suicide had come into the house like a stubborn relation, and it would never leave until it got what it wanted, or until we rid ourselves of it, and what was the likelihood of either? In that way his attempt was an awakening like the one during our honeymoon, when he'd stayed in bed for weeks and said nothing. But I didn't think he would die, back there in San Francisco. What had I thought? Perhaps something about his problem being surmountable.

I'll also note that before I took on more responsibility in the house, I had no idea how to contact anyone for help, I had so little power then. All I could do was wait and shake him and hope that he had not broken his back. As I knelt there I thought, *Would it have been so bad to stay in Taiwan? Was it really so urgent that I leave?* I could have gone to Taipei, Taichung, or even Pingtung, and perhaps my disgrace would not have followed. Perhaps it would have been better than this.

After a few minutes he opened his eyes. I didn't think to kiss him, or say that I was glad. Nor did I think to yell. I stared at him and I said nothing.

"Oh God," he said. "My leg." He gestured. Only then did I realize that it looked wrong. And then he said, "I didn't mean to live."

———◆———

The only way I could respond was to be kind. But his attempt to hang himself woke in me an inconsolable fear. I stopped sleeping more than five hours in any night. I had trouble falling asleep, and when I awoke before the sun rose I found it impossible to sleep again. Opening my eyes immediately triggered panic. I started smoking, too, which pushed down the terror a little. He's been gone for months now and I still feel this panic, as it's a fear that never leaves—the fear of the disappearance of things, and of people. This is a fear that all people must have, because we're all dying every second of our lives. Some of us choose not to think about this. And some of us do forever.

Now I have exactly two attachments. Notice that I include the girl. Of course she's an attachment, because I raised her regardless of where she had come from. The question is never whether I agreed to take the baby, but only to make sense of how I am supposed to live my life now, and to ask myself how so much tragedy has befallen me in this way. Knowing that this white woman had suffered at David's hands, I concluded that the baby shouldn't be punished for its existence. I told David right away, while he had his leg set, that I forgave him. What choice did I have about any of it?

He had me call Marianne, who was staying in a hotel in Sacramento. He thrust the phone at me like a weapon. She began to cry as soon as I said hello. "My baby," she said.

"I want to take care your baby," I said. She kept crying, and in hearing her cry I was angry at being surrounded by so much weakness. I added, "I will love your baby like the child is my own blood."

"God bless you," she said.

David disappeared to aid Marianne in the birth when the time came, and he came home with a baby in his arms. That was Gillian, and when I saw him come into the kitchen, holding her with a tenderness that I'd never seen before, I nearly screamed, but I was sitting with William in my lap, so I did not. William reached for her with wide eyes.

———————◆———————

David said she was beautiful, but I had no opinion. She had only light fuzz on her scalp when she came into our home, whereas William, as a baby, had plenty of dark, thick hair. Her eyelashes were so light that it looked as though she had no eyelashes, and her cheeks were rough and flushed. I told David that I thought she had a rash. He said that was the way babies looked. *Not* our *baby*, I wanted to say.

For some time we were on two teams; Gillian's presence soothed him in a way that I couldn't. He carried her everywhere. He fed her. He changed her diapers. To make up for this I doted on William. Two-year-old William was at first intrigued by the baby, but before long he'd repeat "Where's Baba? Where's Baba?" if we were alone together, and he began to say it even if all four of us were in the same room, which I think says something.

I wanted to be generous to Gillian, I really did. I struggled to overlook where she'd come from, and I sang Chinese songs to her, which was my version of kindness. After she lost her redness and her white hair came in, I saw that she looked like the angels of magazine advertisements, and David claimed that she would be a stunning woman in her years.

But golden sons remain their mothers' flesh long after they've grown. This is truest for immigrants, who have no homes either in country or by blood; immigrants only have the homes that they create. I knew as soon as I first held William that he would cause me pain as a man because he would leave me for his own life, as David left Mrs. Nowak with my hand in his years ago, and I'd have the same frightened, angry look to my face when he did, the departure of a son from his mother being the worst betrayal of all. What would I do when William grew up? What would I do when he wanted a girl of his own? I've become so frightened of having nothing. I need to have my hands on everything at all times to make sure that it won't disappear. "Never leave me," I used to whisper to William in the bed, when the three of us slept

with our limbs everywhere and touching, and he'd laugh his father's old, bubbly laugh as though I'd said a great joke—because
I brought him pleasure and milk; because he loved me most.

After the first try I'd look at David and think, *You're leaving me.*
He'd go out into the woods and I'd think about what it would
be like if he never came back.

I thought of Fatty, the failed *tongyangxi*, the girl who wasn't
beautiful, not like Gillian; yet she'd brush her lips against the
back of my neck, and my heart would respond with quickness. It
would be easier for my children. Gillian could be William's bride
if he loved her, if I raised them right. Yet for years my notion of
reprising the old ways remained only a notion: I still hoped that
David would live.

———————◆———————

While downtown he talked to storekeepers about the price of
milk. He chatted with the kids about a green Cadillac, or a tree
crowded with invisible birds. William and Gillian each moved
in strollers, with each parent pushing his or her favorite child,
and the kids absorbed who knows how much of it. But they liked
his attention, as I did. We all wanted his light, which showed its
face and lingered in his mood at times despite everything. So he
would live, I thought, as long as I kept that light going, as long
as I could stoke the flame.

But for him it was an exhausting act. It took no time for me
to see how tired it made him, and in the spaces between having
to interact with others he went dead. In the Buick, especially,
on the drive home, that silence became petrifying, and I would
have thoughts about him jerking the wheel and plunging us off
a cliff, or heading straight for a tree, because cold, still silence
meant no boundaries and no rules of behavior. He was similarly
comfortable with us at home. He was the most frightening when
the showmanship left him and he felt no need to please, and I'd
never seen someone get so dangerously quiet. I'm not saying that
his silence was a prelude to beatings or storms. He *almost* never
struck us. He never threw tantrums. It was the silence. It was
either listless and half dead, or tense and unable to be loosed. In
the beginning of it I thought, *David is not himself when he is quiet.*
Then I realized that the real thought was *David is not himself in*

town. We would come home and he'd go straight to the couch and lie there. He was too tall for the couch, but he would tuck in his legs slightly and stay.

It was no surprise, then, when he announced in bed one morning that he no longer wanted us to go off the mountain, because Polk Valley was full of idiots. His main example was Sam, a mechanic from the gas station who had the magical ability of showing up wherever we went.

"He is not bad," I said.

"That's not the point," David said. "I'm tired of seeing his face."

"How are we going to get anything if we don't go to town?" I asked.

"I'll go by myself. If you want something," he said, "you can tell me and I'll get it for you."

I said, "I'm going to go for a walk." This I rarely did. He was the one to go out into our property while I cared for the children, but I was suffocated and went into the field. I wandered around the perimeter in the dead field. In my old life I knew the names of plants and birds, but I didn't know them here either then or now. Everything was nameless and I experienced them as they were in my waking dream.

———◆———

David had two projects the year that Gillian came to us. The first was homeschooling. He thought Polk Valley idiocy was the result of Polk Valley schooling. He'd gone to private schools his entire life and there was no such thing in Polk Valley, which he thought was hideous. (When he explained the concept of "private" and "public" schools to me, all I understood was that private meant "good" and public meant "bad.") He had gone down to the only grammar school in Polk Valley to speak to the teacher, and when he came back he was wild with fury about things that I didn't understand, but evidently meant that there was no way whatsoever that our children would go to a Polk Valley school and get a "secular" education. (This also made no sense to me, because in Kaohsiung there were no educational options. If you were lucky enough to go to school, as I had been, you were very lucky indeed. Poor families scrabbled to have their children go to the local school.)

It was good for him to have projects, I decided, in the same way that I had decided that going into town was good for him. He had a small number of books that he had delivered to town for himself, and he brought them into the house with electric brightness in his face. He sat at the kitchen table and made lesson plans in a ledger. He had particular fountain pens that he liked to use with three kinds of ink, which he chose from depending on what he was writing about: green, red, and black. He bought pencils for the children. He also had plain notebooks with cream-colored canvas covers with labels like GENERAL VOCABULARY: WN and GENERAL VOCABULARY: GN.

When he started making these lesson plans, William was two and Gillian was a few months old. David was still using the flashcards with William, but he said that William was too old for *Goodnight Moon* and needed to learn more complicated things. I believe he once said that the most important thing for a parent was to raise his child to be intelligent. How stupid this sounds now, I know.

The second hobby that David took up was stuffing animal corpses, which started when he brought bags with him in the car to pick up the bodies of raccoons and skunks, and took home to empty in the shed out back. I wanted to ask him how could he do something so foul. But by then I chose my moments carefully, and I chose to say nothing. Once I went into the shed and saw his ghoulish animals with sewed-shut eyes on shelves and tables. This was when he was still learning the basic skills of taxidermy, and because he was a beginner the animals lacked their proper shapes and looked distended like monsters. I emitted a small scream and backed out of the shed.

"I saw the animals," I said one morning, before either of the children was awake. Watery light rushed through the kitchen window, over our feet and shins. "Why do you want them? The animals in the shed."

I thought this was a safe thing to ask, but he scowled. "It's not a question," he said.

I was confused. We were in a corner again. "Promise me, you lock the shed. I don't want the children to go in there, get into trouble or get scared."

"Fine."

"And," I added, "lock on the *outside*."

It wasn't so bad all the time, but I remember certain things that are impossible to repeat without ruining his face. The children were sometimes afraid of him. He would say, later, that he had never had a happy day. In the worst of it he would forget that he had ever experienced happiness, however fleeting, and we argued. *But what about this time?* I would ask. *When you did such-and-such? No,* he would say, *that was fakery, it was pretend, that wasn't actually happiness.* It was not a lie so much as a sincere belief in an untruth. At least I imagine it this way, because I can't stand the idea that he was never happy. He said this and it felt like he was being cruel. I wanted to ask him if he was happy when we were first married, or when we lived in San Francisco, but I was too afraid of what he would say. For comfort I told myself that it was a demonic trick of the spirit, but I recall this argument as one of the worst. I had left the house. William ran to the back door and I yelled at him to go back inside, I didn't want him—it was one of the worst things I could say.

Happy things. We had Easters and birthdays. David loved Easter. We dyed eggs by making wire loops and dipping them in Rit. But the game, it turned out, was in hiding the eggs. He insisted on hiding them in tree branches so that the children would have to climb. We celebrated everyone's birthday. We did not celebrate the Lunar New Year. I worry that this is harder than I expected it to be. By which I mean, the difficulty with which I am trying to remember our joys.

So when you say, "Did you ever wish that he would just end it?" do you expect me to say yes? What do you see me as? How human do you think I am?

Now that he's dead I wonder why it terrified me so much more than, say, the threat of illness or a car accident, why his repeat attempts made me frantic at almost every moment of our married life. The impending suicide of my husband was a fear that was completely unlike, say, my worries that William would suffocate in his sleep. With David I learned that suicide was an utterly uncontrollable act disguised as the most controllable death possible. I have seen Western movies, and I will say that my marriage was like riding on a horse alongside a man who is on a horse that is not only unbroken and wild, but also has no care for itself, and will buck in any way possible to get its rider off. David had his hands on the reins, but the horse didn't care. He could stay on for a while but only for so long.

It made me miserable to be on guard always, to never say a word that could be interpreted as unkind, to do everything he wanted whether I liked it or not, to encourage him, to shield our children from his madness and yet to be unsuccessful in my poor attempts, to feel useless, to live with him, love him, be a dutiful wife, and know that it made no difference.

And what difference did it make? I would have gladly been miserable forever if I could only ensure that he would die of the flu. So I was doomed to ridiculous mental calculations and pleas: *David, could we remove the ceiling beams? Could we have a knifeless household, and tear meat with our fingers? Can you not go into the shed with that razor blade? Could all the belts go into a locked box; could all the shoelaces be removed and disposed of; could I have you hand over that tie because you don't wear ties anyway? Please can I follow you from dawn till dawn so that I know you're all right?* A few times he snapped at me. He said, "I'm not a child," and I said quickly, "Of course not," but it would have been so much easier if he were a child, and I could trap him in a room forever.

———◆———

The children were eating 稀飯. Steam rose from their bowls in the cold morning kitchen. William had one knee up and had propped his forearm on that knee while he blew on the spoon. Already he was starting to develop David's broody look, which I thought would please my husband. While the children and I ate 稀飯 with pickles—they were American pickles and not the right pickles, which are small slices with a green-black exterior, but American pickles were better than nothing—David stood by the sink. He had said he wasn't hungry. He had lost weight, and I was worried about the way his bones were showing through his open collar.

"Ai, sit properly," I said to William, "you look like an animal."

William kicked his legs under the table. "What kind of animal?"

"Not Noah's," David said.

"What?"

My husband said, "No, you're not."

(I did know, at that point, who Noah was—David was reading to them from the Bible. He was starting from the old book first. But I didn't know what he meant when he spoke of Noah then.)

David reached to his side and threw an orange at William's head. There was a fruit bowl on the counter by the sink; we kept it there to remind the children to wash fruit before they ate it. The orange hit William in the temple with a muted, dense sound, and then the fruit hit the table, clanking and heavy, and William, who had poor reflexes, reeled. To his credit, he didn't cry, and the orange rolled onto the floor.

It could have been a moment we could have ignored, however difficult it would be. It was almost funny. It could be read as funny. But David said, "I hope you drown, I hope you drown," and he began to head out the back door. We were all so stunned that none of us did anything, including Gillian, who was looking with round eyes. I mentally begged David to come back in and apologize. But no. He was on the porch, and it was snowing. He was in his undershirt and worn khakis. He was not wearing shoes and we all knew that this was ridiculous. The three of us called for him to come back. The orange was under the table, forgotten. He had never hit any one of us before. Had he meant to hurt William? The entire incident seemed so devoid of emotion, like an inversion of a Beijing opera. I told William to watch his sister, grabbed my coat, and put on my shoes. I ran out to follow David into the field. I kept thinking about how cold his feet must be. I was worried about frostbite.

And as I chased his back I thought, my heart banging like a fist on a door, *If he goes away, Gillian can be William's tongyangxi. I will not be alone. Gillian is beautiful. She will be William's tongyangxi. They will love each other as David and I do, together in our home, and I will not ever have to be alone.*

◆

Now when I enter the children's room, and they are lying in their beds on opposite sides early in the morning, with the curtains drawn and their faces barely showing, I can hear their breaths in tandem, the sound of one sound. William can't sleep when his feet are showing; he must always have them covered. Gillian's developing breasts form small hills beneath her sheet. Here is her hair that I brush one hundred times every morning. I adhere to the sound of their sleep not just because I know they are alive when I hear their inhalations and exhalations, but because in sleep they are simply there.

◆

After the incident with the orange I told David that I wanted to learn things. When he asked me what I meant, I said, "Well, you never taught me to drive."

"What else?" he asked. His mind would wander off at times, but sometimes he seemed to be present, and when he was present, he was less upset. We were in the bathtub. At that time he refused to bathe unless I was in the bathtub with him. I think he was afraid of the water. I always got in with him, and I washed his hair in the manner that I washed, say, Gillian's. In the bathtub I couldn't help but look at David's body. He was never in the mood for sex anymore; yet while the two of us were in the bathtub, naked and wet, I felt myself stirring and unable to help myself. I still lusted after him, can you imagine? If I forgot that he in fact looked awful and I didn't see his bones rising through his skin and his wasted and soft muscles. And I was no longer conscious of his hand, which he kept wrapped in bandages most of the time now. He was making small gestures toward sanity. He tried; he really did make efforts. I still loved him.

"Mostly I need to learn how to drive, so that I can go into town. I also need to be able to get money if I need it," I said. "Right now I need to ask money from you when I need it."

He was quiet. He stirred the water with his good hand; the other hand was draped outside of the bathtub, where I couldn't see it.

I knew that this was tricky. By asking him these things, I was letting him know that I no longer felt safe having him in charge. I was telling him that he was troubled and that I knew it. I may have even been hinting at the worst. If he said no, I had little recourse. I'd have to accept it or force it, and I doubted I would be able to do the latter.

He said, "You think I'm not going to keep you safe."

When he said this, I wanted to take it all back.

"I want to have skills," I said.

David sighed. He was behind me in the tub and his legs were on either side of me. He took his good hand and put it on my pale knee, which was sticking out of the water. I had paid so much attention to his bad hand for all of those years that I had forgotten what nice hands he really had. He had long, thin fingers, not knobby; the back of the good hand was smooth, with blue veins below the surface. There were hairs, but not many. They were hands that knew pianos and the skins of animals and a body. My body.

"You're a good wife," he said. "But you know what this means, don't you?"

"I'm not giving you permission," I said.

"I don't need your permission."

"Don't say that."

"I'll teach you anything you want to know," he said.

"Promise me," I said, and that was all—because I couldn't bring myself to finish, because I knew he wouldn't answer.

◆

He took the Buick around the side, on the dirt and gravel, and I followed on foot. He nosed past the house to the field out back, knocking over a garbage can in the process and spraying trash over the dirt, and when he got out of the car he gestured at the driver's seat. "Here you go," he said. "Just sit right here." I went to him, and I wrapped my arms around him without rising on my toes. "What?" He said this softly. He kissed the top of my head, patting my sides with his hands.

In the passenger seat he drank an icy bottle of Coca-Cola. He spoke calmly about the ignition, which I used to bring the car to a rumble. He informed me about the gearshift. "Shift slow," he advised.

I stuttered the Buick around the field, rocking across its bumps and molehills, pressing the weight of the vehicle into the frosted grass, making maps of where I'd been. And even though I would call his mother later that day, and Mrs. Nowak would beg me to help David with so much force that I would have my husband sent to Wellbrook the day after that, which seemed like a sign of hope; even despite this, I could see the end already as clearly as I could see the far trees beneath the sky, with white above and white below. David slurped at the soda with his lips hooked over the glass mouth, and then he kept the empty bottle between his thin legs. I stopped the car occasionally, trying to park, and then, after releasing the parking brake, I would turn the ignition again.

"Ease into it," he said.

PART III

WILLIAM
AND
GILLIAN

THE ARRANGEMENT

WILLIAM (1972)

Our father was in Wellbrook Mental Hospital from 1962 to 1963, and he made a few shorter visits after that. As I recall, Wellbrook had a brick facade crawling with patches of psoriatic ivy, wooden white front doors, and, over the entrance, an enormous half-moon of a stained-glass window that read HYGIENE OF THE MIND in black across an autumnal mosaic. This is where the doctors attempted to scrub my daddy's psyche clean, and this is where he lived for seven months, upstairs, off of one hallway-spoke from the nurses' fishbowl station. Every room had a sad little bed screwed to the floor, green-gray walls, and a wardrobe, which is where Gillian hid the first time we heard the too-close sound of screaming. Back then, I put on a brave face while Ma coaxed her out.

The fact that he was there drove Ma crazy. "I don't know what they can do for him," she'd say to us in Mandarin, "and they're talking about *shocking* his brain." (Gillian and I conversed almost exclusively in Mandarin or Taiwanese with Ma, especially in public, but we are primarily English speakers when together, as we were with David.) Ma was in denial, but Gillian and I knew plenty of the devilry that our father had pulled in his throes, including the incident with the spiders and the one with the orange, and we didn't understand how she seemed so capable of ignoring them, let alone appealing to have him released. The doctors said that he was sick, and didn't everyone want the best for him? Of course they did. Of course we did, if we were sensi-

ble. There was nothing Ma could do but smoke her skinny cigarettes with a moony face and pace around the house and cook
more food than we could possibly eat, all in an effort to distract
herself from the fact that David had, more than once, wandered
in the woods in his underwear all night, and on one occasion
returned claiming to have seen Jesus Christ our Lord and Savior
cooking hot dogs by His very own holy fire pit, and what is there
to say to that?

There was one particular Friday visit. Gillian had prepared a
song-and-dance routine. Ma did her hair in French braids—Gillian, for as long as she's been old enough to have long hair, has
had her hair in all manner of configurations—and that day her
twin tails were tied with red velvet ribbons, secured by elastics
beneath awkward bows. She wore a red-and-white dress with a
collar and cuffs, and the skirt of her dress flared out like a bloody
swan's tail as she twirled to the Buick.

I wore a button-down shirt and trousers, though I had a morbid and aesthetic distaste for buttons. Ma told me that David
liked to see me in a button-down shirt; he'd left a life of East
Coast privilege, but signifiers of that privilege lingered, and in
his lucid spells, my father even wanted me to wear collar stays.
So I dressed ten times my age to go see my father, who was too
out of his mind to care about what I was wearing. I could've
doffed a top hat or donned a trash bag for all he cared, but I still
ironed my own shirts, and I got every last wrinkle out. I also
tied my own ties. So we were a sartorially excellent threesome
standing in a row in front of the first-floor nurses' counter: two
handmade dresses and a small, neatly knotted tie in a place none
of us wanted to be in.

"David Nowak," Ma said, and took out her purse, preparing
to show her identification. Beside me, Gillian hopped on one leg.
But before Ma could say or do anything more, the woman behind
the counter told Ma, apologetically, that David Nowak would be
having no visitors that day.

It was rare that I saw Ma encounter conflict with a stranger.
Strangers were dangerous, she'd always said; they didn't understand us. So I nervously watched as she drew herself up before
this woman like some puffed-up bird.

"No visitors?" she asked.

"That's right."

"But I am his wife. I brought our children to see him."

The woman sighed. "I'm sorry, but that's the way it is."

"Why?"

"It's not a good day for a visit, I'm afraid. I'm sorry, but I don't feel... comfortable discussing such matters, under these circumstances." She looked down at Gillian and me. Then she crooked her finger toward herself and cupped her hand to the side of her mouth, and Ma leaned in, reluctantly, to listen.

The day that we were turned away from Wellbrook was the day Ma assembled us in the master bedroom. She'd been tense the whole drive home, chain-smoking and periodically rolling down the window to throw her cigarette butts out before rolling the window back up again, clouding the Buick interior with suffocating smoke, and neither Gillian nor I said a word or coughed for fear of blowing her up. At home, in that sparse room of theirs, she told us that Daddy was very sick, and that Daddy would want her to tell us that she and Daddy had big plans for us. She told us that Gillian was my *tongyangxi*.

"What does that mean?" Gillian asked.

"Well," Ma said, "it has to do with the fact that someday you will be happy together, so happy together, for the rest of your lives."

In Taiwan, where Ma had come from, this would mean that Gillian and I would be married, but we were in America now and therefore would not be married, though we would be in a very special relationship when the time came.

"You love each other now as brother and sister," she said, "so think of this as an even more special love, a love that will bind the two of you together forever, the kind of love that Ma and Daddy have." (I did not know what this meant, nor did I ask. I assumed it had something to do with the way they touched each other, which was simultaneously fascinating and disgusting.) We were not, under any circumstances, to mention this to Daddy, or something terrible would happen to us. She would send us away, perhaps to hospitals of our own, and we'd never see either Ma or Daddy again. Continuing, she explained that we could not comprehend the complexities of why such secrecy was so important just yet, because we were children. We were too young to understand, but we would understand later, when we were older. Daddy might have to stay in Wellbrook for a very long time.

"How long?" Gillian wanted to know.

Ma shrugged.

"Will it be much longer?" Gillian asked.

"I don't know," Ma said, "but I can't get him out right now." She picked up the burning cigarette and ashed it in a coffee mug with a big orange flower printed on the side. The coffee mug was half-full of cold coffee and a bluebottle fly, floating.

We'd barely been exposed to the world, and post-Wellbrook, as David put us through our academic paces, beginning with the Bible, I wondered if we were meant for a fate such as Abraham and Sarah. Still, David and Ma remained mum about Gillian as my *tongyangxi*. Soon it began to seem as though Ma had never said anything about it at all, as if it were a hallucination I'd caught from some other crazy within the Wellbrook walls.

He died just when things seemed like they were getting better. He was eating at the table with us, and letting Gillian in the shed with him when he worked on skinning and stuffing his animals. He was even playing with us again.

"Fish verbs," he said one morning, coming into the kitchen.

I looked up. "Flounder," I said.

Gillian said, "Char."

He grinned and gave us each a quarter from his mysterious pockets. I thought of my father as an unpredictable and skittish animal. I thought of David as a year of storms and blizzards stuffed into one man.

I knew what was going on as soon as the phone rang that day, sounding like a scream, because we never received calls, and the phone was only for emergencies.

Everyone was raving mad for an intolerable duration, especially Ma and Gillian. I'm not saying that I was immune to the effects of my father's death, but it was true that I was never his favorite, and I mostly felt merely tolerated by him. If I think about it too much—which I have, over the years—I could also say that I was scared of him. Mostly I worried about Gillian, who was his beloved, and who was too small to be confronted by something so big. When David died Gillian cried under her bed until she couldn't move, and as she lay there I walked up to the bed. Then I squeezed myself under the bed with her, and we held hands while she cried and cried, and I thought, *How could you do this to her?* to a ghost.

Ma was angry. She was quiet and she was angry. Her gestures were sharp. Every drawer was closed with too much force. I thought she would take the doors off their hinges. She shouted, "Fuck!" when she dropped a pepper or a fork, but for the most part, she let her actions shriek for her.

Let me try again; honesty is not my strong suit. He didn't love me as much as he loved Gillian, but his death also meant that I wouldn't have the chance to prove myself to him, which was my goal until the moment the phone rang. My father was the smartest man in the world. His sickness betrayed us, and then he betrayed us. That's all. Death makes for incoherent fools.

It wasn't a time to talk about romantic sibling arrangements. I'm not saying that we ever really got over his death, but his death was the event that set things in motion, and when all the hullabaloo had come and gone, approximately five or six months after that terrible July, the idea of having a *tongyangxi* for a sister came up again, and actually came up very quickly.

By then I knew that what Ma meant was sex. This was the thing that had bonded my mother and my father. This was the adult thing that held their relationship together. The idea confused me, as my own body had barely begun to change. I was masturbating, but did so to ghostly images of women from diagrams. I had little sense of what stimuli aroused me; all I knew was that some low brain function commanded me to touch my body, and I lacked the will to ignore the command of ambiguous desire. Sex, though, was frightening. Why? When? How?

"How will we know when that is?" I asked.

"Her body will change," Ma said, "and she'll become a woman."

I was thirteen. Gillian was eleven. She was a girl all over, flat and gangly. I felt myself becoming older, growing beneath my skin, and therefore more responsible for her than ever.

By fourteen, I began to see my sister differently. I can't say whether Gillian is *conventionally* attractive. She is four inches taller than myself, a perfect five-foot-nine. Her skin is the color of cream in the winter and a burnished gold in the summer. She doesn't burn or peel. She has slender arms and long legs, taut and brave with muscle. She occasionally wears Ma's jasmine perfume. She has a broad mouth that smiles easily, even when she's in pain, and a loud, honking laugh.

As for the ineffable claim of beauty, I have no concept of what Helen of Troy looked like. What made her beautiful? What singular or combinatory fact? Though I dreamed of it, I'd seen Gillian's pubescent, unclothed body only once. I was fourteen and in my first mad flush of a crush, and I accidentally-on-purpose walked in on Gillian in the bath. Imagine Gillian's exposed expression when she caught me gaping.

A number of other memories, originally innocent, have taken on the tinge of sex. When I was six years old, we had a large sandbox in the shape of a turtle out back. I'm pretty sure David purchased it in one of his bouts of paternal largesse. Not to say that he was stingy, but he needed to feel a true *need* for almost anything he bought for us. I don't know what possessed him to buy the turtle, which was an eyesore, but it brought Gillian and me much pleasure for exactly two years, until one of us forgot to replace the shell and it became, in the rain, a breeding ground for mosquitoes. Gillian and I leaned over the turtle's shell-less, vulnerable back and watched the threadlike larvae wriggle in the wet sand. David disposed of the turtle's guts, but when summer arrived, mosquitoes clouded the air and welted the hell out of Gillian, whose blood was sweet ("Probably type B," Ma said)— our parents and I remained relatively unharmed—and David covered her with a thick layer of calamine lotion. For the rest of the summer Gillian remained pale pink and quarantined. In my memory she is wearing nothing but her underwear. I still remember the way her scratches made bloody marks across her flat, pale chest.

How about this: as an amateur apothecary at the age of eight, I convinced Gillian to pick flowers with me. I took a ceramic bowl from the kitchen and mashed the petals into water. Even now, walking past a rosebush, I'll rub my fingers over a petal with my eyes closed. I do find that the feel of flowers is unbelievably erotic. Was that what did it? How did I fall for her so very completely and all at once, like diving off a cliff? Dear God, how will I approach her for that intimate act?

———————◆———————

These lustful years continued without much acknowledgment until the week when Ma came into the bathroom in her kimono, calling my name as I crouched in the tub. I hadn't yet removed my clothes as I penciled a reply to Gillian on the wall (which is, and has been for years, littered with little messages between the two of us, including *A grout time for soap, Grout to see you,* and my newest addition, *I'm agrout to take a shower*). "Are you busy, *guai?*" Ma asked. I was, in fact, *agrout to take a shower*, but said it could wait. She pulled down the toilet lid and sat.

"You and Gillian played the most beautiful polonaise this morning."

"She seemed pleased," I said, finishing the *s* in *shower*. The polonaise had been Gillian's idea, a sort of aesthetic compromise. When we duet Ma sits on the sofa with hands folded and leans forward, eyes closed, and she never applauds at the end of anything. David thought applause was tacky. He said that when a man clapped, he was producing the sound of an idiot covering up the lone marble rattling around in his head.

Ma said, "Well, of course. You're both marvelous players, and she loves you as much as you do her. I know everything about you two, don't you see."

I turned in the tub, crouching, with pencil in hand.

"Why do you look so surprised? Such a beautiful, charming girl—of course you would be stimulated by her presence. And we've known since you were children, haven't we? You were always meant for each other. You know this."

My silence must have indicated concordance, because she stood then and began to fish through the medicine cabinet, the long arms of her garment dangling. A baggie of cotton swabs fell off a shelf and into the sink, which she ignored. "Daddy wasn't too keen on the idea of having another child after you were born. Not because of you, but—oh, well," she said, and pulled out a pack of cigarettes, which she proceeded to begin to smoke with the aid of a matchbook from her deep red pockets. Waving her hand in front of her face, she said, "But you seemed lonely, and so we had Gillian to keep you company. Just like with my girl-hood friend—who ended up being quite happy, I'll add. Such arrangements have their advantages over matchmakers, or the

American way. But now you truly love her, don't you? You feel sick inside when she says your name, just as you feel incredibly happy when she does it, too, and you don't know how the two mean the same thing?"

"Well," I said, my hands twisting at this bit of monologue-as-explanation, with parts of it blurring into nonsense, and not knowing what to say next.

Ma moved on to say, kindly, "I couldn't be happier at the way things have turned out. Love is a beautiful thing..."

Here a plume of smoke approached me, and I coughed, grateful for any excuse to postpone a response.

"... and so I'm making a trip to Sacramento. Longer than usual. Because Gillian has officially reached maturity. And so this is the week of... your honeymoon. At last." ("Honeymoon" spoken in English.)

"Honeymoon," I echoed. What I really meant was "Honeymoon!" but I was also shocked, and surprised. I knew what a honeymoon was. I'd heard glorious stories about David and Ma's honeymoon, when they'd taken the Buick to places I couldn't possibly imagine, and had sex in all of those places. It was a romantic idea, and one that I couldn't replicate, but the house would be a place better than all of those other places. I would finally get to lavish my adoration upon Gillian; this idea pleased me.

"A week should give you plenty of time. I expect that things will be very different between you two by the time I come back, hmm?" And I pictured Gillian moving down the cold hall in a silk slip, the white fabric clinging to her small breasts.

"Is that all right?" I asked. "I mean, for Gillian? Will she be all right with that?"

She told me that Gillian knew that the time had come. She told me not to worry about that. But I had all sorts of questions, the step-by-step sex act itself being foremost. From the bloodied tissues in our shared wastebasket, combined with our excellent education in human biology, I also knew that Gillian was now, finally, fertile, and I couldn't bear the thought of impregnating her yet, because the idea of Gillian becoming swollen and heavy went against all the lovely limpidness I loved so. And I certainly wasn't ready to become a daddy myself, lacking so many basic skills required for the position, including how to write a check or open a bank account, let alone drive myself to the bank in the Buick.

Still, I was self-conscious enough to stay quiet about these matters, and I was relieved when Ma reached into a pocket beneath her kimono and said, retrieving a box, "Birth control, so you don't get her pregnant. You must be careful. Pregnancy would complicate things. You could go to prison—understand? Are you listening?" With utter matter-of-factness she removed a foil square from the box, opened it, and pulled out a disc, which she then unrolled onto two fingers of her other hand. I nodded. "You put *this* on your penis when it's hard. When you squirt out the white substance, you pull yourself out of her body before your penis becomes soft, and you roll this, the condom, which is the birth control, off. You tie off the end and you throw it away. Very easy."

She tucked the box into the medicine cabinet. "Is there anything in particular that you want me to get from the city? Some sort of food? Razors?"

"No," I said, "no, no."

"I'll get you some pears. You like pears." She paused, staring at her reflection. "But besides the condom, there are other things you should know. You take off her clothes. You kiss her on the mouth while you take off her clothes, you kiss her wherever you want, until you put your hand to the place between her legs and feel that she is wet. This is when she's ready for you to put on the thing I just showed you, the condom. Yes?"

I nodded.

"You put the thing on. You don't have to go so fast, although you might want to go fast. There might be blood, the first time, when you put yourself inside of her, where the wetness is. The wetness should help you get inside. It helps the movement. You move so that it feels the way you want it to. Okay? Any questions? You're not stupid. Neither of my children are stupid."

"No, we're not. Don't worry."

"But you're concerned. You're holding something back. Don't think you can hold anything back from me. I know you best." And she pulled out another cigarette and lit it, as if to signal that she was settling down for another round. I was afraid to ask her what I was truly thinking—that Ma seemed to want this very badly, although perhaps not as badly as I did, and I didn't understand why.

"It's a good thing," I said.

"Of course it is," she replied.

"Yes, a good thing." I looked at the faucet. My face was swollen and distorted in the silver. "I think I'll take that shower now," I said, and she, who was leaning against the sink with her hip, nodded, shifted upright, and left, still puffing at her cigarette, and I began to worry about everything. In my ardor I dug through the bathroom garbage can. I found Gillian's damp and drying bloody tissues and crushed them to my face. I loved her so. I *love* her.

◆

The day that Ma drove to Sacramento she woke up early, wrote down her inn number, made us porridge, which we ate with fried eggs and pickles. She dressed in trousers and a white blouse. For most of the morning she checked her suitcase, but by eleven she was ready to go, and when Gillian and I stood in the hallway to send her off Ma told us the following: that we must be good while she's away, meaning we mustn't go into town by ourselves, and most important, she repeated that I must take care of my sister. We all knew what she meant most when she said we must be good, and the slight cut of her words when she said "take care, be safe," switching to gently accented English, was there, too, though I didn't turn to see Gillian's face at that moment, when Ma reached down and picked up her suitcase. She then kissed and hugged us in turn before opening the door with her free hand. Ma and her plots for which my pulpy heart and I have no argument.

The door closed. Gillian and I looked at each other, our faces lost. Suddenly the door latched and locked with a rattling click, punctuating Ma's absence and the onset of our honeymoon.

Gillian smiled. "So it begins," she said, and I made a strangled laughing sound.

◆

Two identical uprights stand back-to-back in the living room. I cannot let my little sister sit at her piano without sitting at mine and cranking out some sort of response. She never minds. She'll tilt her head up and smile while delivering fifteen measures of bravura that make me all wet in the eyeballs. At times we duet this way. Her musical preferences, mostly ragtime, are different from my Sturm und Drang, but we grew up with the same teacher—one woman in Sacramento, a big-haired, petite chain-smoker named Mrs. Kucharski—so I do know her Scott Joplin as well as she knows my Beethoven, which is to say, beyond decently.

Mrs. Kucharski! It is hard for us to play anything without remembering her. Her metronome, which sat on the modest piano, also an upright, ticked back and forth with the click of her tongue at her teeth. She noticed that I liked Bach and Beethoven before I did, and unexpectedly gifted me with record albums to take home and play, which I did, mesmerized by sounds that were as inexplicable as Heaven.

While Gillian shuffles around in the kitchen, china and silverware clanking, I sit at my bench and plunk out a graceless version of the opening measures of *Pathétique*.

The sound summons her. Soon she appears with a bowl and spoon. "Ew," she says. The spoon she sticks into her mouth and pulls back out with a pop. She breathes on it, then attempts to rest the spoon on the tip of her nose—an old trick of David's. It clatters to the floor. She says, "Don't know why it didn't work." Bends down to retrieve the spoon, drooping cloth, revealing the space between pale breasts. She rests her bowl of cornflakes atop my piano and lays her utensil beside it, finally settling beside me to reassert the confident opening notes. Her upper thigh is a millimeter from mine, downy and pale, unexposed to sun; her leg hair is the same color as the silky bun pulled loosely from her scalp. Strands leak around her ears. I want to put my palm on the top of her skull, cup it like a ball in my large hand. But I'm afraid. For years I've been afraid of touching her; I've longed for accidents of skin on skin, though what I truly want is to be able to draw a slit from sternum to pubic bone and hide inside her rib cage—the thought of which makes me both loathe my base self and flush with excitement all at once.

"You know," I say brightly, for lack of something better to say, "David would lie underneath the piano while I played this. Do you remember?" She shakes her head. "I have a distinct memory of being, oh, six, seven or so, and him crawling underneath to lie on top of the pedals. I never asked him why he was doing it. I remember being afraid that I would accidentally kick him, though. There's not much space under there, not even for a seven-year-old's legs."

She very nearly trips up on a tremolo, I can tell. Her hands spread across the keys. She reaches across my chest, the sleeve of her cotton nightgown brushing against my shirt, the imagined warmth of her arm seeping through the cloth. I consider stopping. It isn't a good memory.

"He liked to watch you play. He got a kick out of your ragtime. When he was feeling superb he'd ask you to play 'Down Yonder,' and he and Ma would dance around the living room like goofballs, swinging their arms. I don't know if you remember that."

"Nope."

"You were pretty young. It was worse when he came into our room in the middle of the night and dragged you out of bed, totally out of his mind. You'd cry..."

Her hands lift. Silence. The appendages move to her lap, one crossed over the other, before the top one begins to worry itself—the thumb scratching the index finger. A spot blooms pink on white.

"He'd insist you play 'Down Yonder' or 'Maple Leaf Rag' at three in the morning. You don't remember this? I guess you were four."

"No."

"Babbling. Pretty much incoherent at a mile a minute."

"Stop."

"I'd try to get him to leave you alone, but what could I do, really? Who knows where Ma was. I remember going into the living room with the both of you. I think I was wearing footies. You'd cry and play, and then he'd ask you to play it again and again, until you and I were both crying, more out of fear of him than sleepiness or sleeplessness, I think."

"I don't remember this."

"To this day, it gives me the chills."

"So you choose to bring this up now," Gillian says, still rubbing, maybe bleeding soon.

"I'm sorry."

"I just don't know why you brought it up right now. You'd think you would have said something sooner."

"I guess it was sitting here and seeing you play," I say. "I never meant to tell you."

She says, "It's a horrible story."

"I'm sorry."

———————◆———————

Later Gillian sits out on the porch in her bare feet, leaving the light off to discourage moths and mosquitoes. While I stand behind the closed screen door I see her back, illuminated from the hall light, the ichthyian swell of the vertebrae at her neck, and, just beyond her and the porch steps, a clump of nearly invisible boulders. I open the door and walk toward her. The ninety-degree day has descended into the thirties, and when I sit next to her on the steps I'm shivering as much as from the chill as I am from proximity. At this close range I can see her face; my eyes adjust. I fondly observe that tiny freckle above the right corner of her lip.

We barely move, careful not to disturb the encroaching perimeter of potted cacti. I ask her, carefully, if she's thinking about David. She shrugs. Then I ask if she's thinking about our honeymoon week. Emboldened, my hand moves to her exposed thigh. Immediately she flinches, almost imperceptibly, surprised. I withdraw, apologizing. "No," she says, and then she grabs my hand and plants it on her knee, which is cold, colder than I'd expected—cold as a river-wet rock. We sit in silence.

"At least I made him happy. Didn't I?"

"Of course you did."

"I'm nervous, *ge*. Are you nervous? Do you have a case of the nerves?"

"Of course."

"But are you very nervous?"

"It's a big thing, what we're doing, small duck."

"I'm very nervous," she says, and swats at her arm. She says we ought to go inside. I squeeze her knee. For a few seconds, I hold on tight.

———————◆———————

Morning. In the kitchen she's standing at the counter and sink in a sleeveless red dress. The window on the far wall is open and a bright breeze filters through the yellow curtains, letting the light cut across the table to the floor.

"Why'd you stop playing?" she asks. She looks up. "It was an excellent background for omelet-making."

"I thought I'd come help," I say.

"Chop, then," she says, "and I'll put something on the turntable."

Ma has left us with a week's worth of groceries, including two tomatoes the color of poppies, ham from the deli that's swaddled in paper and sweating, six eggs, a hunk of yellow cheddar. I assist as Gillian rubs her long fingers across the tomatoes, as though screwing open a jar, in the faucet's stream, and passes them to me. We two are extra careful with knives, forcing whoever is in the role of assistant to slowly slice. Gillian wipes her hands on her dress and crosses the room to operate the record player. Soon the opening notes of the *Hammerklavier* spin and crackle. The hem of Gillian's dress reaches midthigh, exposing the delicate line of vastus lateralis, which appears and disappears as she backs away from the side table and raises herself on tiptoe. She has always had strong legs, which I suppose is from a lifetime of running barefoot, though at the moment her feet are abnormally clean. "Pay attention," she scolds, "you'll lose a finger." Next I peel back the ham's paper and withdraw four slices. *Chop-chop.* Beat the eggs. She takes the bowl from me and pours the milky-yellow liquid into the pan, surrounding the omelet's insides. We form one omelet, then a second.

Moments later I see a wadded thread hanging off the back of her dress, swinging against her skin. With trembling fingers I try to snap it off. She shrieks as I touch her, a plated omelet in her hands. "That's *cold!*" she cries, jerking away.

We sit at the wide wooden table. Two kids, two omelets. Gillian cuts her omelet with a fork, spears it, and then moves head and hand toward each other for feeding. Her glasses are hazy with grease.

"*Mei*, your glasses are filthy," I say.

"Oh? I suppose they are."

My enigmatic sister, at once crude and delicate, has betrayed only the mildest flirtations since Ma departed.

"I'll clean them for you. Here, hand them over."

Gillian pauses, fork in one hand, glasses in the other. She hands the golden spectacles to me, revealing her naked, open face. I take the glasses and I walk to the sink and turn on the water. I rinse them in the manner of Gillian rubbing a ripe tomato.

All at once I hear a clatter, and then her arms are wrapping around my waist, a cue taken from the days of David and Ma. When I turn, Gillian's mouth is on mine. She kisses me—I think I hear the sound of sucking and smacking—and then she sinks her head into the space between my head and shoulder, emitting a whimper, snatching her glasses from my limp hand. Her height creates an awkward stooping effect, but I am lost in the hard swell of my groin, the scalp-tingle, and trying to recall what her mouth reminds me of.

"So there's *that*," she says, putting her glasses back on. I move my hand up to her breast, feeling the ghost-sensation of her nipple before she whirls around and returns to the kitchen table.

I laugh, a bit crazily. "It was... amazing," I say.

She eats. I pour myself a second cup of coffee and drink it at the counter, invigorating my senses and burning my tongue in the process. So it will be this simple, this wonderful, this *easy*.

"Save your flattery, and finish your food," she says.

"Of course, of course..." I reply, and return to the table, vibrating with excitement.

"Kisses for fishes," Gillian says. She brings her plate to the sink to rinse.

"Hugs for bugs."

"Are you finished? I'll wash your plate," she says. "Or you can come wash these dishes, and I'll eat the breakfast that you abandoned in order to kiss me. *Hao ba? Okay?*"

Though I abandoned my omelet to clean her glasses, and she was the one to deliver the smooch, I don't argue. I eat the omelet. She washes my plate, kicking her legs from side to side to the music.

◆

I want to kiss. She wants to read. I ask if I can read in bed beside her, and she is amenable to this. Gillian's room is slightly larger than mine even though our beds are the same size, which grants her more space—a bearskin rug, one of David's creations, spreads out like a blot of ink; her wardrobe of delicate dresses and lingerie stands in the northeast corner, with clothing leaking onto the floor toward an open trunk filled with taxidermied animals, including a snarling bobcat. Gillian lies faceup on her mattress amid a nest of gauzy gray sheets. She is reading the Bible. (My grandfather's feminine inscription, in sepia ink: *For unto every one that hath shall be given, and he shall have abundance: but from him that hath not shall be taken away even that which he hath. And cast ye the unprofitable servant into outer darkness: there shall be weeping and gnashing of teeth. —Peter J. Nowak, 1949.*) I settle next to her. She moves to turn a page. Her arm touches mine, and I grow warm all over. I turn to kiss her gentle elbow. She laughs and returns to reading.

"Do you remember," she asks, "that this was one of the first things Dad had us read after he got out of Wellbrook? When we really started to learn? I was fascinated with any part that had to do with animals—Jonah's fish, fowls, swine. You were obsessed with the Crucifixion. I think that says a lot about us, don't you?"

"Mmm," I mutter, stroking her hair. "You know, I've loved you for years."

She says, "I love you, too."

I move my face so close to hers that I can smell, faintly, the sweet scent of food emanating from her mouth before she turns away. The book swings to the bed. "Agh," she says, sitting up, the sheets falling all at once from her body, "*please* let me read for a bit. There's this passage that I've had on the brain all morning—'before Abraham was, I am'—and it's driving me nuts to not be able to get it down—"

"Of course," I say, "go ahead, read." And I settle back down, inches away.

A few minutes later, in the middle of our silence, she says, "Bunchability. A bouquet of tissue flowers."

"Good one, fishlet."

"Thank you."

———◆———

The fourth day. I sidle to my piano, and in a booming forte, I start Mozart's Fantasy and Fugue in C Major, K. 394. As predicted, Gillian appears in the entryway a page in, itching at the insides of her elbows with both hands as she watches—Gillian, my Constanze! But though I'm sure that she understands my desirous cipher, she doesn't touch or so much as move toward me, and before the fugue is over, she turns and returns to her room without saying a word: *she* is the cipher.

Later she outlines the shapes of shadows onto a sheet on the kitchen table, drawing new lines every time the shadows change. Every so often she nudges the bridge of her glasses with two fingers. Adorable! Despite growing up together, there's still a sour mystery there, a tangle of thoughts and wants that keeps her separate from myself. In the last few days it seems that the natural wall between us, splitting two souls into two bodies, has become harder to see over.

"What is that?" I ask, putting my finger on one of her jagged penciled lines.

Gillian raises her lashes. "Not sure. That dirty bit in the corner, I think. Or the broken branch. Too dark to be the spiderweb."

"We ought to dust before Ma comes back."

"*You* can dust before Ma comes back," she says. She hates to dust. Never does it, saying it makes her sneeze. She prefers to mop, sweep, do the dishes, scrub our tub with her rump in the air.

I say, "Speaking of which, small duck." No sign of recognition from her side of the table as she continues to drag pencil across paper. I reach out and cover her drawing hand with mine. The skin between her knuckles is unbearably soft. "Speaking of Ma coming back. What, exactly, did she tell you this week was for? Gillian? Look at me," I say. "What did she tell you before she left?"

"She told me that I was to love you," Gillian says. Without removing her pencil hand, she flutters her fingers beneath mine. How her body betrays her; David's did the same.

I say, "Ma said that?"

She nods. Her eyes return to the shadow paper. "She said I was ready to be a proper *tongyangxi*," she says. "That she met David when she was only a little bit older than I am now. She says that she had you when she was twenty."

The light tumbles across the large wooden table and onto our hands. I squeeze hers. "And?" I ask.

"I dunno," she says, shrugging. "I suppose it will happen at some point."

"What point will that be?"

"When I *feel* like it," she says, freeing herself from my grasp. What makes her so afraid? In our lives I've never known her to be afraid of anything.

I lean forward, focusing on the obligation. I tell her that Ma expects us to perform certain physical acts by the end of the week. I don't concentrate on myself and my wants, but on the task at hand.

She says, "I don't know if I'm ready."

"She'll want to know what we've done when she gets back."

"We could lie."

"She always knows when we're lying. Are you afraid of me? Is it the physical part that scares you? It's when I don't know what you're thinking," I continue, "that we're at our most separate. That terrifies me. It terrifies me to think that you're hiding things from me, especially when it comes to this one very important thing."

Gillian stops moving her pencil. She's listening.

"It's a very important thing, Gillian, not just because our parents told us so, but for other reasons. Deep reasons. Matters of the spirit. Have you thought of those reasons? Have you thought of the possibility that we are meant for each other not only because of *what* we are, but also because we are absolutely, completely compatible? You are smarter than those idiots out there, you know—precocious, gifted at the piano—even David couldn't speak Mandarin. I do. But, as David did for Ma, do you know—have you discerned that I love you like they do in books?"

She sighs and finally puts down her pencil. "I'm sorry I've been so awful. I don't know what's wrong with me. I want to do it, and I will. Really. You've been nothing but grand to me. Nothing but patient." And she kisses me on the cheek.

———◆———

I will admit that a darker thought crosses my mind. As Gillian goes to her King James on the sixth day, I go to my *Ars Amatoria*, where Ovid speaks of the female as necessitating a firm hand:

> *What wise man would not mingle kisses with coaxing words of endearment?*
> *Should she not surrender willingly, then take what is not given.*

And:

> *He who seizes kisses, if he does not seize all the rest,*
>   *will deserve also to lose that which has already been yielded.*

I could force myself upon her. I imagine myself a different William, a meaner, less loving young man, seizing her roughly as I pull her dress up, and she will, without entirely meaning to (or maybe she will mean to), extend her arms over her head so as to facilitate the revelation of her body—I would mash my mouth against hers, and run my hand up her thigh, between her legs... Could I do it? But I want the romance, and I want the tenderness. I want to wrap her in my arms. If I take Gillian's maidenhood from her, and if I've done so with even a hint of reluctance on her part, there will be no joy in it. And how could I ever induce joylessness upon my sister when I love her, and when I want both of us to be happy?

———◆———

I am tired the night before Ma comes home. All day and night I've been wearing headphones, drowning out the sound of Gillian moving through the house, drowning out the sound of her at her piano, her tinkling vibrations. This keeps me close to the rolltop desk near the corner of my room, and I rest my forehead on the tabletop. Periodically I shift in order to replay Wagner (*wie sie fassen, wie sie lassen*). One day left. My eardrums throb. I remove my headphones and stand. I walk around the room in bare feet, twitching my head from side to side. A selection from the bookshelf: three Latin dictionaries and a book of verbs, the *Oresteia*. The rest of the books are in a shelf in the living room.

I take out my small pink French dictionary and open it in the lamplight to a random page.

endolori
endommager
endormi
endormir

Translation:

painful
damage
asleep
put to sleep

There's an old snapshot of myself at the river, taken by David, I think, and curled at the corners. The photograph is stuck to the wall with a loop of tape. A yellow-toed dirty sock, dirty trousers, flowered bedsheet; a window above and parallel to my bed, suggesting the possibility of rolling out in my sleep; a box of large knives from David's collection, which I occasionally and idly sharpen. David used to demonstrate the sharpness of his knives by shaving the hairs off his forearm. I don't.

The knives are, of course, a morbid reminder. Some sort of authority at the Motel Ponderosa where David stabbed himself to death took the knife that killed him, but the others remind me of better, though still bloody, times. For example, Gillian and I watching him unzip the belly of a deer behind the house, flies swirling around the carcass... But thinking of David's death puts me in an even more dangerous mood. I return to the desk, where the record has stopped circling. I gather some things, go to the bed, and begin to carve a whale from a bar of soap with a paring knife. The door opens. She comes in, bare feet creaking on the floorboards, and her hands are on my every nerve. The curtains are open. I am working by moonlight and Gillian smacks her gum behind me. Her mere appearance in my room feels like a victory, though I'm careful not to look in her direction.

She sits down next to me. The mattress sinks. Gillian smells sweetly of jasmine and jonquil. Must have snatched some perfume from Ma's room.

I peel a long shaving from the whale's belly. She puts her hand on my knife-hand and gently pushes it down. Immediately my prick responds to her touch. Not necessarily to the skin on skin. To the gentleness of her movements. The knife and the whale fall to the floor with a clatter, and I am weak-limbed and silly. She asks, "Can I kiss you?" I nod. She leans forward and puts her hot mouth on mine. The lenses of her glasses press against my eye sockets. I can feel her nostrils exhale as she pauses there, our lips frozen together, and then she moves backward, forming a gap of steaming air, before gently leaning forward again. A small hand makes its way to my lap, where it rests on my clothed hipbone, and I grow still more aroused to the point of discomfort.

"Wait," I murmur as I extricate myself—with difficulty.

"What?"

"Ma gave me some things," I say, heading wardrobe-ward, unsteady. I begin to sift through the top shelf. "So you don't get pregnant. You can't get pregnant."

"Oh."

Standing at the foot of the bed with the box of condoms in hand, I remove the first square, placing the rest of the box on the floor, and try to tear the package open with my trembling fingers. Next I try it with my teeth. I am half drooling onto the slippery surface, but still the foil gives. Holding the half-foiled condom in one hand, I undo the drawstring to my trousers with the other; they fall to the floor. Gillian watches with an opaque and shadowy expression. Next I pull off my briefs. To my surprise, I feel no embarrassment. Rather, it is a thrill—half naked, exposed and dizzy—has the blood in my head truly all gone to my groin?

"Won't you take off your clothes?" I ask. And, oh God, she does. She pulls her dress over her head and there are her small breasts, her pink panties, Gillian sitting with her knees pressed together and her hands properly folded in her lap. I climb onto the bed and put the condom beside her body because I am desperate to touch her, and there is so much flesh to revere; I am stroking her soft, concave belly the way she does, at times, the bear rug on her floor. I try to kiss her everywhere that I can see. Her naked form is constructed of sinew and bone, with broad shoulders curving upward to a graceful neck; her arms are taut, her waist narrow, her hips wide and boxy. Her navel is an abyss. I grab her curved hipbones.

"What are you doing?" Gillian asks.

"Shush," I say, though it seems that breath has left me. "Lie down," I say, and she does. I tug at her panties and yank them to her knees, revealing her tawny pubic curls, and as I push her legs apart I quickly see her soft and strange womanly parts. Dizzily I lean into her, inhaling the dank scent of those delicate lips, filling my brain with a muddy brown-black sensation. Involuntarily my hand moves. I squeeze myself and moan.

She asks, again, "What are you doing?"

"Don't worry. Ma told me what to do. Just stay like that." I stroke her shoulder. Before I remove my hand I realize that she's shaking. The realization pulls me out of my reverie.

"You're shaking," I say.

"I'm sorry."

"You—you don't have to be sorry. It's okay, just stay like that. I'm going to put this on now, I think. Hopefully I'll be able to figure it out." I fumble. I am aware of my breath hitching. "This is confusing. I think I put it on wrong. I don't think I can use this one."

Here she is, right in front of me, and I can't even get inside of her. I go to the floor to get another one. Gillian is still lying on the bed where I left her, panties around her knees and trapping her legs akimbo, her parts gaping. She watches as I unwrap the condom, again with my teeth, and roll the rubbery disc on.

"Maybe we should kiss some more," she says. She pulls her legs together and tries to sit up, but I'm on top of her, pushing her thighs apart with one hand and manipulating myself with the other. "Wait a second?" she says, and then we're having sex; or at least I am pushing my way inside of her, briefly stopped by what I presume is her hymen, and then, with one final, desperate thrust I am filled with bliss. My body seizes. I utter nonsense and immediately ejaculate inside her, eyes closed and flooded with starlight.

But she is saying something. She is saying my name. The timbre of her voice compels me to open my eyes, and to my horror, mixed with the remaining fog of pleasure, I realize that she's turned her head to the side and is crying. I immediately remove my body from hers and she curls like a pill bug, making small sounds. "It hurts. Why did you do it?" she says, and moves her hand between her legs. When she lifts her fingers to the moonlight we see a shadow, we see blood.

I embrace her. I sink my face into her perfumed neck. "Oh, sweetheart, don't worry about the blood. Ma said that might happen. But I'm sorry I hurt you, *xiao mei*—I never meant to hurt you..."

◆

When I awaken the morning after our consummation, I think for a moment that I'm still dreaming. David's dragged Gillian out of bed again and she's at it in the living room. It is, indeed, my sister playing, and in fact, a sunken part of my brain recognizes it straightaway as Scott Joplin, her favorite. But Gillian rarely gets up before I do—loves to sleep in. Moreso, she seems to have skipped her exercises. Finally, there's something essentially wrong about the way she's performing whatever it is that's waking me up at four thirty on the day that our mother returns.

I sit up in bed and pull off the sheets. Immediately I think of the night before and that clownish pleasure, the prelude to a lifetime of love with her, and I grin to remember the look and feel of her body. She'd gone to the bathroom afterward, turning the light on as she left, and came back in a T-shirt and underwear with clean thighs and a toothy smile. (Her teeth, small and pointy, giving any smile of hers a bizarre gleam.) "Sorry about that," she said, leaning against the doorframe. "The blood shocked me, is all." And then she told me she loved me and wished me a good night.

I dress and go to the living room, where Gillian sits with perfect posture at her bench. The lamp is on. This morning she's dressed in a dreamy, silky thing with no sleeves, exposing her burnished shoulders, which reminds me of how mad I am about her shoulders. "Is that 'Bethena'?" I ask.

"Yes."

"Bethena," the song Scott Joplin wrote for his wife, Freddie Alexander, after she perished because of complications from a cold. So Mrs. Kucharski told us, which I have never forgotten.

"Isn't that a little fast for 'Bethena'?"

"I thought I'd play it a little fast today," she answers.

"It sounds all right," I say. "The syncopation is awkward." Her hands swing at the wrists, back and forth over the keys. Suddenly her comportment dampens the thrill I'd felt in bed and replaces it with unease. "Ma said she'd be home in the evening today," I add. "I'll start cleaning the kitchen. Are you okay?"

"I'm all right."

"Nothing's troubling you?"

"Buddy," she says, "what's troubling me is trying to hold forth while playing this song to completion."

I go to the kitchen, rebuked. For the rest of the day I am desperate to have sex again, the memory of the night before causing a strong and frequent recurrence of arousal. On occasion, in between jabs of mopping or sweeping, I put my hand on her hip or on the small of her back. She neither recoils nor leans into me. *What a fickle, strange girl,* I think, but I have, of course, no complaints, and I kiss her tenderly on the back of the neck as she wipes down the counters; I touch her side, and then the inside of her thigh. Finally she says, "There's a lot left to do, *ge*," and though my fingers linger for perhaps a few more seconds than they absolutely ought to, I pull them back. "Maybe a little bit of kissing, if there's time," I suggest. There is not.

◆

In the late afternoon, before the sun begins to drop out of sight, Ma arrives. "Take my suitcase, please," she says, using the phrase *bai tuo*; the suitcase is at her feet. I pick up the suitcase. Gillian stands behind me, and Ma looks over my shoulder at her as she adds, "Gillian, tea?"

My mother takes a step farther into the hallway and closer to the bare, hanging bulb, kicking off her shoes and nudging them toward the wall, which is already crowded with shoes and sandals.

Gillian retreats down the hall to the kitchen, and I follow Ma into her room, left exactly as before except for the removal of a few spritzes of perfume, where I place the suitcase flat on her bed and wait for the inevitable interrogation. After David died the master bedroom became a shrine to his death, not in framed and nostalgia-soaked photographs, or trinkets from their four-teen-year marriage, but in absolute ascesis. The scroll ink paintings of chickens and other fat and feathered friends, the landscape oil paintings, blobbed and scraped—wall decorations, in general, gone. So when I say that I sit on the bed without the engraved wooden headboard, which I enjoyed tracing with my thumb as a small and less desirous boy, I mean that I am sitting in a very nearly empty room (bed, vanity table, dresser—all ma-hogany), on a bed with one pinned bedsheet and one flowered comforter that is the cheeriest thing in the room, waiting for *How was the initiation, the coming together? How are you and your sister doing, ge?* Or maybe she won't ask at all. Maybe she'll let me tell her first, or maybe she'll merely watch for touches or looks. She seems tired and slightly stooped. Ma sits next to me, pulling a matchbook and cigarette pack out of her skirt pocket, and lights a cigarette.

"How was the city?" I ask, moving behind her to rub her shoul-ders. Her head lolls to one side. She moans. I ask her about the city every time she goes into Sacramento to buy tofu and other things that she can't get in Polk Valley. Every time, I expect and receive the same answer.

"Oh," she finally says, exhaling, "it's never any good, really. Thank you—that feels wonderful. William, you can't get much done in the city that you can't get done in town, and you can't get much done in town that's better than being at home. And how was it, being here for the week? I hope I left enough food?"

"We ate well. Things were fine."

Inhale. Exhale. "What about you and Gillian, then? I expect you bonded?" (I have translated what she actually said to the silly word *bonded*, as though the physical act stuck us two like glue. As it happens, her tone was equally blasé.)

"We did."

"Good. That's enough, thank you." I shift beside her and she smiles, brightening, and pats me on the arm. "You'll be sharing a bedroom from now on. It will probably be Gillian's because of the size, and we can use your room for the altar. Move some things around. It's so good to see you"—and here she embraces me tightly, even with the burning cigarette in her left hand—"and to see your sister looking so well. I really missed the two of you. And I won't be doing that again, I promise. All right. Let's go have some tea, *hao ba?*"

In the kitchen, Gillian is sitting at the table, stripping strings from pea pods. The strings go on the table; the pea pods she drops into a bright blue bowl. "Ma," she says, "how was the city?"

"Well, I had a terrible time sleeping in my hotel," Ma says. "Sirens kept me up all night long. I'm lucky a bullet didn't come through the window while I was lying in my bed."

"How horrible."

"There's something about being away that pretty much steals everything good from your memory. I'd almost forgotten how quiet it is here." Ma crosses the room to sit. I wonder if she'll mention the bedrooms or if I will have to reveal our new situation to Gillian, who has her eyes half shut under Ma's touch, a pea pod in her right hand. It does make me nervous when Ma goes into town. Our lessons with Mrs. Kucharski ended when she, shortly after David's death, fell down what Ma explained was an "elevator shaft"—a terrible accident and a nightmare of bad machinery that we had not and would never experience, thank God!—plunging her into darkness and leaving her body crumpled and broken below.

When the teakettle shrieks Gillian opens her eyes, drops the pod into the bowl, and, with great reluctance, moves toward the stove, which she does by uncoiling her legs and stretching them in the direction of where she means to go. Minutes later we all have tea in small white cups with small white handles. Gillian is sitting across from Ma and me now, with her brow furrowed adorably as she cups the tea in her hands. A greasy strand of hair has fallen across her right eye, and I can see from a distance that her glasses are smudged as usual, but it only endears her to me.

"Ma says that I'm to move into your room," I say.

"I see." Her thumb rubs the circumference of the white cup, back and forth, eyes fixed on the wooden table.

After tea I go to the sink with my cup. Gillian comes up behind me to do the same. I am very aware of Ma watching as my hand alights on Gillian's shoulder.

"So we'll start moving things," Gillian says. "My room is a mess, though. Might not get it all done tonight," and then she pecks me on the cheek.

Before we move Gillian asks Ma if they may speak in private. They go into the master bedroom, closing the door behind them, and I go to the bathroom, where I stare into the small tooth-paste-speckled mirror. I already look steady to myself, a young man ready to take on the responsibilities of having a *tongyangxi*. Still, looking at myself in the mirror compounds a niggling anxiety: that Gillian mightn't be attracted to me at all, and that this face and body are nothing arousing to her.

In the fluorescent bathroom light I straighten my shoulders. I brush my bangs from my face.

Hold steady, Captain, I tell myself, *hold steady.*

We start moving things that evening. Gillian shoves her rickety wardrobe to make room for mine; she pushes her trunk of dead, wild things against the far wall and beneath the windows. We talk a little, but not much. "Is this okay?" I ask occasionally, not wanting to invade, though that's exactly what I'm doing as I cram my postcards in the blank spaces between hers, forming a mosaic; take up space in her bed and on her bear rug; and I'll have her body, too. No—not just her body, but her soul, which is a slippery thing by comparison. When I lift a slip to toss it into the wardrobe, she says, almost plaintively, "Please don't *hurl* my things, William," and, as if I won't notice, rearranges my drawing of a dandelion such that it's below her meadow Polaroid. At one point she disappears into the bathroom and reemerges with her face wet, her nose rabbit-pink. But then again, she does smile at me all night, and when I smile back at her I feel the connection solid between us. Ma fries up slices of tofu with soy sauce. We eat, Ma beams, and it's all extremely pleasant. After we've played a nocturne together (Ma falling asleep, one arm dangling off the sofa), I wash up while Gillian dresses in a new, flimsy night-thing, probably brand new from Sacramento, and I ready myself for bed.

On this night, I am more prepared for the event of her body, though its power over me remains the same. It's not her breasts, though I do enjoy them, which are fist-small and firm, with large pink nipples. I favor the crook of her elbow, where I drag the smooth part of my fingernails. Though her breasts are not my greatest pleasure, I do like the space between them where her bone presses against the skin; but I like the white marks more, I like the way they ripple crooked in the dim light; I like her belly, soft and slightly round, with a smattering of blond hairs leading from navel to groin. But most of all, it's the smell of her that kills me; the top of her head smells like oil and lemony shampoo. Tonight, I pull her to her feet. I kneel and she stands silently as I tunnel up under her filmy skirts. I press my nose against her cotton panties, which are adorned with bows and polka dots the color of red, yellow, and orange button candies. I yank them down.

"Oh," she says.

My face turns upward between her thighs, and she cries out, "Please stop—"

"What?" I ask. My voice sounds harsher than I'd intended. "I'm sorry. What?" I say again, softening the word so that the punctuation afterward resembles a comma, an ellipsis.

"It—it frightens me," she says. "Please—don't..."

"I frighten you? How?"

She hastily pulls up her panties. She says, "You become someone different, is all."

I blush. I wrap my arms around her legs and kiss her wrinkled white knees; I lean my forehead against them. My arousal has gone completely. I let go of her, moving to the bed. I don't know what to do with my hands or eyes. "I'm sorry," I say.

She murmurs, "It's okay."

"I must've temporarily lost my mind."

"Maybe we should send you to Wellbrook," Gillian says, and I am relieved to see a faint smile. I crawl under the covers and say, "I'll leave you alone. I'll stay right here. A foot of space between us." How could I ever make her unhappy? Slowly I inch closer to her and fall asleep, with my face muffled against the soft space between her shoulder blades.

Tonight I awaken, stirred by noise, and she is across the room from me in a moonlit bookcase shadow. She is absently crouched over a sketchpad with a pen in her hand. I look at her and the soft frankness of her pose, the way her knees splay indecorously, touches me. She doesn't look up or notice. I make no sound. She draws or writes—though, by the gesture, it seems like drawing—and pauses, lifts the pen to her mouth, and sucks on the tip, ink spotting her tongue and lips. The pen returns to the paper at her feet.

Gillian looks directly at me. "Hey. I didn't mean to wake you."

"You didn't."

"I couldn't sleep," she says.

"Come to bed," I say, but she shakes her head and pulls her legs into a more ladylike, cross-legged pose. "Come on," I say again, "come to bed. You need your beauty rest."

"I'm not tired."

"It's three in the morning, *xiao mei*."

Gillian sighs. She puts her things down and slinks to the bed, sliding under the covers with her back to me. But when morning comes she's not in the room, and in the haze of half-awakening, it's like Gillian never existed. The songbirds are chirping, *Come to me, come to me...* I quickly dress to leave, surrounded by her dirty underthings and her stiff and glassy-eyed animals. Foreboding fades into a daydream. She will be in the kitchen, eating, or in the living room, looking at a book. Perhaps she will be sitting next to Ma on the sofa. What a treat it is, to be able to anticipate a day with such fervor—to have something (someone!) spectacular to look forward to. And now the chirping cheers me, and the sunlight is less garish and more pleasant, even as I leave it.

But she's not in the kitchen, though the kitchen smells like coffee and bacon, and the dirty dishes are beneath a thin sheet of cloudy water. She's not in the living room, and she's not, as I look through the peephole, on the porch or boulders. The house is eerily quiet. So I go to the other end of the hall, but as soon as I reach the door, it opens. Gillian steps out of Ma's room. I am relieved and unnerved. She stares at me. Pushes up the bridge of her glasses. She says, "Let's go outside."

There are three boulders out past the porch, and they are arranged in a perfect triangular pattern such that the largest rock is at the northernmost tip. As children we found the rocks perfect for games of Lost on an Island. As young adults we lie on them to be alone. Gillian stretches out on the biggest one, maneuvering carefully so that her feet are pressing against the second-largest rock for support. I do the same, but I begin to clench up, expecting her to make a revelation. The thing about lying on the big rock together is that there's no room to move anywhere but down, eliminating the ability to turn and look at each other or otherwise be in any position other than the one you're in: staring at a circle of clouds and sky, bordered by the tips of evergreens.

I now know her body more intimately than anyone has ever known it. Yet the intimacy seems to have created an inverse relationship to my knowledge of her deepest self. So I wade into the conversation carefully. I ask her what she was doing in Ma's room, but I make sure to keep my tone even.

Instead of answering, Gillian says, "Why does she care *so much* that I do a good job as your *tongyangxi*?"

My heart tightens. I say, "Isn't it obvious? I should say because it's the best thing for us." When I receive no answer, I forge on: "We're so compatible—in music, in our education, even in our language. I can't imagine any two people more compatible."

"You wouldn't know," she says. "And neither would I."

"There's a reason for that," I say. "Other people are different. Significantly different."

"When we see them."

"Yes. Consider the dullards we meet when we go into town. They're nothing like us. It stands to reason that they would relate to one another differently."

She seems to consider this, or is ignoring me, watching some bird circle. Finally: "You might be right."

"I know I'm right."

"What it actually is," she says, "is the best thing for *her*, isn't it? She'd be lonely, you know, without us."

"That isn't particularly romantic."

"No. It's not."

"David wanted this, too."

"Yeah."

"You act as though she's being selfish, as though we don't need her, or as if she doesn't give us anything. She does everything for us. What you're saying doesn't make sense. And since when have you been thinking about all of this?"

"I think," she says, "because there's nothing else to do. But haven't *you* thought about any of this? Nothing to do? Nowhere to go? There's a snarl in my gut—things are changing, and it makes me nervous."

What a strange mood she's in today, and I hope that it passes quickly. Chalk it up to hormones. Estrogen gone haywire in her pituitary. Never mind letting her words permeate, though, of course, they do, with our situation working to my advantage, and Gillian's discontent worming its way into my brain, though she's incorrect in that we have had no choice. We are not calves, after all, locked up in crates. She could walk out that door any time she wanted to.

◆

It is two weeks after our honeymoon. In the grass behind the house Gillian and I blow up half a bag of white balloons. The balloons are a gift from Ma, who bought them in Sacramento during our honeymoon week, and though they're an odd choice—balloons are for birthdays, for Easter—Gillian is eager to try them out. So we stand in a field of low golden grass and I am, after puffing my poor pale chest into six balloons, ready to call the whole thing off. But Gillian persists, and insists that we blow and scatter till the palm-sized bag is empty. We stand in a pond of bobbing pearlescent teardrops.

"My cheeks," she says, and rubs them with the tips of her fingers. "I'm more than a little bit light-headed. Golly."

A sudden breeze comes. The balloons rise a few inches and dance before settling on the grass. Gillian bends over and lifts one with both palms, bouncing it, keeping it aloft. She bounces it to me, and I barely graze it with my fingertips, sending it back, which makes her giggle as she leaps to bat it in return.

Later, when the sun begins to set, she frowns. "Do you smell that?" Gillian asks. I don't smell anything. "On the wind," she says, and the balloons rise again.

———◆———

The next morning the sky is slate gray and tinted orange. In the kitchen after both turns at the piano, eating toast and eggs with soy sauce, Gillian points to the corner of the window, in the direction of the woods. The forest sprawls backward, sloping up to the horizon and spitting smoke. She says, opening the window, "That doesn't look good."

"Ma knows."

"Glad to hear you're so concerned for our safety."

"I can't imagine a fire reaching us, sweetheart."

She sighs. "The sky looks awful."

"She'll get us out if we have to leave. The Buick can outrun a distant fire."

"Distant. Really? You say that's distant? Ugh, that *smell*," and she bangs shut the window.

I pass in and out of the room, flip through books, carve notches of baleen into a soap-whale. An hour passes. The slate gray reconfigures into floating ash like snow, tingeing the grass like an old photograph. Ought we to be worried? In our life I've never had to evacuate, though David instilled in me the ground rules of home protection: stack wood away from the house; maintain an irrigated greenbelt; reduce the density of the surrounding forest; mow the grasses and mow the weeds. After all, our property is so flammable, and it is in hot, dry August that the burning bush ignites. But we believe in our imperviousness, and in our invincibility.

At around three o'clock Gillian comes to our room, anxious again. I sigh. She raises her eyebrows, exaggerating her plea to self-mockery and back again to sincerity. "Come on," she says. I put my knife down and go with her to Ma's room.

"Is everything okay with the fire?" Gillian asks.

"It's fine." Ma is sitting on the bed cross-legged and sorting through a hatbox of photographs. Her kimono pools around her. Gillian's eyes go to the box and to the scattering of snapshots on the blanket, which is a shock because we don't look at photographs of our former lives. There are no photographs in the greater house except for the ones on the altar, which are all of David, and meant for the purposes of prayer. This particular hatbox, though usually hidden on the top shelf of Ma's closet, is not unknown to us kids, who poke and prod Ma's bedroom in her weekly absences; but this is the first time that Ma has acknowledged its existence, let alone exposed its contents to us.

"The fire is far away. It's not a threat," Ma says. "Here, look at these photos with me. You too, *ge*. Sometimes it's quite nice to look at old photographs."

I move to the bed next to Gillian, and Ma pushes the box aside to make room. "Look," Ma says, removing a photograph, "this one is of the three of you at the river. You all look so happy. I bought you that swimsuit from a garage sale for two cents. It was such a bargain. It still is a bargain."

Gillian's mouth is thin again, but she takes the photograph and examines it. I know this photograph without looking—Gillian in a striped swimsuit, too young to swim, still just a baby. Her fat legs glow in the water with an ethereal light. Ma sighs. "Ah, look at this one. Daddy and I in Kaohsiung. I was eighteen in this picture. Wasn't I pretty?"

In this photograph Ma is wearing a full striped skirt and a prim blouse, sitting on David's lap. Her long hair is carefully molded into curls. They're frozen in laughter somewhere indoors in front of a dingy wall; a neon sign reading TSINGTAO shines above their heads. They appear shockingly young. I can't imagine them like this, cannot animate them in my mind into walking, talking creatures with wants and hopes; I look and look at David's face, trying to find death in it.

"Before we got married," Ma explains.

I know that Gillian means to speak further about the fire, but here is an opportunity. Ma never talks about her life with David before I was born, and especially not about life in Taiwan. We vaguely know that Ma was born with a different name before she became Daisy Nowak, and that her hometown and birthplace,

Kaohsiung, was in Taiwan, which is an island that we have located in our atlas, but that's the full set. Gillian once asked, as a child, how our parents had met, and Ma had interrupted David by saying, "It's not your business." None of it was our business: how our parents met, how they fell in love, anything about Ma's family (did Ma grow up with parents, or did she hatch, fully formed and adult?), how Ma and David came to live in our woods. Gillian has been dying to know these things. She's always shown more interest in the hatbox than I have.

"What's Tsingtao?" Gillian asks.

"Alcohol. Your father used to drink it."

"Daddy was in Kaohsiung?"

"Yes. He was the only white man who wasn't a sailor. It was impossible to know that he had so much money—he looked like all the rest of them, all the rest of the men in their uniforms. I thought he was old because of his hair, but it was really very blond. White blond. I'd never seen hair like that before."

Gillian asks, reflexively touching her own hair, "Where did you meet?"

"I want you two to remember that with your father gone, we are all we have in this world," Ma says. She slides the photograph to the bottom of the box.

"Who's this?" Gillian has grown bold. She holds a photograph of a girl with a strange-looking arm and a grim expression. I barely glimpse it before Ma snatches the photo and puts it in the box. She tops it with its lid and says, "Didn't you say you were interested in coming with me into town?" Calm as calm can be, and her calm absorbs us and we are calm; we absorb her beliefs when she elides the (unimportant, nonthreatening) fire to stimulate our interest in going into town, which doesn't take any convincing for Gillian, of course, at all, or even me, whose pit of stomach leaps to hear the word, and I know that Gillian will uncover the hatbox later, to examine the photographs for clues.

———————◆———————

Soon the Buick clings to the mountain wall, and Gillian and I are in the backseat. I droop my arm over Gillian such that her left shoulder is in my armpit and observe with her our usual, once-monthly route to town, which is presently curling its way down Sycamore

Road. We pass the Pine Ridge Trailer Park, its sign demarcated by a sloppily painted green triangle with a brown line attached to its base. The trailers gleam with great humped backs. A long-legged mutt is tied to a leaning pole. "Look at the pup," Gillian says. "Do you like it?"

"I do."

The mutt barks soundlessly as we pass. Gillian takes her hand and crosses her chest with it, wrapping her fingers around my yellow arm, adolescent forehead smudging glass. Gillian, the budding amateur anthropologist, the cataloger, observes the movie theater, the diner shaped like an Airstream trailer that promises to make you LICK THAT GREASY SPOON AND LIKE IT. I have never been inside of a movie theater or an Airstream trailer; these are merely glimpsed references. I happily smell her scooped collarbone. This is the third trip in the two weeks since Ma's return, and the thought of town keeps Gillian glad.

Polk Valley is a place of brambly woods and mine shafts, tucked like a finger between the Sierras and the Yuba River of Nevada County, California. What I know of it as a town comes entirely from our monthly errand-runs and the gray pages of a hardbound telephone directory, kept in a kitchen drawer with receipts and a corkscrew. The population of Polk Valley in 1972 is 2,100. The average temperature is 84.3 degrees Fahrenheit in the summer and 32.1 degrees in the winter. Twenty churches. One public library. We are not to be confused with the neighboring state of Nevada, though we are close to Lake Tahoe, which is sliced in two by the state border and also the largest alpine lake in North America. Other towns in Nevada County include Shyville, Lockstep, and Killington, as well as the apocalyptic duo of Devil's Thumb and World's End. During the Gold Rush, Polk Valley was the largest source of gold in the country—hence the town's historically-minded fascination with the Old West. So I've read.

This fifteen-minute drive is almost all that we know of the world, though I do remember long drives from home to the city. On those drives, through the sun-streaked windows, I saw the landscape of groves and orchards, hand-painted signs in dripping red that David read aloud to us kids in the backseat, not because we couldn't read, both of us being taught to read at a young age, but because David loved the sound of EGGS ASPARAGUS and CANDY NUTS PEACHES. FRESH STRAWBERRIES FRESH

PICKED DAILY amid alfalfa bales. "Doughnuts and liquors," he said as we passed a storefront with a neon doughnut and a martini glass. Once he was driving us home from Mrs. Kucharski's in a thunderstorm and said, "Don't worry about the fireflies. They'll just pull out their umbrellas." Another time he explained to Gillian and me what trains were as we stopped at the tracks, bewildered as a locomotive brought its long string of cars across our road and made mechanical, and somehow also animal, sounds.

"Where do they go?" Gillian had asked.

"Other places," David said. "Places we don't go, kiddo."

He had a rhyme that we chanted on the way to lessons:

Highway and right on Cedar Street,
Right on Elm three miles to meet
A mighty oak, and left you'll see
Samson Drive, 1-9-8-3.

Dry grass flat to the blue-and-white Sierras. Black cows grazing under trees, coats glossy as oil; granite quarries gray against the orange earth. "Amador County Fair, well, that sounds fun, doesn't it?... Jack Dunn Water Well Drilling, Pine Grove Stage Stop, Sierra Baptist Church, Four-Square Gospel Church of the Healing Word." Gillian never talked much on those drives because of her motion sickness, but she loved it, she told me later, she loved all of it, just as she melts at that dog and those trailers and, now, the National Auto Gas Station at the outermost corner of Main Street, the slender, stick-straight road flanked by nineteenth-century storefronts and signs. Ma parks behind the K & Bee Grocery, slipping the Buick between a white truck and a low orange car. From the window we can see families, townsfolk, clean-cut, the kind of people David once explained as retirees out looking for a little plot of bramble to turn into a lawn. An old man in a plaid shirt shuffles down the sidewalk with a walker, the brim of his hat shielding his leathery face. Little girls run and give chase, shrieking, as a woman hollers behind them.

———◆———

Gillian jitters in front of us, taking quick, clipped steps around the side of K & Bee to the entrance, passing a woman and her little boy in dungarees. We must not ever touch in public; this is a rule that underscores our difference in this world, as well as what makes us special. The K & Bee logo, painted on a hanging awning sign, is of a big red *K* alongside a big-eyed bee. We know that it's a male bee because he is wearing overalls, and his path of flight, indicated by a dotted line, swirls around the backbone of the *K*. K & Bee and the Apothecary Rx have become the only establishments in our regular rotation since David died, the remnants of a circle that's fragmented over the years. These are the essentials of our lives: food and cheap toilet paper, new toothbrushes when the bristles have half fallen out. And unlike home, these things change, are mutable; brands add MORE CLEANING POWER! or become HEALTHY! HEARTY! GOOD FOR YOU! Gillian was, at thirteen, devastated when K & Bee stopped carrying Apple of My Pie fruit pies, which caused me to question her maturity but, in retrospect, seems to speak to some extended need of hers for consistency in all things she loves, even sickly sweet, rectangular fruit pies.

Gillian drowses to the rightmost aisle and snakes her way through. I am at her side. Ma allows us this as she follows behind with a small and clattering cart. In the canned-food aisle Gillian's fingers, outstretched, brush against tins of corned beef and sardines. I follow and watch as she pauses to examine this thing or that, expecting to hear her marvel, but today she doesn't say much, just looks and touches, and my heart swells at how I can love a girl so easily pleased on a monthly basis by three sorts of corn niblets and an equal variety of peas, this being so different from the brittle housewives moving in buttoned dresses, bare-legged for summer, hands holding shopping lists of scrawl, and thrusting objects into their carts with native finality; women toward whom I have fascination but no attraction. We look at bloody meat chilled in cases and racks of bottled Coca-Cola, Friskies Dog Food Meals, soup cans and signs. Ma asks for her standard three pounds of ground beef at the meat counter, and while she waits Gillian walks around the corner to examine a display of root beer (BE THE KING OF YOUR CASTLE WITH OLD CASTLE!). I follow. When a stock boy in an apron appears from behind us, pushing a tall thing of red crates, muttering, "'Scuse me, 'scuse me," I move closer to Gillian without thinking, pulling her to me as we squeeze against the root beer display. Immediately my body awakens.

The stock boy—one we've never seen before, with spots on his face and orange hair—turns to look at Gillian, his eyes subtly roving over her from head to sandal-shod foot as I attempt to conceal myself. But he couldn't care less about me or my engorgement. He smiles. He carefully dissects her parts, as though he can't decide which way to mount her first, and then he considers her legs, twisted slightly inward at the knees, with calves pulled down to delicate ankles (not seeing the scars from scrapping in the brush with me), the swollen small breasts, her pinkish-white face.

"Good afternoon," he says. "Haven't seen you around here before."

Gillian replies, slowly, "We don't come often." And then she stops. Speaking to strangers is not a thing we do.

"Pity," he says. "I just moved here for the summer to be with my cousin. Make some money before I go back to Killington. You ever been to Killington?"

"How nice for you," I say. "Good-bye."

He laughs. "Aw, what—you two sweethearts?" The stock boy has righted his dolly and is leaning against it now, making him the same height as Gillian. From here I can smell his nauseating perfume, and I can only imagine what sort of filthy smells he would emit otherwise. I want to say, *Yes, we're sweethearts, and I knew her last night, you moron,* but I am suddenly very aware of Ma's ominous presence. She appears with the package of meat and cart, watching. What could Gillian possibly be thinking at this moment? Gillian and I are usually ignored, nonentities; we don't make eye contact. But she is now half smiling at him with a kind of stunned—or is it starstruck?—look. My belly roils. If I'm unaware of what conventional female beauty is, I'm still more dubious in regards to what arouses my sister, and it could be this stock boy covered in blotches.

I could grab her arm and say that there's something urgent that needs attending to, though if she's enjoying this encounter, I'm not inclined to anger her. The truth is that if her interaction goes much further, these happy jaunts will undoubtedly be put on pause for a month, or maybe more, which is not devastating to me, certainly, as I imagine myself with her sans distraction, but Gillian cares greatly about going into town. And I want her to be happy. So I say, *"Mei..."* in the quietest voice that I can muster, and when her eyes turn to meet mine, I mumble something about our mother needing help with a bag of Friskies. Then I hear the cart again, and Ma steps toward us.

Ma says to the stock boy, "Go away, please."

His lips part slightly. His brow knits, and Gillian snaps out of her daze. She smiles at him. "Time to go," she says. He says good-bye and blinks one eye, as though he's got something caught in it. Reflexively, I try to do the same and find I cannot. Ma doesn't say anything. We continue to walk, and behind us the cart be-gins, again, to rattle and squeak. Whether we've passed muster with Ma I'm not sure, but I am sure that we will be heading home more quickly than usual now, and when we get home, I will get Gillian into our bed, because I am still aroused, perhaps more now than I was before we spurned the red-haired kid—aroused, perhaps, as a result of triumph. Then again, I'm not entirely vic-torious, though I will be soon enough when I get the stock boy out of her head and mine.

We walk. I see Gillian stop to pinch a cellophane-wrapped loaf of white bread, hard.

"You know not to speak to strangers," Ma says quietly.

"I didn't say anything to him," Gillian says. She is standing next to the ice-cream case, a sheet of cloudy glass behind her. Ma pretends not to hear. "I didn't *say* anything to him," she says again, and Ma pushes the cart to the frozen vegetables.

We begin to put our groceries on the checkout counter, and the cashier looks up at us. The two women exchange pleasantries while the cashier calculates a total cost, and with her head down in concentration, she says, "Terrible about the fire, isn't it?"

Ma takes out her wallet and prepares to write a check. She has a photograph of our family in the window where a driver's li-cense ought to go, turned with the back facing out so that it just says: KODAK KODAK KODAK.

"I hope you folks stay safe. A fire like that..." The cashier shakes her head, and not one of us looks at one another, or says anything in reply.

◆

At the car Ma settles into the driver's seat and switches on the ignition. I am standing next to my sister and can barely hear the car stereo, which emits a solemn voice and not the usual swell of classical radio. A man is announcing a "fast-moving forest fire." I'm carrying a bag of groceries alongside the Buick. Gillian's hands rest on the cart's scarlet push-handle. The announcer drones on: all residents of the wooded northeast corner of Nevada County are to evacuate to the community center at St. Joseph's Church in downtown Polk Valley, immediately. (Gillian says, in Mandarin, "That's us.") All residents who have no mode of transport are to call such-and-such a number for assistance. This is a mandatory evacuation due to a fast-moving forest fire. All residents of the northeast—

Ma turns off the radio. The Buick is parked on the outside edge of the small parking lot, facing a row of scrubby bushes. Both of her hands rest on the steering wheel at the eleven and one o'clock positions, and the three of us look to the gray-yellow sky.

"Did he say that we had to evacuate? Does that mean we have to leave?" Gillian asks. "Right now?"

"All right," Ma says calmly, the door still open, "get in the car."

But Gillian continues, looking again at the sky: "Should we turn the radio back on? So that we know what's happening?"

"In the car, please."

The simplest next step would be for Ma to take us to the community center. How do we know that this will happen? Because it is the logical thing to do? I set the grocery bag back in the cart and go to the car. I put my hand on the car door. Perhaps Ma will take us to the community center. Perhaps Gillian will get in the car.

But this is not what happens. While I open my door my sister pauses a long while, considering, and finally says, "No," shaking her head. "No, I'm not coming," she says. Not firmly, but the opposite of that. "What about the groceries?" she adds. There's an edge to her voice. She's backing up and pulling the cart with her, making that rattling sound. I turn and look and her hand is on an exposed box of cornflakes. She is almost still. In her stillness she is absurdly, heart-meltingly beautiful, a ragged scrap of a lovely dream. Her naysaying head sways.

"We won't be able to bring them to the center," I say. "They won't have a place to put them. There's no point. And I'm sure they'll feed us there."

We stand and watch the smoke and the sky turned apocalyptic. Here is the back of Ma's gently curled hair and the naked bit of bone-white scalp beneath black wisp, her spine so straight that we could plant a ruler behind it, lining vertebra by vertebra from inch to inch, and I know what Gillian knows. It suddenly seems crazy, absolutely crazy, to consider what will happen if we get into that car and let our mother drive us home, the way that she has been driving us home for all of our lives. But what choice do I have, really? So I don't consider it.

I open the door and get inside. It smells of dust and something spicy and candy-sweet. I remember David sitting in front of where I am presently sitting. His thin—he was more substantial when he was well, but in my memories he is almost always bone-thin—body would lean back in the seat. He'd stretch one arm out to the steering wheel and hold a cigarette in the other, and he'd be driving with his right hand, the one with all the striped and spotted scars, some thick like twine and some merely dark against the skin, those scars that we felt such conflict over—tenderness, fear, confusion. He'd said, when we asked why his hand looked like that, that he'd been hurt, and hadn't we ever gotten hurt before? And we'd learned to fear it only after we realized that others feared it, and withdrew from that hand. I'd even seen Mrs. Kucharski flinch, once, when he handed her a wad of bills from his wallet.

Inside the car Ma and I watch Gillian through the window. The shimmer of Gillian. The tremble of pink flowers against her body from a breeze.

Ma unbuckles the latch on her seat belt. The loud click. She climbs out. *"Guai haizi,"* she calls gently, and closes the door. I can't hear anything from inside the car. I whip around in my seat. She walks to Gillian and takes her hand. Gillian doesn't pull away as Ma pushes the cart aside to make way for the Buick's retreat. Ma leads and Gillian somnambulates to the right side. Their torsos are framed together: one white, one pink and patterned, in the window. Here is Ma opening the door, and here is Gillian climbing in, so very slowly, without looking at me.

———◆———

On our way up the mountain, Gillian erupts into tiny, wheezy sobs, which unnerves me more than any fistfight would have. This even unnerves me more than the fact that we are going in the opposite direction of a caravan of cars crawling down the skinny road toward town, some of which are honking, or the silenced radio, which tells us nothing at all. But Gillian's hands are balled into child's fists. Gillian is in a universe of her own.

The trailer park dog, as I purposefully neglect to point out to her, is gone. The trailer park itself is evacuated both of cars and of people. Up the winding road we go. The sky darkens the windshield with either ash dusting the glass or the view of the sky from inside the car, but with windows up, it's hard to tell.

I can see the interiors of other cars going down the mountain through the haze. Some of them are full of people and nothing else. Most are crammed with things like suitcases and cardboard boxes with presumably valuable lamps and enormous leather-bound photo albums sticking out the tops; these boxes sit on people's laps. The people's faces are steady and serious; these men and women look like people who know in this moment that their homes are already on fire. The people are young and middle-aged, mostly, and some of them are old. There is one old couple in particular—the skinny, bald old man is driving and the skinny, white-haired old woman is sitting in the passenger's seat, but the old man's right hand is resting on the back of her neck as though she were a child. There is nothing in their backseat.

At some point during our drive, when the road suddenly develops a bulging bit of dirt on its right edge, Ma makes a turn off the road and parks the car.

"Get out," she says.

Nobody moves.

Ma says, "Listen. There will be things to stop us ahead. There will be policemen and fire fighters. So get out."

Gillian is now in keening hysterics. I briefly consider whipping open the door, getting out of the car, and running away. All we need to do is run in the opposite direction. Gillian may doubt this about me, but I have no death wish.

Yet I can't bring myself to run. If I ran, would Gillian follow? If we ran, what would happen to our mother? If we ran, and she gave chase, what would happen if she came on us like a wave, and grabbed us by our collars? Already she's brought us to Sycamore Road. The familiar dirt banks and signs make this much clear. Perhaps she's bringing us back because there are things that she wants to rescue. Items of sentimental value. The hatbox. The photograph of my parents beneath the TSINGTAO sign. Perhaps she knew from that moment that she might end up here with us; that the fire might get this bad; that she wanted to share with us, by showing us the hatbox, the only part of her history that she felt comfortable revealing. Perhaps she is only after sentiment. Or she can't imagine rebuilding the house that she and David bought together, can't fathom living a new life after an incineration. An impulse or instinct to go home, unplanned. Gillian is sitting and crying with snot slick down her face, sobbing, her sobs interrupted by sharp, shuddering inhalations, and she does not bother to cover her face with her hands. Ma gets out of the car and walks around the rear to Gillian's side. A nauseated fear grips my guts as she opens the door; Ma reaches over Gillian's body and unbuckles the seat belt. Ma yanks her out and Gillian doesn't fight, but plops onto the ground, and oh, she cries. She still cries.

I open my door and go to Gillian. I tell her to come with us. To defend my choice I think of home and Ma, and of how we know nothing else.

But Gillian says that she won't. She'd rather die here, with people watching, rather than at home alone with us. "It's not safe," she says. (The smell of the gray air.)

Ma grabs her by the arm and skids her a foot along the dirt, dusting up her dress. Her soft thighs scrape against pebbles and earth. I say, "Ma, please, don't." Gillian's unwillingness is not like her occasional unwillingness to succumb to my ministrations, or her unwillingness to play the piano after David's death, but something more difficult than that. What she means by playing this particular card, this still-stuck statue, is to say that she will not climb up into those trees and run toward the house, but neither will she scream for help or run toward the town that she's so long considered a splendid possibility; she will choose nothing.

No one stops to help us, and why would they, those concerned, terrified Polk Valley citizens fleeing from a fire that might swallow up their beloved cabins and homes? Our drama goes on. My beautiful girl is on the ground, blood smearing her dress, and forgive me, Gillian, forgive me, but I go to her with Ma's voice in my ears. I wrap one arm around the back of her neck and the other beneath her knees, but she doesn't fight me. She is taller than I am, and I think stronger, but as she cries and convulses I find myself growing quieter between the ears. Somehow, I manage to lift her.

In my arms she goes limp and heavy, pressing her damp face against my chest.

"Up here," Ma says.

We have no choices. We never have. I thought I was choosing for Gillian, but I had no choice myself. Nowhere to go—and Gillian, poor thing, knew this long before I did. She throws her arms around my neck. Weeps into my breast. I find my footing in the dirt, in the rocky slope with stones like steps. I carry her up and into the trees. Ma is saying, "Hurry, hurry, hurry..." Is this how David felt at the end of it, his briefcase in his lap, his hunting knife, the shades drawn? Here the smoke burns my eyes. The smoke makes them water and tear.

WHIMPER

GILLIAN (1972)

I'm sure it's the dog from the trailer park coming over the horizon. I believe the word is *brindled*. It trots over the clean line, because all a dog with stocky legs like that can do is trot, a white-chested, broad-shouldered silhouette that rises and falls and stops right under the birch tree a few yards from me. With needle in hand I'm mending a yellow sundress that'll be too small for me in a few months, with dry grass pressed against my legs. In a few months I'll have to stop wearing this dress, as well as the green gingham one, or I'll suffer William giving me that peculiar look with his wheedling eyeballs; never mind that I like the feeling of limbs dangling everywhere and the sun's heat on me, too. What and now here's this dog, watching me with its paws crossed and its head resting on crossed paws. Looking at me like I have something it wants, but I'm used to that look by now.

We didn't lose the house—not that I ever thought we would, simply because it would have been too easy. The flames spread in such a miraculous manner that they curved exactly to the edge of our property and then just *stopped*. I mean, they didn't stop on their own—the uniformed men stopped the fire, the same men who found us in the brush and brought us by force to St. Joseph's Church till we were allowed to go home—but the fire surrendered right at the border of our land, as though even the fire wanted me stuck. I feel a softness for the dog, set free by someone, I assume, unto death but now just free. In the field I'm alone because, post-fire, Ma and I have struck a bargain. If I do what she tells me, and if I content myself with good behavior on twice-monthly town outings, I am now also permitted to roam the property for exactly one hour every day without oversight. This bargain strikes me as to my advantage, and I am pleased that I've behaved well enough to have my restrictions loosened, although my gut is full of sourness, and even the quiet can't shut down the noise in my brain that tells me, *You were all so close, you were all so close to being obliterated for some purpose no one will explain.*

I weave the needle into the hem and my hands fold. In the middle of Polk Valley August it's hot, but soon the air will turn sharp and clean. The dog is in the shade and I can't see it well enough, but I call out, "C'mere, c'mere, pup, small pup," even though it is not actually small, and its ears rise. It comes up on all its legs and walks toward me. Comes closer and I see that it's a lady dog, and she's been scrapping with something that delivered a torn ear and scratches along her muzzle. The dog has no collar or tags. I name her Sarah. I will bring her home and mend her, too. It doesn't take a genius to figure that, in a way, I'm both the most and the least powerful person in the house, though the thing that makes me strong makes me weak. So I name her and I try to get her to follow me with my yellow dress draped over my arm. The *guai baobao* has been through a fight, but she doesn't whine. She suffers her wounds without a whimper.

At the porch William is sitting in the rocker, brushed-hair and barefoot. He's not doing anything in particular—not translating, not reading—just staring out, waiting for me. "I see you have a friend," he says, and he gets up from the chair to wrap his arms around me. He holds me close and he kisses me on the neck, and then in the hollow of my sticky collarbone. His kisses are inexplicably wet always, and I always want to wipe them away, but how rude would that be?

"She's in bad shape," I say.

"A regular St. Francis. Are you going to ask Ma about it? She's in her room," he adds, "getting dressed and undressed, reapplying her rouge. Hey, girl." He crouches and holds out his hand.

"Her name is Sarah."

"Sarah. Nice."

I make William watch Sarah while I go inside with my heart beating fast and poke around in the kitchen. We do not own animals; my father was far more likely to stuff a creature than to feed it twice a day. All I can find that might be good is a pound of ground beef wrapped in butcher paper. I feel daring and take half of the cold, soft pinkness to put on a proper plate, thinking of Ma in the next room doing, as William says, God knows what.

"Gillian," she calls as I squeak around the corner of the kitchen door, and I say, "What?" trying not to sound like a girl with ground beef on a plate. She asks me where I've been all morning. I say I was out in the long meadow, which is something that my father used to call it, and I always liked to hear the phrase "the trees in the long meadow" as a result. "I was mending a dress," I say, "just enjoying the sun," and I hear Sarah whimper from outside, I hear her bark, and William says, "Whoa."

And of course Ma comes out of the bedroom one-fourth of a second after the bark. Her hair is in sea-green curlers, the kind with foam and a grip, and she asks in Taiwanese, *"Na shih gao-ah?"*

"Shih."

"And that? Meat's not cheap," she says, pointing, switching back to Mandarin, and though she doesn't outright pull the plate from my hands in this moment, I wouldn't be surprised if she did a second from now, when she thinks I'm not aware of her gears churning. But I wouldn't let go. There would be meat on the floor and I'd clean it up because that's what I do. I'd pick the meat up and put it back on the plate, and I'd head right outside. Ma says, "Well, go ahead, then," and she comes with me.

Sarah is at my feet right away, her tail tentatively wagging as though she knows she shouldn't, but can't help herself. Her tongue, spongy white and pink, is hanging out; she comes to the plate, which I put on the porch, and she snuffles into the meat straightaway. It hurts me to watch her, Sarah, who is trembling like her sturdy build isn't enough to keep her upright.

William says, in English, "Sarah, nobody's going to take it *away* from you." And then, "Gillian, please get your dog to relax. She's going to choke on it."

"In Taiwan," Ma says, "we had dogs like this everywhere. Street dogs, eating out of the garbage, chewing on their own tails." She goes back inside and William goes back to the rocker and watches us. I don't touch her yet. What would our father say about bringing a dog home? He'd let me, I think. He'd let me have this thing to love. Always he was so good at loving, so good at making me feel like the best girl in the world. A girl who could, and should, have everything—everything within reason, but still—everything.

————————◆————————

Sarah sleeps outside. Sarah eats the leftovers that I put on the same plate I used the first day, and she'll eat practically anything, but is happiest with meat. Sarah has hydrogen peroxide and a bandage put on her muzzle, her paws; she doesn't try to bite. Sarah looks sad all day and is especially sad when I go inside at night, when the mosquitoes come for me, and Sarah sounds a low whine that I can hear through the closed door before she goes quiet. Sarah is on a long rope tied around a post. Sarah is a hopeless creature.

In the mornings, at approximately six o'clock, she begins to scratch on the front door, a faint sound like rats scurrying in the walls, and William, who sleeps more heartily now because of exertion, doesn't hear and doesn't wake up earlier than I do to play the piano. I'm the one who gets up and goes to the kitchen, poking through the refrigerator, and whatever is left over and will draw the least amount of criticism from Ma is what goes on Sarah's plate: fish heads, wilted cabbage. I assemble a meal until the fridge begins to look emptier, and then I put the last offending object back. When I open the front door, while the screen is still shut, Sarah is already waiting for me with her front paws high, standing precarious on her hind legs, wobbling like pudding, jerking her head with her tongue hanging loose out. If I try to touch her she'll back away from the plate by my feet and won't eat till my hands are hidden or relaxed at my sides. I sit in the rocker and watch her approach. She investigates the food with a few sniffs, eats with her lips back so that I can see her big teeth. She licks the plate and then, with a satisfied half-whimper, half-groan, trots to me. After a week, she lets me touch her gently behind the ears, where the fur is surprisingly soft.

Sarah solidifies my place in the world. I was mending a dress in the meadow and conjured her alone. I spend so much time with her that they worry. What worry, for what purpose?

One night I come into the bedroom to change into a nightgown and William says, "Haven't seen you in a while."

"We live in the same house," I reply. I go to the wardrobe and open it, facing the mirror glued to the inner door. I see myself and my tangled, matted hair, and I see part of William on the bed with a book open on his lap. There's a bloody spot on his chin where he's popped a pimple, and when he catches my eye in the glass he touches his chin briefly, as if to hide it from me.

"That dog is getting better," he says. "She's probably practically healed under those bandages, you know. You won't know unless you take off those bandages."

"She's not healed."

"And her ribs don't show anymore. You feed her better than you feed yourself."

I say, "It's sweet of you to care."

You're more important is what he's thinking, but he doesn't say it. I unbutton the dress I'm wearing down to the waist, one of the few dresses I own that isn't feed-sack: a red-and-white swirling cotton print. He's so good at undoing my undergarments with one hand or his teeth, unwrapping me, but these days I don't give him the satisfaction. I'm either dressed or undressed. Here or not here. In or out.

In the cold bed under cold sheets he first turns toward me on his side—piped pajamas off, underwear on—and kisses my left breast. "You like it," he says, "don't you, kitten?"

"I like most things," I say, not lying, exactly, my thighs tingling in an anticipatory hurt.

Sarah is sleeping on the porch by now, or maybe she's waiting for me, like I'm waiting for William to put my hand where he wants it. And when he finishes I can go to our bathroom and put my hand into my underwear and jiggle my fingers around, in the cold, with my forehead pressed against the sink, until my muscles spasm and my head turns to air. That's what sex is.

I do wonder if there can be an alternative to this. There are marriages in our books that are not like this one—people wed without the bond of family to tie them, although there is still love as there is love in this room. I am the problem here, but perhaps I would not be the problem somewhere else. And why consider it? It's not as though I can be someone other than who I am. I am born as I am and I live as I am.

When our dad died I cried under my bed for hours, days maybe, and while I lay there I saw William's feet pad in. He said, "No, it's *not* okay, and that's why I love you." I can only assume it was a different love then. He was thirteen, and unlike me, he always wore socks—but now we both know that he likes to be completely naked with me when we are in "the act." His feet are cramped, sad. Little hairs on the toes. I do try to find him charming. The way he speaks is our father all over, but with flourishes. They have the same features stuck in opposite faces: the foxlike versus the jowly walrus or bony antelope.

(William's fingers are inside me and working with diligence; he never rotates his wrist.)

William brushed my hair when I was too small to remember, but he tells me that he did it and I believe him. He's very fascinated by my hair. The way I know that William and I don't see eye to eye is that natural quality of fascination, or non-fascination, with each other's details.

(He sinks his face into my hair and inhales with fingers still moving. I try to relax. With his other hand he rubs the tips of my long curls between thumb and forefinger. Seconds later he grips the back of my skull and pulls my mouth to his. Our teeth click and I feel myself resisting the urge to pull back. He crooks his fingers into the gap beneath my shoulder blade like he wants to pry it off.)

What more is there? Stave off repulsion; replace with tenderness, longing, the ever-elusive *love*. We kiss and his eyes, close up, are inarguably beautiful—William's eyelashes even longer and curlier than our father's, and so muddy that I can barely distinguish the pupils. During our honeymoon week I often looked at his eyes and thought, *These eyes are beautiful, and his hands are slender and strong; he has an open face.* So I counted the qualities in him that I thought I could love. He can't hide a feeling, for example, to save his life. So I loved his vulnerability.

(He removes his fingers from inside of me. I envision the river, which is my pathetic attempt to hasten wetness, which Ma explained to me is so important, but instead I spit in my hand and put it to myself, thinking momentarily that Vaseline would perhaps be a better solution, and I pull William's chest to mine.)

He thinks he runs the show, but when I told him a month ago that I was afraid, his face shrank into itself. Really I hadn't meant to hurt him. It was all of that *desire*, you know, spilling out of him and making him ugly. Really I had just meant for him to slow himself down, to let me find my own pace, because he didn't understand that our future depended on a mutual understanding—and in those weeks between the end of sex and its reintroduction

I saw him wither. I said to him over eggs, "When are you going to play today," and he said, "My hands hurt." When I looked at his hands the veins stood out like crippling wires, with his fingers splayed out and stiff. "My God," I said.

I know all the places that will make him emit miniature moaning sounds. I've known since I was three the keys to press to form a dominant seventh. I coax his penis to me and he lets it happen, wiggling his hips as Sarah does: with eagerness. For a moment, as he props himself above me, I think I hear her whimper.

◆

September. The leaves shaking themselves off the trees onto the floor of what's left of the live wood. When I bring them back and scatter them onto the kitchen table, William tapes them to the windows, the way that he will tape up paper snowflakes when winter comes.

Sometimes I ask myself how William doesn't get bored with the house. With doing the same things over and over again. So I think he's as stupid as he is smart. The only really smart person I've ever known is our father, whose brain worked so hard that it killed him. But take this thing with Sarah, for example. William doesn't seem interested in her at all. When I sit on the porch and play with her, I can tug on a sock between us for an hour. Everything seems so interesting and pleasurable and easy when it's just us two, and William stays away, calling her "it." He sits at the kitchen table, staring out the window at the mountains; he plays the same etudes and reads the same books. How can he not yearn for something different?

Sarah is my something different. But then again, what am I? I clip sweaters to the clothesline behind the house and she comes to lie in the grass beside my legs, a tall dog for a tall girl, and I feel William looking at me through the screen door. I don't think he's jealous of Sarah, though it would be easy enough. As the sun sets the night is ready to push down on my shoulders with both of its heavy hands, and I think, *From now till we die our lives will be the same except for the patterns of weather and the gray growing in Ma's hair, so it's best to work at being happy with what we have.*

I go inside, whispering good-byes to Sarah, and put raspberries on a plate and take a fork from the drawer. I sit at the table and look at the leaves stuck to the window with tape. William has left the atlas on the table, splayed open page-down. I eat the raspberries one by one until the plate becomes wet with red juice. Yes, it's a good thing that I am a fool. If I weren't a fool, I would be dead.

At dinner there's a knock at the back door and everyone startles. We are so accustomed to being left alone that the idea of someone knocking at our door seems dreamlike and ludicrous. Sarah, though she is tied at the front porch, is barking like a scream. I look at William and then at Ma, who sets down her chopsticks and goes to the butcher block, where she pulls out a knife. She leans against the counter with the big knife in her hand, and no one makes a sound. After many minutes there is shuffling, and then more knocking at the back door. William moves to close the curtains. I see his hand pause before he can pull them shut. If he pulls them shut we might draw attention to ourselves. Any person at the back door won't be able to see the curtains close if William closes them right now.

The three raps have come and gone. In the silence we're unable to tell whether the source of the knocking is still standing at the door, and yet it seems likely that the source of the knocking has not left, because there has been no clear sound of footsteps away from the house. Two flies swirl around each other at the center of the table.

But I'm not scared. I feel calm. All I can think is *Gabriel is at the door.*

We sit for a long time. Then William gets up from the table and walks to the door, and I am surprised when he opens it. There's no way that whoever it was can still be there, but on the back porch stands a man about the same height as William, with dark hair and dark eyebrows. He's a pale man, but not of the same cream-and-flaxen complexion as I am, or of our father.

The man says, heaving his knapsack farther up his shoulder such that we can see it from inside, his voice loud enough to sound above the barking, "I'm sorry to bother you folks, but I lost my home in the fire, and I was wondering if you could spare some—"

"*Go away!*" William shouts, and slams the door, locking it, which we do not do, because no one ever comes to our property, and we do not understand how this man has appeared thusly.

William comes back to the table. When he puts his hands on

the table I can see that they're trembling. Ma still has her fingers wrapped around the large knife. Her wedding band glints thin like the edge of the blade.

"The dog," I say, and stand to go to the front door, which someone must also lock.

"Sit down," Ma says. "You just sit down. No one is going to any door. We are going to sit here, and if that man comes back, I am going to kill him."

On the kitchen table is a bowl of apples sliced into wedges, three bowls of rice in various stages of emptiness, a pan-fried trout staring up with its marble eye. I want to sweep everything off the table and scream.

"Ma."

"Gillian."

"I'm worried about my dog."

"Your dog is an animal. It's not part of our family."

"He could still be outside," William says, "listening to us talk."

"He doesn't know what we're saying," I say. "But he could be hurting Sarah. She could already be hurt."

William says, "I don't want him hearing our voices."

"He knows we're in here."

"I know."

It's more than a mutt that a strange man could carry away. It's me, the princess in the high tower. How else to explain this oddness, this jealousy from William? And what about Sarah? The growing desperation that comes with impending loss. I know before I get up and open the door hours later, as Sarah moans and comes to me with her wide muzzle nosing at my legs, that one day she'll be gone. Taken away by a stranger, just as we've always been told about bad men, the wolf at the door.

———◆———

Ma says, "Listen to me. You're never allowed out again. You're never leaving this house without someone again. You come right here." She grabs my arm and pulls me into the hallway, down the hall and into her bedroom. The plain room smells like her perfume, as though she's been spraying to cover some other scent. She puts her hands on my shoulders and pushes me down so that I'm facing her chest as I sit on the bed, the made bed, and the flowers on her dress are shining under the lights. She climbs on top of me and pins my wrists so that they're pressed against the bed, and I start to cry because it hurts and I'm surprised. I think my wrists are going to break. She shakes me. The mattress squeals. "You are a girl and you are not safe and you are not going anywhere."

William, where is William? Hiding in his room? Watching from the door? Listening from the hallway?

"I'm a good mother," she says. "You've never been hurt. You've never had to sell your body before you even grew breasts. I've kept you safe." She lets go. "You smell terrible. Go take a bath—your hair smells like a greasy pan."

When I see William in the hallway his face is both closed and open.

"I'm going to take a bath," I say. And I go into the bathroom. After I strip off my socks and my cotton dress I turn on the bathtub faucet. I climb into the tub and feel the cold water pool around my body until the water runs hot at my feet, which are grayish and dirty under the toenails because I am an animal.

The door opens and William comes in.

"Let me be alone for a little bit," I say, but he doesn't go. Instead he sits on the toilet seat and runs both hands through his hair, gripping it, holding his small head in his hands.

"I heard her yelling at you," he says. "I'm sorry."

"Yeah."

"She's going to make sure the doors are always locked now. I think that's a good thing. And she's worried about you, you know, because she loves you. She doesn't want anything bad to happen to you. I think she's worried you're going to run away."

"That's stupid. I don't even know how. I don't know how to live out there."

"Promise me you're not going to run away."

"I'm not going to run away."

"You promise?"

"I promise."

"At the fire you wouldn't come."

"At the fire," I say, "we were going to die."

"It doesn't matter," he says.

I turn off the water because the tub is about to overflow, even though I would rather leave it on. I want him to leave, but I don't want to be alone.

"I'm sorry that I scared you," I say in the echo chamber.

He stands up and comes to the tub. The water ripples around my body, splashing. He sits cross-legged alongside the tub and rests his head against the side with his hands in his lap as though begging. Or maybe he's just tired.

The water is burning hot by my feet and cold at my back, so I swirl it around in order to mix the temperatures. William doesn't move.

"Tell me," he says, "about something fun that we did when we were little."

"Noah's Ark. Jonah and the Whale."

"Those were fun."

"They were."

"I liked to play Noah's Ark," he says.

"That's because you were always Noah."

"I did the voices of the other animals."

"You got to do the voices of some of the best animals."

"I did?"

"But," I said, "you always let me be the deer."

William is silent. A rush of love roars out of my heart like a locomotive from my dreams, so strong that I feel like I'm going to faint from its whoosh sprinting from my body. I have never loved anyone like I love William; I have never *known* anyone like I've known my brother; I will never know anyone as deeply and fully as I know my idiosyncratic, bombastic, impossibly flawed kin. The only way that I can think of to honor this is to match his silence. So I touch the top of his head with my wet hand, anointing him. I am so confused.

After he leaves I finish my bath, pouring the plastic bucket of water over my head to give my hair a cursory washing. I wrap myself in the crackling towel hanging from the towel hook and let my hair drip all the way to our bedroom. William is lying in bed with the covers up to his armpits, his hands sprawled over the sheets. His eyes are closed, but open when I sit on the corner of the bed, patting my body dry with the towel.

"Come here," he says. "Please."

"I'm very wet."

"But I like you."

"I know."

I crawl into our bed, wrapping my hair in the damp towel, and still my hair sops the pillow so thoroughly that I'm convinced it's soaked to the mattress beneath it. He puts his arm around me. I make my breath go slow. Ma always tells us never to sleep with our hair wet, it'll get us sick, but I lie and lie forever with my hair never getting any drier, and William begins to lightly snore with his face pressed against the nape of my neck, which tickles, and is incredibly gentle in nature. *It's not so bad*, I tell myself. *This is good, to be loved.* Why would I not want this—to be loved, to be loved more than a person loves himself, to be loved so much by people whom I also love, who want to keep me safe and close to them. Isn't that what life is about? Isn't that what was meant for us?

In the middle of the night William wakes me, and for a second I don't know where I am. "You're doing that thing with your teeth," he says softly. The lights are still on. "It woke me up."

"Sorry," I say.

"Don't be sorry. Just relax. It's bad for your teeth. Wears down the white."

He puts his hand on my naked back, making small circles with his palm—small, small, circles—until sleep takes his hand and he stops, dropping into slumber, but now I'm awake and I don't want to be naked in this bed anymore, I want to put on a nightgown or turn off the light or something. But I'm afraid that if I crawl out of bed, I'll wake him up. So I stay.

———◆———

In the early morning, on the front porch, barefoot with scissors in hand, I can barely see anything. Birds are calling—trills, appoggiaturas—and I sense a flock shifting in the sycamore five yards from my face. (Immediately before Wellbrook my father's visions all involved birds, particularly crows and ravens. At dinner he'd duck, hands slamming on the table so hard the plates rattled.) Sarah is restless, pacing in the dark and perhaps hungry. I gather my hair in a makeshift ponytail and lop it off. I snip off the remaining hair. The sibilant cutting is louder than I thought it would be, and when I finish I pat my head all over with my free hand. It's very short. The sky is now a purplish blue and I can make out the snickering outlines of trees and bushes, the J-shaped curls of my locks on the porch, and then I sit among the potted cacti to watch the sun rise.

The door opens. Sarah barks once. William says good morning, a little nervously, and adds, "Your hair. My God."

"Do I look like a boy?"

"Sort of. Not really. That's quite a mess you made there."

"That's why I did it outside. How did you know I was out here?"

"I heard you leave."

Am I less pretty now? is what I want to ask, but instead I say, "I needed a change."

William says, "Did you sleep all right?"

"I didn't have any dreams."

"The best kind of sleep. I had awful dreams. I've never been so happy to wake up."

He pauses, as if waiting to see if I'll ask him about his dreams, and I know that he's not going to leave me alone.

"I'd better sweep this hair off the porch."

He says, "You're breaking my heart, kid."

I go to the side of the house where the broom is, a splayed mess of bristles and dust, and come back to whisk the remnants of my long hair off the porch.

"I mean, gosh," he says, "it just breaks my heart. Let's go inside. I'll practice, and you can make some breakfast, all right?" He puts his cold hand on the back of my freshly naked neck, and I lean the broom against the wall.

"I need to feed Sarah," I say as we go inside. He sits at the table and I go to look for something to give her. There is half a hunk of ground beef. I calculate an amount that could be taken without incident or perhaps even notice and put it on a plate, plus a fish head. As I turn to go outside William says, "Ma," and Ma is standing in the doorway of the kitchen, watching me. Her face is as blank as a flat palm held out, and though I feel a ticklish warning in my solar plexus, I am with the plate and I open the door. Sarah sees the food and is eager, tail swaying. Something moves behind me; my arm jerks as Ma reaches for the plate and pulls it out of my hand, out a long throw so that the plate whirls far with the sound of food hitting the dirt. I don't make a sound. She tells me to come inside, and I do.

Ma in her robe and perfectly curled hair stares at me over breakfast. Her gaze makes me feel like I'm coming out of my body, rising a few inches above my corporeal form. I can feel the slip of skin against flesh, bones wet in air. When I pour myself a cup of coffee I catch a curved sight of myself in the pot, which surprises me. The absence of hair makes my features more prominent. I look like I have an enormous and pointed nose. The glasses are another feature. The dimple in the center of my chin is reminiscent of a potter's careful thumbprint on the bottom of our ceramic mugs. She says nothing about the food, the plate I will have to retrieve and bring inside to wash. I take my coffee with a little bit of cream and no sugar, and the entire time I sip from the mug I think of the girl in the coffeepot, looking out.

It is possible that Ma thinks I'll be headed to Wellbrook next. I've had long hair my entire life. And I cannot recall another epoch of such anger from her except when my father died. If I could only feel the tenderness that suffused me in the bathtub last night. But it was hard to find, hard to wrap my arms around, harder still to recapture. All the furniture looks smaller today.

"I don't want Sarah to stay tied up out there," I say, and though William's eyes are widening, I continue: "Her legs have got the itch. She needs to go on a walk."

Ma shakes her head.

I say, "With William. We'll go together. He can keep an eye on me, make sure we come home in time and don't go anywhere we shouldn't."

"That dog just eats our food," Ma says.

"I never give her the good food," I say, which is not entirely true.

"It didn't even keep the bad man away. Barks to the heavens."

"Ma, I'll take her," William says. "She wants to go."

Ma's face pinches up as she considers, perhaps thinking of the togetherness of such an activity, and then she says, "Stay in the field. I'll find you a whistle. But you can always stay in here. There's plenty to do inside. You can unstring the beans. You can memorize a poem or ten lines of Chinese verse."

"We'll stay in the field," says William.

"Or wash the dishes. Why don't you wash the dishes first," Ma says, rising, clanking them into the sink. "If you don't wash the dishes the egg yolk is going to stick to the pan and to the plates and to the spoons and everything, and it's never going to come off."

What she's said about the egg thing is true, so William goes to the sink and starts to rinse the dishes. His arms move vigorously as he scrubs the plates with his bare hands. I get up and start moving things around on the table, like the salt and pepper shakers, just so I can have something to do. Someone has loosened the top of the saltshaker, probably to be funny. Probably it was

William. Maybe it was me, but I can't remember. I screw the sil-ver top of the saltshaker back on and feel validated; I'm a useful member of the family, no matter what anyone thinks.

I go over to William and whisper, "Thanks."

He shrugs a shoulder. Then he turns his head to kiss me, his hands poised in the sink, the running water shushing us as it slides over everything.

When we put on our shoes to leave, Ma hears us from the back porch and stands in the doorway. She hands William a whistle on a string, which he wears around his neck. She hands him a knife, which he puts in his pocket, and it hangs heavily there.

"Don't go too far," she says.

"All right, Ma," William says. "We'll be as safe as two buns in a basket."

"If you see anyone, don't talk to them. If it starts to rain, head straight home. If you lose the dog in the woods, don't follow it. Never leave your sister alone."

We say okay and head into the field, holding hands. Sarah trots ahead of us on her rope. She stops to smell patches of interminable grass, and who knows what she's sensing, who knows what invisi-ble messages she's gathering from the land. She turns her head oc-casionally to look at me: *Are you still there?* I look into her eyes, *Yes.*

"You know," William says, "I did this so that you could leave the house." He is proud of himself, but not cocky. He stops walk-ing and hugs me. The sky hangs low overhead. "I love you. I love you so, so much. Did you know? I love you so, so, so much."

"Oh," I say. "I love you, too." I hug him back. The hug is a hug that lasts forever. I can feel his love trembling beneath his skin, like he's plugged into an outlet and love is running like elec-tricity through all of his nerves through the ends of his fingers, and when he touches me I can feel the shock, like we're going to explode. Why is it so easy for him and not for me? Maybe I'm not wired right. Maybe the bleeding isn't enough and I'm not mature yet. Maybe I'm unripe.

When we disengage from each other, I crouch in the meadow, softly calling Sarah to me; Sarah turns her long head and her mouth opens into a grin as she comes to nose my armpits, to lick my face until I laugh.

William says, "You really love this dog, huh."

"Yeah."

"Do you mind if I ask why? I don't mean to pry into the inner recesses of your heart, but you seem to love this dog all out of proportion. As if we've had her in our lives since David was around. You barely know her, and yet you spend hours with her."

"I suppose because she's mine."

"She's no one's, really. She was someone else's. Then she ran away. She seems to be a rather itinerant pup. Ma was kind enough to let you keep her in the first place. It was probably against the rules to begin with."

"Fuck the rules," I say.

"Gillian."

"I mean it!" I pull myself up. "The *rules* are of no benefit to me."

We walk farther into the long meadow, and all around us there is nothing except for a tree here and a tree there, twisting trees that have lived longer than either of us and will outlast us, too. I watch my dog's shoulders pump up and down, alternating, and after a spell of whirling thoughts—the rules, Ma's rules, the rules for me and about me—I have a wild hair about going into the woods or to the river. Why? This is the sort of thing that Ma fears: the lure of the hook and reel. I can't tell William; he'll go to Ma. William loves me but his loyalty is not to me. His heart belongs to me but his blood and bones belong to our mother.

"We should head back," he says.

"No," I say. "I want to keep going." I'm close to tears but I bite them back. I hate crying in front of William; I know it makes him sad, and I hate to look weak. I'm overcome with a sadness violent as downpour, am soaking with it. I touch the back of my neck, and for a moment I'm surprised by the lack of hair. Then I remember.

"Oh, honey," William says. "You look miserable."

I turn away. "Leave me alone—"

"I can't, honey, I can't. I'm supposed to be with you. I told Ma I would."

"Just for a second," I say, "I'm not going anywhere," and then a sob slips through my lips so that I'm choking on it; a sob is an act of violence that the body self-inflicts. I can't go anywhere. I stand and feel my body grieving without my permission to do so.

William, thank God, watches me cry without trying to put his arms around me or kiss my neck or any such thing. Sarah, who had momentarily wandered away on her rope, comes back to me in silence.

This time I don't argue when William says that it's probably time to go back. We walk back through the long meadow. I see the house, and William slips his hand in mine. "Wait. Look at me," he says. I look at him. He wipes my eyes before we go inside, wipes the tears off my face, removes the evidence, says, "Honey, chickadee, it's okay."

———◆———

These are the new rules: I'm not allowed to leave the house without Ma, William, or, preferably, both. I am not allowed to go into town. Therefore, William is not allowed to go into town, because I am not allowed to stay at home alone. Now we are having family meetings every day. In these family meetings, we talk about things that are unifying us and things that are dividing us. We are striving for things that unify us (naturally). Things that divide us must be eliminated. At this family meeting is where the rules are defined. We sit at the kitchen table. William has arranged his face in a semblance of nonchalance, picking at the table with his thumbnail. There exists an interminably mythical story about my father buying this table and having to enlarge the doors to get it in. It's one of my favorite stories about him because it seems so outlandish, and makes my father seem grand in a manner that has nothing to do with madness. One of Ma's ideas is to string bells along the top of the front and back doors, and the windows, too. She disapproves of Sarah—"the dog"—and wants me to reconsider caring for her, to which I respond by casting my eyes to my hands and refusing to look up. The night of the day that the bells are strung I wake up after some hours and it's like I never went to sleep. William has one arm flung over me, and it rises up and down like a boat on the sea.

Running away is the thought that's been whispering in my head since Ma pinned me to the bed, and it will not go away.

———◆———

In my dream the river is crowded with naked ivory bodies. They glide through the water and swim froglike, with their arms and legs sweeping outward and then retreating back to the sources of themselves—the bodies swim on and on, and they never stop or decrease in number. All of them are the same, androgynous, having not-quite-wide hips and no signs of budding or budded breasts, being not broad-shouldered and neatly bald. Odder still, I realize, is the fact that they never come up for air, but keep swimming; the river is teeming with them like ants on sugar. I call to them, as though we could communicate—*Where are you going?*—but none of them reply; still they do not come up for air, still they move with fluent urgency. And slowly the water darkens, as though a shadow has come overhead—the sky is cloudless and merrily blue—now wine-red water, darker still, now terrible blood. The stench is appalling and I clap my hand over my face, but the reek of filthy blood is not as appalling as the white bodies, which now thrash and buck and cause me to realize now that they have no faces, the fronts of their heads are as smooth as the scar on my lower back: a childhood incident. The bodies are trying to get out of the blood but cannot, and yet more bodies arrive until the inhuman bodies are crammed together, arms flailing, legs kicking, a Gordian knot of limbs, and I watch them die, their perfect white bodies now saturated in the *coeur*-color of my heart, suffocating, drowning, and yet I feel nothing.

———◆———

We are in Ma's room and the shades are pulled shut, and the lamp is on although it's morning, suffusing the room with orange. "*Xiao mei*, I feel," she says, her pale face shining, "that as your brother's *tongyangxi*, you do not fully understand the essence of the situation. The clear purpose of this life is that you and your brother will be, when I am gone, all that is truly meaningful in the world for each other. Therefore, you must learn to rely on him."

She is standing and holding a marbled aqua silk scarf, which dangles like a half-flopped fish in her hand. William and I sit on the bed side by side, our hands not touching, our hands resting on our knees. She has her back against the armoire, and the mirror reflects us. My hair surprises me. I see that I've dropped weight, evidenced by my emerging cheekbones and the scoop of my collar, and I look ugly to myself; I remind myself of the way Sarah looked when I first found her, starving, with ribs showing, and lost. I can feel and see William's tension from where I sit—he is still and stiff, the good child, but nervous, perhaps, on my behalf in anticipation of whatever is to come.

Ma says, "We are going to play a game. I will blindfold Gillian. I have placed a ten-dollar bill somewhere in the kitchen. It is lying in plain sight, and yet Gillian won't be able to see it. William, you will sit in a chair and direct Gillian by speaking to her. You can't tell her where she is in the kitchen. You can't describe to her the surroundings—you understand? But you can tell her how to move in the room. If she puts her hands on anything that is not the ten-dollar bill, she doesn't get the money. If she puts her hands on the ten-dollar bill, I will buy her something that she asks for, within reason, when I next go into town. See. It's very simple, and there is a reward—not just the money, but a way to show that you are connected."

Ma moves toward me with the scarf-turned-blindfold. An easy game—child's play, of course. But why not put the blindfold on William to show him that he needs to rely on me as well? If I succeed, there's a ten-dollar bill that can buy me a treat, and I could use a treat—I am subsumed by ennui and there is that idea of beginning taxidermy, for which I could use supplies. But something whispers inside of me: this is not what I want, and I don't like the tone of her voice, which bubbles with danger, and swells with impending punishment. I envision a burner left on on the stove, broken glass on the table, my hands cut to shreds as I pathetically attempt to grab for cash.

Ma holds the blindfold to my face, blue spilling over my eyes like water, and as soon as the cool silk touches my forehead I snatch it without thinking and I shove her with even less thought. Ma slaps me hard and I ball the scarf up in my hand, but I don't cry and there is no such thing as pain.

William says, "Gillian," and I wait to be struck again.

"I'm sorry that I hit you," Ma says. She touches my stinging cheek. "Come here, *xiao baobao*," she says, and wraps her arms around me. "I only wanted you and your brother to be closer. It was a game that a friend of mine played with her brother when she was younger, before I knew her. She was his *tongyangxi*. Come on, *ge*," she says, "give your sister a hug. Show her that you love her."

He does. I feel like a crazy person.

"Let's try this again. I will blindfold you. Yes?"

I nod. She wraps the scarf around my eyes and ties it. She takes my hand—her hand is soft, fleshy, and warm—and walks me into the kitchen. The scent of oil, herbs, salt. The warmth of the stove. I feel the dirt beneath my feet, crumbs underneath the pads of my heels, the cold sun hitting my knees. She takes my shoulders and turns me around and around. For a while I can maintain a sense of where I am. But she keeps turning, and I keep turning, and I lose my bearings; I can no longer be sure where the sun is, and probably the feeling of its light was imagined in the first place.

I hear William sit behind me. "Yes. I see it," he says. "You can do this, sweetheart. Keep your hands behind your back so that you don't touch anything. I'll tell you when to reach your hand out. You'll do it slowly, so that you don't touch the wrong thing. I'll direct you with utter specificity. All right. So take a step forward. This is going to be very simple, sweetheart. Go slowly. Take another step."

I move. I shuffle as he guides me—first forward, then to the right.

"Okay, love," he says, "now this is the tricky part. Slowly take your hand—I suppose your right hand—and lift it about a foot, maybe shoulder height. No, lower a bit. Keep your hand close to your body—I don't want you to touch anything you shouldn't. A little bit lower. All right. Now, move it slowly forward. Keep your hand flat... don't move your hand up or down. Oh—it's hard for me to—it's hard for me to direct you from here; it's hard to see where—well, where your hand is in relation to the money..."

"No standing up," Ma instructs.

William says, "All right. Well, let me think about this. It's hard to do it from this angle, but I think you need to move your hand an inch to the right. Then slowly down. You should be touching the money then."

I move my hand an inch to the right. I move my hand down, but my fingers touch a smooth and metallic surface. Strategically I slide my hand a millimeter to the right, and this is when I feel the familiar sensation of clothlike paper beneath my pinky.

"I have it," I say. "Look, I have it, I have it." I'm surprised by how relieved I am.

Someone comes up behind me. I can smell Ma's perfume: jasmine and jonquil. She removes my blindfold and says, "You didn't win." She takes the money from me, and I'm standing in front of the counter, facing the traitorous bread box.

"We'll play again next week," Ma says. "Maybe you'll do better then."

I say nothing. I am ready to walk out of the room when Ma says, as if it is an afterthought, "And you are no longer allowed to feed that dog from our refrigerator. We only have so much food every week, and to watch you take good food and give it to an animal is ridiculous."

"It's not so much food," I say, but I know this isn't the problem. We could have an infinite supply of loaves and fishes, and Ma would still not want me to feed a distraction. The dog is an outsider as much as are the outsiders who shuffle and shove and grunt in town; the dog does not belong in the orderly paradise of our home, or with the trinity of Ma and William and me.

My eyes burn. I walk out of the room, half thinking she'll grab me, but I walk past her and neither she nor William touch any part of me; I go out the front door, where Sarah, who was curled up on the porch, suddenly leaps up to greet me, and I kneel to bury my face in the fur at her neck where the rope is loosely tied, inhaling the scent of her. She is wild with excitement, enormous, rising up to put her paws on my thighs. She licks my cheek. I startle and gasp and then I laugh, without thinking, at this pup who has come for me, and then I untie her from the post. I kiss her on the head; I tell her to go.

———◆———

Nighttime. A sea of crickets warbles in the darkness. William is presumably in the bathroom when I enter our room with cold feet and cold hands. The sheets are bunched in a heap against the wall; I shut the door and climb under the covers, where my exhalations are. William and I used to play Caves of Adullam this way. There wasn't much to the game besides being under the covers together, where we declared that we were hiding. A girl and a boy, sister and brother.

If I had a sister, what would she be like? Would we play Caves? Would she be as much of a hassle as me? It would just be the two of us. Two girls to play and not touch bodies except to cuddle, to braid hair, to kiss without next steps.

Sarah is gone. For a time she stayed, untied, hours spent lying on the porch. Her suppertime came and went with no supper to show for it. I heard her paw at the door—Ma heard it, too, and grimaced, shaking her head. With the pawing came a soft whine. And then—I don't know exactly when—she took off and left me here. In the cave I press my face into the mattress, but I can't seem to cry. I worry that if I start to cry William will come in and notice, and then he'll want to talk about it. He'll want to comfort me when his comfort is the last thing I want.

I predict that he will come in to talk to me but he doesn't. Even in the room, under the blankets, I hear him talking to Ma.

He says, "I don't think it was right."

He could be talking about the blindfold game, or perhaps he is talking about Sarah.

Ma replies, "I know more than either of you do."

William: "She's not a thing you can just play with!"

Ma: "Listen to yourself. Don't let her bad influence get to you. You know better than that."

William: "She loves me. I know she does. You don't have to play these kinds of games with her. You upset her. Can't you see that?"

Ma: "I love you both too much. That's why I do what I do, and that's why you rebel. You don't completely understand love—neither of you do, but especially Gillian. My job is to make sure that both of you are full of the right kind of love. Until then, you're vulnerable to bad things."

William: "She loves the dog."

There is a long pause. "I know she does. The dog will not be a problem for much longer."

They must be in the kitchen. I don't want to leave the cave, but it's getting hard to breathe. When William comes into the room we do the following things: play a few games of Rime Riche, listen to Bach's Partita no. 6 in E Minor while on our backs, hold each other, and then we take our clothes off.

———◆———

In the morning I play "Dynamite Rag" and "The Louisiana Rag" over and over again with a soft sweater over my pink slip in acknowledgment of the fall, my bare feet tapping and occasionally soft-pedaling as William sits on the sofa with a bowl of oatmeal, his hair disheveled in a manner that I might consider wanton, but choose to see as an extension of his overburdened IQ. Because who could care about one's hair if one is busy, as he is, with taking on the task of learning all of Beethoven's sonatas—the exception being the *Hammerklavier*, which he has not yet tackled, and is saving for when he is older and his fingers are wiser. Because he has his whole life to do so. On the other hand, I have no project. My project is to live until I die. Or maybe I can take up a hobby, like embroidery or crochet; more realistically, I've decided, I can take up my father's old love of taxidermy, and add to my trunk of corpses. I think that I could be good at that. When I was small I watched him take apart animals and stitch them back up, and his taxidermy manuals and pamphlets—*Amazing New Methods for Mounting Decoy Owls, Nothing Spared—Boat-Caulking Cotton and Fine Bone Winding*—are still tucked into the bookcase. I could start with a rabbit's foot, and work my way up to entire creatures. My musty museum in the making.

I don't know why I continue to play the piano these days. Habit, I suppose. It brings me no pleasure. There's no pleasure even though I'm good at it. I'm not like William, whose body seems to be wired for the pursuit of two things: myself and Beethoven. I think that after my father, and then Mrs. Kucharski, died, I really did stop caring about the piano. Over the last few days even the sound of it has begun to rub at my nerves, because the piano is coming out of tune, and I hear this new sound emerge like a hatchling; but I play it anyway with determination.

"I think, buglet," William says between songs, "that we've got a bit of a tuning problem. When did we last address your piano?" he asks, because we are the ones who tune the piano, we are the ones who were taught by our father to strike a tuning fork, to turn the tuning lever gently and slowly, to never settle for a cheap instrument, and besides, I have perfect pitch, which William does not.

"It's sort of been a gradual problem," I reply.

"I guess. Crept up. Well, we ought to do something about that," he says, scraping the sides of his bowl, "before it gets any worse."

When Ma comes into the living room and sits next to William, adjusting the neckline of her robe, William says to her, "Gillian's piano is out of tune—we were just saying."

"Well, then fix it. Easy enough."

"We will. We can work on that tomorrow while you're in town."

While you're in town. A flash of bitterness crosses my eyes at the casual drop of news. I will be minded at home; William will be busy minding. I see the K & Bee projected onto the white-and-black backdrop of keys, and the market's gorgeous cacophony of tins and bags: *buy me, look at me.* I want to buy and I want to look at the tinned meat and the women with their long hair and long skirts. The boys with pale skin and sunny hair. And I have lost my dog, the dog who provided me with such electric joy over the last epoch of my brittle life. The feeling of bitterness—so closely linked anger and sadness—melts to ache. So we'll have a few hours without Ma. He'll want to pursue intimacy. An hour of sex, an hour tuning the piano. The word *tune.* The sound of the word *two* encased within the hard *d.* To tune the body. To make it accurate, strip it down to its essential nature.

I saw Sarah in the morning. I did. I saw her at dawn. Was it my imagination, or did she already look thinner? I did not feed her because I knew that Ma was watching. If Ma wasn't actually in the hall, gazing out at me, she was staring from a crack in her bedroom door. She would know what I had done. As she said to William, she knows more than either of us does; she always knows everything.

"It is time to clean the kitchen," Ma says. "Come."

My brother stands, holding his bowl and spoon. He smiles at me.

"I'll be there in a second," I say.

Ma goes into the hall, her sturdy yet slender body dragging the too-long robe behind her, and William, not knowing yet whether to follow, stands in the living room entranceway. "What are you doing?"

I answer, "A consultation."

I go to the bookshelf. William begins to hum—the "Adagio Cantabile" from *Pathétique*, his particular sign of pleasure. I take out the *OED* volume that houses the word *tune. Tundra, tundrite. Tune.* Common meanings: "sound or tone." Here it is. A former meaning: "to close, shut; to fence or enclose."

"What were you looking for?" he asks as I put the book away.

I tell him nothing. I believe in the predictive nature of language.

Sarah is noticeably thinner through the window. She comes still to the house and paces the porch, whining, and will sometimes sound a bark. She is wondering why I won't come to say hello and to feed her.

Days and nights slither by and Sarah still comes with hope.

She comes and comes, and I know the *guai baobao* is more faithful than I will ever be.

One night I lie in bed for a few minutes, listening to William's steady breathing, and then I move his arm without waking him. I slip off the bed. I move into the kitchen.

It's dark. Everything smells like dank and wet wood and is cold to touch. The bells are strung across the tops of the doors and along the windows, an eternal celebration. I sit in the middle of the kitchen, on the floor, and I try to summon my courage; I could walk out that door. I could make the bells ring. I could run faster than either of them—I could run like a deer-girl, a cervine escape artist. Around the house, down the road, down the mountain, down the hills, both deft and light of foot, faster than a car, faster than anything. I don't know how to drive or write a check, but I do know how to run—always have. I practically sprinted out of the womb—I was eager to get into the world. I could find refuge at St. Joseph's Church, where the men brought us during the fire, where it is the job of the holy to take in the helpless. I could find a tendril of bravery inside myself to breathe upon, to make into a blazing flame. It is difficult to be a girl because girls have wills, but no control. It is difficult to be a girl because girls are full of wondering, and then they want to go out wandering. The question is not *Will I get away?* but *Is it really so bad?* If I start to feel foolish on the floor, with my legs folded in front of me, maybe it is better if I slink back to my room like a shy thing, climb back into bed, feel the sourness in my belly turn hard onto itself, become a better version of myself, feel more kindness, show more love.

Though I have never prayed in earnest before—not when my father was so sick—so, so, so sick—and I have never thought of God as a constant presence in my life, and though I've always wanted to believe in the existence of God, instead of in the existence of nothing, I mouth, *Please, let me love. Please.* I go to the refrigerator. I open it as silently as I can. I take a plate from the dish rack, and I say, *Our Father, who art in Heaven, hallowed be thy name. Thy kingdom come, thy will be done, on earth as it is in Heaven. Give us this day our daily bread, and forgive us our trespasses, as we forgive those who trespass against us, and lead us not into temptation, but deliver us from evil.* I gather a bone and some withered vegetables.

I almost drop the plate because I'm so tired, but I don't drop it and I close the refrigerator door. In my head I say the Our Father again. I unlatch the locks on the front door. I open the front door in increments, so slowly that I've breathed a hundred breaths before there's enough space for me to shimmer through. The bells are silent and hang across the room, hang across the right side.

———◆———

In the morning William lies half naked in bed—his slumber the result of orgasm's peculiarly soporific effect on him—and I am reorganizing the furniture in our room, because sex has the opposite effect on me, and makes it both hard to fall asleep and jittery in conscious life so that I must do something with my hands. I should be playing the piano, but Ma isn't awake, isn't wandering around the house or sitting at the kitchen table with her tea, and I don't feel like playing for no one. Perhaps this is what amplifies the jitters today: unfamiliarity. The house is the whole world; one thing out of place sets everything else off its axis. I thought I heard Sarah barking in my dreams, but I haven't gone to see her yet. Instead I am arranging several mason jars along the lip of the wide windowsill, which I've filled with various things: creatures' teeth, bleached white bones, pearl buttons. I am waiting for the familiar sounds; I am waiting for Ma's footsteps. I'm a good girl, and Ma will know this soon enough, and she will treat me as she treats William if I do the right things. She will be glad to know that William is asleep and that I am being good. And maybe she'll buy something for me after all, despite the fact that I didn't win the game—maybe a little sweet treat, or something new to play with.

Instead I hear a yell, or perhaps a cry of anger. I take my hand off the last jar and go into the hallway. Light from the half-open front door tumbles into the house, and I see Ma standing to face Sarah, who is at her plate of food, my miracle born from prayer.

But at once each second pulls my nerves along a crescendo. Ma curses Sarah with a line of Taiwanese. She bends to take the plate of food and Sarah leaps at her, and there is a clatter and a scream, a half-birthed scream that barely escapes her throat and is suffocated before she screams again, more loudly this time, and then there is no screaming because Sarah's jaws are clamped around her neck and she falls. I watch this with hot terror leaching from my bones as Ma's blood comes now in great gushing gouts. It's the screaming that wakes William; it is what drags William out of sleep, along with the sound of horrible thrashing, the sound of something banging into floorboards again and again, and gurgling, too. And when Ma emits her thin, watery scream again, William jerks to sitting and scrambles off the bed in his underwear, his thin figure suddenly shot through and wild with electricity, and I, too, am shot through with it to see him leap off the bed and onto the floor, where he runs out the bedroom door and we both stand in the hallway listening. William is too far away to watch, but I am still near the half-open door. William moves toward it.

"No," I yell. "She's going to attack you, too. Stop!"

And I slam the door shut. In doing so I am committing the greatest act of treason I can think of, but whatever is happening out there is not safe, and—dare I even think this—it may even be Fate. By listening to Ma's death and staring at William in the way that I do I am possessed, possessed with the deaths of all the firstborn sons in Egypt, from the firstborn son of the Pharaoh, who sits on the throne; to the firstborn son of the slave girl, who is at her hand mill; and all the firstborn of the cattle as well. I feel my body stiffening, and then I begin to shudder uncontrollably. *Please* mark lamb's blood on the doorposts of every door. Dear children, death children, please mark lamb's blood on the doorposts, and I will keep you safe. Here is the knife with which to slice open the throat of the lamb. Dear children: weep not at the death of the adorable lamb. What otherwise? Suffer the destroyer to come into your houses and smite you.

William and I stare at each other as the world pulls itself away. This is the moment when one of us could exit this house and do something. We could potentially shift the course of our mother's destiny. I challenge him with my eyes to do it, to walk past me and open the door and make his bid as savior, but in my look I'm now stronger than I've ever been before because I am a part of something bigger than myself. I am the whole world stuffed into one girl's body. I have oceans for blood and skies for eyes.

He does nothing. Neither of us do anything. After many minutes the timbre of the air has changed. William is crying hysterically and I've never seen him this upset—certainly not when our father stabbed himself in the stomach and bled out in a motel room, nor when Ma came back from Sacramento with bloodshot eyes and told us that it was over; but right now this is over, too—it is over. Of this, I am certain.

MISSIVES

WILLIAM (1972)

*D*ear Gillian,
  I don't know where you are presently. I realize that if you never return that this letter will have been written in vain. I have no one to talk to if I don't have you, and so this letter will serve a function, whether you come through that door or not. (Will you come through the front door or the back? Will you climb through the window? The world is full of interminable mysteries, small duck, and we both know that many of the world's mysteries are foggier to us than they are to most.) If you disappear, I don't know what I'll do.

First of all, despite our fight, I will say that I am not "angry" at you with regards to Ma's death. (Do you think that the dog—I apologize for using the word cur, *and I was angry—is coming back, do you think? I refuse to speak its name because I am being superstitious. I know you think me ridiculous but, I think, it is better to be protected than not.) I cannot be angry when you thought that you were doing the right thing by keeping me from seeing the scene. And I especially cannot be angry when you love me, and I love you.*

Still, I might add that you did not have to bury Ma, and though I insisted on doing it myself, the fact that I did adds an extra burden to me that I deem unfair, if it is not ultimately terrible of me to say so. Her face was ravaged. Our mother had become, for the most part, a nightmare. Her eyes, fortunately, were for the most part untouched, but I couldn't get them to close. I put my fingers to her eyelids and brought them down, but they would not stay down, and I buried her with a wound for a face—Gillian, I won't say anything more about it, but it seems appropriate that some of it be mentioned, if only so I am not the only victim here. If that dog digs up her body—well. Let's not venture there. I do not know where you are and this makes me more nervous than you can possibly know, kitten. When you disappear like this I don't know if you'll ever come back. I'm not an idiot; I know that your life, and especially your life as of late, has been less than satisfactory to you, no matter what you say. When you try to be kind, I mean, I can sense it. But I am older than you and wiser than you, and I'm afraid that you are vulnerable to mistakes and misconceptions.

Last night's fight upset me a great deal. We have both been upset. The echo of David's loss is still familiar to me. To have Ma gone so suddenly has been, I might say, worse for us than that one. I have thought at times that we will not be able to continue, or that I will awaken to find myself in Heaven with all of us there, because it seems so unfathomable that life should stumble on.

But if I didn't know any better (and I do, remember, I do) I would say that you were glad... and I can barely bring myself to write that word, glad, but I won't scratch it out. That's why I shoved you the way that I did, with that force. It was the phrase "act of God" that did it. I was out of my mind to hear it, as much as you were out of your mind to say it.

It killed me, sweetheart, to see the bruises! To know that I could hurt you in any way is deeply troubling to me. That is not the brother I am and it is not the husband that I want to be.

And so could I be surprised, really, when I opened my eyes this morning and, after reaching out, found that you were missing? Despite my bad act, don't you think that you're being a little—no, more than a little—cruel?

It has been a week since I buried Ma, and still I find myself thinking of her decay more than of our survival. We will survive, somehow. We will keep the house. What kind of rejection are you plotting, when you say that you're, as you put it, "unsure" of our position now? Whatever you might say, I fear that it cannot be borne.

I love you, and no one else will ever love you as much as I do—because no one else will ever know you, or our differences from others, as deeply. Don't be foolish. Don't forget.

W.

———◆———

She enters the house from the front with her short hair live and wispy around her face, her arms hugging a full paper bag to her chest. I recognize the brown bag when I see its logo: she left, she went to the K & Bee, but she has returned. Her presence in the doorway, and then in the hall, reminds me of lucid dreams I've had in which I reenter my body after going to the stars—the tumbling, and then relief and resettling into the self.

"You had me worried," I say. And, embarrassed by the break in my voice, I add: "You and I, we need to set some rules, Gillian— we need to set some rules."

"You," she says calmly, "are not any sort of parental figure to me." And she slips off her shoes, which forces me to look at her long white feet. She has painted her toenails pink with polish gotten, no doubt, from Ma's bedroom, whereas I don't dare enter that tomb. I do not recall seeing Gillian's toenails painted prior to this moment, and how was I to know that she was even interested in this, this minor thing, this feminine superficiality of painting one's toenails, if not for my pleasure? She begins to walk, slightly waddling, to the kitchen. The house is so empty with only us in it. She is too strong to be really waddling under the weight of the bag, although she must have been walking for hours to get from town to our home, and this bag can't have been light. I realize that she must be waddling because the soles of her feet are blistered.

"And you got food, I see," I say, following her into the kitchen.

"Someone had to do it."

"You could have gotten lost."

"I knew the route, shockingly enough, because I pay attention to things."

"Still. Something could have happened to you. Muggers. Rapists. Murderers. You know this."

"I knew the route," she says, "better than you do, I'm sure of it. And I brought a knife." The bag is on the floor now. She sits in her favorite kitchen chair and pulls the knife out of her dress pocket, waving it at me—the sight of it makes my stomach curdle—before placing it on the table. "But by golly, am I exhausted—be a darling and unpack the groceries for me."

"You're avoiding the subject."

"So how was your morning," she says.

"For example."

"Please unpack the groceries."

I hate this frivolity. Gillian has *changed*. Or perhaps she's anguished, the sort of anguish that can't look itself in the face. We've both cried since the death. I'd say that Gillian cried more hysterically than I did, and though it was no show, its abbreviated nature strikes me as bizarre; she walked around with swollen eyes for days, and then suddenly her grief was over before it had barely begun. She asked, "How are we going to get to town? How do we drive? Who's going to gas up the Buick? How are we going to get food?" "Let's just mourn, all right?" I replied, feeling lost. Again I reference last night's fight. I'd accused her of horrible things, hurling accusations at her and that mutt. She'd bristled and screamed. We are both a mess. It's true, though, that she's gone to some trouble to get these groceries, which we did need. The refrigerator was empty save for an apple and a chunk of hardening cheddar; I think bitterly, momentarily, of all the food she gave to that bitch. I sit on the floor, the way that Ma used to after a day of shopping, and lift things out of the bag. We are in a strange limbo with regards to Ma's death. Even I, the one who buried her, can't believe that she's underground. I know this because Gillian pointed it out last night, during our fight—the fight partially regarding the issue of practicalities, because I seem to have no interest in practicalities. I am sure that we are both in some form of denial, with Gillian's denial being more severe than mine. She did kill her, after all, though I'd never say this gruesome fact aloud. I danced around it and her immature obsession with that damn mutt last night, even in my anger. I have no idea how this denial came to be; our mother was here, ever present, and then she was not here, and is completely gone. If I imagine David, he seems so far away as to only exist in myth, while Ma's death is so fresh that it seems she's only gone to Sacramento, and left us to our own devices for a second honeymoon, a sweet caress. If only I hadn't tried to close her eyes! Even then, it seems that she is only momentarily absent. I cannot reconcile the face in my memory with the wet wound that tries to shove its way in.

"How are we going to get money?" Gillian had asked. "How are we supposed to live? Are we getting jobs, William? Do you want me to, hmm, work? Oldest profession in the book? Because I know it so well by now..."

"That's not funny."

"You have no sense of humor. I'd forgotten," she'd said, turned cruel.

Where did these hard edges come from? From my soft sister, the one who played jaunty songs for her Daddy.

"We can't mourn forever," she'd said. "And we can't be trapped in this house forever."

I have no interest in practicalities because Ma will rise out of her shallow grave and come back into the house. She will come out of her tomb and tell us what we are to do, because I have never known what to do, and for whatever morbid reason my sister seems to be more concerned with issues such as driving the Buick and achieving financial security than she is with explosive tragedy. Even the word *death* seems inadequate and overly soft. I remove a bag of red peppers, which are expensive. There's a soft, wrapped thing that smells like fish, and when I read the scrawl it is fish, a lukewarm rainbow trout.

I say, "You bought fish."

"We always eat fish. What's wrong with fish?" Gillian runs her fingers through her hair, picking at her scalp with her fingernails. She finds some clogged pore or piece of dried skin and examines it at the tip of her finger before flicking it away, her long arm flying.

"You don't know how to cook fish."

Brown potatoes—we can always do with potatoes—and eggs. She has selected a few stalks of broccoli that look good and fresh, with cut white ends.

"Rules," I say again.

"Don't leave the house?"

"Without me. I'm not trapping you anywhere; I'm simply asking that I accompany you if you want to go into town. I have the right to leave the house as much as you do."

"And the property?"

"The property is large. I don't think it's safe anymore."

"Not since the man came, you mean."

"That's what I mean, and because Ma is gone."

She lifts one foot into her lap and begins to rub it. Her fingers move carefully around the sore spots. In her loose dress I can barely see the shape of her body beneath, but it doesn't matter because I know it, and it belongs to us; it is our shared property. I can see the blisters on her soles. Tentatively she presses her finger into one of them, and then releases the bubble. This blister belongs to us as well.

Milk, cans of mandarin oranges (a special treat), a smallish bag of rice.

"No rules," she says without tone. "I'll just break them. I'll live how I want."

"And how do you want?" I do not append an endearment.

"I'm still figuring that out."

"Oh, come on."

"All right. I want you to move out of my room. My great hope is that, before long, it will look like nothing ever changed. I think that the expression on your face is more than enough to let me know how you feel about that, but I want my own space again, and no one is alive to govern where I lay my head."

"That makes absolutely no sense. Everything," I say, "is completely arranged in the room as you like it. All of it is yours, your things are everywhere—there is *barely* anything in there that's mine—"

"It's not my room. It's our room, where I am your *tongyangxi*. Which has been made completely clear to me over the last three months."

"And so you'll sleep in what was my room, and live in yours?" As the words roll out I realize that this is a fatuous question. Of course she will not. What this really means is the end of her body's relationship with mine, which feels like a violation and a broken promise, both. "What you're saying is that you're ending things?" The question is not a question, and then I say, "This is massively wrong. No, you can't do this."

"Oh?"

"Yes! Our lives are written out in a certain way, and just because we're alone now doesn't mean that we're free to do whatever we like. It's not a matter of rules or an immature rebellion against rules. This is a commandment you're violating."

"But why the commandment? Why was it written out that way?"

"What kind of question is that—"

"A legitimate one—"

"I've explained this a million times!"

"It shouldn't need explaining," she says, and now she's moved her body forward such that the force of her physical presence is turned at me. The honesty, the brutality, of her body kills me. "I don't want to do it anymore."

"The serpent's got you," I say.

"But I was already gotten." And maybe there's a bit of sadness to her voice. It's possible that there is sadness there, or perhaps it's sadness that I want to hear.

I say, "I can't stand it."

"You'll overcome it," she says. But when my eyes blur, she comes over to me. She wraps her arms around my body, and the smell of her dusky body, unperfumed and sweaty, makes me choke. "Sorry," she says. "That was mean." She kisses me on the temple, on the cheek, on the corner of my mouth. Without thinking, I shift my face slightly such that my lips press against hers.

"Dammit, William," she says, and turns her face away.

She needs to know that this is wrong. I could also slap her, but did I not just promise that I'd refrain from physical force? She is stronger; still, I could smash the back of her skull with a skillet, though I am sure that both crying and striking are the wrong avenues to walk—too weak, too off-putting, or both. What she needs is to be unbitten, and this I don't know how to do.

———◆———

At night, to know that she is two doors down, but not available to me, makes my skin itch. I press my face into the sheets and smell the bleachy, musky scent of us commingled, the sheet starched from the liquid of my insides. I haven't washed the sheets since our honeymoon. Here is a mark of deep black from when she was bleeding, and though she cramped and gritted her teeth we'd made love anyway. I hug my knees to my chest. Mentally I go through the sheets, crawling over every inch of our atlas. The saliva spots of my mouth pressed and moaning against the pillow. The smell of clean hair, and of greasy hair that's gone unwashed, which I love because it is completely her stench.

I don't know how long this goes on. Forever. Hours. I climb out of bed and sneak into Gillian's unlocked room. In the shadows she is snoring slightly at a low, steady octave. I can't see her in the darkness, but I know that comforting sound. Her breathing staggers and slows. I lie on the floor beside the bed, hoping that the floorboards won't creak, and I feel myself on a deerskin. The skin is short-haired, and when I press my body against it I try to derive sensations of life from it, a bed of flesh, but it is cold and smells like dust. I am falling asleep, and as I fall asleep lights flash behind my lids like a punch to the head. I am dazzled.

The next thing is Gillian shaking me. I am immediately awake. The beginnings of her exclamations are at first a haze. Then: "What are you doing here?" She repeats this a few more times, as though I'm incapable of English and she's making sounds at that dog of hers. But then I hear her words curl themselves around my neurons and I realize that she's angry, she's quite angry, one could even say that she's furious with me for coming into her room. She kicks me. Not hard. She lectures me about violating the borders of her room, where she was sleeping alone. She says "alone" pointedly. She tells me that I appear to have not understood her previous declaration. She says that I'm a jerk, but I hear a thread of fear running through the warp and woof of her voice. I've caused that. I apologize. She sighs. She says, "Don't do it again."

Dear Gillian,

I am embarrassed and annoyed that I'm having to resort to these envelopes and letters again, and taping them to your door as though I'm some sort of missive-bearing dove with a branch in its beak. I feel, to be honest, much less dignified than that bird. But when you spend the majority of your time away from home, and the rest of the time that you're not out who knows where in your room, where you have made it interminably clear that you don't want me, and I get your horrible looks when I do try to come in—so here I am, writing these letters, getting the tape, pressing them to your door. I can call this communication. Well, this is the second letter. It was hurtful for you to slip the unopened envelope under my door. I presume this means that you could do it again. So I could be writing this pointlessly. You may never read this letter, and I have to come to terms with that, as I've had to come to terms with everything these days.

I miss you. I don't think I've made that clear enough. When I say that I miss you, I don't mean to make you feel guilty or otherwise ill about yourself, simply because I'm miserable without you. I'm telling you that I miss you so that you'll fully understand that I'm not just after you for the sexual reasons. I understand that you might feel as though I've forgotten about who we were before the honeymoon, but I never, ever did, Gillian, my sweet-as-sugar dearest heart, my wordplay part-

ner, the doe to my dear, the treble to my bass. And I could go on, about how I am one-half of a duet without my partner piece.

Such as: I could tell you that I remember the time that you first ex-amined my dreams. Do you remember this? You were very, very small. You were three. I'd had a dream that Ma took me dress shopping in Sacramento, and in the dream I was excited to the point of having the faints. I woke up from the faints, which was waking up in the dream, and when I told you that I "woke up" in the dream (this was complicat-ed for a five-year-old to explain to a three-year-old, I understand now) you asked me, "And what color was the dress Ma bought?" Something like that. I said, "It was black, with a bird painted on the skirt." You said, "The dress was black because you're afraid Daddy will die and Ma will fly away." I swear that you said this, and you probably won't believe me, but you said this. Perhaps you are a prophet.

So you can see that I remember things—I remember that, and I re-member the games we played, and I remember how happy we've always been. We have always been happy.

W.

This letter is then slipped under my door again, unopened. I rip it into pieces—not small enough pieces, in my humble opinion.

◆

Something in Gillian has changed, but an increase in happiness doesn't seem to be it. She does seem more solid, as though she were porous before and is now achieving heft. When she eats fruit at the table she is really there and she is really eating fruit. When I say she doesn't seem happier I mean that she doesn't smile, or laugh, but she does seem to be more in the here and now. The flippancy that disturbed me earlier has simmered down, and in its place is a girl who still spends hours in her room with the door closed, but is present. I can't explain it. When Gillian comes out of "her" bedroom, sometimes it's like we're strangers in a hotel. I've also never been in a hotel, but apparently our parents spent plenty of time in hotels when they were first married, and I've heard enough about them. The concept is bizarre to me, the expression something like "A home away from home," as though you were attempting to escape something, but why escape, and why are you escaping to something that is like home, but can't be as good? And you pay for it, apparently. Gillian accuses me of not thinking enough, but that is stupidity.

Such a lovely girl, with such meanness available to her. She comes out of Ma's room, holding a fistful of envelopes with the tops torn. "We have to think about money," she says. As soon as she says it, I realize that there are small, forgotten things about Ma ad infinitum as yet unspoken, such as the fact that she was the one to get the mail, and we were never allowed to accompany her when she went down the mountain to retrieve it. Here is Gillian with the envelopes in her hands, the stripped envelopes with the stern typewriting between her fingers. I start to panic.

"Were you snooping in there?" I ask.

A growl rises from the back of her throat. "It's not *snooping*, it's trying to survive. Look. It looks like we have some receipts here. I imagine they're from... checks that come from somewhere."

She hands me a folded piece of paper, on which there are things like "Total Balance" and "Investment Returned" and "Allowance for 9/1/72–9/31/72." The numbers are big, but big compared with what? There is a name, and a signature.

"Alan Topor?" I ask.

"I don't know. He seems to deal with our money," Gillian says. "I think. All of these envelopes have his name on them. And they all say an address with NY. Maybe he knew Dad back in New York."

"Mmm."

"Money, William. We need to think about money. Doesn't this seem like a lot of it? Thousands of dollars of an allowance? Compared to a week's worth of groceries? Are we rich, do you know? Can you imagine that we're rich?"

"Do we seem rich to you?" is what I say. And then, "This is profoundly, profoundly morbid. I can't believe you were snooping in there."

She ignores this. "We'll be fine as long as we keep getting the mail."

"Are you listening to yourself? You don't know the first thing about how to use a check. So you take it to the bank, if you can figure out where that is. We don't know the first thing about banks. Can you just show up and get money? How will they know we're Nowaks? We don't exist outside of the property."

"I'm sure we can figure it out," Gillian says, and stares at the envelopes again. "I'm honestly not trying to be morbid. You've got to realize that this solves so many of our problems—you've got to see that we're in an enormous amount of trouble if we don't figure out what we're doing. If these come monthly, we're not going to starve. As long as we can figure out the money situation, we'll be all right..."

Why don't I care about such things? Is it because of the rejection and sleeping alone that I've fallen into despair? She's still reading the letters, looking at the receipts. I don't even ask her to hand them over. She is flipping through the papers in her hands and pulling sheets out of every envelope, examining, and in the haze of my fear I see her in my mind's eye using the bedroom phone to call up this Topor fellow and getting money out of this somehow, after which she runs away and leaves me here, oh God.

"At some point, we'll have to go through all of the things in her room," she says.

"We?"

"Yes. As in you and me. There are probably plenty of things of importance in there."

"It's morbid," I say.

"You're incorrigible," she says. "But if you won't do it, I will." She pulls back her lips in a faux snarl, and there is some food caught in between her teeth, something soft the color of bread, which reveals itself as she smiles. Faintly, like a burp: disgust, an unfamiliar feeling. I reach out and grab the papers from her. Then I begin to tear them as I exit to the kitchen, with Gillian yelling behind me.

"What are you doing?" she screams.

I turn on the burner and drop the pieces into the flame, and they curl and disappear quickly into ash.

She slaps at me, her hands on my shoulders and upper arm, but I barely feel them. Her eyes are lit green.

"I may love you more than anyone on this earth," I say. "But I'm not helpless."

Gillian whirls away from me and out of the kitchen. Ma's bedroom door slams, its lock clicking into place. I am triumphant, though I know better than to gloat now that I, for once, have the upper hand. Should another letter come in a month, as Gillian anticipates, I'll deal with the new intrusion then. Much can change in a month, I remind myself.

Gillian tersely cooks trout as I read, and when she calls me to dinner there it is, laid out: the trout on a platter with soy sauce, two bowls of wet-looking rice (off-putting, but perfect for xi fan), and a bowl of withered mustard greens, cooked in the same garlic-and-soy-sauce combination as the trout was. We eat everything like starving children, proving to ourselves that we are all right alone and even fully capable of being human beings and almost adults, even if the fish looks slightly underdone. Gillian eats the eyeball. I have the tender cheek. We suck on delicate bones and pick the skeleton clean. I finish the too-salty, bitter greens. Then I wash the dishes while she sits at the kitchen table and sings to me, and I marvel at her shifting moods as she softly croons "O Rupakach," but something is still not feeling right. I sing along, badly.

Later we are sick. Sick as dogs, sicker than we've ever been before, and we take turns vomiting into the toilet as the other expels into a gray bucket. We have runny bowels and then alternate the use of the toilet for that, until we are vomiting and I feel my bowels clench and expand simultaneously in multiple spasms, but Gillian is on the toilet with her face in her hands; I run out the back door and, undignified, am rudely, horrifyingly sick outdoors by a tree in the dark. This illness goes on and on with no time by which to measure it. With my pants half-down and my body convulsing I want to die; and it is nighttime, so the insects are investigating my vulnerable body and disgusting rump, though my spasming intestines take precedent over the vague and growing itch. After the sickness abates I practically crawl into the house, weak and trembling, down the hall, and pass out on the living room floor with my trousers up, unable to summon the consciousness needed to wipe myself clean with something to be buried deep in the yard later. I dream of climbing a tall ladder against the side of the house. Ma is telling me to do something on the roof. I'm too afraid to climb up the ladder and do whatever it is that she wants me to do. When I look down at her I notice that her face is blurry beyond recognition, as though it's been smeared by an upset thumb.

I awaken, feeling sick for multiple reasons. The sun isn't up yet; the light against the windows is a bruise. Soon it will be cold. In the bathroom I see that Gillian is curled up against the tub, and the air is fetid with the expulsions of our insides. I want to carry her out of the room and be alone to wash myself. It's the first time that I've wanted any kind of separation from her since the sweetness of our honeymoon week. Instead I go back outside, my movements shrouded by darkness, to use the hose, where my skin prickles in the cold air and the icy water sluices down every insect bite and every sensitive part of my body—a beating—an admonishment.

In the morning it's mostly shame that drives Gillian's movements as, after she bathes in the plentiful stream of the tub's faucet, she takes the altar into the master bedroom, and is it that shame that has her searching for a suitable photograph of Ma the way that she does? This is her own private project. At around two o'clock—I have been sleeping fitfully in a cave, scratching till my fingernails catch blood beneath them—she shakes me. She calls me into the bedroom to genuflect and say prayers. On the vanity she's arranged space for framed photographs of David and Ma, as well as a grapefruit pyramid on a plate. Here is the joss sticks' scent, and my tongue sticking to the roof of my mouth.

"A mi tuo fuo," she says. "Guanshiyin pusa."

The photograph of Ma is an old one, no doubt taken by David. A portrait with the focus only on the face. She is, what, twenty-five, thirty, sad eyes, a smiling mouth.

How many joss sticks are there left? How will we ever have enough without eventually going into Sacramento? This is what I think as I hold my stick between my hands next to Gillian and bow, my bangs floating into air. In my head I see my parents next to each other on the couch, kissing. My mother, with such love toward David. How could I ever understand such infinite affection, such deep love, for someone whom one has not known for a lifetime? Ma has her hand on the side of his head and is cupping his cheek and ear as she kisses him, a gesture that I believe I have mimicked with the girl beside me in a poignant moment. Gillian stands. I have forgotten to mournfully think about my dead parents. Gillian is still repeating "a mi tuo fuo, a mi tuo fuo." Now we are both genuflecting, and my forehead is damp against the floor. My buttocks itch from the insect bites and rub against the seat of my pants as I genuflect. I'm trying to think about the catastrophe that has befallen us, made clear by the fact of food poisoning. This is our fault. Or this is her fault, and not mine except by the fault of not being strong enough. I waş never strong enough and Gillian did not know how to cook the fish and here we are, trying to cleanse ourselves with ritual and be pure.

Gillian is trembling, and I put my hand on her back. Her body shakes under my palm, and I cry, too. Now Gillian says, "I'm sorry," in Mandarin, and then in English, "I'm sorry." Her throat bubbling and childish. She crawls to me and her arms are around me. With the joss stick still in one hand, and the smoke wisps around my head. Maybe now it falls to the floor. Again I feel like vomiting, but all over her shoulder now. Things are changing.

———◆———

The thought is a worm at first, and then grows heavy and fat. It begins with the memory of carrying Gillian as I stumbled up the hill with smoke in the air. I carried her and Ma was calm as she led the way, occasionally looking back to make sure that we were following. And of course we were following; but of course we would follow. How could she think anything different? I carried Gillian and we went so far as one slanted peak, until the rocks became vertical and I would have had to put her down for us to go farther. She would have had to get down out of my arms and by her own free will *choose* to climb up the rocks to the next slanted peak, where we like animals would claw our way to the house, and we would, in the house where we had grown up, I imagined, sit at the kitchen table with David's picture in the middle, holding hands, waiting for the fire to gulp us whole. I could see this even as I let Gillian go and screamed at her to keep going. And while we wasted time, because Gillian refused to move after I put her on the dirt, two men in fire suits stood at the top of the hill and saw us, and that was the end of our little hurrying toward death.

What I am fastened upon is the epiphany that we would all die together, and the lack of terror I had when it came to facing this truth. I felt profoundly more mature than Gillian in that moment because I was willing to face our inevitable end under the circumstances of losing the house, which is presumably the reason; Ma would not know how to find a new place for us, is how I read it, or perhaps she was simply panicked and saw no other way out. Though I can't imagine Ma panicked about anything—and it is likely that she was full of clarity that day, just as I am beginning to be full of clarity now.

As clear as anything, I realize that we actually have to leave this life as we've known it. It can't go on like this, if only for the joss sticks, the Buick, the groceries, the soap to wash our bodies, the fact of bleach, the confusion of the insertion of gasoline into a vehicle, our clothes that will disintegrate, the end of thread, the fact that I can't face the beginning of a new life. Because she will fall in love with someone, a stock boy, perhaps, and let him inside of her, and she will shun me, as she has already begun to. Ma is dead and she killed her and I had to close her eyes, and Ma would have understood. I know that she would have implored us to do the very same thing, if her ghost could materialize.

Knife to the heart, in the back, in the chest. Slice the throat. If I had a gun I could make it quick, but I have no way of making it so swift. God knows how angry Gillian would be to see me staring! She's been examined enough. A wash of pity—Gillian is such a child, and she is still unaccustomed to my love. How happy she would be, if I could leave her alone. I think of the knives I keep in the closet, lying like corpses in their trunk. I should end it and let it be ended.

I wipe my eyes with my palms. No. I can't do the inevitable, or at least, not today. So I will leave her alone for now and go into my room. My gift to her is to let her awaken and to see that I have left and not harassed her.

◆

When I've decided I've had enough of leaving her alone, I go into the hall, ready to have a civil conversation, and there is music playing from Gillian's room, the door closed. I find a letter taped onto my room's door, and the sight of this letter, a piece of paper, some kind of communication, startles me.

William,

Please forgive me for what I'm about to do. I need to get away, and for that I'm sorry. Don't try to come find me. I'm attaching a map of directions to town and to the mailboxes.

I'm really sorry. I know you won't believe this, but I love you—just not in the way you, or anyone else, wanted.

Gillian

"Oh," I say. I rush to Gillian's room with the letter in my hand. I bang on the door, call her name, say that we must talk about this. But there is too much quiet beneath the sound of Mussorgsky, and I know. I push the door open and in, violating our contract, and here are her things, her animals, sketchbooks strewn. The spinning and tinny turntable. I search the rest of the house. I look in the closets and the bathrooms. Half deliriously I look in the cupboards. Back in her bedroom I break into tears, kick over the turntable, which exclaims and dies; and then I plead to every familial ghost to bring my girl home.

NOIR

GILLIAN (1972)

Highway and right on Cedar Street,
Right on Elm three miles to meet
A mighty oak, and left you'll see
Samson Drive, 1-9-8-3.

How funny is it that I remember this old, singsong rhyme of my father's? I am more adept at memorization than William is, but I was also more captivated by the journey to Sacramento than William ever was, just as I have always been more concerned with the way to town, or interested in the brands of cereal that the K & Bee makes available to its customers. Certain things I have chosen to pay attention to, primarily things of the world, including this shred of instruction, and I must make the most of it. *Samson Drive, 1-9-8-3.* A young man comes down the aisle with a rucksack over one shoulder and stops with his hand on the train seat beside mine. He's my father's height and nearly as thin as when my father was most ill. This boy's hair is neatly parted and dark; every strand is in its right place, so smooth that it shines like liquid, and he has dark eyebrows to match the mole at the corner of his upper lip, which becomes more visible when he turns to face me and says, "I'm sorry, but—I've been looking for a free seat for *forever*." He pauses. Finally he gestures to the seat beside me. He would like to have a seat offered; he would like for me to offer him this seat.

"Yes," I say, even though I know that the seat is not free. I had to pay for mine with money I took from Ma's room, counting the bills aloud as though I'd done it all my life.

"Thanks." He lifts his rucksack to the shelf above our heads and sits beside me.

So you leave because you want to sit next to morons like this fellow, sneers William. *Xiao mei, you leave me here alone. You ignore the commandment "Honor thy father and thy mother."* On my journey to the train station I thought I saw William everywhere, which is an odd thing to think of a uniquely created young man such as my brother—but still I thought I saw him in the shadows of buildings and amorphous in the darkness of alleys, waiting to punish me. *What,* William asks, *do you mean by all of this? What in God's name do you think you are doing?*

"Hey, I'm Randy," the young man says, and reaches his hand out to me.

I say, "Sarah."

He retracts his hand. If Randy's face were a sculpture, I'd show William its image in a book. I'd say, *This is well made,* although I wouldn't be able to express objectively what makes it so. Perhaps this is attraction, as I would be curious to know the gut-wrench of attraction for myself. I listen for any unusual tones from my heart and hear only blood ringing and ax striking wood. Randy asks me where I'm headed, and I tell him Sacramento, Sacramento being the only other place I've been, Sacramento being home to the Kucharskis. Mrs. Kucharski is dead, but perhaps I can find her husband, although I have never met him, and during our lessons I never even saw a photograph on display. But I am grasping at all possibilities. I must find a way to make a life for myself away from my upbringing, and a heroine's journey is both the only and the grandest gesture I can think to make. Randy says that he's going home to Vacaville from St. Christopher's, where he's a student. I nod, recognizing the saint. "Just started this year," he adds. "You're a student, too?"

I nod again.

"Where," he asks, "do you go?"

What a strange question. Where do I go? Well, I go into the woods, and I go into the shed sometimes, and I go into my bedroom, and I go into the kitchen, and I go into the living room.

"I go wherever I please" is my answer.

Randy laughs. He has a pleasant laugh that sounds not quite grown. If his laugh were a tree it would be a sapling and years from bearing fruit, and I like it, but I know that he is years older than me. The way he carries himself is self-assured. He is not quite clean-shaven.

I ask, "How long will we be on this train?"

"To Sacramento? One hour. Maybe a little more or a little less, depending."

"I'll have to sit with you for one hour?"

"Unfortunately for you, yes. Although," he says, "we may have to go more slowly than usual. Weather man says storms. So you could be trapped here with me till Christmas."

The train cries out. We lurch forward, which causes me to grab at the arms of my chair, and I let out a small, hysterical laugh. Randy laughs, too, although I'm wondering, *Who is this weather man, and are there people born to know the weather before anyone else does?*

◆

In the dining car we drink sour coffee from paper cups and eat sandwiches wrapped in wax paper. He asks if the topic of religion makes me nervous. One unpalatable triangle of my egg salad sandwich, complete with wilting parsley, comes in and out of shadow on a plate in front of me as the lights sway and sway and sway.

"Why do you ask?"

"When I said grace before eating my sandwich. It was the look on your face—the averted gaze. Don't worry, you won't offend me. At this point it's more out of habit than anything else. Sometimes I find myself thanking the Lord before I open a bag of sunflower seeds. So, no hard feelings."

"You're very observant."

"I know. My ex told me it was creepy."

"Ex?"

"Ex-girlfriend. From high school. You're good at changing the subject. Are you going to eat the rest of that sandwich?"

I shake my head. He takes the remainder and bites from one point, causing the filling to plop out from the other side. He gestures at me: *Keep talking.*

"My father was religious," I say. "He was brilliant. He died when I was a kid."

Randy makes an apologetic face but says nothing because of his full mouth, which he's covering with one hand. I keep talking about my father, though I'm not sure why this stranger needs to know about him—better not to tell the stranger anything, just as I've stayed quiet around strangers all my life. Yet there's something exhilarating about speaking to Randy beyond the violation of a taboo or commandment. Perhaps it's being able to tell a complete unknown about my father that's liberating; if I can watch someone else have a reaction, I'll see what kind of response I ought to have. I can't say everything, but I can say some things, so I tell him, "He used to disappear for days at a time. I was very small when this happened, but he would come to me in the early morning, in the dark. I shared a room with my brother then. My father would be quiet about it—he would come to me with a rucksack, and he'd say, 'I'll be leaving for a few days.' He called me Flopsy sometimes. 'Flopsy,' he'd say, 'I'm going to go talk to Jesus.' I don't know what he carried in that rucksack, but it would last him for however long he was gone, and then he'd come back and just pray for hours, he'd pray all day with the shades drawn, in the dark, and when he was done he'd find me and say that Jesus had found him and made him invisible. He'd only become visible again because he left the woods. When I was older my mother told me that it was his mind that was talking to him, and not God."

"You believed him, though."

"I didn't have any reason not to believe him. He was so brilliant about everything. He taught my brother and me all kinds of things, so of course I felt like he knew everything. It wasn't until my mother started acting like things were wrong that things *felt* wrong. He was in the hospital a number of times."

"A mental hospital."

"Yes. It was in Sacramento, actually. It was a terrifying place."

"And were you terrified of him?"

"No. Never. I loved him."

"Sure, sure you loved him. But I'm curious as to why your father chose you to be the one he revealed his—whatever you want to call it. His mystical plans. Why it was you he chose to reveal them to, when you were so small. It seems rather unkind, or, at the very least, irresponsible of him."

"I don't know. How am I supposed to know? And how dare you judge a man you've never met?" I stop. Randy looks pained, and

I immediately regret my actions for causing that pain. "I'm sorry. I'm not used to talking about my father."

"We don't have to talk about him. We were talking about religion. Although religion is probably the worst topic for strangers to start with, second only to dead fathers. There I go again, being awkward."

There is lightning and thunder and still no rain. The dining car is nearly empty except for three others: a dark-skinned couple two rows back and diagonal to us, their skin the color of mink, with the man's hair curiously fluffed around his head; the lady has her hair in tight and tiny braids. He laughs, *huh-huh-huh*. A white-haired woman sits by the door alone, picking from a paper boat of french fries. What an unusual sensation, to be housed in a place with unknowns.

"Did your girlfriend die?" I ask.

"What? No. She's at you-see-allay."

"I see what?"

"What? It's a school. A college in Los Angeles. Do you know about Los Angeles? No. Wow. Where did you come from?"

My face is hot. I've erred, of course, in a situation designed for mistakes. I say, "Leave me alone." He tells me to hold on as I rise and walk past the old woman with her french fries, who is looking at us with a passive expression. I yank open the doors to get between the cars. The space is frighteningly open, and loud with the sound of wheels churning over tracks. I stumble backward slightly; it's raining now, too, and cold.

"Come on," he says. "It's fine. Really."

I close the door. I look over at the old woman, who stares back at me, her face-skin like the back of a dried apricot. It upsets me that I can't interpret her reaction to our little drama, and consider my deficiency to be a result of everything—everything that came before this moment.

"It's completely fine." He guides me back to our seats. "Look, I was surprised, is all. I'll tell you about my ex. Her name was—*is* Cassie Winters. She was devoted to the theater, which I tried to love. I went to every single one of her performances. She'd have five performances of *Guys and Dolls* in a week and I'd go to all of them. I'd bring her flowers for every performance, and she'd act embarrassed in front of her castmates, but she insisted that I keep bringing the flowers because it was making her friends jealous. That was the kind of girl she was. But she was a really good actress. I didn't love the theater, but I could tell that she had star quality."

I roll the parsley on my plate between my thumb and forefinger to make it a small, slender stick. "What did she look like?"

Randy closes his eyes for a few seconds. When he opens them, he says, "Dark, curly hair. Pale. Her real name was Rachel Winzer. As in she was Jewish, and really *looked* Jewish, which drove her crazy. She said all of the good parts in Hollywood went to the WASPy types, so she went by Cassie Winters. She was very practical that way. She was going to have her hair done and get a nose job after high school."

"Are you Jewish?"

"No. So we had a lot of problems. I loved her, though. I was crazy about her. It didn't work out."

"Why not?"

"It didn't work out." He sighs. "I don't want to talk about it."

"You said you would tell me about your ex-girlfriend."

"I did. I didn't say that I'd go through every single horrible detail."

"Did you have sex with her?"

Randy sucks his breath in through his teeth. "Geez."

"I said something wrong."

"Yeah, I'll say you did."

"I'm sorry."

"You're a very pretty girl, but strange," says Randy. "I don't mean anything by it. Just be careful what you say to people. Some won't be as patient as I am. See, you make me want to have a cigarette. I quit, though." He looks mournfully at his right hand. "Don't ask people about sex unless you're asking for trouble."

"I don't want trouble. I've had enough trouble."

"Right. Keep your nose clean."

The charade of being normal is exhausting. There are things I want to ask him: about Jewish people, or about the jobs of noses. I lean my head against the window and close my eyes for an indeterminate amount of time, holding the Bible inside the tote on my lap with the word *Sacramento* on my lips. When I awaken I look over and Randy is writing in a notebook. Despite my sleep-blurred eyes I catch, without meaning to, *her ankle* in blue ink before he looks over at me. He snaps his book shut. "I don't let anyone read my notebooks. What did you see?"

"Nothing."

"Yeah, right. What did you see?"

"Just 'her ankle.'"

"Uh-huh." He tucks the spiral-bound notebook into his ruck-sack. "You were asleep for forty minutes."

"Wow."

"I hope I wasn't what woke you up. You seemed tired."

"I guess I was." The train is still. Our grim sky throws sheets of rain sideways in unceasing turns. "Are we stopped somewhere?"

"Yep. A tree fell across the tracks."

"Can't they move it?"

"Sure. But it'll take a while. This kind of thing always takes forever. Is someone expecting you?"

"No."

"No one at all? Who are you seeing in Sac if no one's waiting for you?"

"It's complicated," I say. I can barely deal with it myself—only this afternoon did I slip out my bedroom window; only this afternoon did I leave my brother in my childhood home to do who knows what by himself. And who knows if I'll ever go back to that place, which is a notion that I can't entertain without panic—since the honeymoon week, I have managed to preserve my sanity only through making the mind into boxes and rooms, and entered hardly any of them.

He says, "I can deal with complicated. Cassie was very complicated."

Somehow I managed to sleep without moving my hands at all in their configuration on the Bible. When I open my hands to look at my palms I see that there are deep red impressions from the hard cover.

"You're very mysterious," Randy says. "Like a runaway."

"Yeah?"

"Yep. Though I've never met a runaway before. It's more of a concept that I'm familiar with."

"How long is it going to take for the train to move again?"

"It really could be hours. So is it a guy you're meeting?" Randy asks. "Do you have a boyfriend you're trying to get ahold of or something?"

"You ask a lot of questions."

"You can tell me to stop, if it's bothering you."

"Please stop."

Randy goes quiet. He reminds me of Sarah, Sarah who wanted to be adored and whose body vibrated with that desire. I wonder where she is now.

"There are certain things that I can't talk about," I say.

Next there is a strange wailing sound, and I whip my head around without meaning to and don't see anything except for parts of people through the windows between cars, reading newspapers, and couples leaning into each other, heads on shoulders, and people reading books, and then, finally, a mother and child on the other side of the dining car.

"Babies hate storms," Randy says. "I should know. I grew up with five brothers and sisters."

I sit on my hands. How could I possibly tell him, or anyone, that I've lived my entire life without hearing a baby cry? And then: How can I tell *anyone* about the house, the two pianos, the life without playmates, a destiny without the possibility of exes?

Randy says, gently, "You okay?"

The baby is being soothed by its mother, who coos: "Yes, good boy, aren't you my good boy—you're my good boy, good boy, shh, my good boy, aren't you, aren't you?" and the baby is quiet, for the most part. I smooth my skirt with my hands and wonder why the baby must be told that it is good—a baby must be told that it's good so that it knows that it will naturally be quiet and not grow up to love a dog that kills its mother, or run away. I turn my face toward the rain-slicked window and I cry some more, not caring that I look abominable, because who knows anyway if I'm a beauty; I've been told, but telling is just words, and I have learned better than to believe in words, and who is this Randy anyway? What does he want from me?

A godlike and scratchy voice comes on from above: "Hello, folks." Everyone except for the baby is silent. "Looks like it's taking longer than we thought it would to get this tree moved. The estimated time of departure is now—eh, it's about ten P.M. We apologize for the inconvenience."

"Worse than I thought," Randy says to the back of my head, as my forehead is pressed against the glass. I begin to hiccup. "Ten P.M."

I'm still thinking about the voice, the top of the train car; thinking about where the voice came from and if every car could hear it, what made the voice scratchy. *Hiccup.* I can't wonder about too many of these things or I'll make myself crazy.

Randy says, "I have a trick for the hiccups."

Cold glass, cold heart.

"What you do," he says, "is to say the name of someone you love, but really pissy, like they're in trouble or you're angry with them."

"I'm not going to do that."

"Why? Just someone. Anyone. It doesn't have to be, like, a *romantic* thing."

"No."

"Hey. Sarah. I don't want to be... presumptuous. But if you don't have a place to stay—you can stay with me, if you want. We have a spare bedroom, and I doubt my parents would mind. I can do that, if you want."

"I can't."

"Why not?"

"My mother," I say, "would hate it."

He pauses. "We could call your mother. I could explain, or you could explain, and put me on the phone."

"She barely speaks English."

"Oh."

"I told you. It's complicated."

"I'm trying to help you."

"I lied. My mother is dead."

"I'm sorry."

"It was terrible."

"I'm sorry."

Still talking into the window, I say, "Tell me about your brothers and sisters."

"Sure. I've got a brother who's older, one younger brother, and three younger sisters. The littlest sister is about six or so, though I may have missed a birthday recently. I call them the Ghastly Trio. In good fun, of course."

"Why ghastly?"

"Oh, because they're *really* well behaved. Impossibly so. Do you want to hear a story?"

I move from the window, turning abruptly to face him. "Yes."

The train car lights up white, and the thunder sounds with frightening enthusiasm. "Um. Okay. Christmas is a big deal in the O'Brien household. My mom goes crazy over decorations. I always complain, because she almost kills herself doing it, but everyone would secretly have a meltdown if she stopped. This is actually the first year I'm not going to be around to see her put it all together, because of school. Anyway, so one year my brother Thomas—Tom, the older one—thought it would be *hilarious* if he woke up really early one morning and took the good stuff out of the girls' stockings and put lumps of coal in them. I don't even know where he got the coal. It's not like we grill or anything. Are you getting this?"

I nod. I know a little about Christmas.

"I didn't know about this, by the way. I would have never let him do it. Anyway, so it's Christmas morning, la-di-da, and we come into the living room and people are going to their stockings. Bridget is the first one to go into hers, which my mother had hand-embroidered with a small Nativity scene when Bridget was in the womb, and Bridget pulls out this coal. She stares at it and then she looks up and says, really bravely, 'Well, I perhaps put my elbows on the table more than I should have this year.'"

"What did the other girls do?"

"I don't remember, exactly. I just remember Bridget, who was eight at the time, with a very thoughtful, serious look on her face and saying that she put her elbows on the table too much. Who *does* that? Even Tom felt bad when she did that. It was worse, he told me later, than if she'd just cried like a normal kid. So I call them the Ghastly Trio. They love each other."

"I like that story."

"Yeah. I decided when I started college that the only thing that I'd actually kill anyone over are my siblings. But especially my sisters. I see the way girls get treated at school, with those macho shitheads..." He stops. "Be right back." He gets up. I notice that he brings his rucksack as he heads out of our car, probably so that I won't read his notebook.

I look around. Two women, presumably strangers from the looks of their disinterest in each other, walk in and settle themselves. One reads a magazine. We had one magazine in the house: a fashion magazine called *Luxe* that Ma saved from the pre–Polk Valley days. This one looks to be about the same—a slim woman in a strange arrangement on the cover, wearing a fur coat and heels. My dress is childish in comparison with the clothes worn by the women in long coats on the train—my clothes with the floral print, the silly lace collar. The reader looks up at me and glares.

Randy comes back, violently plunks his rucksack on the floor, and sits down. I know boys and their foul moods, so I keep quiet and look out the window at some men who are standing around in the rain in slickers and gesturing.

Finally Randy says, "Can I ask you a question?"

"Okay."

"Why do girls act like they care—*throw* themselves all over you to show that they care—and then! And they say that *guys* are the assholes. I'm the nicest guy on the West Coast, probably the country."

"What?"

"Never mind." He evacuates his notebook and a stubby pencil from his rucksack and begins to write, vigorously, before he says, "I called her, is all."

"On the telephone?"

"Yes. On the telephone. This is a train with a pay phone in it. Fourth car, if you want to call your... whoever you need to call."

"Okay."

"Pay phone. You need coins?" He digs into his pocket and hands me a few. His hand is warm and soft like Sarah's belly. "You use these in the little slot."

"Okay."

He goes back to writing.

"Randy?"

"Yeah?"

"What if you don't know the number of the place you're trying to call?"

"Um. Dial zero for the operator. Give her the name and city, and she'll connect you." He adds, "Godspeed."

———◆———

The phone is demarcated in the fourth car with a sign that reads PHONE at the top of a small booth with no door and no privacy. Already someone—a small, compact brown-haired girl with a cap on—is in it, and when I awkwardly stand around waiting she gives me a sharp look and covers the receiver with her hand. A few minutes later she hangs the phone vertically on its hook before adjusting her cap so that the brim is low over her eyes—I don't think she can even see—and then she scoots out of the booth. The slot is there, just like Randy said it would be. I look at the coins in my hand. I sit in the booth, folding my long legs in, and I pick up the receiver, which is still warm from the other girl's hand. I put in my coin—do I put the other one in now, or later? The other one I return to my pocket. The number is 0 for *Operator*.

"Operator."

"Hi."

"Yes?"

"I'd like the phone number for the Nowak family. They live in Polk Valley."

She pauses. I envision an enormous book on her lap, her fingers flipping heavy pages. A book with all the phone numbers in the world must be like an atlas of epic proportions.

Says the woman, "Unlisted."

"Unlisted?"

"No number. This number can't be found."

"Why not?"

"Why not? Some people ask to have their numbers unlisted, so they can't be called by people who don't know them. Some people don't have phone numbers."

"But I know them."

She sighs. "That doesn't do anything for you, hon."

"Oh. What about Mr. Kucharski? In Sacramento?"

Another pause. "Also unlisted."

"K-U-C-H-A-R-S-K-I."

"No. There is no such name here."

William. Poor, poor unlisted William. Poor, poor unlisted Nowaks. Gone and unlisted Mr. Kucharski.

Back at my seat, Randy looks up at me with his pencil still in his hand and the notebook still in his lap. I take great care not to look at the notebook directly. He has a lovely face. A *beautiful* face like a robin's, black-eyed and bright.

"Good call?" he asks. He lifts his legs to let me slip by, and the backs of my knees rub against his stocking feet.

"No."

"Me either. Cassie said that she's not going to see me. First time we're home since school starts and she's not going to see me." Randy closes his notebook. "Have you ever loved someone so much that you thought it would just kill you? That's how I feel about Cassie."

"What does that mean?"

"That it would kill me? I feel like my insides are being torn up. It's like I'm having a heart attack. I don't know. I feel like an abortion." He opens his notebook again. "You should *hear* some of the things she said to me. I'm recording them for posterity."

I wait for him to read them to me, but he doesn't. Instead he reads to himself, silently, growing increasingly agitated.

"Maybe you should stop that," I say. "It's making you upset."

"Ugh. I *know*. I can't seem to stop."

"Here. Give me your notebook. I won't look at it; I'll just keep it from you until we get to Sacramento."

He looks at his notebook, which has a crisscrossing of pale lines across its front from creases, and a maladjusted spine of wire spirals. Quickly he hands it to me. I put it in my tote.

"Thanks," he says.

"It's no good to look at things that will just make you upset," I say.

"I know, I know. I shouldn't have called her. I knew that it wouldn't go well. I'm a real idiot sometimes. Another problem with never seeing Tom anymore is that he's never around to tell me that I'm being stupid. Hey, " he says, "don't let me call her again, okay? I sort of feel like calling her again."

"Why? What would you say?"

"I don't know. Something to make her change her mind. I haven't thought it through. I guess I just want to hear her voice."

"Don't call her again," I say—and here is that hook of feeling again in me toward him, a complicated sharpness and softness at once—or maybe he just reminds me of a sillier, less highbrow version of William. At least they have the same passionate sense about them, and I can protect Randy; I can keep his notebook, I can keep him from calling his Cassie. What is it about these boys and their girls?

"It's from being in the theater, I think," he says. "Her voice, I mean. She knows how to use it. She *wields* it. She has a very vibrant voice, even on the telephone, even when she's not talking loudly."

"Don't call her," I say, "and don't talk about her. You're making yourself sick."

He stares at the seat in front of him. He puts his thumb and forefinger together, forming a loop, and moves the tip from the right side of his closed mouth to the left side of his closed mouth. Then he gives me a fresh look.

"Let's go back to the dining car," he says. "I'm allergic to crying babies."

As we walk back to the dining car I'm reminded of my father. "The left hind foot," he says, "is the lucky one." He's separating the foot from the dead gray rabbit with a small knife at the wrist. He holds the foot in his naked hand and inserts the tip at the top, pulling it down to the dark pad. I am suddenly dizzy.

We're in the middle of an empty dining car when Randy turns abruptly, stretching his arms overhead with a small grunting sound. The bottom of his T-shirt comes up, exposing an inch of white, with a path of thick hairs extending to the waist of his trousers. I don't know how to feel about this, or how to feel when he reaches his hand out for me, walking me to the far end of the car beneath a swinging light. He says, his voice throatier now, "Sarah, I know this is weird, but... d'ya think you could see yourself loving me, if you were Cassie? I know you don't really know me. If you did know me, would you love me? Because I don't know if I can go on when I get back to Vacaville, and she won't say boo to me, you know? It'll just—it's just going to kill me." He reaches over and drags the backs of his fingers against the upper part of my arm. I can feel every finger on my skin. So it is impossible, and yet it is inevitable, that my hand goes to my tote bag and pulls out the bowie knife. I press the tip of it into his sternum.

He startles. We stand, a tableau, with the knife between us, large and with only one intent, until he finally says, "I don't know what you think you're doing, but you need to put that away."

But I keep my hand where it is. I think of pushing it through the layers of skin. What am I supposed to do? How do I keep myself safe? What will the consequences be if I take this knife and slide it down his chest with a terribly exact amount of pressure? After all, I have nowhere to go. I don't know where I am, I don't know where I would run. He is saying words, but I don't know whether to believe him. I don't know if anything he's told me is true.

PART IV

MARIANNE
AND
MARTY

BLESSINGS

MARIANNE (1972)

O *ne time,* I told myself as he left the convent. *It will have to be only this one time. He's married, and he has a child. Beg for forgiveness from Our Lord and Savior; pray that your stupidity doesn't ruin you.*

———◆———

When I failed to bleed the next month, and then the next, I knew. I packed my things and told Sister Angeline that I would leave in the morning. I'd not yet begun to show, but my body had softened as my heart was hardening. I said nothing about the reasons for my departure. Sister Angeline said that she would pray for me, but as I left her small and austere room I could feel all prayers fading for me forever.

And when I later saw David, and when he gave me his largesse, I was making a deal with the devil; I was conscious of the bargain as I made it. I could never ask him to leave his wife and boy for me, because my only claim to him was our history and a few afternoons and now this child inside of me, and I asked, and still ask, myself *why*. What kind of insanity infected the life of the church I'd tilled for myself. Was it his familiarity? Was it the fact that I'd loved him once and could love him again, or that I actually did love him again, had never stopped loving him? Was it the wine that parted my legs? I don't know. I hated him for it, but I hated myself more. He was only doing what he wanted, and who could blame a man for pursuing his desires? I should have, as the expression goes, known better.

My child was so well behaved even then, allowing me no morning sickness and barely any discomfort. The discomfort I did endure, such as back pain, I accepted and even welcomed as punishment. With every month I grew larger, the stretch marks on my soft belly snaking toward my sides. I was not one of those fallen women who could pretend that she was not pregnant—it was as evident to me as it was to everyone I encountered when I left the house to buy groceries or simply exercise my sore legs. Women stopped me in the street and gazed at my pregnant body, saying things like "I carried high like that" or "How far along are you?" No one asked, "Is this a bastard child?" I suppose because I seemed reputable enough, although this may not be a question that people ask if they are polite. I was completely aware of the baby every second of every day.

I was the one who named her Gillian. It is a form of the name Julian, meaning "belonging to Julius," but I gave her that name because Gillian was my mother's middle name, and my mother was perhaps not an exemplary mother, but endured so much that by the time I left home she had earned herself a steely exoskeleton that I couldn't blame her for. I thought that by naming my baby Gillian, she might inherit some of my mother's better qualities. On a more delusional level, I thought that by naming her, I was staking a claim. But I couldn't have what I really wanted, though who was to say what I really wanted; nor could I care for a baby on my own. And yet the larger Gillian grew inside of me, the more inclined I was to keep her, even in poverty.

But it was the call David's wife made that undid me. *Daisy*— what a name. I heard a goodness in her voice, and I've been clinging to that sound of a good soul for the last decade and a half of my life. Yes, I told myself, she would be Gillian's mother. They would live in that house, that homey house in the great wide woods, and they would have the Nowaks' resources to clothe and feed her. Her! Gillian! My offspring, a Nowak after all. I could give her nothing, and they could give her everything; she could be happy, she could wear nice things, she could read good books, David would teach her the piano, she would learn Latin, she would live a good life and grow up to be a better woman than I.

And months later my baby was in my arms in the apartment that David had rented for myself and the midwife, my baby a tiny squalling thing with a bright pink face that I loved with an immediacy more painful than the labor itself. I was twenty-two, penniless, husbandless. In labor I had lost all recollection of any sense but agony, but birthing Gillian put me solidly back into my torn and bloody body, and all I knew of it was that my love hurt like an echo of Hell and I did not want to let her go.

"Please," David said. His hair was thinning. He was old in a young man's body, his grotesquely scarred hand twisting between the fingers of the other. "Daisy and I will give her a good life. I promise you. Don't make this harder than it has to be." The midwife, a softly shaped Russian woman with ivory hair, remained expressionless in the face of our unshared emotion.

I sobbed. I said no. I held Gillian to my breast, and she pressed against it, hot and wailing. I swear she was saying, *You are mine.* But in the end I let him leave with our child, and because of this I had to believe in David's fundamental goodness. I trusted—had to trust—that she would be all right. For a time after he took Gillian from me, I fell into melancholia, and there was no one to catch me—I had no friends, I lived alone. There was no one to implore that I wash my face or brush my teeth or, Heaven forbid, take a shower; there was no reason to eat, and I lost twenty pounds, and had to tuck a cushion between my knees before I slept because in lying on my side, my own bones hurt me. I cried until my eyes hurt, and then I waited and more tears came and I cried some more. At times, I plotted getting Gillian back. I imagined that I'd go to their home in the middle of the night and thieve her from her crib, but these dreams were countered by the self who looked into the mirror on the way to the toilet and saw a gaunt, oily-haired woman with feral eyes, who clearly could not take care of herself and therefore could not take care of a child.

Once the melancholia lessened enough for me to function, I fled the apartment. I moved into a small home in Sacramento with David's money, receiving calls from him every so often with updates, and when William and Gillian were feasibly old enough for a music education, I begged him to bring the two to see me, which is how the piano lessons began. He brought our daughter and his son for instruction every week as a concession, as a form of custody. I would sit on the sofa with my hands gripping my knees and stare at the door at one fifteen, knowing that they would be there by one thirty. The doorbell would sound its chime; I'd open the door and there they were, the child I had lost and the half-Oriental child that was David's, both wearing white linens and clutching book bags of sheet music, while David smiled at me and said, "Good afternoon, Mrs. Kucharski," which was my pseudonym in those days.

Every week I had to hold myself back from tearing little Gillian into pieces and stuffing them into my mouth, to not touch her too much or touch William too little. Instead, I carefully hugged her hello. I held her at arm's length, examining her shape and the contours of her face that looked so much like mine. I did the same with William, although my attention was always elsewhere when I was with William; even when I taught William his lessons I had half an eye on Gillian in the living room while she read, or drew with crayons on the sketchpad I made available to her every time she came.

I always looked through her drawings. I do still have them. She had an eye for detail, even with the clumsy crayons. Her tigers always had stripes that seemed authentically placed.

Every week I cried after she left, pressing my hand to the door and the other to my belly as if ready to birth her again. Despite my broodiness, I was eating and washing myself—I made sure that Mrs. Kucharski would be a charming figure to the children, and then I shed her skin as soon as they left. It was likely bouffant-headed Mrs. Kucharski who applied for, and was rewarded with, a job as a secretary at a real estate agency. Mrs. Kucharski was asked on dates to which she never said yes.

On two occasions did David betray himself to me. The first: Gillian and William were halfway out the door. I had said my customary good-byes. "The bright spot of my week," I managed to say, and David flashed me a look of such longing that I couldn't have misinterpreted it, no matter how many times I replayed it afterward. David always had a particularly legible face.

The second time occurred a month before he died. "Don't get yourself into trouble while we're gone," he teased. He was helping Gillian with her coat. Their drive home was a drive of microclimates.

I said, "I have no one to get into trouble with."

He did not look at me, but replied, "You know I love you," before turning away, his hands perched on his children's shoulders. What possessed him to say this in front of them, I do not know. I don't think they were listening. The door closed so firmly that it was like he hadn't said anything at all, but the words remained with me. I even whispered them to myself at times, as if by doing so I could keep the fluttering thing alive.

I loved them both, and in both cases I imagined my wounds might fester less if I tried to harden my heart fully. But the truth is that I never made an honest go of moving on; I was constantly looking back.

His wife called me one night after I came home from work at the agency. She had never spoken to the persona of Mrs. Kucharski, and when I heard her voice and introduction on the line I nearly dropped the phone. I responded in a voice that was not entirely in my normal register for my role as the piano teacher. It was audibly different from the way I'd answered the phone, but that had only been the one word *hello* and it didn't matter anyway, because Mrs. Daisy Nowak was calling to tell me that her husband and daughter had died in a car wreck.

"William will not come for lessons," she said.

I couldn't breathe, and then I was crying before I could stop myself. If she hadn't suspected me before, she suspected me then.

"How terrible," I said, barely choking out the words.

"It is terrible."

"I'm—I'm sorry."

After a long moment, Daisy replied, "I understand."

A tin of ashes arrived in the mail a few weeks later. I scattered them in my garden, amid the rosebushes, and the piano lessons—Mrs. Kucharski—and my life ended then.

———◆———

When I arrived home from work and saw her for the first time in four years, Gillian the ghost, fifteen years old, was sitting on my sofa with a TV tray and a glass of milk in front of her, looking grown, looking much the same as she did when I last saw her with her small hand in David's as they left this Sacramento home. Her hair was hacked short. Her gold glasses were slightly crooked, and she squinted despite their presence on her face. She looked like a beautiful farm girl—healthy and nourished, with lean and muscled arms and shoulders—but her floral, no doubt homemade, dress hugged too tightly at the armpits, and though its hem was let out and ragged, the skirt still rode up her thighs.

"Mrs. Kucharski," she said.

"Gillian."

"My mother said you were dead, but I came to your house anyway. I didn't know where else to go."

I reached for her. Without being fully aware of doing it, I touched her hair, her face, her hands. Her whole body was cold like marble; she didn't move. I worked to stop crying as I sat next to her with Marty watching from the kitchen, judging the girl who was my daughter and the daughter who was a Nowak all over her face, a Nowak in the slight hunch of her shoulders and the gold of her hair. It was a miracle; I couldn't dissect a miracle.

But I asked her if something happened. I asked her how she got here. She shook her head. "I walked to town," she said, "and asked someone how I could get to Sacramento. I took a train, which was... I'd never done that before. And I remembered how to get to your house, sort of. One-nine-eight-three Samson Drive."

"You're here."

She wasn't dead. I had to remind myself of this. I was not being pursued by an angel, but by my flesh-and-blood daughter, who had come to find me.

"I feel like I'm dreaming. I'm so absolutely tired," she said.

"Are you hungry?"

Gillian nodded. Her hands crossed, one over the other, in her lap, one scratching its partner. Not hard enough for me to tell her to stop, but hard enough to make pink lines on the skin. I still wanted to touch her, to put my hands on her, to feel her solid body under my fingers before she vanished. My mouth watered as my eyes leaked; I was tired of crying, had wept too much over the years, but this made no difference to my body, which made the tears as fast as I could shed them.

"Marty," I said, "is there anything? Leftovers? Sandwich fixings?"

"I think there's meat loaf," Marty said.

"Please."

He went to the kitchen. I said, "Where is your mother? Where's William?"

She looked to the side. "She's dead," she said. "Ma and William died in the Buick on the way to town. I wasn't with them."

"I thought it was you and your father who had died." A proliferation of alleged car accidents, one crashing after the other. But she herself was not dead. "Are you sure?" I asked, and then corrected myself. "No—I'm sorry. Of course you're sure. What about your father? Where is he?"

"He's dead," she said simply.

I asked, "How?"

"He stabbed himself. Didn't you know? I don't know why you'd think *I* was dead." She turned her head. "What's that sound?"

"The microwave. It's heating your meat loaf."

"Microwave. We don't have one of those."

"Not everyone does."

She looked around the room. I tried to see it through her eyes: green walls, botanical illustrations in frames, refurbished furniture bought on resale. We remain frugal with David's money. Blood money, Marty calls it with hatred, and yet he has no job and lives off it all the same, having been dishonorably discharged from the navy for years now.

"Everyone is dead," she said.

"What?"

"Ma and William were in the Buick and a car hit them. I'm all alone." She stared at me. Her eyes were, I realized, the color of mine. They'd changed over the years from hazel to a brighter shade of green, and they gleamed as she said, "I came here, Mrs. Kucharski, because I didn't know where else to go. You're the only other person I know."

Everyone is dead. David killed himself. I'd wondered for all those empty years if it was going to happen, his self-obliteration, and there it was. He was dead, had stabbed himself. I tried to imagine it. As a teenager his demons had repelled me, but with age came a deeper understanding of demons. Always there had been that potential death. Here it was. Everyone was dead but Gillian. In the end, Gillian was left behind for me. The occasion: an extraordinary one, and terrifying if true; I had wanted her returned to me, and perhaps it was my endless desire that tangled up truth and fiction, the succession of accidents that were simultaneously true and false. I was her old piano teacher, and she'd had to come a long way to reach me. She hadn't called. She hadn't even written a letter. Surely there would be someone else who could help an orphaned child—someone who saw her regularly, perhaps a schoolmate's parent or her own teacher. This was a miracle, I thought again. She is here *because of a miracle*. And then I wondered if this was what a miracle felt like—to be commanded by an archangel and to encounter my phantom daughter being the same thing, all things considered—a miracle thus inducing the swollen hot lump between my ribs and forcing electricity along my limbs.

Marty brought the meat loaf into the room and put it on her tray next to the milk. Gillian picked up the fork and cut herself a piece, and then she began to eat ravenously, gulping it down. Once the plate was clean of meat, she scraped the sheen of ketchup onto her fork and sucked it off the tines, and the entire time I didn't look at Marty and I knew that Marty was looking at us and trying to see the resemblance. She had my hair. It was the color of David's, too, but with a wave to it like mine.

"It was good?" I asked.

"Yes. Thank you." She hesitated.

"Do you want more?"

She nodded, not shyly.

"I'm tired," she said after a moment. "I'm really very tired."

"You must be. You came from Polk Valley?"

"I came a long way. Rainstorms on the land for a good while, too. Where's your bathroom?"

I told her. Gillian went, leaving her canvas tote. The living room suddenly felt devoid of life. Out of curiosity, I lifted the drooping tote and peered inside. A Bible, a change of clothes, a drawstring coin purse, a notebook. An enormous knife. I stared at the clean, heavy blade and its worn handle, not comprehending the implications of this weapon, because what could it be but a weapon and a danger to myself and to Marty. And yet the fact that she *had* a weapon compounded my guilt for snooping; I stared at it, not knowing what to do, and Gillian returned as I put the tote and its knife back on the sofa. She wiped her hands on her dress. "You have a nice bathroom," she said. "I like the green tiles and the bottles." She sat down again, touching the glass of milk. "We don't drink milk at home," she said.

"Would you like something else?"

"Yes. Water."

I knew that Marty wanted me to pry. Why was she really here, and how long did she intend to stay? Someone must miss her back home. Her school would be inquiring. I did not want to tell Marty about the knife, which would remain a secret; if he knew about the knife, he would never let her stay. He was suspicious of her, but I couldn't afford to be suspicious of her. I had been the one to let her go, after all, and I was her mother; it was my job to protect her from everything, and if my brother was one of those things, so be it. So be it, I thought, as Marty came back with the glass of water and Gillian swallowed it down. She wiped her mouth with the back of her hand, and I saw for the first time moon-shaped marks on her palms. Her eyes kept darting to Marty as she ate the second piece of meat loaf, a bit more slowly this time, and then she said, "I'd like to sleep now."

I said, "You can have my bed. I'll sleep on the couch."

"I want the couch," she said. She paused. "Please."

When I returned with some linens and a quilt I saw that she was lying on the sofa on her side, reading a notebook with her head propped up on one hand, and Marty had gone into his room, which was one relief.

"Do you keep a journal?" I asked.

"No." She closed the notebook. "It's not mine."

I tucked her in. Had I dreamed of this? Had I imagined the movement of my hands with a blanket gathered in them, lifting the cloth over my daughter's body to say good night? As I wrapped the blanket around her, she said, sleepily, "Why are you crying?" She put the notebook on the TV tray and my heart bled full into my chest. Could I kiss her forehead? I dared not. Instead I sat on the floor, next to the sofa, and though I hadn't prayed in years, I did then.

In my diary on that night, I wrote: *She came home.* I waited for something more to come to me.

At six thirty Marty comes into my bedroom with coffee. He hands me a mug and says, "We should do something fun today. Bring that crazy kid of yours. We could take her to a diner. Visit a museum. Chuck pennies from a balcony at strangers."

"Mmm."

"What?"

"Nothing. Yes, let's do something—something fun."

Marty says nothing. How I hate this adult habit of his. I think it may come from years of psychoanalysis. Conversion therapy. He, of all people, ought to understand perverse desires.

"It's hard," I say.

"What's hard."

"She's here. It's a dream come true in the most literal sense."

"But..."

"But all the old things come up..."

He makes a noise between a throat clearing and a snuffle. "Are you talking about what I think you're talking about?"

"Let's forget I said anything."

"No," he says, "really. Just say it. Go ahead."

I'd spent the morning thinking of David. I didn't want to, but he was as present as our daughter in the Orlich home.

I said, "I'm not angry with him. I mourned Gillian—I was devastated about Gillian—but he did love me, I'm sure of it. We did love each other. There was no way we could be together, but he loved me. Isn't that worth something?"

"Like what?" Marty asked, and I can tell from his tone that I've made an error in judgment, but he has begun to respond and it is too late. "It couldn't have been any clearer to him that it was a bad idea. He was *married*, for God's sake. You were going to become a nun. A *nun*. He let his prick get the better of him, and then he had the stones to go ahead and say, 'Okay, I'm rich, and you live in a garret, let me take your baby. But don't worry, I'll let you see her once a week, and if you're lucky, maybe you can hug her on her fucking birthday.' Annie, I don't call that love. I call it bullshit."

"Let's talk about something else."

His voice softens. "Loving your daughter, that I understand."

"She'll be awake soon." I press my fingers to my throat; I don't want to cry again. I am so tired of my own pain.

He pats my knee and squeezes it. "All will be well," he says. So the saint said.

———————◆———————

She is on her knees, leaning over the back of the couch with her hands parting the gauze curtains at not much of a view. The bottoms of her feet are made of rock, calluses on top of calluses.

Even the lines that carve through are calluses themselves. Canyons. Marty is gone; he takes walks to clear his head before coming home to write, or he goes to see Leo—his lover, the printer.

"Good morning," I say.

Her head turns. "Good morning," she says, serious.

I boil water for oatmeal while I call in sick at the office.

"Eleven new articles came in over the weekend," says Rob. "We go to press this week."

"I'm really sick," I tell him.

"You sound fine. Healthy as a horse, in fact."

"I might feel better by Wednesday."

He sighs. "I expect to see you by ten. *Today.*"

When I hang up, Gillian is in the kitchen doorway. "Who were you talking to?"

"My boss. Everything's fine. I'm not going to work today," I say, and smile. "I'm going to spend the day with you."

"How can work be a place?"

"Work... is a job. My job."

"A job is where you do things to make money."

"Yes."

"My parents didn't have jobs," she says. She looks out the window for a moment, as if they're on the other side of the glass. "But we had money anyway."

The water boils. In go the dry oats, cascading like rain. "Your parents were in an unusual situation. But your friends must have parents with jobs."

"Yes."

"You'll have to tell me about them."

"Sure." And then, "We're going to have a nice life together."

This last line of hers reverberates, and I don't know how to answer.

I ask, "How do you like your oatmeal?"

"Is that what you're making?" She moves to stand behind me. I feel her height, her shoulders inches above mine. "Oh, *owsianka.*"

"Yep," I say, my eyes stinging, "*owsianka.*"

"This is something my dad ate."

"Oh?"

"Yeah. Ma put a fried egg in hers, and so did William. I did whatever my father did, so I had fruit and brown sugar in mine." She wanders to the refrigerator and opens it, expelling a chill into the already cold kitchen. She leaves the door open for a long time, examining its contents.

"Where's your husband?" she asks, her head still in the fridge. "Did he leave?"

I say, "I don't have one."

"But there's the man who lives here." She closes the fridge.

"Marty? He's not my husband. He's my brother. He lives with me because it's easier."

"Easier than what?"

Easier, I think, and spoon the oatmeal into two white bowls. "We like living with each other."

She goes quiet. I serve her al dente oatmeal with berries and whipped cream, and she eats without speaking, staring into the center of the bowl until it's empty. Her movements are quick, intense, as if her gears and springs promise to erupt into irreparable chaos.

"What are you thinking about?" I ask.

"I never realized that I look so much like you," she says, but leaves it there. So I ask her what she'd like to see.

"I've seen you," she says, "which is all I really came for."

"What about the state capitol?"

"What?"

"The government building."

She frowns. "It wasn't in the atlas," she says, as if that explains something.

I sift through my old clothes for something suitable, and then she emerges from the washroom in a dress that has long since ceased to be flattering on the ever-decreasing flesh of my body. I see that she doesn't fill out the bust, but the waist sits well, and what's knee-length on me hits her thigh, showing off her lean, long legs.

"It looks nice," I say.

She reaches her arms out on either side of her like wings, causing the spare fabric at the bodice to billow and pucker. She looks at her hands and down at her legs, and shrugs.

"I don't like to think about how I look," she says. "But the dress is nice. It smells like you." She lifts an arm to her nose.

I find a purse for her. Gillian touches the thin mahogany leather, running her long and crooked fingers across the crackling edges. "This is nice, too. Am I supposed to put something in it?"

"If you want."

"Do we really have to go?" she asks.

"To the capitol?"

"I don't want to go."

"All right. We don't have to go."

"You'll still let me live with you, won't you?"

"Of course!" What a relief, to be asked something that I can answer with certainty. "I want you to more than anything."

She says, "I'm glad. I wanted you to say yes. I knew you would—you always liked me. I was a good student."

"All we have to do," I say, more to myself than to Gillian, "is go through certain things. It will work out, though, all of the legal things. We'll go to court. Look," I add soothingly, alarmed by the suddenly animal look on her face, "it will be all right."

"Court?" Her mouth twitches, eyes big. "Why are you talking about a court? Just let me live with you. You don't have to tell anyone that I'm here."

"Oh, it's more complicated than that. When I get you a doctor, they'll need to know that I'm your legal guardian—when you go to school here, for example—"

"I don't need a doctor. I have never needed a doctor. And why do I need to go to school? I learned everything I need to know from my father."

"But," I say, trying to surmount this revelation, "if anything should happen to you, the police would need to know that I'm taking care of you."

Her face spasms at the sound of the word *police*, and when I try to put my arms around her she jerks away, slapping me before skin touches skin. So this is how it goes, my own flesh and blood hell-bent on rejection. My skin burns where she's struck me.

Next there is a key in the lock, and Marty enters. I pray that my face gives away nothing. He touches his left ear, the way he does when the air has turned them numb, and then he takes both ears with his hands, rubbing them absently. "Everything all right?" he asks. Leo is not with him.

Gillian says, pointing, "It's because of him, isn't it? He doesn't want me to stay!"

"What's because of me?"

"She's never been to a doctor," I say, not knowing what I mean by it, but needing to state it as a fact aloud. "She's never been to school, Marty." And I think again of the knife that I will not mention, which looms now in my mind as I make the decision, again, to not mention it. For a girl who has never been to school, who has never been to a doctor, a knife can mean so many things, and I presume the knife is safety for her. I tell myself that the knife is for self-defense and nothing else.

"You don't understand." Abruptly she stands. "That's not my life. I don't do those things. No one can make us do those things. That's why we don't go out...We Nowaks, we don't do those things. We're not like other people..."

◆

After a bout of wild sobs she passes out on the sofa, a lump beneath a quilt. I go to the bathroom, open the medicine cabinet, and down a handful of Valium while refusing to look at my face in the mirror. I go into Marty's room and shut the door. His room is always at least seven degrees warmer than the rest of the house—he's always cold, and cranks his space heater to maximum year-round. His room is also small, and crowded with things collected over years, most of which allegedly have sentimental value to him, but the importance of which he never bothers to explain when I ask. I sit on his rickety bed. He sinks into the easy chair.

"God. It's like you dropped your baby off at the freak show, she's raised by the mongoloids, and then..." A cough. "Sorry, sorry. I know I'm not being much help. Shit like this, I don't know what to do with."

"Shit like what?"

"Oh, I don't know! Life's various complications. What are you going to do with her?"

"What do you mean, what am I going to do with her? She's my *child*."

"She's brainwashed."

"It sounds so terrible."

"What else did she say to you before I got home?"

"I don't know. Things about not going to the doctor. Not going to school. I already told you." Panic rises from the soft place between my ribs, but I push it down with effort because panic will do me no good at this moment. I must maintain some kind of control.

Marty says, "Christ."

"I tried to hold her. She froze up like I was going to hit her." I say nothing about being slapped.

"Well, you don't know how she's been living."

"But I saw her until she was ten. I saw her every week. She seemed fine. Adorable. David obviously doted on her—she was, without a doubt, his favorite. I even felt a little sorry for William. I thought, *Everything's turned out okay.* As if things were better for her. Oh God. I should have never..."

Marty reaches into his pocket and pulls out a pack of cigarettes. He lights one and hands it to me. I take it.

"Do you think she's really an orphan?" he asks.

I wipe at my eyes, suck at the cigarette. "Does it matter?"

"It wouldn't matter if she were, say, a scrappy black Lab who followed you home. It matters if she has living parents and a brother who've called the cops, and it turns out that you're harboring a lying runaway. For all of her craziness, she's . . . healthy. She doesn't look malnourished or neglected, although she does have a terrible haircut."

"Marty!"

"There's no way that a normal girl goes out in public regularly with a haircut like that."

"You're trying to tell me what to do."

"I'm trying to keep you out of trouble. And you're going to hate this," Marty says, "but I do have one suggestion."

"What?"

"You said that Rob used to be a lawyer before he started the magazine."

"I'm not getting Rob involved in this."

"Bring it up as a hypothetical. Say it's your friend."

"Marty, that's what people say when they're obviously talking about themselves."

"All right." A cigarette flick into the air. "Preserve your precious *ego*. We'll see how this goes."

"He was a *criminal* attorney. It has nothing to do with my ego. Isn't there some other way to find out if her family is..."

"Dead."

"Yes."

"Obituaries. You could call her house."

"No, that was never an option—their number was disconnected years ago, after the wreck. I guess there wasn't... that wreck.

Another wreck happened, but not that one." With this, the car accidents jumble in my brain again. David and Gillian died. They did not die: David killed himself, and Gillian lived. But then Daisy and William died in a wreck, and Gillian lived. Gillian lived, lives, is living, is in the next room with a knife in her bag.

"I know some of it. But not the details..." I can tell before I speak that my voice will come out irritable and bordering on cruel: "No, I didn't tell you details. You can't stand to hear his name—why would I tell you anything about any of them?"

"Fine. I'm glad he's dead. But who knows? No one seems to stay dead in this story." He looks at the door.

"David's wife called to say that he and Gillian had died. She'd met me when I was pregnant. She knew me as Marianne, but she didn't know that I was teaching her children piano. It was the whole *ruse*—I was Mrs. Kucharski, teaching her children music in Sacramento. She was never supposed to know it was me. She never came to the lessons. And maybe she'd known all along, but I was a mess as soon as she told me about the accident, and she was smart enough to guess."

"She blamed you for having sex with David."

"No. I don't think that was it. It seemed that way in the beginning, but she never said a harsh word to me. And you know about the ashes. The ones in the garden. A week later, I called to try and see if there was any way she could be convinced about having William come back. I didn't want to let them go, but the line was disconnected. I tried to find them through the operator, and their number was unlisted—if they still had a line. That was the end."

Marty says, "You should have gone out to the house back then, if you really wanted to see them."

"He was supposed to be dead."

"Maybe. But if you cared about William so much... Or did you doubt the wife?"

"I cared. Did I doubt her? I had the ashes. Bone fragments. Why would I doubt that? I cried for months."

"You should call Rob."

"This is going to sound stupid," I say, having smoked my cigarette dead, "but I'm afraid to call Rob."

Marty sighs.

What I want to say is, *David loved me,* and then, *What power that word has over us pathetic mortals. I love Gillian, and where will that get us?* Marty stubs his cigarette on the arm of the chair, adding to a pointillist array of ash.

◆

Gillian is still sleeping when the phone rings; I dash to answer, afraid that she will wake.

"Where are you?" Rob says. "These fucking articles are piling up. You said you'd be here at ten. It's eleven fifteen."

"I said I was—"

"No matter what is or is not going on between us, Marianne, I expect you to be professional. We are going to press. Or I really will have to find someone else, which is not going to make me very happy with you. In fact, it may very well cause me to fire you." His threat may be real, or it might not be. Either way, there is Nowak money and there will always be Nowak money. We could live off blood money until we die.

I imagine Gillian on the sofa and smiling in her sleep, her hair the same soft shade as mine.

"I have to go," I say.

"You're not going to have a job the moment you hang up the line," he says.

I hang up.

◆

I had a daydream about the bus, which I took to work in the mornings, and which dropped me off downtown near a sandwich shop that I frequented for coffee. The fantasy always involved me facing the back, where the doors opened, and I would be sitting, alert. I would stop and some maternal inclination would cause me to turn; I would then see a slender girl of about twelve stepping across the threshold, perhaps holding a backpack casually over one shoulder.

Even though what she wore in the fantasy varied (I was never concerned with this detail), she would always take the farthest seat in back so that I'd have to turn to watch her. Her knees would be a soft pink. She would be tall, like David, and charmingly gawky.

I'd know her instantly. I'd say, *Gillian?* And I might even repeat myself, because she'd be absorbed in thought, and ask again, *Gillian?*

She'd look up from her hands—she always looked at her hands, which at first I thought was an attentive piano student's habit, but which I now believe is a reflex born from always observing her father's—and she'd stare at me.

Mommy, she'd say, with complete recognition and a smile.

The fantasy ended there. There was no better climax and no need for resolution. I could and did replay this fantasy over and over. The fantasy was sometimes a way to try to get to sleep, a self-comforting tactic, and sometimes a way that my mind would torture me and keep me awake like a record skipping, skipping. It was one volume in a small library. Perhaps I never believed Daisy when she said that Gillian was dead. Perhaps I felt so much guilt for agreeing to give her up that I forced myself to pay the consequences.

What I didn't realize until Gillian actually showed up at my home was that I'd had no fantasies about what would happen if Gillian were actually in my life. All of them were about the reunion and the surprise and the happy shock. What would I do with real-life Gillian? I hadn't thought of that. What did young girls like? What did adolescent girls like? Perhaps it didn't matter. The thing about a true-blue fantasy is that it's based on the assumption that it will never come to pass.

"I've lost my job," I tell her. She's making a tuna casserole for dinner. I'd told her that we could go out and eat anything she wanted, but she wanted this, so she's boiling macaroni. The touchy subjects of court, of police, of the way Nowaks live—all of it has been set aside for now.

"So you have no job. No work. That's great," she says. "Now you can spend all your time with me."

"Yes." I kiss her on the head. "That's exactly what I wanted."

"How will you have money, if you have no job?"

"We..." There is no way to explain right now where our money comes from. Finally I say, "We have money saved up."

"What will Marty think?"

"Oh, he'll be glad. He'll be glad that I can spend time with him, and glad that I can spend time with you."

"Will he?"

"Of course."

"He won't be jealous of me?"

"What? No, he won't be jealous. He'll be glad that you're staying with us."

She stirs the noodles with a wooden spoon. "Do you love him? I need pot holders." She finds them, and she finds a colander. She drains the pasta over the sink, and a cloud of steam rises and consumes her, making her look like an angel, fogging her glasses. When she puts the pot back on the stove, she says, wiping her lenses with her finger, "Gosh, I can't see a thing. Sometimes I can't stand wearing these, you know? Anyway. I was thinking about William. Do you remember him?"

"Of course."

A long pause. "I don't think I was very good to him."

"Sometimes it's hard for siblings to get along. That's normal."

"I made him miserable. But I couldn't help it. It was like something was wrong with me. I *know* something was wrong with me. I don't know what siblings are like, really, except for us, but now I know I really tortured him. But you're kind to Marty, I can tell. You take care of him, and you let him be happy, which is something that I wasn't any good at."

"I'm sure your brother loved you."

"That's not the point. You understand, because you're a good *tongyangxi*. I can tell." She gives me a sidelong glance. When I don't reply, she continues: "Will we still go to court, Mrs. Kucharski?"

"I don't know. I want you to be comfortable. I don't want to make you do anything you wouldn't want to do. But what was it you said? About a *tongyang*—?" I ask, and she stares at me like she's trying to do complex multiplication in her head. She seems to want to say something, but doesn't. Instead, she turns to the noodles.

When it's time for dinner I knock on Marty's door. He opens it and he stands there in jeans and a white T-shirt under a black sweater with a hole at the breast, his face vacant the way it is when he's been staring at his papers for too long under a too-dim light.

I say, "Gillian made tuna casserole."

"It smells good," he says. He lingers at the door.

"Well, come eat then. I've got plates out for everyone."

He says, "I'm going to, uh, meet Leo."

"Right now?"

"Clear my head." I realize he's got loafers on. "I'll eat some if there's any left when I get back."

After the door closes behind him, Gillian asks, "Where does he go, when he goes away like that?"

"Oh, just around the corner, around the block." I put on a big smile. "I'm really excited about your casserole," I say, scooping her a shovelful. It smells like a home that I've never lived in. Gillian leans in and inhales the steam. She settles down in Marty's chair. And though I haven't had anything blessed in my life for years and years, I say grace with Gillian: "Thank you, Lord, for this, your bounty, our blessings." I squeeze her hand.

Halfway through the meal, which is largely silent, Gillian says quietly, almost casually, "Don't tell Marty, but I almost stabbed someone on the train."

My fork is still in my hand, though my fingers loosen of their own accord. I grip the fork in a fist like a child, laying it down on the table.

She says, "I met a man on the train. He was going to rape me, so I took out my knife to scare him. I know where to put a blade so that an animal will die. I could have killed him if I wanted to, but I didn't want to. I wasn't going to kill him. I only wanted to scare him."

I try to imagine this scene. I see my daughter standing in the middle of a train car, wielding a dagger at some pathetic stranger, my daughter out of her mind with a fear that's multiplied by the confusion that accompanies it.

"What did he do?" I ask.

"He just told me that I needed to put it away. It doesn't matter what he said, only that I didn't do it. But it's true, isn't it, that the world is a dangerous place? You can't tell me it isn't."

BRIEF THOUGHTS
OF WOMEN

MARTY (1972)

I think no one is ever so crazy in love as with whomever they were in love with when they were seventeen, and when I was seventeen I was crazy, I mean positively *loopy*, about David Nowak, of all people. And what draws a seventeen-year-old to the thing that gets him going, that gets his cock so hard it hurts, depends on the kid, and even though I know saying that an infatuation or whatever gets guys "in trouble" is cliché—for example, when a man says, "I saw that girl and I was in *trouble*, let me tell you what"—I do mean it literally. When I first felt that *stirring*, years back, for the athletic thirteen-year-old who shared my new school and my new church and, eventually, even my family, I knew it was all over for me, I might as well have become a murderer.

Because I still remember exactly how, at seventeen, the back of David's skull made me twitch, with the curve of its base leading to those two lines of muscle that came down to his neck, and he had these great arms. And I'm not saying that the men whom I was attracted to after that were all just like him, but they all had certain qualities of his. One or more. I had an encounter in the park with a younger guy who had David's particular forearms, that same dusting of gleaming hair that I could see clearly even in the moonlight. Another cliché: to say someone "made me weak." But it's true that every time I saw someone like that I lost my moral fiber, I fell apart. I felt guilty about everything, especially things that made or make me happy, and it doesn't take much time on the couch to figure out how that started. But when I met

Leo—dear Leo—in Monterey, within three hours he'd already told me everything that I needed to know about myself, including the fact that I thought I didn't deserve happiness. He told me before I even opened my mouth. And how I loved that! How could I not love that—someone who saw myself before I did?

Leo also said that had I loved God, and not men, at seventeen, things wouldn't have turned out any better than they did for Annie. "Had you not *renounced* God," he said, chewing on a piece of sourdough, "you would have shot yourself. Because wasn't your father," he asked, "the sort of man who kept a gun around?" And I laughed. Annie and I knew he kept it in that cigar box behind his two pairs of good shoes. I came close plenty of times to opening that box, even after I'd decided that God and the Bible were full of shit, even though to think that God and the Bible were full of shit, strangely enough, didn't have much to do with how I feel or felt about my desires. And about that Colt .45—sometimes I thought my father would shoot my mother with it. Sometimes I spent nights awake, wondering if he would. I told Leo all about that. We were in the back of a bar in Monterey. Neither of us mentioned that we were homosexual, but we knew all the same.

I remember being dumbstruck by his face. Even though I suspected that he wouldn't punch me for saying it, I was afraid to tell him, as badly as I wanted to, that he had beautiful eyes.

"You want to tell me something," he said.

He was like a palm reader, or like a Gypsy with a glass orb.

I said, "Look. I don't know what's going to happen, but I only let *them* touch *me*," and he nodded.

———◆———

What do Annie and Gillian do? For the first week they do very little except talk, even though I've noticed that Gillian doesn't say much about her growing up. She has stories about the woods and the deer and the insects. She speaks with an odd cadence, and occasional Nowak-isms come out of her mouth that make me cringe. But the ladies of the house don't go anywhere. Not downtown or to Tahoe; not to San Francisco and the Golden Gate Bridge. They are only satisfied by each other. Of course, I want Annie to be happy, but I have doubts. I bring Leo over, and Gillian gets nervous the way I used to when I saw lights flashing near the park at night. She goes into Annie's bedroom and shuts the door.

I've told Leo everything about Gillian that I know, including the near-violence on the train. In my room I put my hand on the sleeve of his long navy overcoat. I look up at the fuzz between his proud eyebrows. Behind his head hangs a framed photograph of our mother in the corner; she is sitting at a table with a fishbowl, the bowl filled with water and one sad-looking goldfish.

"She's got a long road ahead of her," Leo says, "if, in fact, she's been living in isolation, and perceives everything as a threat. And who knows? Maybe she *was* going to be raped."

He removes his overcoat. Leo works in a printing shop, so he comes to me smelling of mineral spirits and ink and hands that never come clean. I'm hit by a waft of chemicals from the coat's removal, and we sit side by side on the bed.

"Did I ever tell you," he asks, putting his smudgy hand on my hand, "that my mother was stabbed when she was a girl?"

"No," I say. I try not to be outwardly surprised by anything Leo says, which I first decided when he told me that he had his first sexual experience at the age of eight. I kept my face expressionless and listened to him tell me everything.

He says, "You know how people say, 'She was never the same after that'?"

"Yes."

"Well. I think my mother was never the same after that. She was a living wound. I could tell that just being in the world hurt her. I'd never met anyone else like that until just now, seeing Gillian."

"Mmm. And what about Annie?"

"Annie's tough. She's been through her fair share."

"Yes."

"You have to be tough," Leo says, "to be a woman. Everyone's out to get you." He lies on the bed and pulls me to him. "We have it easy, you and I, in comparison."

"Yeah?"

"I know you don't think so, but it's true."

"You're right, I don't agree. When you say that, I feel sick."

He kisses the top of my head. "Let me tell you what happened to my mother. She was five or so, playing in front of her house. Her mother had gone inside for a moment. I don't know why."

"To use the restroom. To check on the pie."

"Something like that. My mother was playing and a man came up to her with a puppy on a leash. She was playing with the puppy and the man stabbed her in the back and strolled away. He left the puppy, which is a detail that I find excruciating. The knife remained in my mother's back. She screamed. Of course, she tried to pull it out. Thank God she didn't, or she would have died. My grandmother found her on the lawn with the puppy licking her ear and the knife sticking out of her body. I don't know how she didn't die. But you know how some people take a thing like that and never talk about it? My mom talked about it. She talked about it all the time. She showed me the scar. Marty," he says, "be glad you're not a woman." I didn't ask Leo what had happened to the puppy, although I wanted to.

◆

The first man to take me in his mouth was another sailor. His name was, appropriately, Richard. He sucked me off and I fucked him in the fields; he seemed to have no control over his body, which went every which way, but God help me if I could give a shit. And then there was the lieutenant. After that, there was no stopping me from *officially* being a pervert. I was dishonorably discharged for being caught drunk and naked with another man on my ship. Still. Being caught was a relief, in a way. For a stretch of time I traveled Asia alone, and when I was tired of Asia I thought of my sister.

I found out through our mother that Marianne was already living in Sacramento at the time. I suggested, somewhat hubristically, that I join her, and she had no problem with that; in fact, she asked only a few questions, perhaps because she had her own secrets to keep. In the car on the way from the airport she told me about the second set of keys that she'd made for me. She told me about the job she had, how she was making her way as a secretary and then as a copy editor. But by the time we were having coffee in her kitchen she said, "I have something to tell you," and then she told me, without going into detail, about what had happened with David. She was vague. I was jealous, though I tried not to be, that she had gotten her hands on him. It wasn't until later that she mentioned that a baby was involved.

I told Leo a little bit about David, but not very much, and it was Leo who'd asked about it in a different way, saying, "Who was your first love?" I wanted to tell him, *You,* but the only thing that I know about love is that it makes you sick and starving, and Leo doesn't make me feel that way, so I was honest, and he just smiled at me as if to say, *It's not a test.*

He's the one who first made friends with Gillian. I let him in and hugged him; he walked to her and handed her something small and green, Gillian with her tangled blond head in Annie's lap.

"*Leaves of Grass,*" he said. "It's a book of poems."

"I thought we had all the books," she said, and we didn't say anything about this but knew what it meant, and when we tried not to look like she was wrong she knew that she was.

Leo brought her books: poems, cookbooks, plays, novels. After a week of this she asked him to stay in the living room and talk about e. e. cummings, which was like nothing she'd read before, she said. So they read together. While Leo read, Gillian looked at her hands, and Annie and I looked at each other—how the hell were we to react to any of this? And then Gillian started talking more, in a way that seemed like she was getting comfortable around us, but she still wouldn't leave the apartment. Leo said that Gillian had left one life of isolation for another, and that Marianne knew this but seemed unwilling to change it.

"When I was trying to find your house," Gillian said to Annie, "I saw things that scared me, but I knew that I had to get through them if I wanted to find you. But I remembered. I'm clever. Now I'm here, and I don't see why I have to go anywhere."

We celebrated Thanksgiving, which Gillian had never done before. I'd wanted Leo to have his Thanksgiving with us. I'd even asked him, as stupid as it was, and he smiled sadly at me and said that his daughters love Thanksgiving, which was something that I didn't want to hear—but it was my fault for asking a stupid question. I try not to ask those questions. I try not to make things worse for him than they have to be.

I must have looked sad during the Thanksgiving preparations, mashing the potatoes with an air of melancholy, because Marianne turned to me and asked, "Marty, have you ever asked him to leave his family?"

"What?"

"Leo." She blushed, not looking at me. "I was just wondering if you've ever thought about asking him to... leave them. To be with you."

"No," I said. "No, never."

"I see how happy you are together, that's all. And things are changing in this country."

I didn't say anything after that. Not about the politics of homosexuality. Nor did I say, *Leo loves his daughters and would never, ever leave them.* And especially not, *Being happy together has nothing to do with it,* even though it's the truest thing I could have said, or could ever say, about us.

So on Thanksgiving it was just the Orlichs and the single Nowak, gathered around the table with the biggest turkey that Annie could find. I watched Annie carve the turkey, her face glowing.

"There is much to be thankful for," she said.

Gillian nodded, and I said, "Hear, hear," which could have been interpreted as sarcastic, but I did want Annie to smile, and there hadn't been so much enthusiasm in the Orlich household in years and years.

"Wait," I said, "let me get the wishbone for you," and I pried it from the carcass while Gillian watched.

"You take one side and I'll take the other," Annie said. "Then we pull. Whoever gets the bigger piece will have their wish come true." They pulled. Gillian won.

"I wished that everything will come out right in the end," she said.

Still, this way of life couldn't last. We all knew that. It was going to be winter, and the beginning of a new season meant Gillian would have to get ready to go to school in the spring, which seemed impossible given her current state, but what else could we do? After Thanksgiving, Annie made a call to social services and told them as much as she could bear to tell them, including a mix of truths and half-truths: a narrative about her biological daughter being unregistered and an informal adoption and a whole slew of deaths both recent and not recent, leaving the unregistered daughter without family, except for herself, the anonymous woman, and what should she do? Well. There would have to be records of the dead family members. There would have to be evidence of the anonymous woman being the unregistered girl's mother. There would have to be an investigation of the anonymous woman's home, to see if it was fit for a child. That was all Annie could remember; she hung up, overwhelmed, without finishing the conversation.

"What am I supposed to do?" she asked Leo and me. We were camping out in my room, whispering, while Gillian made tuna salad in the kitchen. She had an obsession with canned tuna.

"You have to do these things," Leo said. "You—both of you— have to face reality."

But there was no phone number. No way to reach the mother and the brother. The number had been disconnected forever ago. The phone call to social services had been anonymous, and nothing had been said about abuse, so it could be said that it wasn't a *completely* urgent situation. The urgency was the urgency of people, both strangers and non-strangers, who felt they knew best about what Gillian needed, and Gillian could sense it—I knew she could. It frightened Gillian. How could it not? Anything we mentioned that had to do with authority figures scared the shit out of her.

Annie and I told each other that we had time to think about the future, which meant that our concept of the future was of something that would never come. In this state of denied temporality Annie decided that she wanted to introduce Gillian, gently, to the world outside of our home. I agreed that this was a good idea. The two of us could bring Gillian somewhere fun. Perhaps, we said to each other, she wouldn't be so afraid of the life to come, whatever that life was to be, if we took her somewhere benign. It had been a bad idea to suggest the capitol, for example, because the capitol implied government and authoritarian forces; we might as well have suggested a visit to Alcatraz for all of our foolishness.

"Somewhere whimsical," Annie said. "Somewhere fun."

It was her idea to bring Gillian to the Natural History Museum. "She's mentioned David practicing taxidermy," she said. "The Natural History Museum is essentially one giant taxidermy exhibit."

We mulled over this possibility for half a day. The museum was perhaps not the best choice because of the crowds; still, there would be people no matter where we went, and part of the reasoning behind this excursion was to give Gillian the experience of crowds, and of acclimation to aimless groups of other humans. We would go to the museum on a weekday morning, when children would be at school. We reasoned that we could stay and have a gander for a few hours and maybe longer, if Gillian was having a good time, and then we would go home, having expanded her tiny world that much more.

I did wonder whether she'd be frightened to see the animals. It seemed impossible that she'd ever been to a zoo, and even though the museum's animals were dead and stuffed, their corresponding size and realism might scare her. I had no idea what she'd make of an elephant. I tried to imagine the context of the situation, attempting to come to a conclusion about possible reactions, and found it impossible. Small children went to the Natural History Museum. They, too, were unaccustomed to enormous beasts and sharp-eyed birds, and were in fact delighted by them. Small children experienced such things with wonder. Was Gillian capable of wonder?

But Annie was so excited by the idea that I didn't ask my pointless questions, and we piled into the car—I took the backseat—one Tuesday morning so that we could go to the museum.

"You'll like the museum," Annie said for the umpteenth time. I knew from the brittle sound of her voice that she was nervous. I could practically hear the words splintering as she said them, no matter how she tried to infuse the line with enthusiasm. "It's simply remarkable how they've managed to make things so lifelike."

I asked, "Is there any animal in particular that you'd like to see?"

Gillian fidgeted with the ceiling of the car with her fingertips, plucking at the fabric with her nails. I was afraid that she would begin to tear a gaping constellation of holes. "I would like to see a whale," she said.

"Yes!" said Annie. "They do have a whale. I think they acquired a whale skeleton just last year."

"What do you know about whales?" I asked.

"They're like enormous fish," Gillian said. "And Jonah was swallowed by one."

"Yes," Annie said.

We parked at the museum and entered the building, which was, as we had predicted, almost empty at that early weekday hour. The double doors opened into an alcove where an elderly woman with mottled skin and a clearly practiced smile sat and sold us tickets while Gillian played with the pen people used to sign checks, which was attached to the counter with a rope of metal beads. She pulled the pen tight on its leash and then dropped it, watching it dangle, and then she put it back on the counter and rolled it off so that it dangled again.

The Natural History Museum in Sacramento was small. Marianne and I had grown up visiting the one in New York City, which is the most famous of such museums, and I'd come to Sacramento's version only once because I found it so paltry. I saw what Marianne meant when she said that it might be a good destination because of the taxidermy: the opening rooms were entirely composed of dioramas organized by climate and geographical location. North America came first. I followed Annie and Gillian as they walked to the first diorama, which depicted a pair of deer against a two-dimensional, painted background of hills and flat blue sky. I noticed the presence of an air duct disrupting a cloud, and Gillian said nothing, but she stared and stared. I thought that she must have seen deer where she lived; it was impossible to live in an even remotely rural area in Northern California without seeing deer, or even wild pigs. Mountain lions.

She did startle at one exhibit. It was the violence, I guessed, that bothered her in that diorama of wolves and a felled deer. The wolves' mouths were painted a sticky red. The deer bore gaping wounds of the same color. I watched Gillian grab Annie's arm even as she didn't look away from the scene.

"Remember, it's not real," Annie soothed. She put one hand on Gillian's.

"I know it's not real." But Gillian didn't move from the diorama. She reached out over the waist-high wall, over the sign that detailed an explanation of the scene, and lowered her fingers to one of the wolves' backs, at which I said sharply, "*Gillian*, no." I tried to be gentle about it, but Gillian turned to me with a colorless face. I hadn't intended to sound so harsh, or to scare her.

Annie said, "You can't touch them. It's not allowed," and gave me a dirty look.

We saw beavers and sea lions and birds dangling from the ceiling on wires. We moved into the next room and saw lions. I worried about the lions because they, too, were shown attacking an antelope, but Gillian seemed less bothered by this faux violence. She barely looked at the lions, her eyes casting about to find something to snag upon. I had no idea what she was thinking as she saw these things, because she said nothing as she looked at the stuffed animals and the maps on the walls and read the placards by each diorama.

At some point she and Annie wandered over to an exhibit on pea plants. I assumed that it was something about Mendel; having no interest in feeling like a high school biology student, I stood a few feet away and examined a warthog. Leo would have a good time here, I thought. He and I would have a good laugh at these bizarre dioramas that tried to resemble real life, but were art forms in themselves, and not very good ones.

"Marty," Annie hissed.

She was still standing by the pea plant display with Gillian. By the time I reunited with the two, Gillian was staring at the floor, unmoving. I had no idea what was happening. "Gillian?" I asked, and tilted her face up to mine.

"What's wrong?" Her eyes wouldn't focus. I looked at Annie. "What happened?"

"I don't know," Annie said. "We were reading about Mendel. Darwin. Finches." She waved at the air.

"Let's sit down," I said, because I have always been good in a crisis, and I was afraid Gillian would faint. I found a bench and we sat with Gillian at the left, Annie in the middle, and myself at the right.

"Put your head between your knees," I said to Gillian.

When she didn't do anything, Annie repeated what I'd said, and Gillian folded neatly forward. Before long, she was crying. Her head dangled between her knees, which were bony and stuck out from beneath a plaid skirt Annie had dug up from somewhere, and Gillian was making an ugly sound like a baying dog in the quiet museum.

"Christ," I said.

"What's the matter, honey?" Annie put her hand on Gillian's back.

I figured it out before Annie did. At least, I had the hunch. They'd been looking at an exhibit about genetics, and Gillian was clever enough. If she hadn't been educated in genetics at home, she could still likely figure out from a cursory explanation of dominant and recessive genes that her mother and father, the mother and father that she knew, could not be her biological parents; on the other hand, this blond woman, her former piano teacher, a woman with sunshine hair like hers and the same thin mouth, could be her mother and probably was. But neither is Annie stupid, and I suspected her of being willfully ignorant about what had upset Gillian; perhaps she feared this revelation and was pretending not to recognize its arrival—perpetuating the confusion, buying time.

Soon Gillian began to make the sharp inhalations and exhalations of a toddler who's just had a crying jag, and Annie said, softly, "Is it something about your parents?" I could barely hear her. I could see only the back of her head, which was turned toward me. When Gillian nodded, Annie said, in that same small voice, "I'm your mother, Gillian. I'm sorry it was a secret."

Gillian said, "I don't understand how it happened."

So Annie told her, surrounded by scientific exhibits and glass cases full of bones. She told her daughter about knowing David as a child and then being separated from David as an adolescent; about her brief affair with David when he was married to Daisy and living in Polk Valley with baby William; about making the choice to let David and Daisy raise her. At this point her voice became halting, and the words came more slowly. I thought she wouldn't be able to finish the story, but she did, including the tale of becoming Mrs. Kucharski, the piano teacher. She even told Gillian her real name, and Gillian repeated it, the echo cementing them both in place.

"Let's go home," I said. It seemed fitting after such emotional outbursts. No one objected, and we went back the way we'd come, through Africa and North America, to the double doors. I thought briefly of the whale that Gillian still hadn't seen. I wondered whether she'd ever see it now. Annie kept her hand on Gillian's shoulder until we got to the car, where we resumed our positions. The car pulled into the light, and then we were moving steadily into something I could not name.

Ten minutes into the ride back, Gillian said, "William is still at home."

I almost said, *Christ*, but held my tongue. She admitted to lying about the car accident, which Annie couldn't bring herself to be angry about given her own fresh revelations, and we couldn't get Gillian to explain the context for her lies. Annie did ask if she'd known all along that Mrs. Kucharski—if *she*—was her mother. Was that the reason she'd run away from home, leaving William behind, to seek out the long-lost piano teacher's husband? Why, in the end, did she come to Sacramento? But after her initial confession about William, Gillian deflated. All she would say, over and over again, was that Ma and David were dead and that William was alone. "We have to go get William," she said.

"All right," Annie said, and if I were the type of man who would throw up my hands in extremis, I would have.

I was losing what little patience with Gillian I had, but Annie had an infinite supply of patience for her. It was at this point—halfway during the car ride from the Natural History Museum to our little home—that Annie stopped consulting with me. I was no longer part of the little club in charge of making decisions about Gillian, nor was I made privy to Annie's thought process as she decided that the two of them would find out on their own how William was. They would make their own way.

Leo and I did what men do: we performed the physical labor of loading them up in the Ford with snacks and suitcases. I watched Annie grow more agitated, her body twitching at loud noises and sudden movements; at the same time Gillian grew increasingly enigmatic. To me she was but a faint echo of her mother, after all, and as they prepared to leave that echo rang out and faded until it was almost nothing.

"Keep me updated," I said to Annie, and pressed my lips to her palm. Gillian turned her face away. I asked my sister to at least give me the address of the Polk Valley house. "I don't like the idea of you just heading out there, the two of you by yourselves."

———◆———

Now Leo and I are on the sofa, alone in the apartment without the women. Our faces are men's faces in an apartment of lace and green glass bottles. He slouches in his seat, which he never does; his posture is always impeccable.

"What's wrong?" I ask.

"Nothing."

"Tired?"

He looks sideways at me and smiles. "Yeah. Sure."

I say, "Let's go to the ocean."

We take a cab to his apartment—his wife isn't home, is at a doctor's appointment with the children—and we drive his car for hours, through valleys, to Stinson Beach, riding the skinny rope of road until we reach the shore. He parks. I get out and the wind is whipping the hems of our clothes. Barely anyone is around. We are, as always, careful not to touch, not even by accident. I don't believe in God, but this is the closest that I've ever felt to him—in this place, always the same shore, where everything is the same dull shade of gray and holding the earth together with one gluey hue.

A young couple sits on a blanket on the sand, surrounded by twists of kelp and, nearby, one imperious gull. A man walks his black Labrador. I stand with my hands in my pockets next to Leo, who also has his hands in his pockets, and I say what I've been thinking during the entire drive, which is "We should go after them."

"I have to get home," Leo says, "but *you* should." Then he turns and is on my mouth, is kissing me in front of no one and possibly everyone despite legalities, despite what's proper, despite comfort. His lips are cold and chapped; his hands are on my arms, his firmly pressing fingers against my ribs as if we were dying.

AFFLICTIONS
(1972)

I n the car to Polk Valley both mother and daughter are af-
flicted, with Gillian exhibiting paroxysms of guilt: biting the
middle joints of her fingers, leaving deep grooves. Her arms
itch. When she looks at them she sees that hives have sprung up
from wrist to elbow. She scratches the perimeter of one island
and says, apropos of nothing, "I had to leave him." At this, Marianne's head tilts.

Gillian says, "If I didn't leave him, I couldn't have found you.
I never would have found out that I had a different mother all
along. It makes so much sense, though. You were the only outsider we saw for so many years."

Marianne wants to ask, *Why couldn't William come with you?*
but to speak this would be accusatory. She has one eye on the
road and one eye on Gillian, whose ad hoc pixie haircut is beginning to grow out in uneven patches. Again her beauty is coming
through, a light through a crack. Marianne tries not to dwell on
how this beauty reminds her of her own beauty, steadily fading
since she moved to Sacramento, or maybe lost in the convent
or during the pregnancy. Gillian fidgets with the window crank
and rolls it down, rolls it up, then rolls it down again. She has
changed back into her own green dress. She has her tote with
her—her clothes, her undergarments, a bottle of barbiturates
and another of opiates and tranquilizers that she found in the
bathroom among other partially full bottles, her knife, a garnet
ring that she took from Marianne's jewelry box, her half of the
wishbone, her Bible. Objects of safety, is what she tells herself.
Talismans.

She had taken the pills in the middle of the night because she recognized them from the *Physicians Desk Reference*, which Ma referred to every so often for reasons of health, and Gillian knows those pills could kill her if only she took them all. Already she has been preparing herself for arriving at the house, their "home sweet home," and finding William dead by suicide or other tragedy; and should this happen, she would want the escape hatch by which to end her own life; she would want to follow her brother and her mother and her father. A lineage of Nowaks, gone hand in hand from the valley to the shadow of Death, where she would likely go soon enough anyway—beyond what she'd already known from Ma about murder and muggings and unpreventable accidents, she'd found a newspaper on the train that spoke of a man who had killed people ("serially" was the term, he was called a "serial killer"); the serial killer apparently killed for no reason, which was a fresh horror that Gillian could barely contemplate. And this particular escape hatch of suicide is more of an idea than intent. She hasn't thought it through.

Out of Sacramento already, the environs quickly change from small city to suburbs. There are fast-food chains in orange and yellow—colors meant to stimulate the appetite—and homes exactly identical, or mirror images, of one another. Gillian is thinking about William sliding his hands up her legs, pinching the inside of her thigh until it burned pink; and her telling him that she didn't like it, and him saying he was sorry. Always he was so sorry, so easily sorry, so easily made to feel guilty, and what difference did it make? She knows that Marianne Orlich loves her in particular, but was always kind to both children, and Marianne would feel generously even toward a boy she only remembers as somewhat of a piano prodigy and a lover of Beethoven sonatas. Maybe she will remember his thick, thick hair. She will be wondering, Gillian knows, why Gillian abandoned her brother. Gillian will have to have a good answer for this. She is stuck fast to the word *abandon*, not realizing that she is not, in fact, the older and therefore allegedly more independent one; that an outsider may see the situation as the following: William may have decided to stay at the house for his own reasons, or that he may be, in fact, doing fantastically by himself.

She's been reading Randy's notebook. Most of it is about Cassie, whom he calls "C." In the notebook he details her body and behavior with what seems like astounding precision, to the point where Gillian feels she knows Cassie herself—has been *inside* C's body (both sexually and spiritually), has possessed C's thoughts. This privilege unnerves as much as it excites her. What, then, does it mean that Randy and C are no longer lovers? How many of these sorts of obsessive connections is Randy supposed to make before he dies? Exhausting.

"I have to pee," she tells Marianne.

They find a gas station with an accompanying convenience store. While Marianne sits in the car, Gillian goes inside. Marianne can see Gillian walk to the back of the store with stiff and anxious limbs. She can see Gillian trying the knob to the door inside.

In the gas station, Gillian can't help but think about the K & Bee, which felt significantly more dignified than this place—this place with its rows of unintelligent snack foods and candies. Staring openly at her like a stock boy, the presentation of cheap snacks in bright colors is as tempting as that kid with the blotchy face and long limbs, and licks a similar excitement up her belly. While she waits for the door to open she takes a box of Lots-a-Fun Candies and turns it over in her hive-covered hands, looking at the purple box and the oblong shapes. The typography makes her think of someone shouting. These things Gillian finds charming, and she falls into the old reverie. She smiles, unable to help herself.

"Hey, girly. You need a key for the bathroom." It is the man behind the counter with long hair like Jesus.

Gillian comes back to the car, tapping on the window. The passenger door opens.

"You didn't use the bathroom?" Marianne asks.

She slides in, slams the door. "It needed a key."

"No one was there to give you the key?"

"I don't know." Gillian is picking at her cuticles. "Forget it."

"Honey, you need to go. I'll come with you, okay?"

Gillian hesitates. Eventually, they enter the convenience store together. The convenience store clerk—stoned—looks at the two of them, a woman and what he presumes is her daughter. The daughter will grow up to look like the mom. Already he can see it. The daughter's beauty will turn handsome, with lines around the eyes and cheekbones sticking out of her now-soft face.

"The key to the restroom," Marianne says.

The clerk has both elbows on the counter and is leaning forward as if settling in for a long conversation. He looks behind him at the key on a hook beside a sign for cigarettes. "You gonna buy something?"

"Sure."

He hands over the key—a single small key on a thin ring, the entirety of which could easily be flushed down a toilet, and has already almost landed in the bowl several times.

Marianne gives Gillian the key. "Go ahead," she says.

Gillian takes the key and goes back to the restroom. TOILETS, the door says in marker. She slides the key into the opening and turns it before yanking on the knob. She turns the knob the other way. It clicks without gratification. Her panic intensifies; she is unaccustomed to locks and keys. She looks back and sees that Marianne is talking to the clerk, pointing at something behind the counter on the wall, inattentive to her needs.

"Help!" she yells, her panic surprising even herself.

By the time Marianne comes to the back of the store, Gillian is shaking. Marianne hugs her. "Oh, honey," she says. She takes the key and opens the door, hurrying her daughter in. The bathroom expels odiousness; there is toilet paper everywhere, and Marianne sees a shit smear on the floor and maybe on the wall. Gillian looks around, absorbing it all, and Marianne directs her to the toilet, which Gillian sits directly on after yanking down her panties without arranging any tissue on the seat—Marianne doesn't say anything about it, but she thinks about it. If she'd had more time, she would have. The sound of Gillian's pee is remarkably animalistic, and Marianne tries to think of the last time she was with someone like this, them openly urinating in front of her. *This is my daughter,* she thinks. *Things like this happen with a daughter.* She waits to feel a burst of love for this, but no such burst comes.

After Gillian rinses her hands in the sink, which provides no soap, above which there is no mirror, the two of them exit the bathroom.

"I just need to finish buying something before we go, okay?" Marianne says.

Gillian says, "I want to leave right now."

"One minute." She goes to buy cigarettes; Gillian's eyes flick back and forth. She scratches her arms with both hands and suddenly sprints to the back of the store, grabs her candies, and hands them to Marianne. After Marianne takes them Gillian turns away, ignoring the transaction. *Do you like candy?* Marianne wants to ask. *Tell me something true.*

They return to the car. Gillian's hives are intensifying, with a patch on her face growing hot, and then she says, "I said I wanted to get out of there. Why didn't you listen?"

Marianne pulls out of the gas station parking lot and they are on the road again, the sun blurring their eyes. Both are so tall as to almost touch the top of the car—Gillian with her short hair, Marianne with her twisted and lazy updo. "I had to buy something," she says, "because you used the bathroom. When you go to a store and use their bathroom, you need to spend money on something."

"Why?"

"Because—bathrooms in stores are only for customers, honey. People who buy things."

"Why?"

"That's how they make money." She looks over at Gillian. "I'm sorry. Try to take a nap. You can recline the seat and take a nap, okay?" Again, a lump like ice stuck too hard to swallow, making it hard to feel anything but fear. She is in over her head, she is sure of it, and yet she still reaches over and pats Gillian on the knee the way she would pat a strange dog. "Pull the lever on the side and lean it back."

"I don't want to stop again."

"We don't have to stop again."

"I'll hold it. I'll go in the grass."

"Okay."

Gillian looks out the window. "There are no people like me, are there?" she says, thinking of William and the state he must be in now. Has he even left the house? How much food did she leave him? Why did she have to be the maternal one, the one who cared about their fate? She cranks down the window and out go the candies, ricocheting down the road. "I'm a monster," she says.

"You're not a monster. You—"

"No."

And Marianne thinks, *My poor baby, my poor baby who almost stabbed someone, probably for putting his hand on your shoulder, you poor, inconsolable child.*

"Why weren't you *there*?" Gillian finally asks, and starts to cry.

"I'm sorry," Marianne says, wiping at her own face, "forgive me, forgive me." She squeezes Gillian's shoulder as she drives.

The roads turn to highway and they are moving quickly again with the valley all around them, hills the color of awakening grass, Gillian's head turned with a wet face, pretending to sleep but really looking and thinking, *There is so much of the world.* Again one of the Nowak books, the world atlas, comes to mind; Eden was a place, and so, too, were Greece and Rome; so, too, were Africa and South America. And here she is seeing the spaces in between the only places she knows. How much more of the world can there be? The possibilities feel unfathomable, infinite. She pictures herself playing her familiar piano and peering over the top to see William, his head bobbing, his ecstatic fingers leaping, and she remembers him pressing his face against the warmth of her back in the sun in the endless long meadow, and she remembers her father and mother and William and herself sitting around the dinner table with *golonka* and a broiled fish and mustard greens. In her memory William pelts an insult at her for being grumpy: "The crabbiest crustacean of them all."

Mother and daughter left at 12:43 P.M. and it's now 1:22 P.M., with Gillian having just woken from a nap she didn't mean to take. Her hives have faded but aren't entirely gone. While she was asleep, Marianne quietly sang Carpenters songs to herself and smoked one-fourth of the pack of cigarettes she purchased from the Jesus-man's machine; the Camels gave only borrowed calm. On the left and later on the right is a steep drop-off, with only stunted guardrails to keep them safe. When Gillian turns to her, her face light pink, Marianne asks, "How did you sleep?"

"I closed my eyes. It just happened," Gillian says. She sits up straight. "Where are we?"

"Still on the highway."

"I dreamed about my house," she says. "William is going to give up if we don't find him. He's not strong—you don't know him like I do. No one does. *You're* not a *tongyangxi*—I know without you telling me."

"No," Marianne says. "I don't think I am."

"I'm William's *tongyangxi*. I mean, his Eve. I was supposed to be. I was, for a while. I..." She props her glasses up her nose. "Then I ended it... It was about love, but I couldn't do it anymore,

I couldn't keep letting him...It was making me crazy how foolish it made him, but I knew I was the fool because I couldn't. Now I'm thinking, maybe my parents were the crazy ones. I don't know."

Christ, Marianne thinks, and she tries to say something normal. *The two of them. The brother and the sister. What did I do? They ruined her. I ruined her.* She entertains the thought of driving off the road, but catches herself, knowing what a melodramatic and stupid gesture that is. She's not David. She will not commit suicide under any circumstances. She will fix this. No, she won't cry anymore, but waits for her throat to relax and the pain to relent. She nods instead, gritting her teeth behind her lips.

"William, though, I made him so sad. It's not okay, what I did to him. He called me his fish, when he felt like being sweet. Can you go faster?"

Marianne still can't talk and won't shake her head, so she nods again and drives with all of her muscles stiffening.

"What a beautiful day," Marianne says finally. "I don't remember this route being quite so beautiful."

"I'm glad you think so."

"We're going to get William, all right, and then we're going to go back to Sacramento, and then we'll get things sorted. You don't have to be afraid of anything bad ever again, because you have me, and you will always have me from now on, all right?"

"Yes."

"You will always have me. I haven't always been in your life, I know. And you have been through so many things that I can't even begin to understand. But I am your mother, and I will make things right for you. I promise."

But William, Gillian thinks, *will always want me.*

Soon there is a sign: WELCOME TO POLK VALLEY, POP. 2100. The rest of the sign is barely visible beneath a sheet of brush. To Gillian, the words are mystical. She needs to get home and see William, but knows that it's likely William has no food and probably didn't even cast an eye toward the map she'd drawn him; he'll need something to eat, she says to Marianne, so they stop at the K & Bee to pick up sandwich fixings and juice. At the cash register, the woman behind the counter looks at Gillian and says, "Your family still sick?"

Gillian nods. She reaches into her tote and hands the woman a crumple of bills. "They're very sick," she says.

Gillian directs Marianne to Laurier and Sycamore, and then to the dirt roads that to Marianne look like nothing. She can't imagine that she can bring a car up these roads, as though Gillian has invented them. But like seeing a doe among doe-colored trees, Marianne soon learns the casual edges of where cars have been. Several times she thinks she will kill them on the foothill drive—not because it's worse than the mountainous roads, but because the roads, if that is what they will be called, are so much less demarcated. They pass the mailboxes, the trailer park, and the place where Gillian was nearly dragged to her death, which Gillian notices and says nothing about in a small allegiance to Ma.

And here is the house, which seems so small to Marianne now as opposed to how large it was in her memory, but to Gillian it remains enormous, a castle rising out of the fog. The dead grass stands sturdy and yellow. The plants in their pots on the steps. The welcoming arrangement of boulders. Marianne parks behind the Buick, which is encased in a sheer layer of dust, and Gillian jumps out of the car, her tote flapping on her shoulder. She runs up the steps to the door; Marianne has never seen a girl grow so long-legged in her stride. Gillian bangs on the door and calls for her brother. Marianne hefts the groceries in her arms. She was a girl when she last climbed up these steps. She tries to picture herself as that girl as she watches Gillian.

Gillian bangs and calls, "William!" as though she intends to break the door down. She even hops a little on both feet.

The door opens and Gillian sees William. She thinks, *He is bird-boned and sallow, with hair unattended to and like my father's when he was unwell, wearing pajamas, smelling of unwashed hair and body. I am hesitant to believe that I am here, and that he is still desiring me, but that this desire is now beyond lust or love but something that is pretty much killing him.* Marianne thinks, *This is a malnourished boy with no substance to him and reeking of, what else, canned tuna—how could Gillian have left this boy behind, this vulnerable, desperate creature?*

"Gillian," he says, and falls into her, wrapping his arms around her neck, not noticing the alleged Mrs. Kucharski in his passion or exhaustion.

"Hey there. Hey, you." Gillian kisses the top of his head over and over. "It's okay. I came back. It's okay." She says something in their language.

They stand there for what, to Marianne, is an awkwardly long time, until Gillian says, "Let's go inside."

Marianne had never gone to as many estate sales as David had, but she recognizes the smell of a death house when she enters one. The staleness of the air, as if nothing has moved or breathed or spoken for months, is a gas that fills the hall and then the living room where they sit. Where she sat before. The extravagance of two pianos, she thinks. William is still leaning on Gillian. She is someone new now. She holds her brother to her breast, her hand at his shoulder. Marianne stares openly at them—why not stare openly? The word *incest*, which she won't allow herself to think, plays at the borders of her mind. What have they done? What have they done with each other? His face is too close to her chest for Marianne's comfort. There are rotting food smells, too, she realizes. Gillian was right to ask for food. They'll have a brief snack, and then she will bring them both back to Sacramento with her. They'll deal with the Nowak house and this terrible brainwashing later. The paint is peeling and nothing has been cleaned in what looks like months or even years. Even the sofa is washed in gray now. She remembers that peach sofa as having a brighter shade.

"Do you remember me, William?" she asks, setting the bag on the floor.

"Yes."

"I'm Mrs. Kucharski."

"Why are you here?"

"I'm here to help you." She wants to have something better to say, but leaves it at that. She doesn't know what William will comprehend as "help" or "helpful."

"What?" William says, with more force than Marianne could have imagined coming out of his diminished frame. His hands are still on his sister. He looks at Gillian. "We don't need help. Is that why you left?" he asks her.

"Not exactly," Gillian says.

"We don't need help. Not from you or anyone else. I'm glad that you brought Gillian back, but you should leave now. We're *fine*."

Marianne's gaze travels down the hall. "Where's your mother?"

"Dead," Gillian says. "I told you."

William says, "She's right, she's dead."

"You are two children who have no parents," Marianne says. "That's why you need help."

"You'll live with us?" William asks.

"No—I have a home in Sacramento. Do you remember the home in Sacramento? Where you played piano with your sister? You'll come and live with me."

"I doubt that." William grabs Gillian's arm still more tightly.

She had a plan, Marianne reminds herself. Come to the house. Retrieve William. Allow them to grab a few possessions, and then drive them back to Sacramento. She had, to some degree, counted on Gillian to convince her brother to leave; presently Gillian will not make eye contact with her. *But what am I going to do in the face of refusal,* Marianne wonders, *carry them out of here by force? Call the police?* She wonders if this is what Gillian had planned all along: bringing her to this place only to force her to leave—even if Marianne is Gillian's birth mother, even if the children are alone and without resources and have been abandoned to this rotting home.

"Let me talk to my brother," Gillian says. "I just want to apologize to him." Her shoulders, she realizes, are looser now. She'd been clenching them for weeks. *I am a fool,* she thinks, *to consider that we could ever live a different life—I was stupid and a fool to have wished for anything different. It's not just William, or a dirty bathroom, the men who shouted filth, or Randy on the train. It is one age ending, and having no beginning to hope for.*

Marianne stands.

"Please wait out front," Gillian says.

Marianne says, "I'll need the key."

Gillian looks at her brother. He says, "We have a deadbolt that will keep you out regardless."

"I swear," Gillian says. "We'll let you back inside. We really will."

Reluctantly, Marianne stands, convinced she is losing an important battle in an obliterative war. She is the adult, she reminds herself. Here, she is in charge. She walks to the hallway and puts her hand on the knob. "No shenanigans," she says. She is tall and imposing in her olive coat.

The word *shenanigans* is unfamiliar to the children, but they nod, and then Marianne is outside on the stoop. She goes to the car for her cigarettes and matches. *Help me,* she thinks as she pulls open the door in the damp air. The sky is white and dappled gray. She looks out into the trees at one bird. *I'm going to lose everything,* she thinks.

Gillian is quiet. She says, brushing William's hair out of his eyes, "I'm sorry I left. It was stupid."

"I didn't know what to do after you were gone. I couldn't believe that you did that to me."

"I know."

"You're not just changing your own life when you do things, Gillian."

She nods.

The light is coming in through the curtains and shining on William's face. His cheekbones are pronounced, but even more so now in the afternoon light, making Gillian feel as though she's speaking to an exquisitely preserved corpse. She almost shudders to touch him.

"Are you scared?" she asks.

"Yes."

"She's going to bring us to Sacramento. She knows we exist now, and that we're alone. She feels like she has to do this for us. She wants to do what's right for us."

"For you."

"Yes, for me. But for you, too. I couldn't live with myself if I left you here."

"I don't know what to do."

"We have to be brave."

"Despite what you may think," William says, "I am not brave. I don't even know what that means. I waited for you to come back, but that was no indication of strength. Perhaps stupidity."

"That's not what I meant," Gillian says. "There are other ways to be brave. Smarter ways."

"What, you suggest suicide? And what if we don't die? We get shut up in Wellbrook?"

"Look—"

"I don't want to die," William interrupts. "I just want to be with you. I've been thinking about this—about what I'd do if you came back. I've been thinking about..." He gestures a wide arc. "So this woman takes us into the world. Why not let her?"

"Are you listening to me? I *saw* things." And she thinks again, just as she has been thinking for the last few hours, of the things she saw in the Natural History Museum: the wolves and the deer, the hungry lions. She thinks of the mural painted on the wall in the front of the museum, which neither Marianne nor Marty had commented on. They had just walked by as if it were nothing, whereas Gillian could tell right away that something was wrong with the illustration, a timeline, with large and vivid images of animals and hairy, stooped humans that looked like animals. The museum had been nothing to them. It had been one more thing that they already knew to their bones.

"I am listening. Are *you* listening?"

"We can't change enough. Do you hear me? *We can't change enough to be out there.* It's just like when the fire happened. I understand what Ma was trying to do now. She was just keeping us safe here, in this house, with her. I didn't understand then, but I think you did. You need to believe me."

"We could kill her. Run away. Live in the woods."

"We could walk and walk," Gillian says, "until we get to Taiwan."

"We could even walk to Eden," William says.

"But you want us to try to be in the world."

He sighs. "Yes. Maybe."

"She's my real mother, you know," Gillian says, and William turns to her uncomprehendingly.

Marianne opens the door, ushered in by a gust of wind. She is holding the groceries. "It's raining out there," she says, patting her own wet head. "We should go before the road gets sloppy."

Gillian pauses. "There are some things I'd like to pack. Just a few things," she says, looking at her brother, "before we leave."

Marianne watches her carefully. She had anticipated this, the need for the children to bring things from home with them, but is surprised that Gillian has fallen in step with the idea of leaving; she had expected more of an argument. Without one, she suspects that the siblings are collaborating against her.

"I'll give you half an hour," she says. "Pack the most important things, all right? We'll come to get the rest of your things on another trip." She smiles at them. *There will be another trip,* she is trying to communicate—*we aren't abandoning your world for good.* For now, she simply needs to get the children away. Once she's removed them from this place for the first time, she'll be able to acquaint them with new lives. That acquaintance and acclimation is essential.

At the idea of packing, William nods. So the children, owning no suitcases, fill boxes with no plan and a slothlike deliberation.

Gillian sits in her room with a record crate, empties it, and folds clothes to put inside while Marianne watches her. Marianne, no fool, stays close to Gillian as her daughter slowly sifts through her dresser, pulling out an assortment of frocks (inappropriate, Marianne thinks, all of them shapeless and outmoded, she will need new ones for her new life) and more pairs of ethereal panties that are now tinged with perversion. She can't bear to see the siblings together and is relieved that William is in his own room, packing his own things.

Later William wanders into the room with a crate. It appears that the sedimentary crate has a layer of clothes at the bottom, books in the middle, and papers at the top. Gillian doesn't know what the papers are, but if she looked more closely she would see that they're a diary he's kept while she was away. "Will we drive in this weather?" he asks. The rain is clattering against the windows.

"I suppose not," Marianne says. "We can wait for the rain to stop."

"We get horrible storms near winter," says Gillian.

"Well, at least you two seem to have your packing finished. I say we settle in until it's time to head out again."

Gillian says, "The roads will be muddy. Tires slide. We don't take the Buick for days after a storm."

"Days," William says. He sets down his crate for emphasis and sits on it, his knees open.

"I know how to drive in mud."

"Of course you know how to drive in mud," Gillian says. She rises to standing. "But it's getting dark, and I'm sure William hasn't had dinner. I'm going to make some sandwiches. William," she says, "we bought some things for sandwiches. I expect you ate everything while I was gone."

Left alone in the bedroom with William, Marianne says, "I knew your father when we were young."

William ignores her. Her stomach clenches. *You raped my daughter,* she thinks. *She's gone through enough, you bastard.* She hates herself for hating a child. He is a child, even if he is almost an adult in body—he can't know any more than Gillian does about the world, and still she loathes him. "You had sex with Gillian," Marianne says, and William says nothing. He gets up and goes into the kitchen, where Gillian is spreading mayonnaise on sliced bread. She's wearing his favorite dress, the green one with the elbow-length sleeves and ruffles at the cuffs. Her elbows pink. Her hands and their rough motions.

"Will we kill her?" he says in Mandarin.

Gillian sticks the knife in the jar. "I can't do that. I told you, she's my mother. She gave me to our parents."

"What about Ma?"

"I don't know."

"Regardless. You had no qualms about killing *her*."

"Fuck," Gillian says in English, and then, returning to Mandarin, "I didn't kill her."

William, in his button-down and linen pants, comes up behind her. She feels his hand on her arm, squeezing, and he feels the softness of his sister's skin. He kisses her on the shoulder. His breath is unclean.

"I'm sorry," Gillian says.

"We don't have to decide now," William says, but they both know that this isn't entirely true.

Marianne is in the hallway, listening to them speak in the language she can't understand. She sees William standing behind his taller sister, his face very close to her neck, and she wants to shout, *Stop, please stop touching her. Leave her alone.* She turns and walks back to the living room. She had been in that living room once, pregnant and wanting to die, wanting to die and feeling guilty for the desire. She can remember exactly how she and Daisy and David had sat in this room when she came with a fecund belly. She had loved him then, even then, if she had loved anyone. *Marty is at home,* she reminds herself, *Marty is waiting for me to come back, and we will make a new life together, all four of us.* It will be a family that she had never intended, but was in the end meant to be: she and Marty will raise David's children.

Gillian reenters the living room with William at her side, and Gillian hands out ham and cheese sandwiches on napkins.

"It's really raining very hard, isn't it?" Marianne says.

"Doesn't it rain where you live, when it gets to be December? And snow?" asks Gillian.

"Sure."

William looks at the ceiling, holding his sandwich. They eat in a trance.

"I wanted some tea," Gillian says. "It's on the stove."

Marianne says to William, "You loved Beethoven, when I knew you."

"Yes."

"Please," she says, "play something."

He has never not played the piano when commanded to. It is ingrained in his marrow. He gets up and goes to the piano bench, where his hands hesitate and then draw through the air to the keys, striking the notes of the bright opening, the collapse into waves of a climb and descent. He plays for a full three minutes before the teakettle shrieks a long note. Gillian leaves the room with her tote dangling from her elbow, swaying as she walks. The music seems to remain in the air, as if it has stained the dust motes and fading light with a sad hue.

"That was beautiful," Marianne says.

"I don't have the whole thing yet," William answers.

Marianne says, "The *Hammerklavier*. It's a difficult piece. Perhaps the most difficult. I'm impressed that you know so much of it."

He plays more Beethoven while Gillian is in the kitchen with all the stolen pills that will fit in the mortar, smashing them with the pestle, and thinking, *This is a kindness.* She keeps looking at the doorway to see if anyone will appear to stop her, and no one does.

Finally Gillian returns with a tray of cups. They drink their bitter tea, made with the last of the loose-leaf-filled tin that Ma had bought in Sacramento. Marianne wonders if it would be idiotic to try to drive them away from here; maybe they were telling the truth when they said that it would take days before the roads were safe again. Maybe they can spend the night here, and travel tomorrow. Still, she feels the urgency of having to get them away from the poisonous house. The longer they stay here, the more polluted they become.

"With the money you have access to," she says, attempting to be cheerful, "you'll be able to find a really nice place to live. How old are you, William? In a year, if you want, you can be independent. You'll be an adult in the eyes of the law. You'll be able to do whatever you want."

William says, "I do whatever I want as it is."

"This is a small world you're living in, William. There's a larger world waiting out there for you. Freedom."

Gillian echoes, "Freedom," which arouses Marianne's hopes.

"Yes, freedom. You'll be able to learn and do so many things." She leans her head against a cushion. It's been a long day, and she is tired.

William and Gillian sit in the middle of the room in silence. Marianne's eyes are closed. In Mandarin Gillian says, "We could all use a nap."

"I want to talk to you about *her*." He jerks his head. "She doesn't understand us at all. A kind woman, but... Gillian . . ." he says. And he's blinking slowly now, too, so slowly that his eyes actually remain closed for several long seconds. "Something isn't right. You hopeless, hopeless—Gillian. No." He presses his fingers into his eyeballs.

She takes him by the shoulders and gently lifts him to his feet. "Let's go to bed," she says.

They stumble to the bedroom they once shared. He's been spraying clouds of perfume over the smell of fish and apples. She lays him down on the bed and lies down next to him, wrapping her arms around him. She kisses him softly on his sour mouth and he twitches, crying, putting his hand on the small of her back.

"Hey," she says. "Everything is going to be okay."

"I don't believe you."

"It's okay."

"I love you."

"Shh."

William goes quiet. When he hasn't moved for as many heartbeats as Gillian can stand, she gets up and drifts from room to room—

—first the living room, where Marianne is slumped onto the couch, her form becoming ever softer, almost melting, as she sinks into the cushions. A spot of light from the lamp beside her comes over her thinly lined face. Here, too, are all the books in their shelves, and all the places they did not go. Gillian looks at her piano, but does not sit at the bench, nor does she play. There have been enough hours of playing. *If only I loved it more, or loved anything more*, she thinks. She wipes her eyes.

Down the hall, into the dim kitchen. Drawers of tools and errant notes reminding Gillian to do the laundry and telling William to mop the floors. One says, simply, *MEAT*. There is nothing of David's left, not even a reminder to buy orange juice—his favorite. Everything of Ma's left, including her body in the backyard buried not too deep. There are dirty dishes on the table covering years of carved messages. There is a place where an orange plopped onto the floor once and rolled one or two feet, and drawings of mountains scattered on the floor. The record player is silent. The refrigerator is empty.

And out of the kitchen, into the master bedroom. The room still smells like Ma's jasmine and the faint fog of herbal remedies. It smells like cigarettes. The bed is made for two.

Here is the hatbox.

Here is Gillian, looking through the hatbox. She stares at the picture of Ma and David under the TSINGTAO sign, which she tucks into her pocket.

She goes back to the door to their old room and his body is still curled up tight at the side of the bed, having forgotten how to fill up space without her. *Sweet William, make me an omelet*; two kids, two omelets. She is not crying. Inside her head things have gotten very quiet.

When she lights the first curtain she's surprised by how quickly the flame scampers up to the ceiling, a wild thing—her plan being to destroy all of it, her family and her house and, of course, herself, but it happens faster than she imagined, and with far more violence, which startles her. But she moves to the next curtain and lights that one, too, watching in fascination as the fire swallows it near whole. She sets the papers in the wastebasket on fire, and the flames shimmy up in search of something to catch. Her skin is bright with heat as she watches the room burn. Her eyes move to William, who is unmoving in the smoke.

Something in her stirs and then flares. She grabs William and begins to drag him out of the room. She can't let him die. She can't let any of them die; there has already been so much death, beginning with David. It all began with him in that motel room with a fatal knife wound and a piece of paper on the desk that read only, maddeningly, *I'M SORRY*, as if that were enough to make up for his absence. As if life were something that you could just cast aside, a carapace, in favor of something better. And yet she understands this impulse to escape. She is still her father's daughter.

Marty can see the smoke from down the road. He drives faster in the pelting rain, unheeding of dirt turning to mud beneath the tires. He sees the house burning and panics. The panic freezes him; the car jolts and stops. He can see two dark figures in front of the house and stars falling all around them. One of them is his sister, lying in the cold mud. A young man, presumably William, is next to her and on all fours, staring at the house, pointing—

—and that is when Marty turns and sees it, too. It is something tearing itself away from the house, fleet of foot and fast. The house is a live thing and will continue to live for hours, snarling despite the rain, before it puts itself to sleep; but for now, before anyone can fully comprehend what is happening, something is sprinting into the woods, like a deer, or the ghost of something beautiful.

ACKNOWLEDGMENTS

This book would not be what it is without the following people, places, and institutions, for which I am gobsmackingly grateful.

To Miriam Lawrence, who has read this novel almost as many times as I have, randomly quoting bits of it back to me, and generously offered much-needed advice and cheerleading along the way; to Anna North, my former swimming companion and brilliant friend; to the keen mind and friendship of Anisse Gross. Gratitude to the writerly smarts of Andi Winnette and the present and former members of the No-Name Writing Group, all of whom took time and energy out of their busy lives for the Nowaks and me. A special note of thanks to Mira Ptacin, who, without knowing much about me at all, dragged me across the finish line when I was ready to lie down and die.

To my tireless agent, Amy Williams, who believed in this book when it was but a single chapter; to my editor, C. P. Heiser, who offered editorial insight and encouragement, as well as a wealth of support; and to all the folks at Unnamed Press, including Olivia Taylor Smith, for bringing this literary dark horse and its author into the fold.

To the Gibraltar Point Artscape, the Vermont Studio Center, Hedgebrook, and the Kimmel Harding Nelson Center for the Arts, for giving me time and space with which to write; to Sara Carbaugh, the Grass Valley Public Library, and the Nevada County Historical Center, for invaluable research assistance; to Helen Zell, the Hopwood Awards, and the Elizabeth George

Foundation, for their financial resources; to Leigh Stein, Dyana Valentine, Jenny Zhang, Vauhini Vara, Tanya Geisler, Aaron Silberstein, and the women of BinderCon, for friendship, support, and community. To my doctors and counselor, Dr. Grieder, Dr. McInnes, and Grace Quantock, for helping to manage my body and mind.

To Stanford University and the University of Michigan, which gifted me writing teachers and mentors such as Malena Watrous, Katherine Noel, Eric Puchner, Elizabeth Tallent, Eileen Pollack, Nicholas Delbanco, and Michael Byers. To Yiyun Li, for permission. Special thanks to Doug Trevor, my thesis adviser for *The Border of Paradise* when it was in its infancy.

To those I have lost: thank you.

To my parents, and the people and places they came from; to Allen and Claudia; to the parents and family that I married into, and the people and places they came from.

And, finally, to Chris and Daphne, who remind me of everything that is good in this world.

ABOUT THE AUTHOR

Esmé Weijun Wang was born in Michigan to Taiwanese parents and grew up in the San Francisco Bay Area. She received her MFA at the University of Michigan. Her writing has appeared in such publications as *Salon*, *Catapult*, *The New Inquiry*, and *The Believer*; awards include the Hopwood Award for Novel-in-Progress, an Elizabeth George Foundation grant, and the Louis Sudler Prize. She writes at www.esmewang.com.